Children of Fog Island

Mariette Lindstein

Translation by Rachel Willson-Broyles

HQ

ONE PLACE. MANY STORIES

This novel is entirely a work of fiction. The names, characters and incidents portrayed in it are the work of the author's imagination. Any resemblance to actual persons, living or dead, events or localities is entirely coincidental.

HQ
An imprint of HarperCollins*Publishers* Ltd
1 London Bridge Street
London SE1 9GF

www.harpercollins.co.uk

HarperCollins*Publishers*
Macken House, 39/40 Mayor Street Upper,
Dublin 1, D01 C9W8, Ireland

This edition 2025

2
First published in Great Britain by
HQ, an imprint of HarperCollins*Publishers* Ltd 2025

 A catalogue record for this book is available from the British Library.

ISBN: PB: 9780008245436

This book is set in 11.2/15 pt. Bembo by Type-it AS, Norway

Printed and bound in the United States of America

Praise for Mariette Lindstein's Fog Island series:

'Chillingly authentic'
Guardian

'An interesting exposition of the psychology and the insidious methods that govern cults'
Daily Mail

'I loved it – tense and atmospheric, slowly drawing the reader in to a reality that is utterly terrifying'
Lisa Hall, bestselling author of *The Day She Disappeared*

'An intense, terrifying, and utterly believable journey into the shadowy world of cult leaders and cult members. A just-one-more-page thriller that will have you reading late into the night and holding your breath until the very end. I loved it!'
Karen Dionne, No. 1 international bestselling author of *The Marsh King's Daughter*

'This intense thriller completely grips you from the off'
Heat

'A vivid crime novel'
Express

Mariette Lindstein was born and raised in Halmstad on the west coast of Sweden. At the age of twenty, she joined the Church of Scientology and worked for the next twenty-five years at all levels of the organization, including at its international headquarters outside Los Angeles. Mariette left the Church in 2004 and is now married to Dan Koon, an author and artist. They live in a forest outside Halmstad with their three dogs. *Fog Island* is her debut novel and was first published in Sweden where it won the Best Crime Debut at the Specsavers CrimeTime Awards. Mariette now dedicates her life to writing and lecturing to warn others about the dangers of cults and cult mentality. *Children of Fog Island* is the final book in the Fog Island Trilogy.

Also by Mariette Lindstein:

Fog Island
Shadow of Fog Island

Children of Fog Island

Prologue

The girl's scream pierces the howling wind. Vic is holding her wrists in an iron grip and dragging her, on her back, across the barren terrain. I want to stop him, but there's hardly anything to be done when Vic gets like this. He is full of a pulsating energy I know well. He is exhilarated by his own cruel idea and possesses a superhuman strength fuelled by hatred.

She kicks and tries to wrench her arms loose. But Vic is too strong. We're on the slope that leads to Devil's Rock. He pulls her up the craggy heights and I know where he's going. The very highest cliff is known as Old Nick, and he grimaces above us with his loose tooth, reaches clumsily over the sea and nudges the steely grey clouds with his nose.

I cry: 'Not there!' But he doesn't listen.

He yanks at the girl's arms impatiently, but she resists and nearly throws him off balance. Quickly he throws an elbow around her neck and squeezes until she goes quiet. Her arms and legs shake helplessly, then fall slack to the rocky surface.

He lays her on the grassy patch just before the rocks take over, plunging to the sea.

'Are you going to help me or what?' he calls to me. 'We'll throw her over and then we'll be rid of her. Don't look so horrified. No one will ever know.'

My legs will no longer bear me. I fall to my knees on the

slope and bawl at him to stop, but he only stares at me, bold and defiant.

When I look up at him, it isn't Vic I see. That is Father's face, full of chaos and scorn. His eyes are black worms crawling into my soul.

My head is pounding. Something wants out. The pounding turns into something else, something worse and more stubborn. Like a chainsaw biting its way through my frozen brain.

I shout the only words that will come to me:

'Father is going to be furious!'

And as I say those words, I realize they're true.

Vic stares at me, mouth agape, looking panicked. The momentary delight I feel to have reached him transforms into horror as I realize that he has spotted something behind me. I don't have to turn around; I know who it is. The shadow falls across my body like an unexpected eclipse. All at once I'm in the midst of something dark and forbidding. The sound of the sea and the wind has faded. The air feels different, sharper and colder.

I meet Vic's gaze. For a second, our eyes are locked. Something passes between us, an awareness.

That life will never be the same again.

1

The sound of the TV was deafening. *Gusts may reach over 110 miles per hour, the strongest winds ever measured in western Sweden…*

Sofia set the grocery bags in the kitchen, went to the living room, snatched the remote from Benjamin's hand, and turned off the television.

'What are you doing?' Benjamin asked.

'Don't just sit there – do something!'

'But that was interesting. They were explaining how to prepare for the storm.'

'Well, it's no mystery. Go out and bring in the lawn furniture, secure all loose items. I bought enough food to last us a few days. Then we have to gather candles, flashlights, and all that. Do you know where Julia is?'

'No idea. I'm sure she'll be home for dinner.'

He stood up, came over to her, and placed his hands on her shoulders.

'Honey, try not to get all worked up about the storm. Everything's going to be fine. The weather guys are afraid they'll get the blame if they don't warn people. I'm sure it won't be as bad as they say. You worry too much.'

'We'll see,' she said, extricating herself.

It was true she was worked up over the storm. Not just because the meteorologists seemed so concerned; a feeling had crept up on her. An unpleasant sense of foreboding that she couldn't shake off.

She went out to the yard, stood on the lawn, and stared at the lake. It was all so unnaturally still that it gave her the creepy-crawlies. The complete absence of birdsong. The water was a black mirror beyond the trees. The only movement came from an aspen leaf trembling frenetically as it tried to hold onto its twig. A nearly clear sky. Migrating birds slipped silently past like gliders. Everything was so quiet that she could hear a faint rush in her ears. That constant companion.

The autumn air was sharp and cold. Someone was burning leaves nearby; she typically loved that smell but now it made her feel melancholy. There was a sound from above, like a drawn-out sigh. But it was only a gentle breeze moving through the leafy crowns of the trees. Then, silence again. A lump rose in her throat as she stood there.

Everything I love is here, she thought. *My wonderful husband and daughter, my lovely house. Yet here I stand with my heavy, heavy heart.*

She was ashamed of having snapped at Benjamin. In recent days she'd felt so restless and easily irritated. She knew why, but she didn't want to admit it to herself, much less Benjamin. Once again she was having dreams about Franz Oswald, the cult leader. After fifteen years he had inexplicably returned to her dreams. The rape, which she had worked through and mulled over until she felt completely devoid of emotion and wrung out down to her very soul, had begun playing in her mind again. The images had a fresh sharpness to them. She suddenly recalled new things about the incident; she could picture it once more, clearer and stronger.

Her reason told her that Franz Oswald had gone underground. He hadn't made a public appearance in almost a decade and was said to spend all his time at the ViaTerra cult's manor on Fog

Island. The assumption was that he was developing new theses there. There was also a rumour that he had lost his mind. Sofia entertained different, darker hopes. That he had died of some incredibly painful disease and that the idiots in the ViaTerra cult were all destitute and shivering with no electricity at the isolated manor.

There was still chatter about Franz Oswald, though. It was as if the legend of the charismatic cult leader would never die. Even though he'd spent time in prison for sexually assaulting a minor fifteen years ago, there were plenty of people who worshipped him. Sofia tried to tell herself that he had left the limelight for good, was maybe even dead. But her intuition told her something completely different: that he was very much alive.

She noticed her fingers trembling slightly. Must be the cold. She went back into the house, into the bathroom, where she ran warm water over her hands.

In the mirror she could still see the girl who escaped ViaTerra. Twice. Only the crow's feet around her eyes and the laugh lines around her mouth were new. A few strands of grey in her bangs. Did she look even a little bit harried? Was there really any reason for the approaching storm and her dreams about Franz Oswald to knock her so off balance?

Her phone vibrated in her pocket. When she picked it up, she saw a text from Julia light up the screen. *Home later tonight.* As if everything was perfectly normal. As if she had no idea about the storm. Suddenly Sofia had a panicky thought that Julia might not know it was approaching. She tried to call but only got the annoying voicemail message: 'Hi Mom, since you're the only one who leaves me voicemails let me assure you that everything is fine. I'll call later.'

★

When Julia came to the world, it didn't take Sofia long to realize she had given birth to a whirlwind, one that quickly increased in strength into a hurricane. Julia had a type of energy that Sofia – much less Benjamin – couldn't control.

There was not a trace of Benjamin in Julia. She had inherited Sofia's hair colour, dark eyes, and features, but there was something else, more intense, shimmering beneath the surface. Julia went after life with immense delight; she was defiant and completely uninhibited. Like the time last spring when she won a song contest on TV and became Sweden's little darling, only to shrug and say, 'You know, I don't think singing is really my thing.' She said she wanted to take it easy until she stumbled across her 'calling' in life. For some reason, Sofia shuddered to think of what that calling might be.

It wasn't just Julia's appearance that made her stand out from the crowd. She was more *there*. More present. If you walked into a room with a hundred people in it, Julia would be the first one you noticed. She was extraordinary.

And there was only one other person in Sofia's life who had been like that.

She sent a text: *Answer me when I call*. She waited a moment. Then she dialled Julia's number once, twice, three times, until Julia picked up with a snappish 'What *is* it?'

'You have to come home right away.'

'Why?'

'We're getting ready for the storm. It's coming in.'

'Can't you and Dad handle it?'

'No, come home right now. You can't drive your moped in the storm.'

'Oh, they're just exaggerating.'

'I wouldn't be so sure. The meteorologists on TV look worried. They've even given the storm a scary name. Hercules.'

'Fine, I'll be there in a little bit.'

Benjamin was standing in the hall. Filled with regret, she nestled into his arms.

'I'm sorry I blew up at you before. It makes me so paranoid to hear them go on about the storm.'

'It's okay. You look tired, sweetheart. And kind of sad.'

She hadn't known she looked so down.

'I don't like it when things change,' she said, looking up at him. 'But you never do. You're just the same as always.'

Benjamin was the anchor of their existence. In his previous job at a transport company in Gothenburg someone had discovered his talent for logistics and convinced him to start his own firm as a consultant. The firm, which he ran from home, was doing brilliantly. He had no trouble supporting the family; in fact, it was thanks to Benjamin they had been able to buy their house on the island of Orust.

A few years ago, Sofia had left her job as a library director in order to fulfil her dream of helping cult defectors. These days she ran a shelter alongside Anna Hedberg, another woman who had defected from ViaTerra. The shelter received state funding and Benjamin tossed in some money when they needed it. It wasn't turning a profit yet, but she loved her job.

Now she caught sight of their dog, Denzel, who was trembling under the sofa.

'How long has he been like that?' she asked Benjamin.

'Since this morning. I could hardly get him to go out to pee.'

'Do you think he's sick?'

'No, I'm sure he can just tell the storm is coming. Animals can sense these things.'

Sofia knelt and pulled the dog out from under the sofa. She rocked him in her arms for a moment, but he was still trembling.

'Do you want to go out?' she asked, opening the door to the yard. But the dog lay down on the floor and turned his head to the side. She fastened his leash to his collar and dragged him out to the yard, where he dutifully peed and then began to tug at the leash to go back inside.

She noticed that clouds had gathered on the horizon. Dirty grey and deep purple. A faint breeze was rustling through the trees. The white caps on the black waves made the lake look like static on a television. But it was still quiet. No birdsong. No cars on the road. It felt like they had been abandoned in a no-man's-land.

Benjamin came out with his phone linked to a pair of headphones, which he pulled from his ears when he spotted her.

'Hey, they're saying it's going to turn into a hurricane. If it gets as awful as they predict, I'll have a lot of work afterwards,' he said.

'How can you think like that?'

'You have to try to find the silver linings in life.'

Benjamin always did.

'Look, there's Julia!'

Benjamin pointed at the road, where Julia had popped up on her moped. Her long hair was whipped backwards by the wind. She was going so fast that at first Sofia thought she would miss the driveway. But she made the turn and drove up to Sofia on the lawn.

'Happy now?' she asked, pursing her lips sullenly.

Thank God, Sofia thought. *Now everything will be okay. We'll make it through this just fine.*

When they went to bed around midnight, the wind had increased; it whistled around the corners of the house and made the rafters creak softly, sadly. The trees outside the window were bending with the force. But none of it seemed violent or threatening. When the power went out and interrupted the news, which showed a reporter standing in the wind, shivering and being blown backwards, it still seemed safe to go to bed. It felt as though the storm would be over by the time they woke up. None of them wanted to sit around listening to the wind as it tormented the house.

Julia pulled a mattress into their room. They chatted for a while, giggled in the darkness, and managed to fall asleep.

A few hours later, Sofia woke to a crash that was so loud she flew out of bed. The wind was no longer howling; now it was roaring madly. It was pitch black out, darker than the bleakest winter night. The rafters' creaking sounded like the whole roof was about to be torn off. Then came the sound of breaking glass, deafening and sharp.

Hurricane Hercules had made landfall.

This is my story. My thoughts surrounding the events that led to that frightful night on the cliffs. There is a lot to say about my eighteen years of life. Far too much. So I've decided to focus on certain aspects and hope these will make it easier for you to see how things turned out as they did.

I'm not asking for your understanding or your forgiveness. I'm really only writing because there's so much inside me that I have to get out.

Who knows what you'll think. If you even read this.

But I hope you do.

I was born a fraternal twin. It took years for me to realize that Vic and I belonged together. From the very start, we were so different. It was like those twin girls that were born in Australia – one had white skin while the other was dark-skinned. It was kind of the same thing with Vic and me.

I've read up on twins. Tried to find an explanation for the lack of brotherly love between us. In the flood of information, my attention was drawn to one recurring fact: Twins, but above all, individuals.

Most fraternal twins look like siblings even if they don't arise from the same egg the way identicals do. But Vic and I looked like we had totally different parents. Vic was a strapping baby, weighing almost nine pounds at birth. I was a six-pound wretch, skinny and pale.

From these bodies grew two very different personalities.

★

In one of her crueller moments, Fanny, our nanny, told us what happened the first time Father saw us. He had hand-selected her from among the staff because she was 'mature' and 'experienced', not a 'child' like Mama. Fanny was a grim forty-year-old woman with short-cropped hair, thin lips, and sharp, deeply sunken eyes. I can still remember how she would fix her gaze on me, with superiority and a bit of scorn. The idea was for her to teach Mama how to care for us. What really happened was that she got on Mama's nerves with her nagging and her digs about how useless Mama was.

In any case, Fanny was the one who told us about our very first encounter with Father. He was still in prison when we were born. Later I would understand that this was because he had locked Mama in the attic and had sex with her when she was fourteen. That was how Vic and I came to be. But I didn't learn this until much later. When he returned to ViaTerra, Mama had moved into the cottage next to the manor house. We were only a few months old. Mama had spent the whole day waiting anxiously for Father. Even Fanny was nervous. There was a smouldering sort of mood in the house, she said, as though God the Father himself were about to descend from heaven and bless the little children. Someone called from the manor and said he would be there in fifteen minutes. Fanny hurried to bathe us, just so we would smell nice.

When Father arrived, he looked harried.

'They will be raised according to the principles of ViaTerra,' was the first thing he said as he stepped through the door.

We lay naked on the large changing table, ready for Father's inspection. We were babbling cheerfully after our warm bath. We didn't scream once. At least that's what Fanny told us.

Father approached us and cast a quick glance at Vic.

'This one looks like me,' he declared.

Then he caught sight of me and started laughing. Shrilly, making Fanny's heart leap into her throat. He grabbed my foot and gave it a little yank.

'That's the most pitiful willy I've ever seen!'

With these words, he turned on his heel and marched out of the cottage.

Welcome to the world, Invictus and Thor.

Welcome to ViaTerra.

We grew out of these bodies.

Vic was an exact copy of Father. His dark hair and eyes, his broad shoulders, his confident stride, his straight teeth, dimples, even his laugh had the same echoing tone as Father's.

I became a wan copy of Mama. Skinny and freckled. Ginger-haired with long eyelashes. Some people still mistook me for a girl when I was ten.

Vic was the first to walk. The first to talk. He kicked the first ball. Used the potty first. Got the first tooth. Climbed highest. Swam first.

The only thing I did first was get a concussion, when Vic came after me with a bandy stick. And I was also the only one who got braces.

He outshone me in every way, even when it wasn't necessary. It was so clear from the very start that I was inferior.

The sun never stopped shining on Vic, and I was constantly in his shadow. Sometimes it was unbearable. Sometimes it was nice to avoid attention.

But there is one trait I did inherit from Father. His infallible memory.

2

She opened the bedroom door but was thrown back by the wind, which had found its way into the living room through a broken window. Her hair whipped her face so violently that at first she couldn't see. Her instincts told her she was in danger. Even so, she took a few steps forward. Furniture and flowerpots crashed to the floor; some hit the walls with loud bangs.

All her senses were overloaded, but she couldn't tear her gaze from the chaos before her. The windowpanes rattled in their frames. The rafters whined and groaned. She glanced towards the yard outside. The trees were no longer swaying, they were pressed to the ground and whimpering as their branches were torn free. Shrubs fought in vain against the merciless slaughter of the wind as they were ripped up by the roots. The horrid sound of ash trees, their timber dry from ash dieback, cracking in the middle and crashing into the ravine past the yard.

The sky outside was an angry whirlwind of debris and rubble. A greenhouse came flying out of the swirl and only narrowly missed the house. An odd thought came to her: this was punishment for something she had done. She felt thoroughly whipped, completely incapable of moving her body away.

Then Benjamin's hands closed around her waist and pulled her back.

'Down to the cellar! Hurry!'

Julia was already on her way down the stairs with Denzel under one arm and a blanket under the other. Benjamin had a steady hold on Sofia's shoulders. He guided her ahead of him and caught her when she stumbled.

When she got to the cellar, Julia was standing in the centre of the room, pale as a sheet and wide-eyed. She had never seen her daughter so frightened; she was radiating fear. Still, there was a hint of excitement in her eyes. Denzel had curled up in a corner, where he lay shaking.

Benjamin closed and locked the cellar door. They lay down on the mattresses they had brought down earlier that evening. There they curled up into foetal positions, close together, as though they were a single creature. It was impossible to block out the horrible sounds. Objects being flung against the outer walls with massive booms. The wind hurling itself furiously at the house, as though it were angry at its very existence. Furniture and other belongings thudding and scraping against the floor above them. They were terrified and powerless in the face of the violent forces that were tearing their home apart. The barbaric strength of the storm found every last crack in the cellar window casings. Cold, raw outside air pumped into the room. The air was full of static and smelled singed.

They didn't talk very much. They tried very hard not to cry out in fear or make comments that would feed the panic bubbling inside them. But when it sounded like the floor above might crack in two, and when the roar suggested the roof was being torn from the house, they exchanged I love yous. Benjamin had brought a flashlight, which flickered and died after a while. The total darkness made everything even worse.

Time meant nothing. There were only the eerie sounds, the fear, and more sounds – even worse now. She would never know how long they lay there, clinging to one another like a single, warm, pulsating body. Maybe it lasted for a few hours; five, perhaps. Each time the wind seemed to die down, they heard something new: a crash, a bang, an unsettling howl.

But then, slowly, the roar of the wind turned into an even rush. Pale, cold dawn light snuck in through the cellar window. Everything grew quiet. So very quiet.

Sofia extricated herself from Julia, who was in front of her, and realized her daughter had actually managed to fall asleep. Benjamin, who was clutching Sofia from behind, let out a groan.

'I think it's over.'

They got up, stretching their sore, stiff joints. Slowly they went up the cellar stairs. Sofia, in the lead, was afraid of what they would find on the other side of the door.

'Open it,' said Benjamin. 'I hope the walls and the roof are still there.'

Her first thought, when she opened the door, was that a miracle had happened. Even though the living room was a jumble of furniture, broken glass, dirt and decor, the house was still standing. Only two windows were broken. The section of roof over the three-season porch had come loose and was on top of some trees out the back. Other than that, there wasn't a great deal of damage.

The wind was still blowing into the living room; dust whirled up and hung in the air like a curtain. But this fresh breeze felt like a gentle whisper compared to what had raged during the night.

They walked out into the yard. Dawn cracked the sky at the horizon, as though nothing had happened. The clouds moving in cast a shadowy darkness over the landscape, but they were only stragglers from the storm. Several of the lovely linden and maple trees were down, uprooted. The top of the big linden in their yard had snapped off and was dangling. The trees that were still standing bowed humbly in the wind. The only thing that seemed unchanged was the grass beneath her feet.

The shed had transformed into kindling. No cars, no people were in sight. A couple of newspapers blew by on the street. The lake had risen and the water was lapping at the edge of the road. The air was sweeter, milder, and smelled like seawater.

Only once before had she experienced such joy to be alive – fifteen years ago, on a boat, as she fled ViaTerra for the second time. The open bay back then, the open landscape before her now, gave her the same sense of euphoria. *I'm alive. My heart is beating. The blood is flowing through my veins.*

It took three days for them to make contact with the outside world. The internet had been knocked out by the storm, despite a decade's hard work to install underground fibre across the island. Later they learned that the base stations had been damaged by the storm, and they suffered power outages that lasted for several days.

They tried to get down the road on foot to find someone, but the road was flooded here and there with water from the rising lake. In addition, trees had fallen like bowling pins and blocked the way.

At last they reluctantly accepted that they were stuck in the house for the time being. They cleared the yard, put up hardboard over the broken windows, repaired the porch roof, and cleaned like never before. A large pile of rubbish took shape in the back yard. Denzel ran around the property, sniffing, eager to take in all the new smells the wind had ripped from the ground.

Impatient and restless in their ignorance of what effect the storm had had elsewhere, they mostly worked in silence, amazed and relieved to see one another's faces unharmed and alive now and then.

Sofia felt like she would die with worry for the shelter, but there was nothing she could do. It was impossible to contact anyone there. At the same time, her concern about parents and friends grew. It was like being stuck in a bubble after Armageddon.

Their phones were long since dead. On the first day, Julia fiddled with her tablet in an attempt to find a signal, but eventually its battery gave out. Then she threw the tablet on the floor, went to the bathroom, and slammed and locked the door. Sofia could hear her crying in there. When she came out, her eyes were red and swollen. Sofia tried to put an arm around her, offer some comfort, but Julia shook her off.

Sofia let her be. She knew that if Julia were simply left alone, she would usually be back to normal within half an hour.

On the first night after the storm, Sofia lay awake for a long time, listening for sounds, thinking she heard a rumble in the distance, waiting for all hell to break loose again. Each time she heard a noise, it felt like all the air was sucked out of her lungs. On the second night, she was so exhausted that she crashed at eight and slept for twelve hours.

On the third day, they were so sick of eating variations on dry sandwiches and so restless that they started arguing about the most trivial things. But then Benjamin got the idea that he could charge his laptop with the car battery and he managed to get an internet signal. They crawled onto the sofa together, crowded around the screen, and read the horrible news.

Hercules had nearly destroyed all the infrastructure of western Sweden. The losses were incredible.

Over a hundred people dead.

Thousands of houses were a total loss, roofs and walls carried off with the wind until only the cellar was left.

Schools, day cares, community centres – wrecked and totally unusable.

Trains, flights, and ferry traffic were all cancelled, no one knew for how long.

Historic monuments and buildings, which had taken centuries to build up, razed.

It was chaos.

They devoured all the news there was, horrified and distraught.

'Is my school still there?' Julia asked.

'I don't know, sweetie,' said Benjamin. 'It doesn't mention it here. But I'm sure it's fine. It was built pretty recently. I'll charge our phones so we can call around to everyone.'

'What if one of my friends died?'

'I'm sure they're all fine. Soon you can call and talk to them.'

Sofia used Benjamin's laptop to email Anna and her parents. Tears burning in her eyes, a big lump in her throat, she steeled herself to read their responses. The one from Anna came a few hours later.

> Everyone made it through uninjured, but the house was flattened. Nothing could be salvaged.

She cried while Benjamin held her. That beautiful house with its veranda. Their little community. The sense of security for those who had no other home. It had all been carried away on the wind.

'Everything's going to be fine,' said Benjamin. 'We'll rebuild the house. Look on the bright side. Everyone's alive.'

That was so Benjamin.

Sofia's parents' house in Fjelie outside Lund had survived just fine, aside from a couple of cherry trees that had been downed and fell on their roof.

That day, the power came back on. The TV turned on on its own and showed a stream of horrible images that Benjamin became glued to. There was even some footage from their neighbourhood. Slussens Pension was flooded, the veranda and restaurant totally destroyed. The Uddevalla bridge was closed, with portions of its arches destroyed, and it would take a long time to repair. The bridge to Stenungsund was closed, too, but the damage there was less extensive.

The news clips were repeated again and again. With their phones charged, they called family and friends.

Everyone had made it through. Benjamin's sister was in the hospital with injuries from a window that had broken in her apartment, but she would be discharged that day.

Julia's school in Henån had only received mild damage and would open again in a few days. As soon as Julia got hold of her friends she began to get restless. If she wasn't staring at her phone she was pacing around the house and biting her nails.

On the sixth day, she was sitting in front of the TV, half-watching *Extra*, a show about celebrities.

Mostly gossip, it seemed to Sofia, but Julia liked the program.

'Mom, come here! Hurry! Quick!' Julia suddenly called, her voice so urgent that Sofia came rushing over from the kitchen.

On the screen was a man standing on a slope in front of some craggy cliffs, the sea in the background. The camera slowly zoomed in on the speaker, who was dressed all in black.

She recognized him from the first glance. She would have known him from a mile away.

For what seemed like eternity, her heart stopped beating.

It was Franz Oswald.

Her first thought was that it was unfair that he still looked so good.

Her second thought was that all hell had just broken loose.

I think of my thus far short life as divided into two parts: the time before and after Earth's Children. And it's no exaggeration to say that the before time was paradise compared to what came later.

Vic and I were six years old when everything changed. Before this, we rode the roller-coaster of Mama's depression and Father's moods and whims. But betweentimes, we remained blissfully unaware of their strained relationship in the way only small children can be.

And there was a certain freedom in that.

OLD NICK

It's an early-spring evening. Fanny has gone home for the day. Mom is curled up on the sofa with her arms around her knees. She's still in her nightgown. Vic and I are invisible to her. She's in another world, one we don't understand.

We are three going on four. Now that Fanny is gone it feels as if we can do whatever we want, and we take full advantage. I pull a bunch of books from the bookcase and page through them, trying in vain to decipher the letters and tearing out pages that pique my interest. Vic is in the kitchen. I hear the racket as he bangs on pots with a ladle. Then comes the sound of breaking glass and an angry cry.

Mama doesn't react. She stares out the window. Unreachable. She's shivering, even though it's not even a bit chilly in our cottage.

'Stupid pitcher! Mama! The pitcher fell on the floor,' Vic calls.

But she doesn't hear him.

When the front door opens, I reflexively flinch. I turn around to see Father's shoes, a familiar sight. I smell his scent. Sometimes I wake in the middle of the night with that scent hovering above me in the dark. I know it's only my imagination, but it makes my heart pound.

He lingers in the doorway for a moment and observes the chaos in the room. Then he spots me and the pages I've torn from the books. His jaw is clenched, his eyes stern. I try offering a child's placating smile but it's no use.

Vic has heard him arrive too and is in the doorway to the living room with a broken glass pitcher in hand. It broke just beneath the handle. The sharp edges look dangerous, like shark teeth.

Father strides over, takes the pitcher from Vic, and puts it on a table. Then he picks Vic up and sets him down on the sofa. He's rather rough about it; Vic bounces a few times and looks scared.

Mama has emerged from her trance. She seems even more frightened than Vic.

Father hauls her off the sofa and shakes her hard, shouting terrible things. 'Useless mental case!' and, 'You are completely worthless!' I think he's about to hit her, but he doesn't. He only wants to scare her.

'You can keep the kids,' she says in a tiny voice. 'Just let me leave here.'

There was a time when we were allowed to visit the mainland with Mama. A time I only recall as a few faint, almost transparent, images. But Fanny told us Mama wanted to stay there with us, and Father flew into a rage. Mama isn't allowed to leave ViaTerra anymore. That makes her sad, and that's all I know about it.

Father pushes Mama back onto the sofa and says something about how she has to get hold of herself, or else…

I don't understand the last part.

You can keep the kids. *The words still echo in my head.*

Then he turns to us. He's smiling, and when he smiles it feels like winning first place in some competition. Suddenly he looks super nice. As if the mess in the cottage no longer exists.

'Come on, boys! I want to show you something. Get dressed and we'll go outside.'

We can dress ourselves, and it happens fast when Father's the one asking us to do it.

He takes each of us by the hand. My body warms at his touch; some of his energy flows into me. I hold tight to his big, dry hand.

We walk through the front door and over the heath to the sea. Father walks fast. I stumble now and then, but he doesn't get angry. Instead he pulls me up by the hand so I dangle in the air for a moment, and then he sets me down again. It gives me a pleasant tickle in my belly.

Everything is so beautiful out there. It's day and night at the same time. On one side of the sky, the sun has become a glowing drop of bronze sinking into the sea. On the other side, you can see the hint of the new moon. The wind is gentle, yet strong enough to send small ripples across the water.

By Devil's Rock, Father stops and points at the cliff.

'Do you know what the cliff is called?' he asks.

'Of course,' Vic says boldly. 'Devil's Rock.'

'Right,' says Father. 'But if that's Devil's Rock, where is the devil himself?'

Vic and I stare at each other uncertainly. Father laughs aloud. He points to the right of the slope, where the craggy outline of the rocks reaches up to the sky.

'Do you see that big rock up there? Doesn't it look like a face with a tooth sticking out of its mouth?'

I can see it now. The big boulder reminds me of a man in profile, something protruding from his upper jaw. It's as though it was invisible before. Now I can see it so clearly that I'm a little frightened.

'The old islanders called that rock Old Nick,' Father says. 'They said *that the devil himself was watching over the island up there. Devil's Rock was his trap. He lured people there and made them leap to their deaths.'*

Vic and I don't know what to say. It's so exciting that I shudder. A sense of camaraderie has risen between us and Father, an intimate feeling I'm not used to.

'Do you want to go up with me?' he asks.

'Yes, yes!' Vic cries, but I'm more skittish.

We start to climb up the rocks. Father notices I'm falling behind and lifts me up to ride piggyback. This moment of closeness, my arms around his broad shoulders, the warmth of his back against my body, takes my breath away. But Vic doesn't need to be carried. He bounds up the rocks, effortless and agile, all the way to the top.

The heath is bathed in moonlight, lit up like a stage. The water laps playfully at the cliffs far below us.

Father sets me down.

'There now! Go all the way out. I want to see what you're made of.'

Vic runs out, almost too fast; he has to stop short just before he reaches the edge. I totter over cautiously, wanting so badly to show that I'm brave too. When I'm nearly to the edge of the cliff, Father's hands suddenly come up under my arms, from behind. He lifts me high over his head, giving me a great view of the sea. The dark water stretches before me to the horizon. The lights of the mainland shimmer across the sound. I float in the air. A spray of water blows into my face. Father sways without warning and I am suddenly dizzy. My stomach turns inside out. But he pulls me close and holds me tight.

'In the olden days, they threw naughty children from this cliff,' he says. 'Think about that the next time you decide to make a mess.'

The waves thunder out at sea, and his voice is barely audible. But we understand.

Vic looks terrified and dashes away from the cliff and down to the slope. Father carries me down and sets me beside Vic. He eyes us closely. There is no more warmth in his gaze.

But then he starts to laugh and crouches down.

'Don't look so terrified! You've learned a lesson. Come here now, give me a hug!'

But it's not a real hug, it's just a quick squeeze, and then it's time to return to the cottage.

All the way home, my chest feels tight.

The air feels hard to breathe, even though gentle veils of evening mist fall over us.

The nice feeling I had earlier is gone.

3

Sofia clung to Benjamin's hand. The camera had zoomed in on Franz Oswald's face. He looked just as she remembered him: tanned, intense gaze, not a single strand of grey in his black hair. It seemed the only trace left by fifteen years was tiny furrows at the corners of his mouth. From smiling? Hardly.

But now she realized that something had changed about the way he spoke. This was a calmer, more collected Franz. Gone was the role of eager saviour; instead he had apparently taken on a more mature persona, that of a serious father figure who radiated security.

'This is a time of deep sorrow for our country, a time for reflection,' he said, his expression grave. 'What am I doing with my life? What are we doing to the earth? These are questions everyone should be asking themselves today. Climate change is the greatest threat to our existence. There is no time to waste. We cannot afford to be greedy. The fate of all of humanity, and our children's and grandchildren's futures, are on the line.'

He aimed a pensive smile into the camera.

'To those of you who have lost someone you love, or your home. To those of you whose life has gone to pieces. And to everyone who is working through trauma right now. I am with you. It is for your sake that I have come back.'

A gust of wind took hold of his hair and swept it back, but

he didn't react. He looked solemn and serious under the weight of this new burden he'd elected to take on. To help the Swedish people out of the crisis. Now he reminded the viewers that he had predicted natural disasters like this one twenty years ago. If more people had followed the clean-living philosophies of ViaTerra, perhaps it could have been avoided. He repeated the phrase 'Listen to Mother Earth,' and used poetic expressions like 'Her hunger, her thirst, her breath'. Somehow, these all sounded lovely coming from his lips.

Benjamin closed his hand tighter around Sofia's and whispered, 'What a hypocrite!'

'Right?' she said. Experience had taught her that Franz really didn't care about the environment. He'd once told her that ViaTerra's clean-living ideology was nothing more than a way to rope people in. Folks liked that kind of thing. In reality, it was all about his theses, which were only simple self-help exercises he claimed to have invented. The idea was for participants to recall incidents from their past and draw strength and energy from them. Some of the theses had remained completely opaque to her, even when she was on staff.

Julia had bounced off the sofa and was now leaning against its back, apparently enthralled by Franz Oswald.

For a moment, he didn't say a word.

'I understand that life may seem hopeless and unfair right now. That it can be hard to move on after this kind of disaster. But there is a way – ViaTerra, the way of the earth. All are welcome to walk this path with me. Thank you for listening!'

Sofia felt a warm gust, Julia's breath on her cheek.

'Shit, Mom! He's still a hottie!'

Sofia was frozen, staring at the screen. *If only you knew.*

Now the camera zoomed out from the cliffs of Fog Island and the viewers were transported to a studio where a group of people were chatting on a sofa. This was a set the channel had dubbed the 'crisis room'; a few celebrities, a psychologist, and a structural engineer were there to discuss various aspects of Hercules.

But now they were talking about the return of Franz Oswald instead.

'He sent this video to us today,' said the host. 'We here at *Extra* are the first to break the news of his return. What do you all think?'

The psychologist was sceptical and pointed out that Franz Oswald was not the only one to offer warnings about the greenhouse effect, and that he had a dubious past, to put it mildly. But one of the celebrities, a platinum blonde actress, interrupted.

'Come on! You have to at least give him a chance. That alleged rape took place over fifteen years ago. It was the woman's word against his. He was convicted of unlawful coercion and served his sentence. I've heard he has custody of the children he had with that woman, and that he's taking good care of them.'

An older woman, an author, nodded in agreement.

'I think it was clear watching that speech that he really cares. It was like you could see it in his eyes, there's no mistaking that.'

'It's admirable that *someone* is trying to lead people out of this crisis,' said the platinum blonde. 'All the politicians do is spout bullshit.'

The topic turned to all the rumours that had spread about Franz Oswald's disappearance from the public eye, after which they went back to discussing the storm. They showed horrifying images of the damage, some of which Sofia must have already seen a hundred times. Beneath the images was a ticker of statements from celebrities: *My heart is breaking. Hugs and strength to all who have been affected by Hercules.*

Sofia heaved a protracted sigh and turned off the TV. She

wiggled her hand out of Benjamin's, mostly because it was now dripping with sweat.

'This is unbelievable! People are actually listening to him, they believe him.'

'Oh well,' said Benjamin. 'They don't know the first thing about what he did to us. They have no idea how he treated the ViaTerra staff. The last thing they heard about was the trial, where he claimed Elvira was in on all of it. If she hadn't been fourteen, I'm sure he would have gotten off scot-free. There are politicians and other leaders who've been forgiven for much worse. Besides, what can he do? Give a sad little speech out there on Fog Island? His methods are stale.'

Julia was now straddling the arm of the sofa with her nose buried in her phone.

'He's all over the internet!' she exclaimed. 'News flashes, webcasts, all the socials. Hundreds of tweets a minute now. Not *that* stale, I guess. And look! There's a new website too.'

'Julia!' Benjamin said sharply. 'Your enthusiasm is uncalled for, considering what he did to Mom and me, and so many others.'

'Just the thought of his being back makes me want to vomit,' said Sofia.

'Honey, this has nothing to do with us,' Benjamin said, pulling her close.

'The media will make him into an eco-conscious national hero.'

'Hardly. He's not the only one talking about environmental destruction. Besides, he hasn't said anything of value in the past decade.'

Julia seemed completely oblivious to everything they were saying and pulled up yet another image of Franz Oswald. She took it in with a fascinated smile. A smile Sofia didn't like one bit. It felt like all the oxygen had been sucked out of the house. Bolting to her feet, she escaped out to the yard.

It was October. The storm had robbed the trees of their leaves too early, as though the blazing fall colour were a fire that had been blown out in a single breath. The surviving trees reached their bare, straggly branches to the sky. But despite the desolate sight, it was beautiful. The dew had already settled into a silver blanket on the grass. The smell of autumn mingled with the smell of the lake, sweeter and more pungent.

Sofia thought of the shelter and her conversation with Anna earlier that day. It was all gone; it had been razed to the ground. If they couldn't come up with vast sums of money, they would not be able to resume their work. When the storm came through, there had been seven defectors at the shelter. They had fled inland with Anna to ride out the storm in a kind family's cellar for a few days. Now Anna had got hold of an old VW bus and was taking them to her parents' summer home in the Stockholm archipelago. With any luck, they would be able to acclimatize them to the real world as gently as possible from there. Sofia had wanted to come along, but Anna thought it would be better for her to stay behind and explore all avenues for rebuilding the house. Donations, maybe. There was not a chance they would receive more state funding. The storm had caused so much damage that other operations would be prioritized.

Ever since talking to Anna, Sofia had felt as though there was a heavy stone in her belly. Images of the beautiful old house flashed through her mind: summer nights on the veranda, the faces of those they had helped. Although the shelter was only a few kilometres from their house, she didn't want to go there and see the mess. Not yet. The house had been insured, of course, but not against natural disasters. Not against Hercules.

Everything she'd worked for over the past years was in pieces, even as Franz was profiting from the disaster. And here came that smouldering hatred again. The feeling she'd thought she'd put behind her. A desire for redress so strong that it made her dizzy. She wanted to bleed him dry. Destroy him completely.

She lay on her back on the grass, immediately embraced by the darkness, by millions of stars and complete silence. The wet dew chilled her body; it felt like she was lying on ice.

My life is just a brief gasp in eternity, she thought, full of reverence for the starry sky. She closed her eyes, and suddenly she was twenty-one again, just as stubborn as Julia, on her way to Fog Island – to the greatest adventure of her life. Memories of the island returned to her. Sunsets, storms, the chill of those raw winter nights, the ever-returning fog. The buzz of joy at first, her love for Benjamin. Then, being held prisoner and her despair until she was finally freed. It all played in her mind's eye. She thought of how life could so easily slip through your fingers like sand without leaving even the faintest impression on the earth's surface. *I have to save the shelter*, she thought. *Somehow I'll make it happen, no matter the cost.*

A gust of wind carried the sound of Julia's ringing laughter from the house. The moisture had soaked through Sofia's trouser legs, so she stood up and walked back inside. She decided that Franz Oswald's success would come to a sudden end. The media would give him a few days in the limelight, but ViaTerra would never again get a foothold in what was now a broken society. People would focus on taking care of their own business. There was no time for mysterious gatherings or idol worship.

As if I care, she thought.

But she did.

This belief that Father had gone underground. It was almost as though the media wanted it to be so. It made him more mysterious. But he was here all along, and he was particularly present in our lives.

Just before he withdrew from public life, the manor house burned down. At first the police thought it was insurance fraud, and Father was a suspect. But no one was able to prove anything. Now, as I write this, I still don't know how the fire started. But almost immediately the manor house was rebuilt, and the new one was even grander and more imposing. I was too little to remember that time, but I've heard construction moved quickly. Suddenly, everything was back to normal again.

So why did Father stop showing his face in public?

I don't have all the answers, but I know one thing for sure: he was absorbed in a bunch of different projects. Visions of the future he had decided to make reality.

One of these projects turned into Earth's Children.

But before that, there was Grandma. Without her, I never would have been sitting here today, writing to you.

GRANDMA

Mama is having one of her better days. She played with us on the playground outside the house and took us on a walk in the forest. Now we're curled up on the sofa while she reads aloud to us. She doesn't read particularly well, it's slow and stuttering, but that doesn't matter.

We're so fascinated by the book that we don't notice Father until his shadow falls over us.

'You still read to them? When are they going to learn to read on their own?' he asks.

Mama squirms. All at once she looks unhappy.

Her voice becomes childlike and pleading.

'They're only four. And Thor can already read a little.'

I know she's lying, but I don't dare contradict her.

'That's great. Then he can read aloud to me.'

He takes the book from her hands and places it in my lap. I look at Mama, unsure of what to do, hoping that she'll help me out, but she says nothing.

'Read to me, Thor!' Father says. 'I can't wait to hear this.'

I stare at the page. Long, black lines of incomprehensible symbols flow together as I strain my eyes to decipher them. Tears spring to my eyes and soon the page is all blurry.

'The stars shine in the great black sky,' I manage to produce, because Mama read that part not long ago. Father shakes his head in anger.

'It says dark, *Thor,' he says. 'So that's how she reads to you, illiterate bitch.'*

I know he means Mama. All the colour has drained from her cheeks and she chews her lower lip nervously.

Father yanks the book from my grasp and tosses it across the room, where it hits the wall and thuds to the floor. His eyes are furious and he starts to shout that Mama is useless and lazy. He throws things: books, a coffee mug, and Mama's nail polish, which stains the white walls red. I've never seen him this angry before. He aims a vicious glare at me and I'm scared, not that he'll hit me, but that he'll stop loving me.

Fanny comes running from the kitchen and he shouts at her to go to Penance, a word I don't understand yet. Fanny looks terrified as she gathers her things and vanishes from the cottage. Mama stands at attention. Father takes hold of her beautiful long hair and pulls her face close to his own.

'Fuck with me and you'll see what happens,' he hisses.

With one yank he tears open her blouse so the fabric rips, buttons bounce off the floor, and her breasts are bared. He grabs them, squeezing until she shrieks.

'If you hadn't gotten so fat I would teach you a lesson. Now you're not even good enough to fuck,' he said.

He pushes her away roughly and marches out of the cottage.

Vic and I are crying. I'm sure I will never get to hold Father's hand again, or ride on his shoulders or feel the warmth of his body, because now I've both lied to him and shown him how hopelessly stupid I am. Mama starts crying too. Then she makes a half-hearted attempt to clean up the mess in the cottage. I hear her muttering to herself. Goddamn fucking bastard, idiot... *sometimes she uses bad words. Fanny told us Mama is so young that she hasn't learned to talk properly, like an adult. But then Mama says nothing for the rest of the evening. We have to eat macaroni and cheese, again, and she doesn't read us a bedtime story.*

The next day, all she does is sit on the sofa and stare out the window.

Fanny doesn't come. Vic and I must take care of ourselves, and we do, but without making too much of a mess. Neither of us wants to get thrown off Old Nick.

The next day, our miracle arrives. We hear loud voices outside the cottage. I crawl off the sofa and peer out the open window.

An old woman is on the lawn, along with Father. She has long white hair and is tanned and almost as tall as Father. They're shouting at each other.

'How did you get in here?' Father yells.

'The guard let me in, isn't it obvious?'

'You are not welcome here. You are dead to me, you bitch.'

'After everything you've done, you're just as dead to me,' she says. 'But I want to meet my grandchildren.'

'You've never done anything for me. I don't even want you near them.'

Father is so angry, but the lady isn't afraid of him. Her arms are crossed over her chest as she glares at him. They stand there staring for a long time. I'm afraid they'll notice me, but their eyes are locked together. A silent battle is being waged between them.

Something happens to Father. His gaze turns inward, it's as though you can see the cogs turning in his brain. This is what he looks like when he's about to have a flash of inspiration, I know this. He must absolutely not be disturbed when this occurs.

'Okay, you did one thing for me,' he says. 'You taught me to read. Teach the brats to read and write. If you do that you may come here twice a week, but no more. And I don't want anything to do with you.'

He doesn't wait for a response, just leaves the old woman and walks toward the manor. She's smiling now, and even though she's old she looks beautiful when she smiles.

Then she enters our cottage, this miracle who smells good and gives us such long, firm hugs that we can't breathe. We feel embarrassed; after all, we don't know her, but I think it feels nice. Her embrace is soft and warm.

Twice a week she comes, but never when Father is there.

She teaches us to recognize our letters, see how they're different, how they sound, and how to put them together into words.

Each time she comes by, she teaches Mama something new. How to fix other meals than macaroni, how to bake buns, things like that. Mama likes it. She starts to laugh again.

The woman smells good, like a mixture of our woodshed and sweet winter apples. She says we may call her Grandma, but not when Father can hear. Then she tells us she lives in a small cottage where Father also used to live, when he was little. But we shouldn't talk about this either.

'Now I'll need to winterize the cottage so I can live there all year long and keep visiting you two,' she says one day.

'How do you do that?' I ask.

'You put in double-glazed windows and real heat and so forth.'

'Whoa, is it super expensive?' Vic asks.

At that, she laughs.

'Yes, but you're worth it.'

And that sounds so nice that my whole body feels soft, like after a bath, and I am brave enough to crawl into her lap for the very first time.

4

It was one in the morning, and Sofia was tired. Even so, she was glued to the computer in the dark living room.

Benjamin was already asleep. He had been working on clearing the roads all day and had returned home with a euphoric expression to tell her that tomorrow Highway 160 would be open all the way to Stenungsund.

Julia, who was behaving ever more like a tiger in a very tiny cage, had bounced off the walls, cheering for joy.

But Sofia's day had been frustrating. She had contacted potential sponsors and financiers to ask for help rebuilding the shelter. Although she had used her mildest voice, begging and fawning, she had received the same chilly response again and again. Unfortunately, there were more important things that had to be prioritized. They would think about it and get back to her once things had settled down after the storm. Then she began to call around to find temporary spaces to rent, but once again encountered only rejection. There were social institutions that were suddenly without premises, families without homes after the storm. Always the same, stinging implication: *what you do is no longer important.*

After dinner she was exhausted and fell asleep on the sofa. When she woke up, the house was silent, and that's when she decided to search for Franz Oswald online. Just a quick check-in to see what he was up to. With a few clicks she gained access to his new empire.

The first thing to come up was his website, which was incredibly sophisticated and flashy, sporting a new ViaTerra logo. The background image was a picture of the manor house, and it made her gasp. Last time she'd seen that building, years ago, it had been ablaze. That had been her revenge against Franz for raping her. Benjamin and Sofia's best friend Simon had helped her escape over the sound. They had stood on the boat, watching the smoke spread over the island. But now the manor seemed back to its usual self. Grand and gleaming white. The caption under the image read: *The manor at ViaTerra is 100% eco-friendly, hurricane-proof, and built to stand for a millennium.* The website included a video tour of the newly renovated annexes, which served as guest houses.

There were pictures of Franz posing at various angles. He was sometimes serious, sometimes smiling, and one photo showed him gazing out at an indigo sea from Devil's Rock. There was a quote underneath that one: *We can only change the world one person at a time, one life, one rescued soul that now walks the way of the earth.*

There were even clips from his old lectures and a link to video chats that were apparently held each evening at eight. Here, people from all over the world could listen to a short address from Franz, with automatic subtitles in forty-eight different languages. These live webcasts were held in English. At the end of each, he would answer questions. Four of these talks were available to watch, and she clicked on the most recent one, titled 'The Fundamentals of Life'. Franz appeared before a picture window with the sea in the background. Clearly these talks were broadcast from his office.

'Today I'm going to talk about the unchangeable,' he began. 'As we all know, utopians predict a sensational future. Spacecraft that will take us to other solar systems in the universe, neural networks that will outperform the human brain's capacity to make decisions. Some predict dystopian anarchy. But in reality, life doesn't move that quickly. Our limitations are largely due to our bodies. And there are certain unchangeable principles that govern our bodies.'

Then he began to talk about his usual ideas. Sleeping in complete darkness, organic and locally grown food, his typical marketing techniques. He paused for effect.

'And sex, of course; a future without different kinds of sex is basically unthinkable,' he said with a sly smile.

After this there was a Q&A session. A woman from France asked if Franz thought good sex could prolong a life. Franz replied in fluent French, which made him seem to be a linguistic genius. But Sofia knew, of course, that he had lived in France when he was young. He replied that sex was the ultimate pleasure and life is a spectrum running from death to complete ecstasy. So of course sex could prolong a life. The woman then asked if he believed in open relationships.

'Sex is as close to nature as you can get, and I see no reason a person should limit their sexual desires,' he said.

He was in his element now, radiating charm with a gleam in his eye.

Sofia wondered how many women were watching this and dreaming that Franz was hitting on them. If only they knew.

She clicked on a few icons. A new book: *The Power of the Earth and Your Future*, which would be released next year, translated into fifty languages. Praise from world leaders, natch. Celebrity testimonials about ViaTerra. A new sponsor program called Foremost Friends of the Earth, which was built upon different levels of membership depending on how much money you donated to ViaTerra.

There was a list of environmental organizations, with ViaTerra at number one.

Another link led to 'winter programs'; those who wanted to meet Franz were welcome to take part in a five-day conference in the Swedish mountains where they would celebrate the new year and discuss his plans for the future. This page ended with a plucky line: *Want to start a ViaTerra club in your region?* If so, a certain Bella Svahnberg was the one to contact.

Sofia stared at the picture of the manor house again, feeling slightly relieved. It was a good thing that they'd restored the lovely building. But everything else he was up to gave her a headache. She refilled her glass of wine. Typically she wasn't much of a drinker, but right now she needed something to take the edge off her anxiety.

When she returned to her search, she found pages about ViaTerra and Franz on all the social networks and clips from his lectures all over the place. The media had also jumped on the trend, some with positive articles suggesting that he really had being sitting on the answers to many existential questions twenty years ago. Back when he showed up out of nowhere and started preaching his clean-living message.

She wondered if people would believe any of this – it seemed so transparent. But then she recalled how devoted she herself had been once upon a time. Plenty of people would be won over by his charm, no doubt about it. Considering the thousands who had liked his new pages, he was already popular once more.

She filled her glass again and realized she had drunk almost a whole bottle.

Sofia heard steps behind her, and when she turned around she nearly choked on her wine. It was Julia, dressed in a black lingerie set consisting of a bustier, garters and retro-looking nylons. In addition she was wearing long black gloves and four-inch heels. She merely stood there grinning like an elaborate doll, too young to understand how fantastic her body was.

'My Halloween costume. Like it?'

'Are you nuts? You are not going out like that! Over my dead body!'

Julia instantly looked hurt.

'Mom, I'm going as Dita von Teese. Wasn't she popular back in your day?'

'Hardly. Check with Grandma.'

'Well, she's cool again now. Or her style is, anyway. We're going to rent the scout cabin for Halloween, a whole crew is coming from Uddevalla too.'

'You may not go out dressed like that. Not under any circumstances.'

Any other fifteen-year-old would look ridiculous in that get-up, but not Julia. Despite her young age, she already had an hourglass figure.

'Aren't I hot? I'm gonna take a bottle of champagne and pour it over myself, there's a picture of Dita doing that... Oh my God, chill out, Mom, I'm only kidding! I'm going to wear a dress over this.'

Sofia started laughing. It was so like Julia to provoke her this way.

'I think you've got cabin fever. Good thing school is open again in two days.'

Julia caught sight of the screen of Sofia's laptop before she had time to slam it closed.

'Mom! Are you like totally obsessed with that hottie?'

'Not at all. It's just upsetting that people listen to him.'

'But that was ages ago that you were in the cult. Maybe he's changed.'

'Doubt it,' she said, a little too fast.

'Is there something you haven't told me?'

'No, I mean, there are some things I might tell you later. It's complicated.'

Julia seemed satisfied with that. She did a pirouette.

'Okay, I'll put a tight dress on over this, but it's going to be really short and have a plunging neckline.'

Sofia gave a huge yawn and stood up.

'Come on, let's go to bed, it's late,' she said, gathering Julia into her arms. She held her tight and inhaled the sweet scent of her hair.

Sofia had trouble falling asleep. It felt wrong, lying to Julia, but did she have any choice? No one must know that Franz had raped Sofia. It had happened fifteen years ago, when he kidnapped her and kept her locked up in the cellar. She had decided not to report the rape the very day she managed to escape and set fire to the manor house. Ironically enough, Franz had created a perfect alibi for her, one she could use as proof she hadn't been on the island. She had been kept prisoner at ViaTerra twice, and certainly didn't have any desire to be locked up for arson. But she didn't regret setting that fire. It had been sweet revenge. The people who'd helped her escape were the only ones who knew the truth, and it had to stay that way.

And then there was the manuscript that had been languishing in her files for almost a decade.

Sofia had written a book based on a family history by Franz Oswald's paternal grandmother, Sigrid von Bärensten. It was a long, sad story about the fate of women at the manor and how Franz had been tortured by his father at the age of three. Sofia had taken the papers with her when she fled the cult – or, rather, she had stolen it. And then she had used the material to write a book of her own. But no publisher would even discuss the book without having settled the matter of copyright with

Franz. And that was a pipe dream. She wasn't even sure if he knew she had the family history, but now that he was in vogue again, the media would drool over the terrible tale of Sigrid von Bärensten. And with any luck, the same would go for some brave publishing house.

She tossed and turned in bed, staring up at the ceiling. Listening to the silence of the house. The desire to talk to someone about all of this welled up inside her. Franz, back again. The media frenzy. Where it all might lead. She knew Benjamin refused to dwell on the past; he always told her to live in the present moment and put it all behind her. But there was so much on the line.

Her thought wandered freely and snagged on Simon, who had been her best friend for years. They had worked together at ViaTerra, Simon as the gardener and Sofia as Franz's secretary. Later, Simon had gotten a job at the pension on Fog Island. It was thanks to Simon that they had been able to serve locally grown vegetables at the restaurant there. He was the first person she had dared to open up to about the terror of ViaTerra. Each time she escaped, he'd helped her. When everything looked grim and hopeless, she had always been able to talk to Simon.

He would understand.

There was just one problem.

Simon had gone up in smoke five years ago. He seemed to have vanished off the face of the earth.

It was unusual for the staff to be allowed to leave ViaTerra when Father was there. His employees were expected to be on hand in case he needed anything.

When Vic and I were five, we were allowed to visit the mainland with Mama once a month to see Mama's aunt. But only if someone on staff came along. Most of the time, it was Madde who tagged along with us. She was Father's secretary and worshipped him more than anyone else in ViaTerra. She would circle nervously around Mama to make sure she didn't say or do anything wrong. Questions about how we were doing must always be answered with cheerfulness and positivity, and Madde imprinted this in our little heads.

I sometimes sensed discord between Mama and Madde, and that made our trips less enjoyable. Getting to ride the ferry, go shopping, all of that. Because Madde had opinions about everything we did.

We hardly ever got to see Grandpa Anders, even though he worked for ViaTerra. For a long time he was in Penance, and you weren't allowed to talk to anyone in Penance at all. Later, Father felt that Grandpa was a bad influence on us. He called him a 'weakling' and 'slow', an 'opportunist'. Mama called him a 'coward' and a 'betrayer'. She seemed relieved that he didn't visit very often.

So, for the most part, we were isolated with Mama in the cottage. Our time outside was limited to the playground in the courtyard. Soon enough we grew restless and bored.

Which meant it was extra exciting when Father invited visitors and allowed us to meet them.

THE VISITOR

We're wearing nice clothes. Mama is too; Father told her to. There's a lady called Carmen Gardell who's going to visit. Vic asks Mama why this lady is so important, and the answer is that she is Father's advisor. His face to the outside world. Mama tries her best to explain, but we don't understand. Father's face is fine the way it is, as long as he isn't angry.

Vic and I sit in the bay window, pressing our noses to the windowpane and waiting to spot our guest. Just as we're about to give up and climb down, she turns up in the courtyard with Father. She's holding his arm and tossing her head back when she laughs at something he says. They head for our cottage. She's the strangest lady I've ever seen. A very short skirt, high heels, and hair that looks like a birds' nest; her blouse is so tight that her breasts seem way too big for her tiny body.

'Go sit on the sofa this minute!' Mama snaps at us.

Her nervous energy makes the air tremble. I feel nervous too; my body itches with it. But Vic is excited and shoves me so I almost fall over.

'Go hide in the wardrobe, you dork,' he says. 'She's going to think you're a girl and be all gross and cutesy with you.'

I don't argue with him. That would only make things worse. But I don't get into the wardrobe either.

The door opens. The smell of Carmen's perfume is the first thing to enter, and it's so strong I recoil. Father is wearing a suit. He looks so handsome that I get a lump in my throat.

'Here they are!' he says, sweeping his hand towards us. 'Invictus and Thor, say hello to Carmen.'

We dutifully do as we're told.

'Oh my,' says Carmen, looking surprised. Her voice is deep, like a man's.

'You can say that again,' says Father. 'It's like you hardly want to be seen with them in public.'

She eyes us up and down and smiles at us. But it's a cold, calculating smile.

'But you really should, even so,' she says. 'It will inspire a lovely image of you as a devoted family man.'

Father looks annoyed.

'I won't be showing my face in public for many years. And that's where you come in. Because when I do, my image must be spotless.'

'It would also be good for your image if you got yourself a wife,' Carmen says with a saucy smile.

Even though I'm only five, I understand what she's getting at and feel afraid that this scary person will start hanging around with Father. But he just laughs.

'That's where you're wrong, Carmen. It's important for the image I mean to create that I remain single.'

Carmen looks disappointed. She looks even stranger at close range. Her eyelashes are very long and clumpy with mascara. She almost looks more like a character in a comic book than a real person.

She walks up to Vic and ruffles his hair.

'Why, this one is the spitting image of you.'

I feel more and more strongly that she is a peculiar and unpleasant person.

Then Father does something unexpected. He walks up to the sofa, where we're perched, and picks me up.

'I love both of my sons equally,' he says, hugging me hard. His nice smell overshadows Carmen's perfume when I'm close to him, so close that I can feel his heart beating against my chest. For a brief moment I lose all contact with the world around me. I am a pupa, wrapped up in a cocoon. I never want to come out.

Father suddenly drops me to the sofa and looks around the house.

'Is the old witch the one who cleaned up around here?' he asks Mama.

'If you mean Karin, she also taught them to read and count,' Mama says. She shoots us an anxious glance. Don't ruin this for me.

'That's good. They can read to me and Carmen then. I hope it won't turn out like last time.'

Vic and I are eager. We can do it. We want to show him. We fight over the book on the coffee table, and Vic wins, of course. And then he reads – it's a little touch and go at first, because he's nervous, but he does a good job. Father asks me to count to twenty, and I do. Very quickly. We've almost forgotten that Carmen is there. Father praises us. He nods in satisfaction and aims a surly glance at Mama.

'A different story from when you were in charge of them.'

'How often do they receive lessons?' Carmen asks.

'Twice a week, but soon it will be time for them to start school. They will be taught here at home, naturally.'

Carmen looks thoughtful. She stares at us oddly.

'Look, the only thing I think anyone could find fault with is that they might seem a little isolated if they aren't allowed to spend time with other children.'

Father, who had started pacing impatiently, stops short. He shushes Carmen loudly. Something she said has spurred his thoughts into action. That means we must all be quiet as a mouse. The slightest noise might interrupt his train of thought.

His gaze has turned inward; he walks around, stroking his chin as he muses. It's so quiet you can hear the floorboards creak under his feet. Then he stops and fixes his eyes on Carmen.

'I think you have a point. But I won't have them go to any public or private school. The Swedish educational system is pure garbage. They will be raised according to the principles of ViaTerra.'

'Of course,' says Carmen. 'I understand.'

Father goes to the window. He stands still, gazing out at the courtyard. Slowly, thoughtfully, he nods to himself.

'Come take a look at this!' he says to Carmen. 'Look at this property. Can you imagine a better place for children to grow up?'

She approaches the window and stands close beside him, her side pressed to his body.

'It's truly the lap of luxury, Franz,' she says in her hoarse voice. 'A total paradise.'

'We're going to create something great here for the children,' he says at last. 'Something absolutely unique.'

5

Simon.

Sofia had thought about him every day since he disappeared. Of all of Simon's traits, Sofia liked his calm nature the most. Hearing his voice was all it took for her to relax. Whenever she found herself in a crisis, he had always supported her. But then, late one night five years ago, he had called her up, skipping the chit-chat and getting straight to the point.

'I'm out of here, Sofia.'

'What do you mean? Where are you going?'

'I don't know, exactly.'

'Can you stop speaking in riddles and tell me what's going on?'

'I've found someone to replace me at the pension and I'm going to spend some time travelling.'

'For how long?'

'I don't know that, either. I plan to take each day as it comes. Look, you know I like talking to you, but I'm going to be unavailable to start with. It has nothing to do with you. It's just something I have to carry through.'

At first she thought he was joking, but there was a grave note in his voice.

Simon's friendship had been something she took for granted, something she could always fall back on. As soon as the meaning of his words sank in, she felt ill at ease and couldn't produce any sound at all for a moment. It was as though someone had amputated part of her body. This was serious. Simon was going to vanish.

'But Simon, why can't we keep in touch?'

'There is a reason. But I can't tell you what it is right now.'

'You'll come see us before you go, though, right?'

'I'd really like to, but there's no time.'

'Why can't you say where you're going?'

'It's complicated. I plan to be totally anonymous for a while. You just have to trust me. As soon as the time is right, I'll contact you again.'

'I'm going to miss you so much. Isn't there anything I can do to make you stay?'

'Sorry. But I promise you'll be the first one I call when I get home.'

The tone of his voice told her there would be no changing his mind. She wanted to say she loved him. Not like *that*, but he would understand.

She was sure a life without him would be bleak and banal. And at first, it was. It took a year for her to stop reflexively grabbing her phone to call him. She kept sending emails and texts, just in case he changed his mind and wanted to talk to her. But not a single response came. For the first few years, she searched his name online, certain he would turn up somewhere. But she found nothing more than old articles about the pension's gardens, nothing new since Simon took off. A thousand times, she asked herself why. She couldn't come to terms with the fact that he had simply vanished.

In the end, she accepted that Simon was gone, but she never stopped thinking about him. And now, ever since Franz Oswald had surfaced again, she thought of him many times a day.

★

It had been ten days since the storm. Benjamin was out helping clear debris and Julia was at school. Sofia was home alone and feeling restless. The first frost had come overnight, dew transforming into a gleaming blanket that made the ground shimmer. It was a partly cloudy day with a hint of winter in the air. The chill had robbed the air of all its moisture, in its eagerness to frost the landscape. The sun fought its way through the thin layer of clouds and was sparkling on the rime.

Sofia had gone grocery shopping. On the way home, she decided to drive by the shelter, but this turned out to be a terrible decision. The site looked like a garbage dump. All that was left of the house was the foundation and a few splintered walls. Furniture, beds, kitchen utensils and other objects were strewn across the lawn, as though a giant had walked through the house and tossed its contents every which way. She stared at the destruction. A chilly inland breeze blew straight through her thick wool sweater and made her shiver.

A particular sensation overwhelmed her as she stood there – it had been so long since she experienced it that it took her a moment to recognize it. Anxiety. The feeling that something always had to go wrong. This discomfort lasted all the way home. Once she was through the front door and had put the groceries away in the fridge and pantry, she realized she hadn't eaten breakfast. She popped two pieces of bread in the toaster, but when they were ready she simply stared at them on the plate. As though they might suddenly take off and fly away. She had no appetite. She threw the toast in the sink, went to the living room, and sank into an easy chair.

Her phone lit up with an unknown number. Her heart beat faster. Maybe her attempts to secure new funding had brought results.

A woman with a young, pleasant voice said she was calling from the investment firm Stone Equity in Stenungsund – it was a company Sofia had never heard of.

'We have a financier who would like to meet with you to discuss rebuilding the shelter you ran on Orust,' she said.

'But I never contacted your firm – how did you hear about it?'

'News travels fast in the business world. In any case, our financier would like to book a meeting with you today to discuss your situation.'

'Who is it?'

'He would prefer to introduce himself, if that's all right.'

'Sure, when should I be there?'

'At four o'clock, if you can make it?'

She glanced at her watch. Quarter past two – it would work.

'I'll be there.'

Her hope soared. If this benefactor had gone to the trouble of contacting her, he must be interested. Although perhaps he hoped to make a profit on the shelter. He probably didn't know that the shelter ran at a deficit and Benjamin had to pitch in funds now and then. She found all the calculations she'd made of the cost to rebuild and moved them onto her laptop. After a quick shower, she put her hair up in a bun and browsed through her wardrobe for a proper outfit. She settled on a navy blue suit that made her look businesslike, then added high-heeled shoes and some makeup before checking herself out one last time in the hall mirror. Last of all she took Denzel out for a quick pee in the yard and gave him a bone to chew on while she was gone.

Before she jumped in the car, she called Benjamin to ask if he'd heard of Stone Equity, and he had. Their offices were right downtown.

All the way to Stenungsund, she rehearsed what she would say. She rattled off statistics to herself: how many defectors there were in Sweden who needed help, how many they had helped already. She recited a brief summary of their reintegration methods. All this practice distracted her from the destruction outside her car window. So many downed trees. Sheds overturned. The storm had left its mark all over the landscape. She was sick and tired of being reminded about Hercules.

She arrived at Stone Equity at quarter to four. The firm was in a new building with a white plaster façade and large glass doors. Loath to be too early, seem overeager, she paced outside the door for a while. But then she got so chilly that she began to shiver and slipped through the front doors at five to four. The lobby was tastefully done in granite and glass. The receptionist, a very elegant woman, smiled in a way that made Sofia feel important.

'Hi, Sofia! He hasn't arrived yet, but I'll show you to his office and you can wait there.'

She guided Sofia down a long corridor and opened the door to the last room. The office was enormous, with white leather chairs, a large mahogany desk, and a world map done in bronze glass on the wall.

The receptionist pulled out the visitors' chair in front of the desk and Sofia gingerly took a seat.

'Would you like a cup of coffee or tea?'

'No thanks, I'm fine.'

The receptionist's heels echoed off the floor as she left, closing the door behind her. A harsh silence ensued. It was chilly in the room, or perhaps Sofia just hadn't had time to warm up yet. The desk in front of her looked unused. It was empty aside from a white leather blotter and a matching pen holder. A large computer monitor stood on a sideboard and a tablet was charging on the desk. She shifted position, craned her neck, and tried to read what was on the monitor, but it was too far away. Even though the sun was shining into the window, there was not a speck of dust to be seen on the furniture. And the room was completely devoid of any odour. It was like a sterile trap. Something about the atmosphere brought up unwelcome thoughts. Whoever worked here must be so pedantic that he could hardly be interested in her messy little shelter. There must have been some misunderstanding, something she likely wouldn't be able to fix.

She didn't hear the door open – there were just steps, and then his voice.

'Sofia, welcome!'

She whirled around.

It was him. Franz Oswald.

He was almost by her side, so close she could reach out and touch him. It felt like her chair was spinning and tipping backwards into a void. The room went grey and foggy. Nausea welled up inside her as if something had been rotting in her stomach for a very long time, something she'd managed to forget. *For God's sake, don't faint!* She pressed her nails into her palms and the pain drove the fog and the dizziness away. She forced herself to look at him.

'I think you have something that belongs to me,' he said with a smile.

Behind the cottage where we lived was a large meadow where sheep used to graze. When ViaTerra's animal caretaker ran away, long ago, a lot of the livestock was disposed of. These days, most of the food served in the cafeteria was vegetarian. There were only a few cows and hens in the barn. The meadow had been empty for years. Vic and I played there sometimes, until he pushed me into a stand of stinging nettles and I refused to go there anymore.

Just a few weeks after his meeting with Carmen Gardell, Father began a construction project in the meadow. Vic and I were entranced by the steam shovels and trucks and constantly hung around nearby. We didn't know what was being built, and Mama answered our questions evasively. But one day, Father came to tell us. The look on his face was solemn and a bit sly.

'You're going to have your own school soon. And friends.'

Vic hooted with delight. I thought it sounded a little scary and tried to put on a happy face but didn't quite succeed.

'Doesn't that sound like fun, Thor?' Father asked.

'Yes, super fun,' I said, smiling as wide as I could, and finally he took his eyes off me.

I have often thought about the day the parents and children arrived, trying to understand the decision those parents made at that time. Clearest in my memory are their faces as they looked at Father. Full of respect and admiration. It was a different sort of love than when they looked at their children. Maybe that was why they never understood what went on at the school.

But there was so much we weren't allowed to talk about.

THE SCHOOL

Construction on the buildings is finished. One consists of several rooms with bunk beds. There's nothing fun to do there besides jump on the beds. But the other building is large and exciting. Inside is a classroom with desks and chairs, a gym, and even a library. It smells new, like wood and plastic, and the sound echoes off the walls when we run around in it. In truth, we're not allowed to play in the schoolhouse, but no one can keep us away. One day Mama said the authorities were coming to do a school inspection, and we weren't allowed to go there. But today we snuck out early while Mama was still sleeping.

Suddenly she calls for us; her voice is all shrill and she looks anxious.

'You have to come in and put on your smart clothes. We're having visitors!'

She refuses to answer our questions and seems harried. She gets us dressed and combs our hair, tugging and pulling at my unruly curls. It hurts so much I start to cry.

There are excited, eager voices outside and then Father's voice, thundering over everything else. We crawl up into the bay window and right away we see them: a group of people standing around listening to Father. Several children. We haven't met other kids for a long time. Vic gets so wound up that he starts running in circles around the living room. I press my nose to the windowpane and observe the group breathlessly. Three girls and three boys. Some are clinging to their parents' hands, while some are dashing around the courtyard. I feel nervous, unsure of what I'll say to them. At the same time, I want to be outside playing with them. They seem so wonderfully free.

'Mama, what are they doing here?' I ask.

'They're going to come here and go to school with you. Won't that be fun?'

The group vanishes from sight. Mama says Father is going to show them the school, and then we'll eat dinner together.

Dinner takes ages and I feel like the other kids are staring at me weirdly. Father speaks almost without stopping. He explains his pedagogy, his views on education and child-rearing. The parents hang on his every word. Some of them get a glassy look; others nod along the whole time. Even the children gape at him with mouths hanging open.

'You can view this as the most important project ViaTerra has ever undertaken. These children are unruined and unrestrained. With the help of ViaTerra's methods, and by sparing them the destructive forces of public school, they will have opportunities completely unavailable to other children. In fact, I can promise a brilliant future for them. They will likely become the vanguard in the fight for a better world.'

One woman sitting beside him clears her throat discreetly.

'I'm sorry, but I'm having trouble getting used to the idea of leaving her here all week. I apologize for being so hesitant, it's just that as a mom…'

'I understand,' Father says, placing his hand over hers. 'But sometimes it can be good for children to be away from their parents and learn to make it on their own. They'll have competent supervision here. Our educational plan has been approved by the Schools Inspectorate. And they'll come home every Saturday and Sunday, of course. But you're also welcome to spend the weekend here with them. Use our spa, enjoy the organic food and the beautiful nature of our island.'

I can see the woman melting. The image of her face will come to haunt me for a long time. That concerned wrinkle smoothing out. Her eyes when she looked at Father. There's something eerie about that image that I can't put my finger on.

'In any case, I'll stop talking so you can enjoy the meal. But I want

you all to know that I hand-picked you for this meeting. You are the most devoted members of ViaTerra, people I've always been able to depend upon. Thank you for supporting me during these difficult years.'

After dinner, Father goes through the educational plans with the parents and we are sent back to the cottage. I try to memorize the other children's faces. The tough-looking boy with the gap between his front teeth. The girl who was so shy. But mostly, the boy with the kind eyes and curly hair. Just like mine, but dark. Matteo, I think his name was.

The next morning, we're woken by loud pounding on the front door. Mama goes to answer it. Still half asleep, we find ourselves standing in our pyjamas and staring at Father and two people I've never seen before. A fat lady with glasses who looks grumpy, and a man who is tall, taller than Father, and seems very strong.

'We're all set,' Father says cheerfully to Mama. 'The kids are arriving next week.'

Mama mutters something anxious in response. Father tells her to go get herself, and us, dressed. When we return, they're sitting on the sofa. Their curious gazes sweep across us.

'Come here, Vic and Thor,' says Father. 'I want you to say hello to your new counsellor and teacher.'

The guy approaches us first. He seems to be about the same age as Mama.

His hair is blond, downy, and so short that you can see his pink scalp underneath. His eyes are icy blue. His gaze flickers over us. When he looks at me, his mouth crimps into a smile – and not an entirely nice one.

'This is Karsten Hoss. He will be your counsellor. Help you with homework, exercise, playing ball, that sort of thing.'

My heart sinks, because I'm not very good at playing ball. Karsten grins.

'We'll have a good time together. But just so you know, I'm pretty tough. I don't tolerate laziness.' Father nods in agreement and turns to the lady, who studies us thoroughly.

'This is your new teacher,' he says.

She introduces herself as Alice Karlsson, but she says her name so quickly that Vic hears it as 'Alikan'.

Later this will be our nickname for her, 'Ali-Khan'. For Grandma has told us about Genghis Khan, a vicious warrior who struck fear into his underlings. And that's exactly the type of person Alice Karlsson is.

6

She stood up so suddenly that her chair flew backwards and hit the floor with a bang. In a great hurry she pushed past him and headed for the door. At first he made no attempt to stop her, but as she reached for the handle he shouted.

'Stop!'

And she did. Like a dog trained to obey his commands. In the deepest reaches of her brain, she still reacted to his voice.

'Listen to what I have to say. I'm not going to touch you.'

He raised both hands in a gesture of surrender.

'You sadistic pig, I don't want anything to do with you.'

'Please, Sofia, just listen to me for a minute. Not a day has gone by that I haven't regretted what I did. I'm sorry. I was so bitter after two years in prison, and I blamed it all on you. I was obsessed with punishing you. But I beg of you, listen to what I have to say now.'

Later in life she would find herself returning to this moment and wonder why she didn't just leave. But deep down in her heart, she knew why. There was an invisible bond between them. A connection she had desperately hoped he wasn't aware of. *Julia*. The reason she'd thought of Franz Oswald every day for fifteen years actually had nothing to do with the horrific things he'd done to those in the cult. It was all about Julia. For if he suspected, if he had the slightest inkling, she would go to pieces. That fear, always present in her conscious mind like an undercurrent, exploded as she stood before him once again.

And that wasn't all. He didn't look dangerous in the least. If she hadn't known better, she would have believed that was real regret she saw in his eyes.

'Don't you think you can forgive me, Sofia?' he asked.

'No. Never. That's not the kind of thing that can be forgiven.'

'But you did burn down my whole place. I almost went to prison for insurance fraud. Thirty million kronor went up in smoke.'

'Good – I'd hoped it was even more than that. How did you get this firm to fool me?'

'No one fooled you,' he said with a crooked smile. 'I own Stone Equity as one of my investments. This is my office – although I seldom use it, as you can tell. I've got more important things in the works, on a more international level.'

'You're lying. They said you were a financier who was interested in my shelter.'

'Which is true. Now, listen to me. Just give me one minute, and then you can go.'

'What do you want from me? Spit it out, so I can say no and get out of here.'

'It's more complicated than that. The fact is, I think you have something that belongs to me.'

'I'll mail you the family history. Can I go now?'

'Can't you sit down for a moment so I can explain?'

She stubbornly remained standing, leaning against the wall with her arms crossed over her chest. She decided to listen to what he had to say and then take off. He truly did look different. Fifteen years seemed to have taken the edge off the self-righteousness that had once marked his whole persona.

The constant rage that had smouldered inside him had been extinguished. This made him even more present, but probably also more dangerous.

'Sofia,' he said, so softly that she almost couldn't hear it. He took a few steps towards her. 'Not many women get more beautiful with age, but you sure have.'

'Lay off the bullshit and get to the point.'

'I want to donate the money for you to rebuild your shelter. And a publisher has contacted me to say you want to put out a book about my grandmother. I intend to give the go-ahead. If the book is well-written, it will actually benefit me. There is just one condition.'

This is my one chance to leave, she thought. But it was like she was being sucked into the maelstrom of his eyes. The feeling was so familiar that it made her want to crawl out of her skin. Even so, she stayed put. A tiny part of her was curious now, but she was on guard. He immediately noticed her hesitation and took another few steps her way. So close now. She realized he had cornered her. He had switched aftershaves, and this new one smelled like it must be upscale and exclusive. His suit was navy blue and almost certainly bespoke. He had grown stockier, more muscular. She realized she wasn't afraid of him, even though her heart beat faster as he stood so close.

'There comes a time in your life when you have to revisit certain decisions and events,' he said. 'I did just that after the incident with you at the manor. I have honestly turned myself around. I began to regret what I did, and decided I want to make it up to you.'

'I don't want your money.'

'Why not?' he countered. 'It would at least be a consolation. I know how hard you've fought for that operation you run – or *ran*, I suppose I should say. Doesn't it seem logical for me to support a place that helps people who defect from cults? Think about it. All this keeping people from leaving when they want to – I've given that up entirely.'

'Really? Look, we're done here.'

He ran his hand through his hair. In her time working with him, she had learned that this was a sign of stress. That, and when his little finger trembled. But right now it was still. She couldn't interpret the expression on his face.

'Of course, I could also turn this around to my advantage,' he said. 'If, contrary to all expectations, that unfortunate incident fifteen years ago were to come to light, it would benefit me if you and I had made peace.'

'That's not possible. Is this supposed to be some sort of bribe? So I won't talk about the rape?'

'No, not at all. You can talk about whatever you like, under one condition.'

'What's that?'

'I want you to pay a brief visit to ViaTerra. There's something there I have to show you. Then I want to talk about some ideas I've had. As soon as that's done, I'll pay for the shelter. You won't have to have anything to do with me after that.'

'You think I would come out to Fog Island again? Forget it. I don't want your money.'

'You can bring the entire Swedish police force if you feel like you need to. But don't bring Benjamin, I can't stand him. Maybe that Simon could come, although he seems to be awfully busy these days. In any case, you don't have to come alone. There's something there I want to show you. That's all.'

'Just show me right here, right now. Get it over with.'

'Unfortunately, that's not possible. There's something at ViaTerra I want you to see.'

'Why is this so important, after fifteen years?'

'Fifteen years, fifteen minutes – what does it matter? All that matters is that the time is right.'

There was a knock at the door.

'Not now!' he shouted.

The woman outside the office spoke in a soft, ingratiating voice.

'I apologize, I just wanted to check and see if you need anything.'

'I said, *not now*!'

The distraction gave Sofia a little bit of breathing room. Why such desperation? What did he want from her? Something awoke in the pit of her stomach. Her intuition was like a snake, and Franz's presence made it writhe inside her. *He is anything but stupid. He has eyes everywhere. You'd better get out of this, and fast.*

'I'll think about it,' she said. 'That's all I can promise. And if anyone comes snooping around my house, if my computer gets hacked, if anything unpleasant happens to me or my family, I will become your worst nightmare.'

'That would be too bad. I want nothing to do with you when you get like that,' he said. 'Thanks for listening to me. Leave a message here, or call the front desk at ViaTerra once you've made up your mind, and I'll get back to you.'

He took a step back, gesturing at the door. Sofia took a deep breath.

'Stay away from my friends and family.'

'I would never dream of hurting you.'

She hurried out of the office, feeling his eyes on her back. The woman in the lobby smiled kindly, as though nothing strange had happened.

Once she was in her car, her heart began to race. At first, all the anguish she suffered was physical. Dizziness. Shortness of breath. Gagging despite her empty stomach. She was sweaty all over: her forehead, breasts, armpits, between her legs. Then came a wave of shame: why hadn't she simply told him to go to hell and walked out?

Then I want to talk about some ideas I've had.

That was the part that made her skin crawl. And now she wanted to reassure herself that he was still totally clueless. Force him to creep back into his spiderweb.

She took long, deep breaths, fumbling in her pockets until she fished out her phone. For the first time in a long time, she had an impulse to call Simon. Franz seemed to know something about him, was that possible? She called Benjamin and blurted out a description of the meeting in one long sentence. Benjamin didn't say anything for so long that she thought the call might have dropped.

'Come home and we'll talk about it in peace and quiet,' he said at last.

Not the least bit of complaining that she'd gone there in the first place or that she'd listened to Franz. She felt a rush of love for Benjamin so strong that she had to squeeze the phone hard.

'Okay. I'll never take his money, but now I'm afraid he might suspect, he might think…'

'No, I doubt it.'

'But then what does he want to talk about? Why did he say you can't come?'

'He's always been fixated on you. And jealous of me. He hates me. Remember when he made me jump off the cliff?'

'Don't remind me, my brain is already chaos.'

'We'll talk about it tonight. My gut feeling says we should absolutely not have anything to do with him.'

'Mine too. I love you, you know that?'

'Of course I do. Drive safe, now.'

*

After their call she still felt too overwhelmed to drive. She called Anna and told her about the meeting with Franz. Anna was of a very different opinion than Benjamin.

'It's only right that he make amends for everything he did to you. Franz Oswald, donating money to a shelter for ex-cult members, that's priceless,' she laughed. 'We could make all our dreams come true. But I definitely don't think you should go out to Fog Island. Don't meet with him alone. That sounds dangerous.'

'Anna, he almost ruined my life, and so many others'.'

'Exactly! Maybe you can get him to make a public apology for everything he did to us. It's clear to see you have the advantage here. Make the most of it. But don't meet with him one-on-one, promise me you won't.'

'I won't. I don't trust him. The moment I let down my guard, he'll attack.'

The car ride home was annoyingly slow, with a traffic jam on the bridge. She felt odd, as though she were partially outside her own body. Her thoughts wandered between old memories from Fog Island. All at once, her time there seemed more real than the road and the cars in front of her.

When she arrived home, Julia was perched on a barstool, talking to Benjamin as he made French toast. Sofia raised a finger to her lips when Benjamin spotted her, but just then Julia turned around.

'What now? What kind of secrets are you keeping, Mom?'

'Oh, it's just Christmas presents and stuff.'

'Already? Isn't it a little early? Where have you been?'

'I was meeting with a financier.'

'How'd it go?'

'Terrible, to be honest.'

Julia gulped down dinner fast and said she was off to meet a friend in Henån.

'I thought you were going to study,' said Sofia.

'School is still such a mess. We don't have any homework.'

The door slammed behind her. It was dark out. As usual, Sofia felt a passing quiver in her stomach at the thought of Julia being out late at night.

Benjamin got up and pulled Sofia to her feet.

'Listen, honey...'

She was expecting him to scold her, but instead he lifted her chin to pull her face close and kiss her. It was a tender, lingering kiss. His tongue was familiar and warm.

'You look nice today,' he said.

'What did you think about this Franz stuff, though?'

'I already told you. You should stay as far away from him as possible. Maybe I can get a loan. I have so much work right now, it's crazy.'

'It's not about the money, it's about Julia and you know it. I'll do anything to make sure he doesn't suspect.'

'There is another solution. We can do a DNA test. We should have done it a long time ago.'

She burst into sudden, loud tears. Benjamin embraced her.

'I can't. I'm too scared,' she sobbed. 'If it turns out he's Julia's father, I will fall apart. I don't think I could handle that. I would have to tell Julia, even though he's a monster. I would feel like I *had* to tell her, and even him. He would be all over us for the rest of our lives. It's been just fine living in uncertainty for fifteen years. We're happy, aren't we? Why does he have to show up now?'

'It hasn't actually worked *that* great,' said Benjamin. 'You think about it all the time. So do I. But I love her so, so much and I will always be her dad, no matter what happens.'

'You know, there was something strange about him.'

'What was that?'

'He's changed. He almost looked regretful. Would it really be so dangerous to go there? I want to be sure he doesn't suspect anything about Julia. Then I'll come right back.'

'Honey, you really shouldn't go there. I would be so worried. You always overreact. It's time to let this go.'

'He wouldn't be able to do anything to me if I brought someone else for protection.'

'Who would you take with you?'

'I don't know. He mentioned Simon...'

The thought that had been chafing at her suddenly took shape. What Franz had said about Simon. She hurriedly pulled her phone from her pocket.

'Hold on, I want to check on something.'

She searched for 'Simon Ahlgren', something she hadn't done for months.

And got half a million hits.

In the wake of Father's brainwaves always came huge piles of papers. These piles contained notes, words of support, and philosophical statements his secretary was expected to type up neatly. Several secretaries were lost on account of this process. Rumours spread through ViaTerra that the position of Father's secretary was a death trap.

Eventually the piles would be transformed into a single document, a sort of presentation for everyone who would be affected by his latest plan. Which went for Earth's Children as well.

Karsten Hoss and Ali-Khan were holed up in a room in the new building for several days, where they were expected to study Father's plan and learn how we must be raised. When they were finished, Father came and asked trick questions to make certain that they understood it all.

Vic and I were there that night. Why, I don't know – maybe because Father liked to demonstrate for us how much power he had over his employees.

'So what is the most important, most foundational concept in this plan?' he asked, fixing his gaze on Karsten Hoss, who was looking unusually small and retiring that evening.

He hesitated, becoming tongue-tied, so Father turned to Ali-Khan. Karsten cleared his throat and recovered Father's attention.

'That children are like adults, but in smaller bodies,' he managed to say.

Father's face split into the biggest smile I'd seen in ages.

'Exactly. Here's a real leader for you!' he said, turning to us. 'Karsten used to be in the military and knows how to build a team.'

Karsten sat up straighter, feeling proud.

'Remember that my sons are not to receive special treatment,' said Father. 'Quite the opposite, in fact.'

That evening, the doors to our new life were thrown wide open. Roll call, uniforms and hard physical labour. We were woken at the break of dawn and fell into bed at night, exhausted and all alone. They had confiscated our stuffed animals. We were children, but we toiled like slaves.

THE QUARRY

During our first lesson with Ali-Khan, she has us count, read aloud, and answer questions. She says she wants to form an idea of how much we know already. Vic and I are six, and the other children, apart from Livia, are seven or eight and have already spent a few years in regular school before being moved here. So Vic and I do not perform as well. What's more, I was sad and tired even before I arrived in the classroom. Karsten had found the stuffed bunny I secretly slept with and said it had to go back to Mama's cottage. Only babies have toys like that. This was the first time I had ever slept anywhere but my bed in the cottage. The dorm was dark and cold. It sounded scary when the other boys' breathing slowed as they dozed off. Through the window I could see the moon, which looked lonely too, hanging there in the sky.

In the classroom, I feel anxious when Ali-Khan stares at me. I speak so softly that she's always shouting at me to speak up. Once she approaches me and thrusts her face in front of mine and roars:

'Turn up the volume, Thor!'

Her breath smells like smoke and something sour. I force myself not to turn away. Didrik, who is eight and really big, looks at me and smirks. Suddenly I wish Grandma were there. But now that Ali-Khan is our teacher, Grandma can only come on Sundays.

When our lesson is over, we have roll call with Karsten. We must stand in two lines, like a military exercise. In my row is Didrik, a sassy girl called Molly, and Matteo with the kind eyes. Vic stands in line with Hugo, who is skinny and a little wall-eyed, and Sara and Livia, who are sisters. Sara is seven and seems quite prim and proper. Livia is only five, and she's awfully shy.

Karsten speaks loudly, almost shouting. He uses words I don't understand like 'discipline' and 'loyalty'. Then he says we will be responsible for the animals and take care of the school ourselves. When he does roll call he barks our names and we must say 'Present!' loudly.

Our first task is to build a fence, an enclosure for the animals. Karsten has found two small wheelbarrows and tells us we are to go to the quarry and fetch rocks. As we walk there, we must march in line. Vic is excited; he takes command and shouts: 'Forward, march!' The wheelbarrows bounce on the stones and roots that cross the path.

The place they call the quarry is really a ravine. Maybe people once quarried there, because there are loose rocks on both sides of the stream. Some of them have been tumbled by the water until they are soft as velvet. Other rocks are piled atop each other but rest askew. Most of the time Vic and I are not allowed to come here, it's too dangerous, but since Karsten is with us today it's okay. We are divided into work teams. Didrik and Vic will push the wheelbarrows. Livia will count rocks, because she's too little to work. The rest of us will load the rocks into the wheelbarrows. I've never done anything like this. It's hot and humid, and the rocks are heavy. Sometimes it takes two people to lift them onto the wheelbarrow.

Karsten has brought gloves, but they're made for adults and way too big for us. We have to pick up the rocks with our bare hands. All the while, Karsten circles us, bellowing commands. Faster, Thor, stop moving like a sloth! Get that rock onto the wheelbarrow now, Hugo. Quick!

While Vic and Didrik convey rocks to the property we are allowed to take a short water break, but the sun is blazing and it's so hot I feel dizzy. My hands hurt; blisters have formed on my palms. Hugo almost drops a rock on his foot and starts to cry. Karsten takes him aside and chastises him in a stern voice. He says Hugo will get used to this. That soon enough, it will get better. But it doesn't. We work for hours, and just as I'm on the verge of tears Karsten blows a whistle.

'Well done! That's all for today. Run home and shower, and then we'll gather in the cafeteria.'

Us five boys have to share one shower. Didrik and Vic are first out of their clothes and they fight over who gets the shower first. Didrik says he should get to, because he's oldest. When he comes out of the shower again he looks at me standing there naked, waiting with towel in hand.

'World's smallest willy, that is!' he says. Loudly, so everyone can hear. Everyone laughs but Matteo. His willy isn't very big either. My chest burns, my vision goes blurry, but I turn around and manage to hold back the tears. I know it will only be worse if I cry.

Father comes to roll call. He speaks to us in a kind voice. Patiently he explains that the work we do will make us stronger. He tells us we're critical for the future of the planet. It sounds nice, but kind of weird. We're so little. The world is so big.

'When you talk to your parents about the work you perform here, you must always say that it's almost like a game,' he says. 'That you get to enjoy the fresh air and learn things.'

Then he shifts his gaze to Didrik.

'I've heard you have already shown leadership qualities. I will let your parents know.' Didrik straightens his back, proud. Vic looks cross.

'Don't make a fool of yourself, Vic,' Father warns him. 'You're a born leader, so just be yourself. You don't need to try so hard.'

Then Father looks at me. In his eyes I see scorn.

That's the moment I feel it for the first time. A mixture of deep longing, loss, and despair. The warmth from my recent shower drains from my body. All that's left is the chill of the concrete walls around me. Suddenly I want to be anywhere else.

One time Vic forced me to open my eyes while we were watching a horror movie. He put his legs around me from behind to trap me and used his fingers to pry open my eyelids.

That's exactly how I feel now. The only difference is that this time I'm forced to stare at reality.

A moment of confusion follows; I'm too young to analyse my feelings. They're simply there, tearing at my insides until I think I will fall apart.

Father notices. A quick shadow passes over his face and then he gives me a kind smile.

But not even that helps.

7

Julia hit the gas until the moped was speeding as fast as it could. The air was so cold that her face felt like a stiff mask. But her heart was soaring. It was so easy to lie without really lying.

I'm going to meet up with a friend.

He had showed up at school just before summer vacation. This was after she'd won the singing competition; she'd become incredibly restless, sick of school, and impossible to deal with.

One day he was suddenly there. Auxiliary staff, a student teacher. Eighteen or nineteen years old. So handsome it was impossible to look away. He had thick, curly hair down to his shoulders. Deep-set brown eyes that seemed to belong to someone much older. But the best part was his lips. She couldn't look at them without thinking about kissing. He didn't have that wound-up intensity like the teenage boys in her school; he seemed self-confident without being cocky.

Matt Larsen. What a boring name for such a hot guy.

At first he seemed to look straight through her, and it drove her nuts. Even the old-man teachers usually checked her out, their eyes lingering on her breasts. But to Matt Larsen, she remained invisible. The more she hit on him, the more uninterested he seemed. She became totally obsessed with him. When the other girls swarmed him on break, she felt an icy stab in her heart. She hated it when he laughed at their jokes. With every passing day, her frustration grew. Eventually she considered doing something bold, like jumping into his car unseen and throwing her arms around him from behind. She didn't know how he would react, and it might end up earning her a talk with the headmaster, but her dad was good at helping her take care of that sort of thing.

But she's got top grades in every subject. She'll grow out of that kind of behaviour.

Once, just to mess with Dad, Mom had told her about Dad's nickname when they were in the cult. Slippery Ben, that Franz Oswald had called him. Dad was so embarrassed when Mom told her this that Julia felt sorry for him. Still, she couldn't stop giggling. It was so accurate, that was just who he was. In a good way.

All summer long, Julia had thought about Matt. She had hoped he would show up at a beach or café somewhere. She even stopped by her school to see if he was there. But the school building was locked and the grounds seemed sad and deserted.

She revisited memories of him all the time: when she was tanning, when she was partying at night, before she fell asleep. Always before she fell asleep. She was worried he might not come back next term. But he did. And then, one day, she caught him staring at her. She fired off her very best smile and he smiled back.

That's it! I've got you now, Matt Larsen!

That same day, he showed up in his car when she was on her way home. He rolled down the window and asked if she wanted help with her homework. As if she needed any help.

Now they saw each other several times a week, always at out-of-the-way places where there weren't very many other people, but that just made it more exciting.

She tried to get her moped to go faster, but it coughed and continued at the same speed. *Just please don't let my friends be hanging at the gas station tonight.* Although it was probably too cold out. When she arrived, the gas station was deserted, and she was afraid Matt had taken off, that she was too late. But then she saw headlights on the road and recognized his car turning in. He parked off to the side, past the bright lighting above the pumps. When she climbed into his car, it was dark. Her eyes adjusted to the dim light, and then she could see his face and tell he was grinning. There was a sweet smell in the car, from his deodorant and gum.

'Hey, cutie! Thanks for coming,' he said.

'No biggie.'

Her voice sounded much calmer than she felt.

He leaned over her and kissed her, warming her chilly lips.

'Those lips…' he said. 'All the things you could do to me with them.'

Heat rushed to her cheeks; she liked it when he talked that way. Pressure built in her belly.

'Come here,' he said in a low voice. He took her arm and pulled her into the driver's seat so she was straddling his lap with the steering wheel against her back. His lips brushed her cheek and she trembled. His hands slid up under her leather jacket and found her breasts. He gasped as he realized she wasn't wearing a bra. Slowly he pulled her thin tank up to reveal her breasts. Her hands flew up to cover them, but he grabbed her wrists and forced her arms down along her sides.

'You have nothing to be ashamed of,' he whispered.

His pupils were enlarged. His breathing was heavy. Still holding her wrists, he let his tongue slide over her breasts and closed his lips around one nipple to suck, sending a thrill into her belly. She couldn't sit still but squirmed and let out a hoarse sound. He took one of her hands and placed it on his crotch.

'Feel how hard I am.'

She squeezed the hard bulge under his jeans, which made him moan so loudly that she recoiled.

'Don't be so scared. I'm not planning to have sex with you. Not here, anyway.'

She sighed in disappointment.

'Why not? I'm not a virgin, you know.'

'Okay… so how were they? The other guys?'

'Boring as shit. They would come the second I touched them.'

'That's not going to happen with me.'

'Prove it.'

'There's so much I want to do with you first. And we should wait until we can be somewhere more comfortable, don't you think?'

'What if we recline the seat?' she suggested.

He laughed.

'You're going to drive me insane if we keep meeting like this.'

'Why?'

'You have no idea how hot you are, Julia. Those long legs. How did you end up a whole head taller than your mother?'

'How do you know I am?'

'I've seen her around the school a few times.'

'Well, my dad is super tall.'

'Do they know you're messing around with me?'

'They don't need to know who I'm hanging out with.'

'Good. They wouldn't like it. I'm practically your teacher.'

'Student teacher. There's a big difference.'

'I'd probably still get fired, and then we couldn't see each other. So you were saying, reclining the seat…'

His eyes urged her to get back into the passenger seat. She

slid off him, and as soon as she was ready he tilted the seat back and gently pushed her into it.

He brought his hand to her calf, letting it slide up her thigh, under her short skirt; he stopped at her panties. He gently covered her mouth with his own as his fingers found their way in and began to touch her. It was so good that she had to interrupt the kiss and gasp for breath. He rubbed her slowly, until she was breathing hard. The muffled sigh that came from her lips sounded unreal, as though it had come from someone else.

'Do you like that?'

'What do you think?' she panted.

She let him continue. His fingers moved back and forth. The cold autumn air trickling into the car made her nipples stiffen. His lips landed here and there on her body. But the very best part was the sensation in her belly that came from doing something forbidden. After a while, her legs began to tremble and she vanished into deliciousness. Her body arced, then went totally slack. Tiny aftershocks, delicious jolts, vibrated inside her.

But then, far too quickly, she returned to the cold car.

'Was that good?' he asked.

'Yes, but it ended too soon.'

'I'll teach you to hold back. That will make it even nicer.'

'When?'

'As soon as I've found a good place for us to meet.'

'Why not your apartment?'

'I rent a room from one of the teachers. It wouldn't work. Hey, maybe we could go away together over Christmas break, for a few days? Just you and me. Can you get a friend to cover for you?'

'Maybe. Where would we go?'

'My parents have a winterized cabin in the archipelago,' he said with a sly smile.

She wondered if she could trust him. Dare to go away with him, on her own. There was something reassuring about him that made her think it would be just fine.

But there was no hurry. He did something new, something wonderful to her every time they met. She enjoyed every minute.

Still, sometimes she longed for something else, something even more forbidden.

I often dream that I've been forced to go back to Earth's Children. Everyone is there: Ali-Khan, Karsten, and the children. But I never dream about the punishment, threats, or everything they forced us to do. Instead I end up in a tangle of shame and lies. There are eyes everywhere, monitoring me. I can't get away. With each move I make, I sink deeper into some sort of quicksand. Sometimes I wake up with a start and lie still in bed, paralysed by the power of the dream. It takes time for me to find myself in the present, as though I have come through a tunnel full of thick fog.

THE CLASSROOM

It's Saturday. The other children were supposed to go home, but last night Karsten brought a message from Father. In Earth's Children we call him 'boss'. Even Vic and I aren't allowed to call him Father. Karsten said that the children will have to stay here for a month to get acclimatized before they can go home. It will be too much for them to return home before they've gotten used to everything. In a month we'll have a party and show the parents everything we've done and learned.

We've received our uniforms. Grey shorts for summer, white T-shirts, and grey jackets in case we get chilly. The jackets have the ViaTerra logo on the breast and there's a picture of the green-and-white ViaTerra flag on the T-shirts. And we have sandals that chafe when we walk in the forest. It's so hot the sweat makes our shorts stick to us. All morning we've been gathering rocks by the river. The fence is growing. We've gotten better at marching and have learned to obey commands like Halt! and Attention! The heat is so oppressive that we have to drink water frequently. One time Hugo gets overheated and falls face-first into a thicket, but after he rests for a while he's okay again. Sweaty and exhausted when we come home, a little late, and the shower is crowded and unpleasant.

As usual we have lessons with Ali-Khan after our work. She gets math and Swedish over with quickly. Father has written exercises for us, a whole stack of paper that sits on her desk. She picks up the top sheet and gives us a mysterious smile.

'The first exercise is simple. You're going to learn to speak in front of a group. Come stand at the front, one by one, and tell us why what you're doing in Earth's Children is so important. Stand up straight. Speak loudly and clearly. If you practise now, you can impress your parents when they come to the party.'

Vic, eager to participate, hops off his chair and stands front and centre. With the confidence and clear voice of a born leader, he says that when the war comes, Earth's Children will save the world from destruction. Didrik seems peeved that Vic gets to go first and waves his hand frantically. Ali-Khan nods at him to come forward.

'We will become presidents and kings and be in charge of everything. Everyone will obey us.'

'But why, Didrik? Why will people listen to you?'

Didrik looks uncertain.

'Because we have all the answers, of course,' says Ali-Khan. 'What you learn here is the one and only truth. Never forget that. You will help *people by being in charge of them.'*

Didrik seems surprised, but he nods and returns to his chair.

'Who wants to go next?' Ali-Khan peers at us and nails Livia with her gaze.

'Livia, your turn!'

Livia slides down from her chair, which is a little too tall for her. She glances nervously at her big sister, Sara, who nods encouragingly.

'Stand right in the centre there, Livia!' says Ali-Khan. 'Face the group.'

But Livia can't move. She remains by her chair, looking terrified. Her eyes are wide and her face has lost all its colour. Ali-Khan approaches her, takes her by the arm, and pulls her to the front.

'Now, tell us.'

Livia sticks her thumb in her mouth and starts to suck it. Her cheeks are red now.

'Thumb out of your mouth, Livia!' Ali-Khan roars. 'Stop being silly this instant.'

But Livia only sucks harder. A dark spot appears on the front of her shorts; a stream runs down her leg and a few drops hit the floor.

An oppressive silence follows, but then Molly shrieks:

'Look! She peed her pants!'

Giggles break out, followed by cruel laughter.

Something snaps inside Livia. Tears course down her face and soon she's shaking with sobs.

We don't know what to do. Ali-Khan's eyes are full of disappointment, which I fear will soon turn to rage. She gets up and goes over to Livia, avoiding the puddle that has formed around her, and grabs her by the upper arms. Livia twists, trying to get away, still with her thumb in her mouth. But Ali-Khan's grip hardens. She looks infuriated and starts to shake Livia.

'Stop this nonsense! Stop it this minute, you little shit!'

Livia screams and kicks. One kick hits Ali-Khan, who is beyond furious and shakes Livia even harder; her head is thrown back and forth like a rag doll's.

'Let her go!'

That bright, clear voice has come from Matteo, who has leapt to his feet. Ali-Khan lets go of Livia, who slumps on the floor in a heap.

Ali-Khan turns to Matteo. Her eyes flash. Someone gasps loudly. She takes a few steps towards Matteo, who stubbornly stands his ground and stares at her with his big, sad eyes.

'You were hurting her,' he says.

'Oh, you think so, you little fag? And do you also think it's the boys with the tiniest willies who will run the world?'

The terrible silence is broken. We all burst into shrill laughter. Even I join in, although I don't think it's actually funny. But the laughter is freeing, because an unpleasant tension had built up, an electrical force that can only be discharged with a laugh.

I'm sure that Ali-Khan is going to hit Matteo, she looks so angry. But then she turns around and stalks out of the classroom. She leaves us unsure what to do with the sobbing Livia and the puddle of pee on the floor.

Sara goes to Livia, pulls her to her feet, and sits her down on a chair. Molly runs out to get a bucket of water and cleans up the pee.

Ali-Khan returns. She still looks strange; she's breathing heavily and her eyes are darting. She takes Sara to a corner and speaks softly, so we can't hear. Sara nods again and again.

Then Ali-Khan goes to the lectern. She watches us for a moment. Her hands are trembling.

'In this classroom, I am in charge,' she says, staring at Matteo. 'I am the leader here, do you understand? You must never contradict me.'

My head is crowded with emotions. I feel scared in a very odd way. It's like my body is freezing over from the inside.

'The things that happen here are not always pleasant. Sometimes I must use discipline,' she continues. 'What happens in this classroom stays in this classroom. If you have questions or opinions, you will bring them up with me, not with anyone else. Is that understood?'

A dull murmur arises, some sort of assent.

What happens in this classroom stays in this classroom.

But who could I tell anyway? Father would say I was a wimp if

I told him. Mama can't even manage to dress herself these days, what could she do?

Matteo has taken a seat beside me. Beneath the table, I gently stroke his arm.

8

Sofia let out a happy cry and grabbed Benjamin's arm.

'It's Simon! Look, he's all over the internet!'

Benjamin leaned closer and stared in astonishment at her phone as Sofia scrolled through posts about Simon. Articles and video clips from lectures on organic farming he'd held in California. And not just any lectures. He had addressed the CEOs of major companies in Silicon Valley and given talks at respected universities and big conferences. All of this seemed to have started right after Sofia gave up searching for him. She scrolled down lengthy columns of headlines that never seemed to end.

Simon Ahlgren lectures on organic farming
for business leaders in Silicon Valley.

Simon Ahlgren meets CEO of San Jose
non-profit Veggie Solutions.

Turning green into business: Simon Ahlgren gives
a lecture at the University of California, Davis.

'BITE', where technology and food meet: Simon
Ahlgren delivers lecture at annual conference.

Apparently Simon had invented an effective and economical method for growing organic vegetables which was now being exported to developing countries with support from philanthropic organizations. Sofia could not imagine Simon as a public speaker. But there he was on video, dressed up in a blazer, lecturing in English.

Benjamin threw himself back on the sofa and burst out laughing.

'I'll be damned! He's famous in America!'

'But why hasn't he been in touch with us?'

'I'm sure he has his reasons. Maybe we remind him too much of ViaTerra. He's probably put all that behind him. Or else he's too snooty to talk to us now.'

'Not a chance. He would never think he was too good for us. There must be some other reason.'

'Does he have a website, any contact info there?'

Sophia looked frantically but didn't find any website. Instead she started searching for organizations where Simon had given lectures. She sent them emails with her phone number and asked them to forward it to Simon. She kept this up for several hours until Julia arrived home, cheeks flushed and eager to talk.

Simon called on Halloween. It was late evening. Jack-o'-lanterns with flickering candles inside edged the flower beds in the yard. A chilly scent of rain came through a living-room window that was ajar.

Julia had long since left for her Halloween party at the scout cabin, wearing a tight, low-cut dress over her Dita von Teese get-up. Sofia and Benjamin had been invited to a party too but decided not to go. Sofia was exhausted and restless following her meeting with Franz. She was also annoyed that she hadn't heard from Simon. Benjamin sat at his laptop, deeply absorbed in something that had to do with their finances. He said he was going to try and scrape up enough cash for the down payment of a loan to rebuild the shelter.

But then Sofia's phone lit up. Someone was calling from an unknown number.

His voice sounded just the same as usual, calm and a little drowsy.

'I'm sorry I haven't been in touch.'

'Oh my God! It's you!'

'It's so good to hear your voice, Sofia.'

'Same to you. But why have you been avoiding me? You're not upset with me, are you?'

'Of course not. I know you have questions, but I can't answer them yet.'

'Oh, Simon, I missed you so much!'

'I missed you more.'

Benjamin, whose nose had been buried in his laptop, gave her a thumbs up when he realized it was Simon.

'Tell me why you're being so secretive,' Sofia said. 'Is it your new job?'

'No, not at all. Look, it's kind of complicated. And it was important no one knew where I was, that's all. And then I met someone here in California.'

She felt an unexpected stab of jealousy. She realized she didn't want to let anyone else feel the same sense of connection with Simon that she did. But she answered breezily and asked him if he'd hauled off and got married.

'No, nothing like that. But it's complicated. Please, don't make me talk about it yet.'

'Okay. If you don't want to tell me, we'll leave it there.'

Instead the conversation turned to Franz Oswald's return to the public eye. When they were discussing ViaTerra, it was like no time had passed. He was the same Simon she loved talking to. Who never cut her off. Who always understood. Even his gentle breathing into the receiver sounded the same.

When she was finished telling him about her encounter with Franz, he didn't say anything for a long time.

'What do you think I should do?' she finally asked.

'I definitely don't think you should have anything to do with him. And for God's sake, don't accept his money.'

'I'm sure you're right. There are rumours that he's been involved with recovery work after the storm.'

'Sure. But really he's gleefully wallowing in the disaster and in other people's losses and grief.'

'You really do still hate him.'

'Don't you?'

'Yeah, I despise him. The worst part was that he looked so good. I'd really been hoping he would die of some terrible, painful disease.'

They talked for almost an hour. Simon told her he'd taken a shine to California when he visited her there fifteen years ago. That's why he had returned when he left Sweden. First he had taken courses at UC Davis and worked at a couple of different organic farms, eventually developing a new method for producing affordable organic produce. In California it seemed all the financial bigwigs and major companies were involved in philanthropic projects, so it was easy to get grants.

'I didn't really set out to give lectures about it,' he said. 'You know me. I do best when I'm getting my hands in the soil. But then I found out I'm actually good at it. From then on, it was smooth sailing.'

'And you've turned into a suit guy!'

'Never expected to see that, did you? Oh, it's only a costume. I've still got my old coveralls from Fog Island.'

He gave her his phone number and told her to text or call any time of day. In a few months he would come to Sweden and visit them.

'How about your friend, will she come too?'

'We'll see. Maybe.'

Benjamin spoke with Simon for a while too. By the time they were finished, it was half past midnight. Sofia was so worked up that she paced back and forth chattering nonstop, unable to sit still. But then she noticed a look of concern on Benjamin's face.

'What's wrong?'

'I found something unusual about our accounts, something I don't understand.'

'What is it?'

'Now, don't be alarmed, but it's Julia's savings account. A large deposit was made to it recently. Two hundred thousand kronor. Could it have come from your parents?'

'No way. Mom would have let me know.'

'Maybe it's the money from the singing competition?'

'She blew through all of that in a matter of weeks, buying her moped and clothes and… What on earth could it be?'

Unpleasant thoughts came to her mind. What if Julia was involved in something criminal? Could she be dealing drugs? Intrusive images of Julia in a very short skirt, prostituting herself. The cheerful mood brought on by Simon's call was gone in a split second.

'She must be up to something. Oh my God!'

'Calm down. It's her savings account – she doesn't even have access to that, does she?'

'No, that's true, but Julia could hack her way into anything.'

'Let's ask her first, before we jump to any conclusions.'

'But she isn't here, and it's quarter to one! She promised to be home around midnight.'

'Sofia, it's Halloween. She's at a party. We'll bring it up with her tomorrow. If you're worried about her, just call, but don't mention this money.'

Sofia tried calling several times but only got Julia's voicemail. She searched for Julia's friends' numbers in her contact list. After a few tries, Julia's best friend Laura picked up. There was heavy bass thumping in the background and Laura sounded a little fuzzy, but even so she managed to get across that Julia had vanished from the party. Laura was trying to find her because she wanted to head home.

'She's not at the cabin?' Sofia asked in horror.

'No, she must have taken off.'

'And you haven't heard from her?'

'No, but I'm sure it's nothing. Julia is always doing her own thing. I'm sure she'll turn up.'

'Laura, how long has Julia been gone?'

'Like half an hour, I think.'

'I'm on my way! Can you stay there in case she shows up?'

'Of course.'

Sofia hauled Benjamin along with her to the car. Her worry had given way to hysteria so powerful she didn't want to drive. Benjamin, too, looked anxious. Sure, Julia was unpredictable, but she usually called when she was going to be late. Sofia called Julia's number over and over as Benjamin sped down the road.

By the time they arrived at the scout cabin, Sofia had worked herself into such a frenzy that she was on the lookout for the blue lights of the police cars and ambulances she was sure would be there. And the stretcher holding Julia's lifeless body. But the scout cabin looked deserted. A few cars were parked along the road – parents, picking up their kids. A couple of teenagers were making out on a bench. Muffled music poured from the building.

Laura was in the doorway with her father, waiting for them.

After some polite greetings, and assurances from Laura that Julia wasn't there, Benjamin and Sofia stormed inside anyway.

The place was empty aside from a couple of guys gathering soda and beer cans in big plastic bags. The decor on the walls – spiderwebs everywhere, as well as plastic monsters, ghosts, and witches – were hanging askew and looking sad. Not frightening in the least. There was a sour smell of beer and the faint odour of vomit. They walked through the mostly empty, dimly lit room. No sign of Julia. But then Benjamin grabbed Sofia's arm.

'Shh! I hear something.'

And now Sofia heard it too. The distant sound of rippling laughter, somewhere deeper in the darkness. They hurried down a hall that ended at a door to some sort of storage area. They couldn't hear the laughter now, just muffled voices.

Sofia yanked open the heavy door. It took a second for her eyes to adjust to the darkness.

Julia was backed up against a shelf, her breasts bare and her arms raised above her head. Leaning against her was a guy – one who didn't look anything like fifteen – with his hand up her skirt.

Sofia gasped. The guy looked startled and let go of Julia. Julia's eyes went wide as she covered her breasts. Her cheeks flushed suddenly. But then she recovered her courage and glared at them fiercely.

'Did you bring handcuffs or are you going to drag me home by my hair?'

You and I grew up in totally different worlds. As I write this, I wonder if these worlds are so different that you will think my tale is beyond belief. I want you to understand that what they did to us was not evil through and through. They had a conviction that our upbringing would make us better people.

And some got caught in a web of lies they couldn't get out of.

I don't say this to defend them; I only want to make it easier for you to understand.

THE PIGSTY

Ali-Khan has gone home for the day. Karsten looks tired as he perches on a stool, where he's reading a newspaper. His eyelids are heavy. Again and again, his chin falls to his chest. This is unusual for him, but despite his intense gaze and booming voice, we are sometimes too much for him. Today is one of those times – we made a terrible wreck of the common room, overturning chairs and strewing toys all over the floor. We're chasing each other, becoming so hyper that we scream at the top of our lungs. But Karsten has had enough and has somehow managed to doze off despite the racket.

At first we don't hear Father as he enters the room; the sound of our cavorting is deafening. Hugo is the one to spot him first.

'Boss!' he squeaks.

Father is standing in the doorway, eyeing us with distaste. His gaze is black as a thundercloud. In a few quick steps he is next to Karsten; he takes him by the collar and pulls him to his feet.

'Clean this place up this minute!' he barks at us.

And when the boss barks, everyone obeys.

First Father chews out Karsten.

'No goddamn order around here… this calls for punishment, no, consequences… they're behaving like toddlers… you will get a handle on this, or else…'

Then we are sent to the dorms. We don't chatter as we usually do, we just brush our teeth, put on our pyjamas, and crawl into bed. I have the top bunk and must climb a ladder to get into it. Up there, near the ceiling, I have begun to feel safe. If I creep under the blanket, no one can see me. I can pretend I am somewhere, anywhere, else.

Before anyone has time to fall asleep, the door flies open. The light comes on and there stands Karsten.

'This room is a pigsty. Clean it up! You have ten minutes, and then I'm turning out the light!'

Matteo asks me to help him with a stack of books on the floor. It takes so long to arrange them in the bookcase that nothing else gets done. Suddenly Karsten is back, commanding us to get in bed. I haven't even made it up my ladder before the light goes out.

For a while I lie awake with a lump in my throat. My uniform is still in a messy pile on the floor. I consider climbing down and picking it up, but I can feel Karsten's presence in the darkness as he stands there keeping watch over us.

I don't know how long I sleep, but we are woken abruptly by Karsten's shrill voice.

'Out of bed! All children at attention!'

The light blinds me. I stumble on my way down and bang my knee on the ladder. The floor is cold beneath my feet. We stand at attention beside our beds; this is something we've learned to do. Hugo, who hasn't got his glasses on, blinks like an owl into the bright light.

Karsten vanishes from the room and we can hear him barking orders at the girls in the dorm next door. When he returns, he is carrying a small cane. The kind you see at military parades.

'I will now inspect the results of your cleaning,' he says. 'Those who don't pass will get the pigsty.'

I don't understand what he means, but I will soon enough.

Karsten goes to Didrik and Vic's bed first. He eyes the uniforms hanging over the headboards. I am embarrassed to be reminded that my own is in a wrinkled pile by my feet. Karsten pulls back the blankets from their beds and looks under their pillows. Under Didrik's pillow he finds a toy car. I recognize it – Didrik had bragged about how expensive it was. It was a birthday present from his dad.

'What is this doing under your pillow?' Karsten asks.

'Let go of it! It's mine!' Didrik whines, his face turning red. 'My dad bought it for me, you're not allowed to touch it!'

Karsten eyes the car for a moment and tosses it into the trash can with a thud.

Didrik unleashes a scream, throws himself at Karsten, and beats him with his fists. It's almost like the time Livia peed her pants – he's out of control.

'Meanie, meanie, meanie!' he howls.

Karsten becomes scarily angry. He grabs Didrik by the arms and drags him across the room. He crooks one arm around Didrik's throat and opens the door to the broom closet with the other. He brusquely shoves Didrik inside, then slams the door and turns the key that's already in the lock.

'You will stay in there until you have calmed down!' he says.

Didrik howls hysterically and bangs on the door for a long time. But Karsten doesn't move, just stands with his arms crossed. At last Didrik stops screaming. All we can hear is his tiny voice: 'Let me out.' But soon even that turns into quiet sobbing.

Karsten approaches the bunk I share with Matteo. He has already spotted my uniform on the floor and doesn't even look at it, just nails Matteo with his gaze.

'Whose uniform is this?'

'It's mine,' I say, before Matteo can respond.

Karsten turns to me. I haven't been particularly afraid of him before, but I am now. It's something about his eyes. He looks insane.

There's no time for me to explain; there are no excuses that will suffice.

Karsten's upper lip is trembling like it belongs to a furious dog.

'You will sleep in the pigsty tonight,' he says, taking me by the arm. Then he turns to the other children.

'And you have five minutes to clean up your crap. If anything is out of order when I return, you'll be sleeping there too.'

Karsten hauls me out. By the time we get to the courtyard I feel all woozy like after a ride on a merry-go-round. The chill makes its way under my pyjamas and the gravel hurts my bare feet. Karsten tugs at my arm and forces me to keep up with him. I'm too scared to protest. I hope this is just a joke, a warning to the other children.

Not a word passes his pursed lips as he drags me over the courtyard and field. When we reach the barn, I hope he'll change his mind, but then I see the sleeping bag in the old pigsty. No pigs live there anymore. Someone has spread straw over the floor, but along the sides I can see layers of leftover filth from the animals.

Karsten shoves me towards the sleeping bag. There is no pillow.

'You will sleep here tonight. And maybe you will obey me the next time I tell you to clean up.'

He quickly vanishes from the barn, so fast I hardly notice. I stand there petrified, staring at my new bedroom. The sharp odours from the cows and chickens make their way up my nose. It's cold, but I'm not shivering – I'm paralysed with shock.

I crawl into the sleeping bag, which smells like it spent an awful long time in an attic. Shadows surround me. They look like the silhouettes of ghosts and wolves reaching threateningly for me. Then I hear a scratching sound, like claws would make, from a tree whose branches scrape against a window. Nearby, the two cows, the only livestock left at the manor, are sleeping. Sometimes I hear their snorts and their hooves scraping at the stone floor.

But none of this is as scary to me as the thought of what Father will think when he finds out about this. My chilly body throbs with shame.

It's impossible to fall asleep. There's something poking me through the sleeping bag, right beneath my head. When I stick my hand under, I find a screwdriver. I crawl out of the sleeping bag and sit up. The screwdriver must have come from somewhere. I stand up and set off to find a toolbox, but I can't find anything. My eyes have adjusted to the darkness. The moon shines in through a window and illuminates a stall beside the pigsty. I go in there and stand in the hay, enchanted by the lovely blue moonlight. When I turn around to leave, I see letters carved into one of the walls. They're lit up by a moonbeam; a little sloppy but etched deep into the wood.

Sofia, *it says, and there are lots of lines below it, too many for me to count. The sight takes my breath away – the certainty that someone else has been here, just like I am now.*

With great effort, I carve my name below hers.

Whoever she is.

9

Sofia had ended up arguing with Benjamin. It was nearly impossible to provoke him, but this was about Julia, who had locked herself in her room to stew all morning.

It had all started when they asked Julia about the money in her savings account. She claimed she hadn't the slightest idea where it had come from. Sofia was inclined to believe her; Julia seemed just as surprised as they were. But the conversation took an unpleasant turn when Sofia forbade her from seeing Matt Larsen again.

There was no time for discussion – Julia stormed upstairs and soon cacophonous music was blaring from her room.

'We raised her to be independent, so we have no right to be shocked when she acts accordingly,' Benjamin said.

'What? This guy is her teacher, how can you defend a relationship between them?'

'*Student* teacher, Sofia. There's a big difference. He's not employed by the school, he's only working there for a little while as part of his education. You could at least listen to what she has to say.'

'She refuses to talk to me!'

'That's because you treat her like a child.'

'She *is* a child! And yet she's drawn to dangerous older guys.'

'As if you have any right to judge her on that account. First there was Ellis, who nearly turned you into an internet porn star, and then there was Franz, who you thought was so hot. Oh no! I almost forgot Mattias. *He* was virtue personified, except for the part where he drugged you and kidnapped you. A kidnapper, a hacker, and a sadistic psychopath. Yeah, you're an excellent role model.'

She really ought to smack him. But it wasn't often that he said such cruel things, and when he did it was never with the intent to hurt her. He was uncomplicated and clear-eyed. Sometimes things just slipped out of him. Besides, it was true that she wasn't exactly a great role model, although he was blowing things a little out of proportion. Ellis was an ex who had been so bitter when she broke up with him that he posted pictures of her nude online. But he'd also hacked into Franz's computer and helped her escape from Fog Island the first time. These days he was a good friend. Mattias had been a fling in San Francisco who had turned out to be a spy sent by Franz.

Sure, Sofia had a tendency to be drawn to dangerous men. But she reasoned that she could use her own experiences to warn Julia against doing the same.

'Fine, I'll talk to her. Can you go get her?'

After a while, Julia and Benjamin came downstairs together. Julia, wearing nothing but a baggy T-shirt, looked sullen.

Sofia promised herself she wouldn't blow up.

Julia sat on the sofa, as far from Sofia as she could get.

'We have to talk about this, Julia. Come on, sit over here by me.'

But Julia drew even further away, until she was sitting on the armrest.

'I don't get why you're always on my case,' she said.

'I'm sorry, I don't mean to be. I know it's tricky when you have such strong feelings for someone, sweetie. It's not your fault.'

'What do you mean?'

'I think it's extra tough when you're so young. You might know deep down that it's not going to last forever, and that hurts so much.'

Julia let out a burst of shrill laughter.

'Mom, come on! You're acting like I fell for Matt and I want to get married and have kids! I like him a lot, that's all. He's a way to have some fun in this boring place.'

'I don't want you having sex with him.'

'You're the one who went on and on about the pill, and now I can't even experiment a little? Mom! Don't look so horrified. We haven't had sex. Yet.'

Sofia sighed. 'How reassuring.'

Julia got back on the sofa and moved closer. Sofia put her arm around her and realized she was trembling.

'I just like older guys. Exactly like you, right? Dad is six years older than you, and Franz Oswald—'

'Please leave him out of this. It's fine if you like older guys, as long as they don't take advantage of you.'

'I would never let them.'

'No, I suppose you wouldn't. But if you're going to be with Matt, it would be better for you to bring him over here. No more sneaking around in storage closets or other sketchy places. And I don't know what the staff at your school are going to think about this.'

'I'll handle them,' said Julia.

'Yes, you'll have to, because Dad isn't going to come smooth things over with the headmaster this time.'

Julia looked restless; she sighed and asked if she could go. Then she flew off the sofa and dashed up the stairs. Within minutes she was back, fully made-up and wearing a leather jacket, a low-cut tank top, jeans, and high-heeled boots. She didn't even bother to lie about where she was off to, just blew them a kiss and was out the door. The sound of her moped starting brought Sofia's thoughts to her own teenage years. Stolen kisses, secret meetings and lots of drama.

She consoled herself with the fact that Matt Larsen seemed to be a pleasant guy. As soon as he had recovered from their sudden appearance in the scout cabin, he had shaken their hands and introduced himself. He looked decent. There was something honest in his eyes.

For a moment, they said nothing in the emptiness Julia had left behind.

Then Benjamin started laughing.

'She reminds me of why I fell for you,' he said.

'So, what are we going to do with the money in her account?'

'You can't even tell where the money came from. I've never seen anything like it.'

'But it must be possible to find out, right?'

'I'm sure it is. Don't worry. I'm more concerned about you, you've seemed down ever since you met with Franz.'

'I've been worried about this every day since Julia was born. And when I saw him again…'

All of a sudden, she started to cry. The uncertainty she'd lived with for fifteen years washed over her with a violent force. She buried her face in Benjamin's chest and got snot all over his shirt. He put his arms around her, rocking her.

'Shh,' he whispered. 'He doesn't have the right to do anything.'

'I still want to be sure *that's* not what he's after.'

'Seriously? You honestly think he's going to ask you about it? He would have asked you in Stenungsund if that was the case.'

'What else could it be? What does he want to show me?'

'Who knows. Maybe some new bonkers thesis. Or a new

building on the property, a place to hold their nutty seances. Remember when he said you were the only one who understood the depths of his theses? It wouldn't surprise me if it had to do with cult stuff. He's crazy. Don't forget that.'

Benjamin pulled her close and kissed her forehead.

'We'll do the DNA test. We should have done it ages ago,' he suggested.

'I can't. If she's not yours, I will die. It would be like opening Pandora's box. As long as I don't know for sure, I can pretend everything is fine.'

'Same here. But I can't stand seeing you so sad. You really think going there is the only way to find out if he suspects anything?'

'Well, we can't just ask him, can we? He'll definitely bring it up if we go there. If he doesn't, we'll let it go. There's no reason to go digging any further. But we also have to think of what's best for Julia. If he has even the slightest suspicion he will never let it go. I know him. Maybe we have a duty to tell her, in that case. Let her be the one to decide if we do the test. And if I know her, she'll want to. Oh, Benjamin...'

She started crying again.

'Honey. In this instance, our greatest responsibility is to protect her.'

'It was so simple when she was little. But she's growing up way too fast. I bet I can get Franz to promise never to contact us again if we go there just once.'

'All right, then. If you feel like you need to get this out of your system, I will go with you to Fog Island,' he said. 'It has to be me. No one else. Actually, maybe it wouldn't be so bad to see the place again. Get some closure, put it all behind us.'

★

So it was decided. Sofia contacted ViaTerra that same evening, and Franz called her back right away.

'You may have regrets, but you are still a sadistic rapist,' she said. 'So I will never accept your money. But I'll consider coming there one last time to hear what you have to say. If I do that, will you promise never to contact me or my family again?'

'It kind of depends on how our meeting goes, but in theory – yes. If you don't want to be contacted, I promise to leave you alone. Who are you bringing?'

'None of your business.'

Just before they ended the call, she could have sworn she heard him holding back laughter.

Vic and I were eight the first time we faced the Consequences. *These were the punishments for those who disobeyed, who were sloppy or lazy, and they were presented as a policy. Karsten said Father had approved them, that they were penalties for poor behaviour, and that we were not allowed to call them 'punishments' under any circumstances.*

But they were.

Karsten and Ali-Khan weren't the only ones who were permitted to hand out these punishments. Since Vic and Didrik were the leaders of our two groups, they were also allowed to make decisions about us. They often disciplined us for minor infractions, simply to torment us.

If you were disrespectful, for instance, you had to run around the barn while someone kept watch. We called these 'laps'. The angrier the issuer was, the more laps you got. 'That's three laps!' he would say, and you had to set off at full speed.

If you were whiny or grumpy, you would be assigned some dirty, unpleasant chore that was meant to toughen you up. This could be anything from scrubbing the toilets with a toothbrush to mucking out the cows' stalls.

If you were lazy, you had to do push-ups, and that wasn't easy with my spindly arms.

And then there was sleeping in the pigsty, of course, the punishment for anyone who didn't tidy up after themselves.

Everyone was afraid of sleeping in the pigsty, even Vic and Didrik.

Vic scared us with a story about a farmhand who had hanged himself from the rafters a hundred years ago. Now he supposedly haunted the barn. Rumour had it that he ate up little children.

One day, as we waited for Ali-Khan, who was late to our lesson, I told everyone about the name I had found carved into the stall. Sofia. *For once, Vic and Didrik didn't jump down my throat, because everyone thought it sounded exciting. Sara said Sofia must have been a princess who hid in the barn when she was running away from a monster. Molly thought she was a witch who had escaped when she was about to be burned at the stake. After much speculation, Matteo said we should carve our names under Sofia's every time we had to sleep in the pigsty.*

'That way her spirit will protect us from the farmhand's,' he said, looking so serious that we all believed him.

This became a secret we shared. We never revealed it to any grown-ups. It brought us comfort when the chill, the darkness, the shadows, and the sharp barn smells got too scary.

But, back to the Consequences. Sometimes, someone would do something so horrible that the leaders didn't know which punishment it called for. But they were always able to think up a new, even worse, kind of discipline.

That's how they came up with the ice bath.

THE ICE BATH

It's early morning, the sun is shining, and the grass, still wet with dew, smells good. We're working on the fence. Sara is singing as we stack rocks on top of each other. Vic tells ghost stories, but they don't frighten anyone when the sun is out. The wall grows, this creation we have worked on rain and shine. We have come to feel proud of it. Karsten sits in the grass nearby, listening to music on earbuds that are connected to his phone. I'm working with Matteo. He picks up the rocks and I find good, stable spots for them. I feel calm and strong, as if nothing can upset me.

But then there's a horrific cry not far from us. I see Hugo first; he looks terrified, and then I see Molly lying on the ground and screaming. Her face is beet red and she's holding tight to one foot. Her cries chill me to the bone; my blood runs cold and I realize something awful has happened.

Karsten rips out his earbuds and rushes over, falling to his knees beside her.

Soon we've flocked around them. Hugo has dropped a rock onto Molly's foot, which is all red and seems to be swelling and expanding before our very eyes.

Karsten picks Molly up and carries her to the main building, with the rest of us trailing behind. She's still howling hysterically. When we get to the common room, Karsten shouts at Vic to get the first aid kit and barks at the rest of us to go to the dorms. We wait in silence for a long time. Hugo sits in the corner, eerily pale, his lower lip trembling.

When Karsten calls us back to the common room, Molly is lying on the sofa with a bandage around her foot. She's still crying, but it's quieted into sniffles now. Karsten says he has to drive Molly to see the doctor. If any grown-ups ask what happened, we're supposed to say that she fell and hurt her foot.

I don't understand why we have to lie, but most of all I'm worried that Molly's foot is going to fall off. Karsten tells Vic that he's in charge while Karsten is gone. As soon as they leave, Vic says that Hugo has to be punished and locks him in the broom closet. Hugo doesn't protest. He's as limp as a ragdoll as he's shoved in.

Later that evening, when Karsten returns with Molly, we're called to an assembly.

Karsten says that Molly will be fine, and that's she's resting for the time being. But now he's going to tell us how things are done at sea. He was a sailor on a big boat when he was in the military. Clumsiness was not an option out there, because the sea is full of dangers. One mistake can have terrible consequences. The whole ship could capsize. Blundering sailors were thrown overboard, immediately. And the water out at sea is cold. With these words, he sends us to bed.

Hugo, who had spent almost the whole day in the broom closet, seems to have shrunk. He looks so small and sad that I feel a stab of pity for him.

Everyone goes to bed. Lights out. But then Karsten comes to get Vic and Didrik. Just as I'm drifting off to sleep, I hear the sound of the door opening, followed by whispers and giggles and sloshing.

It all happens so fast. The light comes on. Vic and Didrik are holding a bucket. A cascade of water hits the lower bunk where Hugo sleeps. Then comes the clinking sound of ice, and a piercing shriek from Hugo, who sounds like an animal in distress. He flies out of bed and lands on his belly with a sick thud. His arms and legs spasm as though he's lost control of his muscles.

At first I think the water and ice cubes on the floor must be a dream. But Hugo is real. His frantic gasping for air. His hoarse whimpers.

Karsten stands in the doorway, watching.

'That's how it feels to be thrown overboard, Hugo. Now you know.'

He takes a few steps forward and tosses a bath towel to Hugo, who is sitting up in the puddle. I notice that his bed is soaked, with ice cubes on the blankets, and I wonder where he will sleep. But I don't dare ask.

'Molly broke a bone in her foot,' says Karsten. 'Because of your clumsiness. But she'll be fine. And you are forgiven. When you're tossed overboard, the sea washes away your sins.'

10

The fog shrouded the sea like a heavy blanket, swallowing everything in the distance. Somewhere ahead of them, Fog Island was lurking. The sound of water lapping at the hull of the ferry was dampened by the white haze. Sofia stuck out her hand and watched it grow blurry in the mist. Her other hand was holding tight to Benjamin's.

They were sitting on a bench next to the cabin and chatting with the ferry captain, Edwin Björk. He had been delighted and surprised to see them when they boarded the ferry. The last time they had seen him, fifteen years ago, he had helped them escape across the sound in his motorboat. Ever since then, they'd kept in touch over email.

'What on earth are *you* doing here?' he exclaimed when he saw them.

'It's complicated. Let's just say we're taking care of some unfinished business,' Benjamin said. 'But if we're not on the first ferry tomorrow, you should call the police.'

Björk laughed, but his forehead creased in concern.

'You've got my mobile number,' he said. 'If you need my help, that is. If you have time, you should come for a visit. Elsa would be beside herself.'

Björk had aged. His scalp was bare, but he still sported sideburns and smelled the same – of diesel and seaweed. The furrows in his weather-beaten face had deepened, but his eyes still sparkled with mischief. Now he was telling them about the storm. The pier had been carried out to sea and part of the ferry's hull had been damaged. But his friends on the island had helped him repair everything.

'How are things on the island?' Benjamin asked. 'We got the impression from the media that Franz had gone underground and the organization was at a standstill.'

'All lies!' Björk exclaimed. 'That nuisance of a place hasn't slowed down at all. A constant stream of visitors. Although Franz hasn't taken the ferry very often. Last time I saw him he stayed in his car with his sunglasses and cap on, on a cloudy day.'

The faint outline of the island appeared ahead of them, a blurry stain on the horizon. Something inside Sofia tightened, a mixture of anxiety and deep loss she hadn't been aware of.

'I have to dock now,' said Björk.

The fir trees at the highest points of the island came into view, and then the silhouettes of the houses in the village. The hoarse cries of the gulls pierced the fog. The ferry's engine went quiet and they floated silently towards the pier.

They said goodbye to Björk and walked down the gangway.

Up ahead, the village looked just as Sofia recalled, with the fountain on the small square where the houses clustered. The shops were closed aside from the grocery store and the bakery, all lit up and radiating warmth. No traces of the storm were evident. It was as though it had been miraculously spared.

On the ferry, the air had seemed warm, but now she felt a chill settle into her lungs. She shivered, letting go of Benjamin's hand and hugging herself. She looked around for the driver Franz had said would be waiting for them.

He popped up beside them, suddenly just a few metres away.

She couldn't breathe. It was Franz, yet it wasn't. More or less the way he'd looked fifteen years ago, but even younger. The resemblance was so strong that at first she thought she was seeing things – she took a few steps back and trod on Benjamin's foot.

But now Sofia realized that the guy before her was a teenager. He was wearing pressed grey pants and a blazer with the ViaTerra logo on the chest. It all looked expensive and tailored. He eyed her closely. With a blank expression he glanced at Benjamin, then back to her.

'I'm Vic,' he said. 'Father sent me.'

She had already figured out who he was. It was hard to decide what she thought of him. She wondered if was merely his resemblance to Franz that sent ripples of unease through her body. He walked ahead of them to the car, a black station wagon that was badly parked in the middle of the square. That confident gait, that arrogant tilt of the head – his whole body was like a parody of Franz.

Her thoughts unconsciously turned to Julia and what would happen if she met this exquisite guy. The power of that thought made her stop short. She tried to put her mind elsewhere, but her brain demanded she see this train of thought through. At last she told herself that Julia would never be allowed to meet Vic.

On the way to the car, they passed the bakery and the wonderful scents pouring from it. It really wasn't too late to change her mind, grab a treat and some coffee, and head home on the five o'clock ferry. But Benjamin had caught up with Vic by now and was about to get into the car. Sofia sighed and settled beside him in the back seat.

She did some quick calculations in her mind. Elvira's kids couldn't be of age yet.

'You drive?' she asked. 'You're not eighteen, are you?'

'No, not until this spring. I've got my learner's permit,' he

There was a sharp rap at the door, which opened before they ould respond. Franz towered in the doorway. Here on his home rf he looked more imposing and uncompromising than on e mainland. He was dressed casually, in jeans and a puffer oat, and was even more tanned than when she met with him Stenungsund.

'Hey there, Benjamin, it's been a long time!'

He approached to shake hands and thumped Benjamin on e back. Benjamin looked startled; he took a few steps back id withdrew his hand. Franz tried to kiss Sofia on the cheek, it she darted out of reach.

'Can we just get this over with as quickly as possible?' enjamin asked, annoyed.

But Benjamin's chilly attitude didn't seem to bother Franz at l. He radiated a cheerful openness that couldn't be dampened.

'There are a few things I want to show you two,' he said. 'hen I'd like to speak to Sofia in private, if that's okay. Just for few minutes.'

'We'll see,' Benjamin muttered. 'It's up to Sofia.'

Franz led them over the courtyard to the main guesthouse id down a corridor to a room at the rear of the building. Aside om a large table, the room was empty. On the walls were irious sketches and floor plans. Franz pressed a button and the ble lit up in bright colours.

'This is a photorealistic 3D model,' he said. 'It's a composite of vast number of images. Use your fingers, just like on a tablet. ou can navigate and zoom down to the tiniest detail of this iilding. I mean, there's a close-up of every last screw.'

Sofia took a step closer. She tried to absorb the sophisticated odel in front of her. In focus was a large plot of land with house in the foreground. Some parts were illuminated while thers were in shadow. The house, which seemed to be bath said, turning around and firing off a blinding smile. 'No one cares, here on the island.'

She hadn't expected much in the way of small talk from him, but he entertained them with little anecdotes on the way to ViaTerra. He was relaxed and engaging, yet she felt all the while as if his thoughts were elsewhere. Once he caught her eye in the rear-view mirror and winked at her. When he spoke, he radiated warmth. But when she looked into his eyes, his gaze was cold and suspicious.

'What do you do around here?' Sofia asked. 'There's no school on the island, is there?'

'We have our own school,' he replied. 'Beyond that, I work with Father.'

How handy to have a perfect replica of yourself as a successor, Sofia thought.

'I used to know your mom,' she said. 'Is she well?'

He didn't respond to that, simply talked about something else. To their right, the cliffs plunged to the sea just past the edge of the road. It was a sight that still took her breath away.

When the car turned onto the gravel road that led to the manor, she felt a sticky, sentimental sort of feeling, and when the manor house towered up ahead an ache settled deep in her chest. By the time they reached the massive gate, she was so anxious that she thought about skipping out on the visit. Going back to the ferry. But Benjamin put his arm around her and whispered into her ear.

'You can do this.'

All her tension drained away. She focused on what was there before her. The gate looked the same. The guard in the booth was no one she recognized. The rhododendron bushes behind the wall had grown. As they drove through the gate, she felt a flash of panic and having passed the point of no return.

They climbed out of the car. The property spread before them. Good Lord, it was all so familiar. For a moment she stood very still, overwhelmed by the collision between past and present. With a pang of irritation she noted that everything was well maintained. The bare trees were neatly pruned. A couple of stumps from fallen trees were the only traces of the storm. Several windows in the manor house were glowing cosily. Elegant, minimalistic advent stars decorated the windows of the annexes. In the middle of the courtyard stood a gigantic Christmas tree. All for show, to make the guests feel at home. Franz himself hated Christmas. She noticed a new building next to the annexes, an enormous hall with a glass roof. There were also a few new buildings behind the manor house. She recalled that there had once been a meadow there. Her hope soared. This must be what Franz had wanted her to see. New buildings, to show off his engineering skills.

Not a single soul was in sight, and now Sofia wondered if the staff had been ordered to avoid her. Probably just as well. She couldn't imagine what it would feel like to see them again, people who had been working there for twenty years. What could they have become?

'Father said I should take you to the annexe,' said Vic, addressing Sofia and ignoring Benjamin completely. 'There's lunch there. He thought you… might prefer to eat on your own.'

'I would,' she said. 'And I hope there's food for my husband as well.'

'Of course.'

'I know the way,' she said.

Vic handed her the key to room number three. She recalled that this was the suite, the one only celebrities got to stay in. When she turned around, she saw Vic hopping into the car, driving across the courtyard, and parking in front of the gate.

I'm sure he's in a rush to report back to his father, she thought. A
at once it felt like there were eyes everywhere. Watching the

As soon as they were inside, Benjamin took her hands.

'If Franz says I'm not welcome, we're out. Promise me y
won't stay here alone.'

'Of course. He has no power over me anymore.'

The room felt sterile, and the sense was only enhance
the faint and monotonous hum of the heating system. Sh
oddly dizzy and sat down on a chair.

'Benjamin, what on earth are we doing here?'

'Well, that's the question, isn't it. Honey, we can just go
if you'd rather.'

The jangle of the internal phone cut him off. Refle
she lifted the receiver.

'Exactly which part of "don't bring Benjamin" did y
understand?' asked Franz's voice.

The static vibration in the receiver made it harsher.
she worked with him in the office she had learned to t
angry he was based on his tone of voice over the telep

'You're not my boss,' she snapped. 'If Benjamin isn't w
here, we'll go right back to the village and get the five
ferry home.'

He didn't say anything for a moment.

'It's fine. I'll come talk to you after lunch.'

The food was already laid out on a table in the w
Hors d'oeuvres, different types of salads, and home-ma
Bottles of ViaTerra's specially produced mineral water.
said that the sea air had made him hungry and ate
Sofia had no appetite and could only worry down a l

'Doesn't it have any effect on you, being here a
asked Benjamin.

'It feels a little creepy, but it was all such a long t

in sunshine, was white. Beyond the property you could see the sea, rippling and alive. And now she saw the cliffs, the road winding to the house, the formation of trees she knew so well.

It was her shelter as it had looked before the storm. But even lovelier.

'The architect's name is Gerhard Diller,' Franz went on. 'He specializes in 3D models. Isn't it amazing? And it's all hurricane-proof.'

Sofia took a nervous breath. She leaned over and took in the creation anew. The main building was a copy of the old house, but with an extra storey. The beautiful veranda was still there. A paddock for animals. A barn. A pond with a waterfall in the back.

Looking at this model reminded her of all her wonderful memories of the shelter. She had the unpleasant sensation that Franz had stolen her dreams. She whipped about to face him.

'I know you liked that veranda,' he said.

How the hell does he know that?

'Why did you do this?' she asked, her voice shrill. 'What are you up to?'

'I thought I would cover the planning, so you can use your funds for the construction and the operation itself. You can zoom in on the model with a gesture and comment on any part of it. Naturally you'll be the one to decide how everything looks.'

'But why the hell did you go and do this behind my back?'

'I already told you, Sofia,' he said with mild reproach. 'I simply want to bury the hatchet. Just think what you could do with these blueprints. You're so innovative.'

Benjamin was unusually quiet; he was totally absorbed in the model. Sofia had seen him work on similar projects on his computer. He must have heard of Gerhard Diller before.

'I've already told you I won't accept your money. And I don't want to discuss this right now,' she said curtly. 'Was there anything else you wanted to show us?'

Franz, true to form, took complete control. He dragged them on a tour of the property, showing them the hall, the school building and his new gym. He blathered on about alleged miracles they'd achieved with the children using ViaTerra methods. But Sofia was only listening with half an ear. Part of her attention was still back with the model. The sun-drenched house.

This is important to him, she thought. *Why have I suddenly become so important?*

'Where's the staff? And the children?' Benjamin asked.

'In the village, helping with preparations for the annual Christmas party for the islanders. We've got a really great partnership with the church these days. And the municipal council too. It started with the storm – we helped clean up all over the island. Our reputation around here has never been better.'

'I'm surprised you let the staff out,' Sofia said, her voice dripping with venom.

'I told you, I've changed.'

When Franz concluded the tour, they were standing in the centre of the courtyard. Darkness had fallen over the property. Garden candles and lanterns flickered everywhere. The Christmas tree glowed. Their breath puffed into large clouds when they spoke.

'Let's take a break and you can have dinner,' Franz said. 'Then you can come to my office, Sofia. Just for a little while. Is that okay?'

She intended to snap back and say she refused to come without Benjamin. But she also wanted Franz to tell her what was on his mind. And during their tour she had come to realize more and more that she wasn't afraid of him.

Benjamin took an anxious breath.

'You absolutely do not have to do this, Sofia,' he said.

'It's fine,' she said, turning to Franz. 'Five minutes, max.'

He nodded and bowed to her jokingly.

A feast was served in the empty cafeteria. Some sort of curried lentil stew, salad with beets and feta. Prawns. Sofia had a few spoonfuls of soup and a few bites of the rest, but the food seemed to have no flavour.

Benjamin reached across the table and took her hand.

'Don't answer any questions that make you feel uncomfortable.'

'You don't need to coddle me, I know how to handle him.'

'I wonder if he could put me in touch with Gerhard Diller. I mean, that man is a genius.'

'Forget it. That's exactly what he wants you to do – drool over his vast network of contacts.'

They lingered over the meal for quite some time. Benjamin demanded that she call him the minute Franz suggested anything shady.

She dragged her feet all the way to the front door of the manor house and slowly ascended the stairs to his office. The building felt dull and deserted without any staff. Empty, dark offices and hallways. Everything seemed neat and meticulously clean, with a whiff of lemon cleaning product hanging in the air.

She opened the door to his office without knocking. He was at his massive desk and a wolfish smile spread over his face when he caught sight of her.

'Have a seat, Sofia. To think that you're here again, in my office. Want anything to drink?'

'No, I'm fine. Can you just tell me what you want already? I'm exhausted from all the information you force-fed us today.'

He urged her to sit down in the chair in front of his desk, but she elected to stand in the corner of the room. It struck her that his office looked just as it had when she worked there. The only additions were a few easy chairs and a coffee table. But everything was still white, grey, and spartan. No Christmas decorations, but she noticed a basket of hyacinths and Christmas roses.

'A gift from the church in the village,' he said. 'Smells awful.'

She saw that the little desk she had used was gone. He noticed her roving eyes.

'I don't have a secretary at the moment. A stream of incredibly incompetent individuals passed through here, so I gave up. Honestly, you are the best secretary I've ever had. Why did I have to go and ruin that?' he said with a heavy sigh. 'We'll see if Madde manages to smarten up. Remember her? Just as useless as ever. Now there's a room right next door here where I have support staff to type up my theses and lectures and so forth. They'll come at the press of a button. Anything else you'd like to know about my life these days?'

'Nope, I'm not the least bit interested. Get to the point.'

He took a deep breath and stared out the window for a moment. Then he stood up and took a few steps her way.

'This isn't an easy question to ask, but I have to do it anyway.'

'Out with it. I'm not much for guessing games and trivia time.'

He held her gaze steady for a while and then released a long sigh.

'I want to know if Julia is mine,' he said seriously.

For one overwhelming instant, Sofia was on the edge of a ravine, facing a greedy black hole that threatened to swallow her up. In the midst of this chaos came a beam of clarity.

You can dread something every single day for fifteen years, and still not be prepared when it actually happens.

11

Her reaction and ensuing meltdown were not at all typical of Sofia. But as she stood there in front of Franz's massive desk it dawned on her why he had called her there. Out of her safety zone and into his. To a place he expected he could make her feel small. It was all so he could get a read on her. For a fleeting moment she felt reproached and fragile. Then came the rage. She looked around for some object to throw, anything at all, and caught sight of the Christmas display on the sideboard. She grabbed the flowerpot and flung it at him. It landed at his feet in a pile of soil and shards. A couple of hyacinth bulbs flew out and bounced on the floor. A lone amaryllis sailed up and landed on his polished shoe.

'So you don't know,' came his voice from far away, as if from another dimension. 'You're welcome to throw my tablet and laptop as well. They're shockproof. And insured.'

His feet stepped over the pile of dirt and came her way. Instinctively she pulled away, but not fast enough. He gave her arm a quick stroke.

'I know you think I'm doing this to fuck with you,' he said calmly. 'But that's not why. If Julia is mine, I want her to have the option to come to me and get to know me.'

'She'll never want to do that.'

'Why not?'

'Because she's everything you're not – humble, warm, human.'

I'm lying through my teeth, she thought. *She's just about everything he is. Minus the evil.*

'It never even would have occurred to me if I hadn't seen her in that singing competition on TV,' he said. 'That's when I began to suspect. But that was before I knew who she was, I didn't even know she was your daughter. I just felt such a strong connection. So now I'm begging you to do the DNA test. I'm happy to help you with the shelter either way. And, of course, you can publish the book.'

'You could have asked me in Stenungsund.'

'Sure, but it feels more natural here. On our home turf. Where we have a number of lovely memories together. And I wanted to show you the model, as well.'

'You have no rights to her.'

'True. But you're a good person, Sofia. You'll do what's best for Julia.'

All at once, she became aware of the mess around her and felt an incredible sense of relief. There was nothing to lie about any longer; all she had to do now was say no.

'Now, don't make any hasty decisions,' he warned. 'Talk to Benjamin. Sleep on it. Try to consider this from Julia's perspective before you make up your mind.'

'Don't say her name as if you know her. You don't know who she is.'

'I know more than you think. I've done quite a bit of research.'

'Yeah, you're so good at that. Why don't you press your little button and make your underlings clean up this mess now, because I'm going to bed. You won't be hearing from me again.'

'Oh, I think I will. It's been nice having you here. And entertaining!' he said, smiling.

She hurried out of the office, forcing herself to slow down as she headed down the stairs, out of the manor house, and across the courtyard. She could feel his eyes on the back of her neck, dead sure that he was watching her from the window. Sure enough, when she turned around she could see his silhouette there. She flipped him the bird and went back to the annexe.

When she opened the door, Benjamin leapt from his chair.

His expression said it all. He knew. He had realized it was all about Julia.

'Maybe it's just as well that everything has come to a head,' he said. 'So we can stop lying to ourselves.'

Before she even had time to sit down, she burst into tears. Benjamin put his arms around her and held her.

'I never want him to meet Julia, talk to her, touch her. Never, ever, okay?' she said. 'How can life be so unfair? How could something so wonderful have come from something so hateful and degrading?'

'We don't know that yet. Sweetheart, let's go to bed. You look wrecked. Nothing that happened today can change the fact that we have a wonderful life together. It's just old demons catching up with us. We'll chase them off like we always do. No one can force you to do anything you don't want to do. You've got the upper hand here, not Franz, you know that, right?'

'Why didn't I lie and say we already did the test and she's yours?'

'Because you are an honest and good and strong person. All the things I love about you.'

'But he's lying! He said he saw her in the song competition. The hell he did. He doesn't watch TV, and he definitely doesn't watch those commercial programs. He's been digging. For how long, I don't know.'

'Don't get yourself all worked up, honey,' he said. 'Come on, let's go to bed and relax.'

She gave in, sinking onto the bed and settling into his embrace. After a while she decided to take a shower and wash away the sticky feeling Franz had left her with. Benjamin had gotten under the covers by the time she came out of the bathroom. She crawled into bed and let him hold her. He always slept in boxers and a T-shirt, and now she could feel that he was hard against her back. He stroked her breasts.

'I know one way to stop thinking about Franz,' he murmured.

He pulled down the strap of her nightgown and she let him touch her until her rage evaporated. As soon as their lovemaking was over, he fell asleep and snored like a pig. After an hour of restless tossing and turning, Sofia drifted off into a light sleep.

She woke up with a crick in her neck. They hadn't managed to figure out how to adjust the complicated heater, so the room was cold and she was freezing. It was still dark outside, but moonlight streamed through the window and puddled on the floor. She got out of bed and looked at her phone to see what time it was. Quarter past six. Less than two hours before the ferry would depart for the mainland.

She got dressed and put on her winter coat, gloves and boots. Opening the front door, she stepped into the frosty winter morning. The manor house was dark. The tiny shimmering lights of the Christmas tree were the only source of light, aside from the moon hanging magnificently over the manor.

She shoved her hands in her pockets and walked to the small gate in the wall behind the annexes. It opened the second she touched the handle. The moon was like a flashlight guiding her along the narrow path to the field of heather. The air was so cold that it hurt to breathe at first. Out on the heath, the sky was vast, millions of stars hanging on invisible threads.

She climbed down the cliffs and walked to the tip of Devil's Rock. The moon splashed its silvery beams over the sea. On either side of her, the silhouettes of boulders rose against a dark, blue-velvet sky. The cold air robbed her body of warmth. She closed her eyes for a moment and listened to the gentle lapping of the waves.

I'm that young girl again, she thought. *Standing here at Devil's Rock, dreaming of an exciting future, far away from the average life, long before I have experienced pure evil.* She tried to put herself in Julia's shoes. *Would I want to know if a crazy cult leader and rapist was my biological father?* she asked herself. *How would that affect my life?*

She turned around and walked slowly back to the manor, pulling her numb hands from her gloves and blowing on them feverishly. Her heart leapt into her throat as a fox she'd scared dashed across the path. It turned around and looked at her with glowing eyes.

Benjamin was getting out of the shower just as she came through the door.

'It'll be so nice to go home,' he said. 'Where have you been?'

'Out by the Rock. Thinking.'

'Don't let Franz get into your head.'

'But what if he's right, what if Julia should be allowed to find out who her biological father is?'

'What difference would that make, except to give him a thousand new reasons to contact us and keep an eye on us?'

'But maybe it's not about us. It feels wrong, lying to Julia. Doesn't she have the right to know? She is actually like him in a lot of ways.'

'You're wrong about that, honey,' he said. 'Seems you've lost the ability to see yourself through the eyes of others. There is not a trace of Franz in Julia. And not much of me there, either. She is one hundred per cent Sofia Bauman. *That's* why he's so fixated on her.'

*

During the ferry crossing, Sofia noticed that Julia had called several times overnight. But when she tried to call back, she only got Julia's voicemail, so she left a message to say they would be home soon.

Just then, Anna called.

'I've been trying to reach you for two days. What is going on?'

'I was on Fog Island, the coverage there is pretty bad.'

'What? You went after all? How did it go?'

'I'll fill you in later, but the short version is that Franz is just as hateful as always.'

'I see. Anyway, I'm calling for a different reason. Do you remember Peder Santos, the guy who helped us with the yard and all sorts of stuff around the shelter?'

'Of course I do.'

Peder had showed up just when they opened the shelter. Not only did he take care of the grounds, but he could fix anything from a leaky faucet to a jammed lock. Always helpful, jocular, and well-liked by all.

'Well, someone called me from Henån, some worker who was out clearing the roads. He had gone onto our property and spotted some tools and machines that belonged to Peder. So I called him, but got a message that the number was no longer in service. I searched for him online and contacted a few authorities, and now I am totally perplexed.'

'Why's that?'

'The home address he gave us is fake, someone else has been living there for ten years. The more I searched the more I realized he's gone up in smoke, he's untraceable.'

Father stopped spending time with me when I was nine. I hardly saw him anymore. When we were first in Earth's Children, he sometimes spent weekends with Vic and me; he would come up with things for us to do together and always asked how things were going in school.

But one day everything changed. The events of that day live on inside me. The memory will overwhelm me when I least expect it.

It was always strongly emphasized, throughout our training, that we were a team. The roll calls, marching, being divided into work groups and teams to play sports. To reinforce this, they introduced what they called victory songs. Some of them were real songs about ViaTerra. But sometimes they were only a rhythmic chanting of quotes from ViaTerra texts. We would stand in a straight line in front of a large, framed photo of Father and shout his words of wisdom, loudly and in unison: 'I place my life in the hands of the earth', or 'All the strength I will ever have comes from Mother Earth.'

Sometimes Karsten or Ali-Khan would stand in front of us and bellow questions whose answers we were required to shout back.

'Who is your leader?'

'Franz Oswald!'

'What way do you walk?'

'The way of the earth!'

'What is the one true way?'

'ViaTerra!'

'Who are the chosen ones?'

'We are the chosen ones, Earth's Children!'

These exercises went on until we were hoarse and always ended with a round of applause directed at that framed photo of Father. Of all the things we were forced to do, this, applauding a picture of Father, was the most difficult for me. There was something off-putting about it. It felt strange to stare into his eyes and clap. I felt so far away from him at those times, it was so surreal. Who applauds their own father like that?

Eventually I would only pretend to be clapping; I would simply let my hands brush together and hope that no one noticed.

That was what prompted the terrible events of that day.

ISOLATION

It's late at night. Ali-Khan has just dismissed us from a long, boring lesson in which we shouted so much wisdom and so many chants that I'm a little hoarse. Now it's time for the round of applause, and then we can go to bed.

As usual, I can't bring myself to do it. I'm incapable of being swept along in the others' fervour. This time I merely place my hands together as the others clap. I hope no one will look my way. Just as I think I've gotten away with it, Vic gives a shriek.

'Thor isn't clapping!'

Everyone falls silent. The children turn to stare at me with suspicion.

Ali-Khan fixes her hawklike eyes on me.

'Is that true, Thor?'

I stare at the floor and nod; I can't bring myself to lie. I've almost been waiting to be found out.

'Why aren't you clapping, Thor?'

'It feels weird,' I manage to say.

'Don't whisper. Answer me properly.' Ali-Khan's voice has gone

icy. I've already overstepped a boundary. Questioning something that Father has decreed is unthinkable and strictly forbidden.

'Clapping for a picture feels weird,' I whisper.

Vic approaches me. He looks insane, his face blotchy red and his eyes furious. He grabs my hands and whacks them together a bunch of times.

'Clap, you freak. You stupid idiot, clap for the boss this minute!' He shoves me in the chest, and I fly backwards and nearly fall down.

Ali-Khan stares at us, her arms crossed.

'Vic is right. Clap, Thor, loudly so everyone can hear.'

Something inside me has locked up. I can't get my arms to move; they hang slack by my sides. All the air seems to have left the room and I sink to a crouch on the floor.

Just then, I sense Father's presence behind me. I can't see him, but I know he's there. The other children gasp as they catch sight of him. I don't dare to turn around.

'Carry on,' Father's voice says. 'I'm just here to observe.'

At this point, Vic goes crazy. He starts to shout at me and kick me as I sit there on the floor.

'Clap for the boss! Clap, or I'll kill you!'

Ali-Khan comes over, grabs my arms in her claw-like fingers, and hauls me to my feet. The smell of her smoker's breath is suffocating. I sense a certain hesitation in her – Father is there, after all, and I'm his son – but she must act, this can't go on.

Vic senses Ali-Khan's uncertainty too and takes over. He grabs my arms and drags me across the room while shouting 'Stupid idiot! You're going to isolation!'

I'm too scared to fight back. That never helps with Vic, and Father's eyes are there somewhere, taking in everything that's going on. Vic drags me to the broom closet and shoves me inside; I land on my back. It's a minuscule space and I have to tuck my legs in to fit. The door slams and the key turns in the lock. Total darkness swallows me. I can't see a thing, but my hearing is painfully amplified.

'Well done, Vic!' I hear Father say outside. 'Today you demonstrated your leadership ability. The least insubordination from one team member can bring down the whole group.'

I hear mumbles of agreement from the other children and then Ali-Khan's voice.

'Time for bed! Ten minutes until lights out!'

The silence and darkness are about to smother me.

I lie on my back in the closet and wait. Listening for sounds, for the steps that will soon approach, someone coming to let me out. But nothing happens.

The line between day and night is blurred; there is no time. The darkness eats at me until my fear turns to desperation.

My little heart aches.

I swallow my tears; there's nothing to dry them with.

No one comes to open the door that night.

12

Julia stretched, arching her body in an attempt to lure Matt back to the sofa. He was putting on his jeans, and he stumbled over one leg and was about to fall head-first on top of her when he caught himself against the edge of the sofa. It looked so comical that she burst out laughing, and he followed suit.

He cupped his hands around her face, the same hands that had explored every last part of her body and given her three orgasms that night.

'It's always so hard to leave you,' he said.

'Can't you sleep over?'

'I have to be at school super early tomorrow. So if I stay I have to *sleep*, and that means where I sleep is six of one, half a dozen of the other.'

'Why do you always use such old-fashioned expressions? Six of one? No one says that anymore.'

'I don't want to be like everyone else.'

He stood up and managed to put on his jeans without falling over this time. She stayed on the sofa, watching as he pulled the T-shirt over his wiry torso and sat down to put on his shoes and socks.

'When will your parents be home?' he asked.

'Tomorrow afternoon.'

'But you'll be in school then.'

'Maybe. We'll see.'

He bent down to place a kiss on her lips.

'See you tomorrow, cutie.'

'When are we going to have sex for real?'

'I told you. When you turn sixteen. We'll go away together, somewhere, just you and me.'

'Hmm… maybe. But I'm over the age of consent already. It's so silly to wait.'

'The longer we wait, the better it will be. Are you going to sleep like that – naked on the sofa?'

'Yup. You totally sapped me, as the old dorks say. I can't even manage to drag myself upstairs.'

She stayed on the sofa, lying on her back. Moonlight fell through the window, illuminating her body with a faint blue shimmer. She heard Matt's car start and drive off. She touched herself, thinking about him, making her nipples hard and bringing that good heavy feeling between her legs. She decided to go upstairs after all, wanted to be in her bed. She stood up and stretched her body, feeling relaxed and happy and calm.

Suddenly there was a flash outside the window. Lightning? *There can't be lightning in winter, can there?* she thought, peering out the window for thunderclouds, but all she saw was the full moon in a clear sky.

Then there was another flash, several of them, like fireworks. She looked down and felt an icy hand squeeze her heart.

There was someone outside the living-room window. Julia was staring into a pair of black eyes in a grinning mask.

The chill in her heart spread through her nerves and up her spine.

She was paralysed, couldn't take her eyes from the horrid

mask. She heard herself give a screech, but it sounded like it came from someone else.

Her phone! Where had she put her phone?

The face vanished from the window, but her feet were frozen on the spot. Her thoughts leapt from her phone to the front door, which wasn't locked. *Door first, then phone. Police, I have to call the police!*

Her muscles filled with a prickly pressure so powerful that it broke through her paralysis. The adrenaline made her legs explode into violent movement. She stumbled over the rug and nearly fell flat on her face but made it to the door. She locked it twice, just to be sure. She leaned against the wall, trying to calm her frantically pounding heart, and her eyes darted around to look for her phone, which she now recalled she had put down in the living room.

There was a screeching sound from a hanger behind her in the coat closet. A puff of air licked the back of her neck. Before she could turn around, he attacked her from behind. In a single motion he locked one arm around her neck and the other around her waist. She tried to scream but her mouth was suddenly so dry that only a hoarse croak came out. He was unbelievably strong, his grip rock-hard. Her brain had turned off, and some terrified part of her hovered outside her body.

'Do as I say and everything will be fine,' he said. She didn't recognize the gravelly voice, which sounded oddly matter-of-fact and calm. She was breathing hard, but no air seemed to reach her lungs.

'Walk straight ahead, into the living room.'

He nudged the backs of her thighs with his knee. Her panic rose, and she reflexively tried to break free by pulling her arms in and kicking backwards at the same time. He responded by squeezing the elbow around her throat until black dots danced in her vision. She gurgled and hissed, trying to get her arms loose, prise his suffocating arm away. But she was no match for him.

He loosened his hold on her throat and let her suck in air.

'No more trouble. Go!'

He shoved her across the cold floor and past the kitchen island, where he stopped, took his arm from around her waist, and picked up something hard he pressed to her back. A knife? Her thoughts sped up. *Oh God, help me, he's going to kill me!* She was hyperventilating now. Her breath came in tiny gasps.

Once they reached the sofa, he loosened his grip on her but locked her legs from behind with his own. He took a length of rope from his pocket and bound her hands behind her, pulling so tight that it stung. She felt the urge to fight for her life but a voice in the back of her mind warned her off: *He has a knife. You haven't got a chance.*

He left her standing by the sofa for a moment. Suddenly she was ashamed of her nakedness, her butt brushing his pants.

'On your back!'

When she turned around to obey, she came face to face with him. His eyes were cold and focused. She had seen that same gaze before – not on a person, but on the neighbour's cat an instant before it pounced on a baby bird that had fallen from its nest. And now she was the baby bird.

She knew that this was the moment she should start begging and pleading for him to spare her, but all the feelings had fled her body. All she could feel was her pounding heart, her cottony mouth, and her uncontrollable trembling. As soon as she sat down on the sofa, he pushed her the rest of the way onto her back. The rope around her wrists dug into the flesh at the small of her back. The pain was so sharp it made her gasp.

He crouched down before her. She could tell he was wearing a black denim jacket with shearling trim and a black turtleneck.

His chin, covered in black one-day stubble, was all she could see under his mask. He took a piece of black fabric from his pocket and blindfolded her. In the dark her senses were heightened: the beating of her heart against her ribs, her shaking body, the clench of her teeth to keep her jaw still. His steps echoed over the floor. A faint light appeared – from the floor lamp, she assumed.

She heard the sound of a zipper. A fly? No, a longer zipper, maybe on a backpack or a duffel bag.

Something was wrong with him. No panting, no sharp odour of sweat like from a crazy serial killer. He was scentless and chilly, performing his tasks methodically and purposefully.

Do as he says. You'll make it through, just do as he says.

Now she could hear something scraping the floor, and a faint tinkle and the click of something flipping out.

His gloved hands took hold of her calves and pulled until the backs of her knees rested on the edge of the sofa. He spread her thighs, wrenching them apart so hard she whimpered with pain.

'Lie still, just like that.'

No sound for a moment, and then a series of flashes that blinded her even through the cloth over her eyes. The click of a camera, over and over.

He's taking pictures of me!

She wondered if this was the revolting precursor to something even more awful, before he killed her. But she instinctively felt that something else was going on, something she didn't understand. He pressed something hard and chilly against her throat. *The knife!* He adjusted the object over the dip of her throat. Her brain felt like a merry-go-round, the panic spinning around and around and making her dizzy. Suddenly she began to babble, fast and incoherently, the words coming too quickly, some of them missing, fragmented sentences. He took hold of her hair and yanked hard, making her scream.

'Be quiet and lie still.'

Another barrage of flashes, this time closer to her face.

'Open your mouth,' he said, and she obeyed. Her lower lip was trembling uncontrollably. He removed the object from her neck, grabbed her shoulders, and forced her to turn onto her stomach. She let out a hoarse whimper. But making a noise didn't help at all – she was caught in a nightmare and there was no way she could scream her way out of it.

He took hold of her shoulders again, pulling her up so her breasts were over the edge of the sofa. Now another series of flashes, very close.

'Open your mouth, lick your lips!'

Another battery of flashes and clicks, and then it was silent for a moment.

His hands closed hard around her calves, pulling her backwards until her legs were off the sofa and she was on her knees with her ass in the air. Everything spun around her; it was like waking up in the middle of the night with the stomach flu.

'Don't move!'

The degrading position set off another round of trembling; her legs shook helplessly. He placed a hand on the small of her back, pressing hard and somehow, mysteriously, making the trembling stop.

More flashes went off, further away, and then just behind her.

At last, she heard a mutter of satisfaction, but it ended abruptly. She knew he was just looking at her. All she could hear was her frantic breathing. He loosened the rope around her wrists but shoved her brusquely back down when she tried to stretch out her arms. Then she felt a rope being wound around her calves and tightened. He pressed the metal object to the back of her neck and drew it slowly down her spine.

'If you move now, I will hurt you.'

Then came the sound of the zipper again, he was snapping something closed, it sounded like he was putting things in the backpack or whatever it was.

Then came a hard slap on her butt.

'Won't your mama be proud of you!'

His steps echoed through the room, fainter and fainter until all was quiet.

He's gone. He left. Breathe, breathe!

She strained her ears to the limit. But she didn't hear the front door closing or a car starting.

Even so, she knew he was gone and wouldn't be coming back.

13

Sofia thought she had never been so relieved for a day to be over and done with.

It all started on the ferry when Julia called and told her about the attack, sobbing.

Then she had turned to shouting about how Sofia was so hard to get hold of, and where the hell was she when Julia needed her mother? Because Julia had had to handle it all on her own, the stupid police and the psychologist chick who wanted her to run through the attack like a hundred times, and now she was exhausted and wanted them to come pick her up. Julia put on a tough front, but Sofia knew she was upset and shaken.

While the mainland was slower than ever to appear in front of the ferry, Sofia's hysteria dialled up to levels previously unheard of, until she was shouting at Björk to go faster. She could tell that Björk felt for her; he didn't become the least bit irritated and simply explained that the ferry was already crossing the sound at maximum speed.

Benjamin had managed to remain relatively calm, but she could see the drops of sweat springing forth at his hairline, despite the below-freezing temperatures. The whole day turned out to be a chaotic mishmash of police, psychologists, and social workers who wore varying degrees of accusatory expressions on their faces.

But the most upsetting part was Julia's peculiar psychological reaction to what had happened. Sofia could see in her eyes that she was shaken. She trembled now and then. At the same time, she was angry as a hornet and snapped angrily at everyone. She said she had already been tortured by that shithead and now she wanted to go home and be left alone.

When they arrived home, two police officers were outside, shooting them sympathetic glances. Inside the house, a couple of crime-scene investigators were just packing up to leave. Julia said she was ravenous and wanted to eat before she talked about what had happened. After she ate, they sat down on the sofa. Sofia put her arm around Julia's shoulders. Benjamin was there too, but he kept getting up and walking around the house restlessly, looking for doors and windows that needed to be secured. At last Sofia told him to quit it, because the solution was very simple: just lock the front door.

Julia rested her head in Sofia's lap. When Sofia asked her to tell them what had happened, she shut down.

'I don't want to talk about it any more.'

'Honey, I don't understand why you don't want to talk about your feelings. I think you'd better see a psychologist tomorrow so you can deal with this trauma straight away, while it's fresh in your mind. That's really important.'

'I don't need to.'

'But why not? It will help you in the long run.'

'I tried to explain it to the police, but they wouldn't freaking listen. There was something strange about that man, something that makes me feel sure he won't come back, so I'm not afraid.'

'What do you mean?'

'Like, at first I was scared shitless, I was so sure he was going to kill me that I was basically shaking uncontrollably. But once he put the blindfold on me, and I heard him moving around,

I realized he wasn't going to hurt me. He was totally not interested in raping me. It was like… he was only there to do a job. He was freakishly efficient, and then he took off. And he moved the rope from my wrists to my legs, so I could untie it. He could have hurt me easy as anything, but he didn't.'

'But what if this is only the start of something—' Sofia cut herself off. She didn't want to set Julia off, but it was too late.

'Oh, Mom!' Julia whimpered; she burst into tears and clung tight to Sofia. Sofia stroked her hair and let her cry.

'The police will catch him, sweetie,' she said reassuringly.

'They seem more interested in torturing me. Mom, seriously. What if he sells the pictures? The internet's going to be crawling with porn of *me*! Oh, Jesus!' she cried, sobbing once again. Sofia rubbed her back comfortingly. A while later, Julia suddenly sat up.

'I feel a little better now. I'm so tired.'

'Do you want to sleep in our room?'

'No, I want to sleep in my own bed. I don't want you to mollycoddle me. Or ground me or invent a bunch of new rules or anything. This wasn't my fault, was it? I just want everything to be normal.'

Once Julia had gone to bed, Sofia tried to process it all with Benjamin.

'What is going on? Franz pops up again and all hell breaks loose. Peder Santos goes up in smoke, and now this.'

Benjamin frowned, concerned, and thought for a moment.

'It seems unlikely that Franz is behind this,' he said. 'He went to a whole lot of trouble just to ask you for a DNA test. He's definitely a pervert, but I don't think incest is really his style. Then again, Julia's description of this man – short, strong, dark stubble – it does sound a little like Santos, doesn't it? Do you think she's attracted the attention of a stalker? Julia did visit the shelter now and then, after all. Maybe he spotted her there. He wouldn't be the first one to become fixated on her.'

'But why would Santos do something like that? Here I was thinking he had given a fake address because he was in trouble with the Migration Authority. Surely we shouldn't ignore the fact that this is happening such a short time after Franz contacted me? I don't believe in coincidences.'

'Me neither. But this also coincides with the storm. Everyone's life has been seriously shaken up. I think this kind of natural disaster brings out the best and the worst in people.'

The more they talked, the more it seemed to have been a mistake not to mention Peder Santos's disappearance to the police. Benjamin called them, then said he was headed to bed and that she should join him. But she knew there was no way she could fall asleep. Her brain was full of uneasy thoughts and her body was still running on adrenaline.

Although Sofia desperately wanted to blame Franz for all this, she couldn't make it make sense. Ruminating on it was taking its toll, eating her up from the inside. She searched 'Julia Frisk' online, trying to see if the terrible photos were there already, but there were no hits. Then she started searching for Julia on porn sites, until she realized what she was doing. This was nuts. Instead she went to the ViaTerra website, and there she found news. In two weeks, just ahead of the new year, Franz would be hosting a gathering for spiritual leaders from all over the world. The conference would take place on Fog Island, and they would discuss the greenhouse effect and the need for spiritual guidance in an unstable world. The media was also invited. The announcement included headshots of the celebrities who would make appearances that evening.

All at once, a wave of exhaustion hit her. *The nerve*, she

thought. *Closing in like a goddamn hurricane over everything and everyone.*

She managed to get a few hours of sleep, but Julia woke her up, demanding to be allowed to go to school. She looked tired and vulnerable, standing there.

'Stay home and rest today, sweetheart. It's way too soon to go back to school.'

'I don't need to rest. I want everything to go back to normal. I'm not about to let that disgusting shithead get me down. Please let me go to school.'

There was nothing Sofia could do but ask Benjamin to give her a ride. But she made Julia promise to call right away if she wanted to come home.

That day, Sofia kept busy by cleaning. She wanted to scrub away every last molecule of the bastard that had invaded their home and scared their daughter half to death. Between rounds of cleaning she read everything she could online about determining paternity and forensic genetic studies. Again. She was looking for technicalities or loopholes Franz might exploit, but found nothing. Franz had no rights whatsoever, yet she couldn't shake the unease that lingered from her meeting with him. At the same time, she was feeling increasingly guilty about not being honest with Julia.

Her phone rang, an unknown number. Despite a moment's hesitation she answered, because her hope of finding financial backing for the shelter wasn't dead yet. She recognized Franz's voice immediately and resisted the urge to throw her phone against the wall.

'Hi, Sofia,' he said breezily, as though they were friends.

'You and I have nothing further to discuss. Do not call my phone.'

'Where else would I call?'

'You are not to contact me at all. You *promised* to leave us alone if I came to the island.'

'But things are totally different now. I heard what happened to Julia.'

'How did you hear about that?'

'It was in the paper, and after asking around I figured out it was her.'

'Are you behind it? It totally matches your style.'

'Are you out of your mind? Why would I contact you if I wanted to hurt my own daughter? Don't you understand how worried I am?'

'She's not your daughter!'

'I just want to help you. I can offer her much better protection than the police can.'

Behind his usual nonchalance, she sensed a flicker of worry in his voice.

'We can take care of ourselves. Good luck with your stupid conference.'

'Why does it feel like I'm talking to a child? Look, I was thirteen when I figured out who my biological father was. That stuff is important when you're a young person.'

Sofia knew what he was talking about. Franz's journey to fame had begun when he was thirteen. He was the 'bastard' child of the count who had owned the manor on Fog Island. He'd spent the first three years of his life at the manor, but then his mother moved with Franz to a small cottage in the forest. She still lived there, as far as Sofia knew. But when Franz was thirteen, he ran away from the island, tracked down his father, who had moved to France, and forced him to accept Franz as his son. The whole family, except for Franz, had later died in a fire. He had inherited an enormous fortune from them, which he later used to finance his cult. His return to Fog Island had been something of a triumphant act of revenge. In one conversation with Sofia, Franz had suggested that he had set the fire his family perished in, but no one had ever been able to prove it.

'That's right,' she said. 'And when you realized what a jerk your father was you swept him out of the way. You should watch out. Julia sometimes has a terrible temper.'

He gave a heavy sigh.

'I really don't want to fight with you, Sofia. I just want to help.'

'Then the best thing you can do is leave us alone,' she said, and hung up.

He didn't call back. She made up her mind to get a new phone number but didn't have the energy to deal with it just then. Now she was almost certain Franz had nothing to do with the attack on Julia. He really had sounded worried. But that certainty only made her nervous. She had a decent amount of past experience with Franz's cat-and-mouse games. This was something new and unfamiliar.

Later that afternoon, Benjamin called her mobile.

'We have to meet with the headmaster of Julia's school, something's happened.'

Her heart flew into her throat, but he was quick to reassure her.

'Julia is fine, but it seems she caused some sort of incident. Look, it's probably not that big a deal. Let's meet up outside the school.'

It turned out that a boy in Julia's class had accused her of being something along the lines of 'fuck buddies with the student teacher', which had unleashed a fit of rage. It was unbelievable, but Julia had somehow wrestled the boy to the ground and let her fists fly. His glasses were ruined. Naturally, the boy's parents were upset and demanded that something be done.

Benjamin apologized to the headmaster again and again. 'I hope there won't be any repercussions for Matt Larsen,' he added. 'He seems to be a nice guy and I know they haven't—'

'No,' the headmaster interrupted. 'I've already discussed this with Matt. Naturally we would prefer that they had no relationship, but Matt is a good student teacher and thus far we haven't seen any evidence that it's affecting Julia's schoolwork. We can overlook it for the time being, considering everything that's happened. I'm really more concerned about Julia's behaviour, as you can understand. Frankly, I don't understand why she's here today, after what happened just two days ago.'

Sofia went to pick up Julia, who was sitting on a bench in the schoolyard and staring sulkily into space. Together they spoke with the boy's parents, who began by glaring at them with critical eyes. Benjamin explained that it must be a delayed reaction to trauma. That Julia must have been projecting her pent-up rage at the perpetrator onto their poor son. He offered to compensate the boy for pain and suffering, as well as paying for new glasses of course. As usual, he successfully smoothed things over.

All the way home Julia was silent and sullen in the back seat, well aware that she wouldn't be going to school for a while. When they got home, she took Denzel to her room. Sofia resisted the impulse to follow and offer comfort. She could sense that Julia wanted to be left alone. After an hour, Julia came back downstairs with a wan smile on her face.

'Mom, something nice actually happened at school today.'

'Oh, that's good to hear,' Sofia said with a slight note of disbelief in her voice.

Julia scraped her foot nervously on the stone tiles.

'So, you know, we have this religion teacher who's pretty cool, Mette Carlsson. She's organized a field trip two weeks from now. Our class is the only one who gets to go out of thousands of religion classes all over Sweden. Guess where we're going?'

Sofia had the feeling that this wasn't going to be good news at all.

'No idea. Anyway, I doubt you'll feel strong enough to go.'

'Oh yes I will. It's a meeting with a whole bunch of religious leaders from all over the world. We get to listen to them give speeches.'

A wave of dread welled up in Sofia.

'There will be celebrities there too. The conference is on Fog Island, Mom, I finally get to see Fog Island!'

Father treated me like a nonentity for almost a year. I regretted the moment I had stubbornly refused to clap my hands, wished I could turn back time, bring my hands together a few times so everything would be okay. But Father ignored me entirely and instead developed an even greater interest in Vic.

He saw something in Vic that night, something beyond just his own mirror image. Maybe he realized that he wasn't immortal after all and would need a successor one day.

The situation was made even worse by the fact that I was often sick. My body didn't handle physical labour very well. That, in combination with the fact that I was almost constantly depressed, meant that I caught every cold and flu I possibly could. When you were sick in Earth's Children you were put in isolation, but it was a different kind of isolation than in the broom closet. They had set up a room in the barn with a bed and dresser. It was cold and draughty there, the only heat source a small radiator, and it smelled like mould and herbs. After all, we weren't allowed to take real medicine.

In hindsight, I think it was my constant absence during those years that resulted in my being less influenced by the indoctrination, the stories about us and the others, *than the rest of the children.*

US AND THE OTHERS

We're sitting in the classroom. My mind isn't entirely present today and I'm lost in fantasies of Father talking to me again. But in that moment

I have no idea my wish will be granted. I'm trying to tear myself from the daydream and focus on the pictures Ali-Khan is showing us.

The subject Ali-Khan is teaching is called 'world knowledge'. Not history – where you learn about what happened a long time ago – but what's going on right now out in the world.

Ali-Khan is telling us horrible tales that frighten me, even though I'm ten years old and don't believe in ghosts anymore.

On the projector screen she shows us examples of evil in the world – illustrations, or rather caricatures. Psychologists with super-thick glasses and fangs administering electric shocks to people in chains. Journalists with cruel, slanting eyes and drool dribbling from the corners of their mouths. Doctors pouring enormous amounts of pills out of bottles and into the mouths of restrained patients.

Now and then we do exercises based on defending ViaTerra. Although really you're never supposed to defend yourself, only attack those who criticize us. After all, our critics are only the puppets of psychologists and journalists. Their consciences are heavy with sin. We're supposed to say things like 'What crimes are you guilty of, what are you so afraid we will reveal?' over and over until they give up or break down and confess how evil they are.

All of this is spinning in my head. The horrible world outside the walls of ViaTerra and the equally horrible world inside these walls.

Now Father comes in and stops in the doorway to listen. I hear his steps and turn around to see his shoes and trousers, but I avoid meeting his gaze. I feel that I must do something, anything, to make him notice me. So I raise my hand and Ali-Khan nods, although she looks worried.

'What is the difference between us and the others?' I ask.

Ali-Khan doesn't have time to respond. Father comes up to me and places a hand on my shoulder. A miracle has occurred. He has touched me again.

'I can answer that question, Thor,' he says. 'I'm just going to go and get something, and then the whole class can follow me to Devil's Rock.'

I'm suddenly afraid he's going to push me off the cliff, but he doesn't sound angry.

When he returns he's wearing sneakers, jeans and an athletic jacket. In his hand is a large pail with a lid. He says there's no need to march, we can simply follow him in a line.

When we arrive at the slope that leads to Devil's Rock, he tells the other children to stay there but asks me to follow him out onto the cliff.

Now I'm scared. There are rumours that once we turn twelve we have to jump off the cliff if we do any violations, instead of being punished with the ice bath as we are now. It's a chilly spring day. The water looks cold, with little waves spitting and foaming down below.

I follow Father to the place where Devil's Rock stretches out over the sea.

'Stand still now,' he says, setting down his pail. It smells weird, all sour and rotten.

He makes me take off my socks and shoes. The rock surface is cold beneath my feet, rough and hard. His hand does a quick flourish and magically produces a blindfold from the pocket of his jacket, the kind Mama uses when she can't sleep.

He takes me by the hand, leads me further out on the rock, and puts the blindfold on me. Everything goes black and now I'm really scared; I sway and almost lose my balance. It feels like I'm already falling.

'Now walk out to the edge, Thor,' I hear Father say. 'Remember you're a spirit, not a body. You don't need eyes to find the way.'

I take a couple of hesitant steps, biting my lip to keep from sobbing. If I cry now, it's all over. I have to obey, try to feel instead of think.

'Keep walking,' Father says. 'All the way to the edge.'

Slowly, fumblingly, I take one step at a time, but it's so hard to keep my balance when I can't see. I stretch out my arms like a tightrope walker. I have no choice but to obey. If I fall, if I bash my skull on the rocks or fall into the sea, it still wouldn't be as bad as Father's wrath if I don't obey.

A small gust of wind nearly knocks me off balance. My foot lands exactly on the edge of the rock and nearly slips into thin air. I hear one of the children gasp behind me. I quickly pull my foot back and use that sidestep to put myself back in the centre of the rock. I keep moving forward with tentative steps. A sea anemone cuts my heel, but that doesn't affect me nearly as much as the question that suddenly hits me like a load of bricks.

How do I know where the end of the rock is?

I order my spirit to rise out of my head so I can see, but I'm caught in darkness and uncertainty. A couple more steps. I hear the sound of someone coughing. It's Matteo. I recognize that cough, because I sometimes hear it from the bunk beneath my own.

All at once I understand.

'I'm at the edge, boss,' I say.

The blindfold is removed. My left foot is just inches from the edge of the cliff. The big toe of my right foot is a centimetre past the edge.

I'm suddenly dizzy, the world is spinning, the sea below tugs at me and my stomach turns – but I did it.

Father places his hands on my shoulders.

'You *did that, Thor,' he says. 'Feel the wind, the salty air, the freedom here – it's almost like you can float, isn't it?'*

I nod, resisting the impulse to recoil.

'What you felt was your spirit. Your true self. You don't need eyes to see.'

He turns to the children standing on the slope.

'Now I will show you who the others *are. How they behave, while you all live according to the principles of ViaTerra.'*

He lets me take a few steps back and goes to stand at the edge of the cliff. When he opens the lid of the pail, a sour, fishy gust hits me.

'Herring,' he says cheerfully, picking up the pail and dumping its contents into the sea.

In under a minute, a flock of gulls comes flying across the sound. With shrill cries they begin to dive and fight for the herring. Soon another flock arrives, and chaos ensues in the fight for food.

We all stand there staring. None of us dares to say a thing. But no one quite understands why Father is feeding the gulls.

'Those gulls are just like the others,*' he says, making a sweeping gesture at the sea. 'Do you understand now? This is how they behave. Like stupid, soulless robots fighting over a couple of herring. There is no life in their eyes.*

'You all,*' he says, pointing at us, 'are different. Never forget that!'*

14

There was no avoiding the fight. Sofia had to keep Julia from travelling to Fog Island no matter the cost. Benjamin had come into the living room, but at first he just sat there in silence, observing them.

'Have a seat,' he said at last. 'We have to talk through this calmly and rationally.'

Sofia sat down, but Julia leaned against the wall.

'I don't want to sit on that nasty sofa.'

'Of course,' Benjamin said, pulling over a chair.

Then he began to talk about all the things Franz had done to them in ViaTerra. The outbursts of rage, the forced jumps from Devil's Rock, the electric fence, the cameras everywhere, Penance, and Elvira, the girl he'd locked in the attic and had sex with even though she was only fourteen.

Julia listened patiently, although she'd heard most of it before.

'So now maybe you understand why we don't want you to go there,' Benjamin concluded. 'For my part, I think it's indefensible that those religious leaders are supporting Franz.'

'Exactly,' Sofia chimed in. 'It's like everyone has forgotten what happened fifteen years ago. Or else they think we made it all up.'

Benjamin nodded in agreement.

'And it can't be a coincidence that Julia's class was the one selected to attend,' Sofia added, shooting a meaningful look at Benjamin.

'But he went to prison and served his time,' said Julia. 'That all happened fifteen years ago. Nothing terrible has happened since. Don't you believe people can change?'

This is when I have to tell her the truth, Sofia thought. But she was reluctant to do it, and now she wondered if it wouldn't be better to do the DNA test without letting Julia know. Telling her this now, without being sure, and after all Julia had been through, seemed cruel. *And by the way, he might be your biological father.*

'Mom, I'm only going there for a day, with my class. You don't think I'm going to join a cult, do you? It would just be fun to see the island, since you've always said it was so pretty there. And also UnderGong is playing there that night.'

'What's that?'

'One of my favourite bands. They're so rad. I don't get why you have to be so protective. *You* both went there, and you ended up stuck for years. I'm only going to be there for a day.'

'We love you and would do anything to protect you. Under no circumstances are you allowed to go.'

'People *can* change, you know. I've listened to some of Franz Oswald's video chats with my friends. Super interesting. He's done a ton of stuff to help people after the storm. There's even this course called "Our Environment" on his website where you can learn about the ecosystem and how the earth is one big, giant organism.'

'That does sound interesting, but you can learn that anywhere. Even in school,' Sofia said.

'But the way he explains it is so simple, so it's easy to understand. There was one lecture where he said he doesn't have a relationship so that he can focus completely on aid work.'

'He said that? What utter bullshit. He's only saying that so those bitches who worship him believe they have a chance.'

'Sofia!' Benjamin said, warning in his voice.

'Well, it's true! There's an ego trip and an ulterior motive behind everything he does.'

'Mom! Do you even know how much money he's donated to families who lost everything they owned? Doesn't that count?'

'He only does that stuff for the attention it brings him. In reality he's a huge narcissist.'

'Julia, why are you so into this?' Benjamin inserted. 'Looking him up online and stuff?'

'It's the most exciting thing I can find to do in this boring shithole,' Julia sighed. 'I think all that stuff is interesting. This hottie cult leader who went insane, and how you and Mom managed to escape. When you jumped off the cliff, Dad, and everyone thought you were dead. It's like a thriller.'

'Sweetie, life is not an action film,' Sofia said.

'Do you have to be so condescending? Can I go meet up with Matt now?'

'No, it's better for him to come here. You may not go out alone after dark.'

Julia made a face.

'Fine, I'll call him. Was there anything else?'

'No, but this discussion is not over,' Sofia said.

Julia bounced up the stairs.

'This is exactly what I do not need in my life right now,' Sofia said as soon as Julia was out of earshot. 'Franz is insane. I'm going to call him.'

'No! That's exactly what he wants you to do,' said Benjamin. 'So he can start an argument with you. Just think how much he's missed that, and now he's had a taste and wants more. We'll start by calling Mette, the RE teacher. Pull a few strings.'

Benjamin called Julia's headmaster and said he wanted to make sure this class trip was suitable for Julia. The headmaster gave him Mette Carlsson's number with no fuss.

'Do you want to call, or should I?' he asked.

'You do it. I'll only blow up at her.'

After the conversation with Mette Carlsson, Benjamin was perplexed.

'She says she read about the conference online and contacted his PR person, Carmen Gardell. She swears it was her idea. She also said the kids aren't going to meet Franz. They're only going to stay for a few hours and listen to the lectures.'

'Of course she said that. And you remember this Gardell woman, right? Franz's face to the world. So fake.'

'I have an idea,' Benjamin said. 'Let's send Matt along with Julia, say she's been a little fragile after what happened. And before they go, we'll talk to Matt and make sure he won't let her out of his sight for even one second during the whole visit.'

'Not on your life! She is not going. Who knows what kind of nonsense those religious idiots are going to stamp in these kids' brains. I can't believe this is allowed in Swedish schools.'

'They're not lecturing on religion, they're talking about the state of the world. It's about aid work in areas suffering the effects of climate change.'

'So you've been reading about Franz online too. Maybe you'd like to go along?'

'Very funny. Julia would never allow it.'

'She's not going.'

'Then we have to tell her the truth.'

They couldn't come to an agreement, so they decided to sleep on it.

★

The next day, Benjamin decided they should take his pickup to the shelter, load up anything of value, and store it in the barn behind their house. Julia, who was restless, welcomed the chance to get out of the house. Sofia was hesitant, but she figured it would help her come to terms with the loss of that lovely house.

At first glance, the property looked just as it had last time she was there, aside from the frost covering everything and making the place look even colder and sadder. The sky was grey and thick with snow-heavy clouds, but only a few lone flakes fell on them. The north wind was light but stinging cold. The air smelled like metal and smoke.

The first thing Sofia noticed was that the small tool shed Santos had used was totally cleaned out. No tools or machines, not even a single screw was left.

'Do you think someone stole it all?' Benjamin asked.

'Or maybe it was Santos himself,' Sofia said with a shudder.

Sofia gathered anything usable that was strewn across the property, while Benjamin followed behind filling bag after bag with trash. This went on for some time, until they were so cold they were shivering and took a coffee break in the heated cab of the pickup.

It was starting to feel nice to sort through this mess, almost like starting over fresh. Sofia couldn't help but think of the model Franz had showed them. Her dream could be reborn from this rubble, bigger, more beautiful. But just then, a bracingly cold gust of wind blew through the yard, slipping up the sleeves of her coat and clouding her wishful thinking. She would never ever be able to accept money from him. Her train of thought was interrupted by a cry of delight from Julia, who had disappeared over by the edge of the property along with the dog.

'Look what Denzel found, Mom!' she called, holding

something up in both hands. When Sofia went closer she could see that it was a metal lockbox, the kind you might keep money in.

'What if there's a bunch of cash inside?' Julia said, enraptured.

'We didn't keep any cash in the house,' Sofia said. 'This must be something else.'

Julia shook the box. Something hard rattled back and forth inside.

'I guess there's no way we'll ever find the key,' Julia sighed.

Benjamin had joined them.

'Bring it home. I can open it with my tools there,' he said. 'Although I'm sure it's nothing important.'

But Sofia couldn't shake the feeling that something was wrong. She should have recognized that box; she knew every nook and cranny of the shelter. Either it had come from Peder Santos's shed, or it had been hidden somewhere. Maybe it belonged to a defector who'd left it behind when they had to flee from the storm.

No one mentioned the lockbox again until later that night when they were warming themselves by the fire. Benjamin had made char in lemon sauce and Julia was allowed to have a glass of wine for a change; Denzel was lying on the sofa between them, his belly in the air, and everything felt almost like normal.

'The lockbox!' Julia suddenly shouted, and she ordered Benjamin out to the garage to open it. He was gone for a while, and then he returned with an amused expression on his face.

'Just a bunch of flash drives,' he said.

Julia yanked the box out of Benjamin's hands, set it on the coffee table, and opened the lid.

The box was full of USB drives.

Julia picked one at random and stuck it in her laptop.

A bevy of images came up on the screen.

Sofia gasped.

The pictures were of her; it was almost like a collage of memories from her time at the shelter. There she was on the veranda, deep in conversation with a defector; there she was in the yard with Denzel, chopping carrots at the kitchen island, sitting on the couch in the living room. But there was something odd about the pictures. They had all been taken from outside the house.

'What is this, Mom?' Julia asked. 'Do you recognize these pictures?'

Sofia shook her head in consternation. She shot a quick glance at Benjamin, who was gaping at the screen.

Julia pulled out that flash drive and inserted another.

The next set of photos also featured Sofia, but these had been taken earlier, right when they opened the shelter. She recalled that her hair had been shorter than ever before at the time, so short it barely brushed her shoulders. These pictures had been taken from outside too, through the window of one of the bedrooms. She was changing clothes, probably to go to the beach. There were images of her naked body from behind as she pulled on her bathing suit. In one of the pictures, she was leaning forward so her bottom was fully exposed. In another she was pulling up a shoulder strap and her breasts were front and centre. And then there was a close-up of her face.

She whimpered and grabbed Benjamin's hand.

But worse than her nakedness – the fact that someone had secretly taken pictures of her breasts and bottom and lips with perfect focus – was the carefree look on her face.

The fact that she hadn't had the foggiest idea.

15

Julia moved closer to Matt and slipped her hand into his. A couple of her classmates were staring, but it was no skin off her nose.

They were almost to the island. The sea breeze whispered in her ears, showering her with salty kisses and ruffling her hair. The sky was clear. Only a few fluffy clouds rested on the horizon. The sea was a shade of azure and the sun glittered on every ripple of the water. But the chilly breeze made her draw closer to Matt.

It had proved nearly impossible for Julia to get her mother's permission to go on this class trip, but after a lot of nagging and a promise that she would stick close to her teacher the whole time, Mom had given in. But only after Matt had promised to stick to Julia like a shadow throughout the journey.

Julia was exhilarated, although it felt a little improper. Life in Henån, which had been beyond boring since the storm, had suddenly become both exciting and frightening. The attack had shaken her to her core. She was always careful, now, to make sure all the doors in the house were locked at night, and she glanced over her shoulder an extra time whenever she walked home alone. She still got a sinking feeling in her stomach when she thought of what had happened, but she hadn't had any panic attacks or nightmares yet. Mom had explained that a person might experience delayed reactions after a traumatic incident like this one.

Even so, Julia couldn't help but feel a little excited that something had finally happened in Henån. It was like life had suddenly come to a head, and it was mostly exciting – if not for the horror in Mom's eyes when they found those pictures. Mom, who was usually such a bundle of energy, seemed to be wearing a veil of sadness these days. After they'd looked at the pictures on a couple of the flash drives, she had closed the lockbox and said she didn't want to see any more.

Everything had fallen into place that night. The attack, the pictures of Mom, and Peder Santos's disappearance. A stalker had been after them for years, and they'd had no idea.

The police hadn't been much help. Julia had learned that it wasn't like the crime shows on TV, where you could immediately issue a 'wanted' picture to the media. Real life was different. There was nothing to link Peder Santos, or whoever he was, to the pictures or the attack. Even though any old idiot could figure out that it was him. There was no 'concrete evidence'. The police said they would contact the Migration Authority and look through the pictures. They couldn't offer any sort of permanent security, but they would send a patrol car by their place at regular intervals.

'A stalker has been conning us for six years and they aren't going to do a damn thing!' Mom exclaimed when they got home. 'I wonder what he'll do in the meantime, while the police are sitting there drinking their cat-piss coffee!'

Dad had tried to reassure her, but not even that helped. Mom was furious, disappointed, and scared. She was usually so tough, and being fearful really didn't suit her.

★

The ferry was full of people, but the ferry captain, Björk, recognized Julia straight away.

'What's this? A taller version of Sofia Bauman!' he cried, shaking her hand. She liked him immediately. 'What are you getting up to on the island, helping your mom mess with that Franz Oswald?'

'No, I'm just here with my class. There are so many people on the boat!'

'Yes, I've been cruising back and forth nonstop since six this morning. I have to admit it's fun to have so many visitors on the island. Even if I do hate that cult.'

Julia looked around curiously as they went ashore. On the square ahead of them was a huge crowd. There were reporters with cameras and microphones everywhere. The garish colours, the laughter, and the warmth of so many people made her happy. It was almost like this tiny island had become the centre of the world. The idea that something horrible could happen here was totally laughable. She thought about sending a quick text to Mom but realized she had no signal on her phone. She wanted to stay on the square, mingle, find a strategic spot to stand and be caught on video, but Mette quickly herded the whole class to a bus that would take them to ViaTerra.

Before they drove through the massive gate, she felt a quick tremor in her belly. But the courtyard was full of buses and cars, as well as people chatting in small clusters. The white manor house towered up ahead, majestic and vast. It was even more beautiful than she'd imagined.

After a long lunch, during which Julia kept an eye out for celebrities, they gathered in a large auditorium with a glass cupola for a ceiling. There must have been room for a thousand people in there. Mette whispered to the class that the auditorium had been built with this conference in mind. Julia stared up at the glass ceiling, where the pale blue sky arced above them and a couple of gulls sailed on the breeze. At that moment she understood in a totally new way why her parents had been drawn here. This wasn't some weird cult. This was different!

Mette had prepared them well for the conference. She had explained that this wasn't about religion but human kindness and empathy, concepts that stood above religious purposes. The religious leaders would issue promises and set goals for aid work that would be conducted in regions affected by climate change. All this work would be done by volunteer organizations, a sort of 'volunteers without borders'. In this way, hundreds of thousands of people would work towards a common goal: alleviating the suffering of fellow human beings.

Julia thought it sounded nice, but there was no way to know whether it would lead anywhere or whether it was just one big PR stunt. Mette had also gone on and on about how the students were to conduct themselves.

At last came the moment when Franz Oswald took the stage to kick off the conference. There was a screen above him, and several more on the walls, where you could see a close-up image of him. Julia had seen him in so many videos online; she was prepared for how attractive he was, but it was his presence rather than his appearance that took her breath away. As soon as he took his place at the podium, the auditorium became so quiet you could hear a pin drop. He stood still for a long time, taking in the audience. She knew he was over forty, but he seemed eternally young. His symmetrical, tanned face, his well-defined chin and high cheekbones: every part of him radiated vitality. There was a warmth in his eyes and something gentle and heartfelt in his smile.

'Welcome to a brilliant future!' he exclaimed at last.

Cheers and ringing applause broke out in the room.

Laura, who was sitting next to Julia, tugged at the arm of her blouse.

'He's even hotter in real life,' she whispered.

But Julia didn't respond. She was stuck in the moment Franz had stepped onto the stage. When he put everyone in the audience under his spell, robbed the air of oxygen, and made the onlookers gasp for breath – with nothing but his presence.

They were sitting close to the front of the room, right behind the celebrities. A few times, when Franz paused between sentences, she thought he was trying to catch her eye.

She listened with half an ear to the other religious leaders' lectures and dutifully jotted down notes whenever Mette shot her a look. After each speaker, Franz came up to shake hands; he thumped some of them on the back and flashed his blinding smile.

At the very end, they showed a short video of a representative of the Pope, wishing everyone good luck at the conference. *Franz Oswald has become an international celebrity*, she thought. *I wonder what Mom and Dad would think of this. It's so awesome that you can hardly question it.*

Not even UnderGong could draw her attention completely away from Franz, who could make the air in a huge room stand still. Who had kind, warm eyes – not cruel ones, as she had originally imagined. And he had arranged this magnificent gathering, which the Pope himself had given his blessing to.

I want to meet him, she thought. *How can I draw my own conclusions if I don't get to meet him?*

But then she felt Matt's fingers sneaking under her short skirt. She put her purse in her lap and spread her legs, enjoying the last notes of UnderGong in a totally unique way.

Dinner, like lunch, was served as a buffet. There weren't enough seats in the cafeteria. The long tables were piled high with fancy organic food, constantly replenished by servers in grey uniforms. There was champagne, organic wine and mulled wine, which Mette said they were not allowed to drink under any circumstances.

When Julia took a step back she ran into one of the servers, who nearly dropped a tray of cheese. He was around her age and had longish copper hair, and he seemed a little distracted. Her interest was piqued – she had never seen such an amazing hair colour on anyone. He apologized again and again, and their eyes met.

His kind, sad eyes didn't seem at home in this euphoric hall. There was something lovely about him, something she couldn't quite put her finger on. She recognized him but couldn't think where she would have seen him before.

'Sorry I'm so clumsy,' he said with a smile, but the melancholic look lingered in his gaze. He took a plastic glove from his pocket and rearranged the cheeses. When he looked at her again, their eyes locked until she felt Matt taking her arm. A while later, she noticed the server guy watching her from one corner of the cafeteria. Feeling the power of attraction between them, she thought about going over and introducing herself. But then Matt tugged at her arm again; he excused himself to go to the bathroom.

'Don't move a muscle,' he warned her. 'If I lose you, your mother will kill me.'

She promised to stay put but snuck out of the cafeteria the moment he was out of sight. The manor house was calling her name. She wanted to see it without a bunch of people in the courtyard. It was warm in the cafeteria but frigid outside. She put on her winter coat and stuffed her hands in her pockets.

All lit up in the night, the manor house was even more beautiful than in the daytime. Spotlights were aimed at an inscription on its façade: *We walk the way of the earth*, it read. Here and there, a light was on in a window. Lanterns and garden candles glowed all over the courtyard. The lights of a huge Christmas tree flickered to life as she stood there. From some nearby kitchen came the wonderful aromas of cooking meat and mulled wine.

There was a crunch on the gravel behind her. Before she could turn around, she felt a pair of hands on her shoulders.

'I would be able to pick you out of a crowd of ten thousand people,' a voice whispered in her ear.

She knew who it was right away, and whirled around, only to find herself so close to him that she reflexively took a few steps back.

A smile played on his lips as he reached out to shake her hand with the perfect amount of squeeze. He gave off a pleasant scent. His whole appearance – his suit, white shirt and tie – radiated wealth. But there was nothing superior or threatening in his behaviour. Instead he examined her with curiosity and let go of her hand when he sensed her hesitation.

'I'm sorry, the last thing I want to do is frighten you. I saw you in the audience and wanted to say hello.'

In that instant, Julia realized that this was a magical evening. An evening in which all her wishes would come true. She had wanted to meet him, and here he was! All she could do was cut right to the chase.

'My mother warned me about you,' she said. 'What you did to her and my dad was awful.'

'I know,' he sighed. 'But I've changed. I'm truly a new man. You'd better believe I've tried to make things right with her, but she can be so stubborn, your mother. Anyway, I'd rather talk about you, before your… bodyguard comes to get you.'

'Who do you mean?'

'The guy who was stuck to you like a leech all night. Tell me a little about yourself. What do you like to do, besides sing?'

Julia shot him a suspicious glance but couldn't stop herself from answering his question.

'Anything that gets my heart beating in that boring shithole of a town we live in. When I turn sixteen, I'm going to get a motorcycle. But I don't think Mom would like you interrogating me like this. I did want to meet you, though. Find out if you're as evil as she says.'

'She still thinks so poorly of me? Poor Sofia. What do *you* think, then?'

'I don't think you're evil, but I'm sure you're dangerous.'

'I think your mother has demons she needs to work through. I'm not dangerous in the least, as I'm sure you can see?' He threw out his hands in a disarming gesture.

'But I have to admit I can't take my eyes off of you, Julia,' he went on. 'Why do you suppose I feel so drawn to you? Is it the bittersweet memories of your mother, or is there something special between you and me?'

'I don't feel anything special,' she lied. 'I don't think we're at all alike.'

'But that's where you're wrong. You and I, we have no restraint. It's the only way to live. There's so much life in you, Julia.'

Her cheeks went hot. He took a step closer. Before she could even think, he had run a finger across her cheek. She was about to point out that he was old enough to be her father, rebuff him a little. And then she thought there was no way he could be very smart if he thought she was such an easy mark, but it was fun to play along. Plus, it was hot when he looked at her so intently.

Just then, someone coughed behind them.

The magic spell was broken.

Matt was standing just a few metres away. It looked like he was absolutely dripping with guilt.

'Julia, you promised to wait for me,' he said loudly.

'It's okay,' Franz said. 'We were only saying hello. After all, we know people in common. Now I have to go and entertain those avid souls inside. But it won't be as fun as talking to you, Julia. I really hope we'll meet again soon.'

Then he vanished into the cafeteria. She stayed put until Matt came over to her, took her arm, and hauled her along. He was about to give her a stern talking-to, but she put her hand over his mouth.

'Nothing happened. He was only saying hello. He knows my parents, that's all. But I don't think it would be a good idea for you to mention this to them. Can't we just talk about all the fun stuff that's going on here instead?'

Matt didn't say a word, but she could see in his eyes that they had made a pact.

There were some advantages to the fact that Earth's Children was isolated from the world outside. We never came into contact with drugs or alcohol and we didn't get addicted to video games. There was no desire for nice clothes or expensive things, and somehow this made us humble. You have to try to find the silver lining in everything.

And then there was the bullying. There wasn't any one victim in our school – anyone would be an outcast subjected to scorn as soon as you were out of the good graces of Karsten and Ali-Khan, and especially Father. If the boss was angry with you, life became hell in a split second. So I didn't have it any worse than the other children.

When Vic and I were eleven and the older children were thirteen, Father realized we needed to learn about sex and ordered a compulsory lesson on sex ed. He thought it would be best if we were ahead of the curve. The leaders of the new world must not be late bloomers when it came to something as important as sex.

SEX ED

Ali-Khan blushes, as she has done a number of times in the last ten minutes. She stumbles over her words when she speaks. This is a totally new side of Ali-Khan, and we're endlessly delighted – for once we have the upper hand.

She draws a penis on the whiteboard. A shaft hanging over a large scrotum. It looks like a fat worm. Everyone giggles and Didrik whoops, which makes Ali-Khan even more embarrassed. She shushes. Now she has to draw a vulva.

Just as she's completed the first two lines, Father and Karsten enter the classroom. Now Ali-Khan is even more anxious and she starts to stammer. I squirm. The mood is unbearably awkward. Father bursts out laughing, which makes Ali-Khan go purple in the face. But then he looks mildly annoyed.

'Is this what you call sex ed?' he asks, pointing at the penis and the two lines that are meant to become a vulva. 'This is totally nuts. You are not qualified to instruct them in this topic.' Then he turns to Karsten but shakes his head.

'And neither are you. It would be best if I instructed them myself, now that *would be a quality education, but my schedule is packed,' he sighs.*

He paces back and forth, deep in thought. We dart anxious looks at one another and at the whiteboard, where the slouchy penis reminds us that most of what we do turns out to be silly and clumsy in Father's eyes. He starts to nod, which means he's about to have a brainwave, and he speaks to Karsten.

'Put a computer in the little office next to the classroom. Do you know how to put a filter on a computer so that certain sites are blocked?'

Karsten shakes his head.

'Then you'll have to ask for help. Get rid of all the crap they write about me. But they're welcome to visit our webpage. And then you can see to it that they can access some mild, softcore pornography. Boobs and butts, and missionary position, to start with. They'll learn on their own how it works. We don't need someone like her to do this,' he says, glaring at Ali-Khan.

'The only purpose is informational, got it?' he continues. 'They need to know how it works, and that's all. And you must have a confession time with them one-on-one, once a week. So they don't get it into their heads to do anything dirty.'

We don't understand what he's talking about, but we will soon enough.

A few days later, we crowd around the computer. Just this – getting to use a computer – is astounding. Colourful still images, videos – we only have to click the mouse. A new world opens to us. And then there are these naked bodies doing weird things: squeezing each other, panting and moaning. It's both titillating and kind of scary. A good feeling tightens in my groin when I watch them.

Molly, who's usually so tough, is embarrassed. Sara, who's pretty shy, is overexcited and doesn't want to stop watching. Vic and Didrik repeat over and over that it's so cool. Just a few days later, I come across them in the dorm with Sara. She's on a bottom bunk, naked from the waist down, and Vic and Didrik are touching her down there.

They make me promise not to tell anyone.

There's a lot being confessed during confession time. The naked bodies on the computer screen spark a whole lot of forbidden thoughts and new feelings in our bodies.

It's so much that Ali-Khan decides we have to confess in front of the whole class each Friday. That way we'll think twice before doing something dirty. I start to dread those Friday moments. The mood is always tense and awkward.

Most of the time, Ali-Khan has to draw the confessions out of us. Things like:

'I tried to suck my penis under the covers.'

'I touched myself a couple times.' (After this you had to report exactly what you did, and how many times.)

'I squeezed Sara's breasts. But she said I could.'

Everyone has to stand up.

Everyone has to confess something.

Everyone is embarrassed, except for Ali-Khan, who has stopped blushing when she's discussing sex. I almost think she looks a little exhilarated. One day, she realizes that the pornography we watch doesn't explain how babies are made. Then she scares us with a story about a boy who got a girl pregnant and went to jail. She also holds up a box of condoms, but says they're for older boys. Here in Earth's Children, absolutely no dirty actions are allowed.

Sara confesses that Vic and Didrik touched her down there. Vic even stuck a finger inside her. Ali-Khan makes them run around the school ten times and scrub all the toilets with a toothbrush. Even so, no one seems all that angry with them.

It's a different story when Hugo confesses something one-on-one to Ali-Khan, something I hear about later on. Suddenly Hugo disappears from school. When he comes back, a few weeks later, he is forced to tell the whole class that he had terrible, impure fantasies, which he has stopped having now, but they are so disgusting that he's not even allowed to tell us what they were.

'But I'm not a fag,' he concludes, and he dashes to his seat and sinks into his chair with a sigh of relief.

That night Vic tells me, once I've promised a hundred times I won't tell anyone else, that Hugo had fantasized about Father sucking on his penis.

My skin crawls with discomfort.

This sex-ed episode has unleashed a monster in our little school.

16

Sofia and Benjamin were getting dressed for a Christmas party when Anna called.

The last time Sofia had spoken with Anna was the night they found the flash drives. Since the shelter had been razed to the ground, there didn't seem to be any reason for Anna to return to Orust. For the time being she was staying with her parents in Stockholm. But when Sofia told her about the pictures, Anna said she felt like she was letting Sofia down. Sofia assured her that everything was fine, even though it wasn't fine at all. She missed Anna. They had bonded the way people do when they have a traumatic past in common. It was a different sort of closeness than she had with Benjamin, not quite as laid-back, but sometimes stronger. Sofia's years with the shelter were gilded by lovely memories made with Anna.

Just as Benjamin was zipping her up, Anna's name popped up on Sofia's phone.

'I'm here!' Anna exclaimed cheerfully.

'Where?'

'On Orust! I have a job interview tomorrow.'

'Really? Are you kidding?'

'No, I'm not. I'm staying at the pension. When can we meet up?'

Sofia told her about the Christmas party and Anna promised to stop by. She knew the family giving the party.

'I'm a little tired from my trip,' she said. 'But tomorrow we have to get together and talk about the future.'

'Who was it?' Benjamin asked once Sofia had hung up.

'Anna. She's back!'

Benjamin looked a bit surprised.

'What? I thought she was staying in Stockholm. You don't need her here, do you?'

'No, she's applying for a job at the pension. Great news, right?'

Sofia went upstairs to get Julia, who was also coming to the party. Mostly because Matt would be there. Julia was sitting on her bed, the floor covered in dresses, skirts and shoes.

'Who am I even getting dressed up for?' she complained. 'This town sucks.'

'Yeah, so you've said. Many times. In the fall you get to go to the high school in Uddevalla.'

'Another sucky shithole town.'

Sofia sighed.

'Honey. Why does everything have to happen at once? Can't you just have your fantasies without acting them out? You have to live in the real world. Going to school is part of that.'

'Look, I do fine at school, but that doesn't mean I have to like this shit.'

'That's enough. Put on your black dress. At least that one covers your butt.'

Julia made a face and pulled on her dress.

'Don't give me that sass, Julia! You look amazing. Come on, let's go.'

It was just a few days before Christmas Eve. Mild, humid air had settled over Orust, putting a stop to the clear winter days. At least the rain had finally let up. As they walked to the car, there were only a few stubborn drops falling from heavy clouds.

When they got to the house where the party was under way, Anna was waiting for them. Her eyes were lined in black and she was wearing bright red lipstick. Her brown hair was held up by a clip, but a few locks had slipped out to land gently around her face. She was wearing a tight, navy sheath dress and tall boots. Anna seemed to have infinite resources to spend on clothes.

They hugged for a long time.

'And here I thought you'd forgotten we existed,' said Sofia.

'No way. I've missed you so much. But listen, I'm so tired. I've said hello to everyone I know. If it's okay with you, I'm going back to the pension and falling into bed.'

'You don't want to stay with us?'

'It's fine, I'm staying there for free. Tomorrow you have to tell me about everything that's happened.'

'My whole life is a mess, you can't imagine.'

'Yeah, I can, but I still want to hear every detail.'

'What's the job you're interviewing for?'

'They need someone at the pension. A jack-of-all-trades, kind of. The same sort of stuff I took care of at the shelter. Someone there is going on parental leave. I'm supposed to help with the Christmas banquets. Then they'll stay open throughout the off season, for conferences and so on.'

'That sounds perfect. You'll definitely get the job.'

Anna embraced Sofia again.

'I'll come over tomorrow after the interview. Is that okay?'

'Of course. We can go and look at the ruins of the shelter. Then I want to talk about our options for rebuilding.'

'And you have to tell me about your meeting with Franz. I'm super curious.'

'There's not much to tell. He's his same old self, fake and manipulative. I won't be taking any money from him.'

'We can at least talk about it,' Anna said hopefully.

Sofia was touched to have another person on her side in the desperate hunt for financing.

By the time Anna took off, Benjamin had already joined the guests in the living room with a drink in his hand and his most charming smile on his face. Julia and Laura were sitting on the sofa, looking at something on their phones.

Sofia decided to let herself be swept up in the festive atmosphere, but it seemed impossible. Her head was filled with the blaring noise of Christmas carols. The pictures taken by the stalker appeared in her mind unbidden. She wished she had looked at everything on those flash drives before handing them over to the police. At the time she had merely been disgusted, but now she wondered if there might have been some clues among the photos. Something the police would miss. Her gaze was drawn again and again to the windows in the room, and she imagined Peder Santos standing there staring in. She was anxious, restless, and totally incapable of relaxing and having fun at the party.

After a glorious Christmas smörgåsbord she was too full to move and curled up in an easy chair to watch everyone else. Benjamin was chatting with the headmaster and his wife. He was cracking jokes, making them laugh out loud. How did he have the energy? Julia was clinging to Matt in a corner.

A guy came by to serve wine. She didn't want to drink, but he had a non-alcoholic option. She let him hand her a glass. A sudden wave of nausea washed over her and all at once she had a headache. She pressed her palms to her temples, but it was no help. She wondered if she was coming down with something and decided to go home and sleep off the headache, enjoy a quiet house while Benjamin and Julia were at the party.

Benjamin had no objections. He said that he and Julia could take a cab home and handed her the car keys.

When she got home and climbed out of the car, something felt off. Everything looked the same, yet something didn't match up. The rain had stopped. The house was shrouded in eerie shadows. A raw, cold gust of wind swept past her head. There was something unpleasant and strange about the yard, as though the darkness under the trees and around the hedges was whispering warnings. The air was heavy with a presence. She was sure she had left a few lights on, but now it was pitch black inside the house.

She couldn't find the key in her purse. Her fingers trembled almost spasmodically and her stomach was in an uproar. She put her hand on the door handle and the door swung open. Chilly air rushed to meet her. She took a tentative step across the threshold. Her foot landed on something hard that was crushed beneath her shoe.

'Hello!' she called into the darkness, feeling instantly foolish. She turned on a light in the front hall. The pane of the bay window was broken, and the floor of the entryway was strewn with glass shards. A chilly draught came from an open window somewhere.

When her eyes adjusted, as the details of the living room took shape, she gasped.

It was one big mess. Not like after the storm, with overturned furniture, but a systematic sort of mess left by someone searching frantically for something. The doors of the display cabinet were wide open; the drawers at the bottom had been pulled out and their contents emptied onto the floor.

She really didn't want to go in, but her legs stumbled automatically across the floor. The kitchen cupboards were open and the contents of the drawers had been dumped: whisks, silverware, knives and ladles in one big jumble. She slowly dragged herself through the room. Every part of the house was the same, as though some senseless lunatic had gone through like a tornado, searching the whole house.

What the hell were they looking for?

She sank to a crouch in the guest room on the first floor. The bedsheets had been torn off and the mattresses were crooked. They had searched everywhere – under the sheets, mattresses, and pillows. The drawers with spare sheets and pillowcases were pulled out.

She frantically searched her purse for her phone. Sobbing hysterically, she took a deep breath and let it out through her mouth.

There was a creak from another part of the house. Then came the sound of running feet, glass being crushed under heavy footsteps, and the front door thrown open so violently that it crashed against the exterior wall. All while she sat frozen on the floor. It was impossible to move. Her fingernails dug into her palms; she pressed them harder to calm her panic.

From somewhere far away came the sound of a car starting. She was paralysed. Her heart pounded frantically. She managed to get her hands working and searched her purse for her phone. She found it at the very bottom and dialled 112. Tears fell onto her dress.

'There's been a break-in,' she said when the dispatcher picked up. But she accidentally gave the wrong address. She couldn't concentrate.

'Are you going to help us this time?' she shrieked. 'Or are you going to keep not doing a damn thing while this bastard harasses us?'

She really didn't want to be shrill, but her voice was stuck in falsetto. The dispatcher said something about sending a car.

Now the room was spinning fast, like a dryer, and the woman's voice faded away as she asked questions Sofia couldn't answer.

'He was still in the house when I came home,' was the last thing she managed to say before the phone fell from her hand.

I know all about shame.

About being ashamed of my shortcomings, lack of devotion, and keeping of secrets.

Each time I saw Grandma, I was ashamed because I lied about what went on in Earth's Children. And I could sense that she felt guilty for never asking for more details. Being allowed to see us meant so much to her. She didn't dare risk Father sending her away. As long as she pretended not to notice our weary eyes, the callouses on our hands, and the bits of straw under our shirts after a night in the pigsty, she didn't have to ask any questions.

Even so, it hung in the air between us. Shame.

I have been ashamed of so much, for all my life.

But never of Father. Not until the night he came to fetch Mama.

MAMA IN THE ATTIC

It's Friday evening. We're standing on the rocks with Mama, looking out at the sea. Darkness falls over the bay. The moon is bright and casts shadows so long that mine looks like it belongs to a giant. The lapping of the waves below feels reassuring. The taste of salt on my lips is freeing.

Suddenly I'm filled with an intense longing to be somewhere else. The lights of the city sparkle on the other side of the sound. I can almost feel the warmth of the people who live there.

Vic and I start to chase each other around the slope. The wind whips at my face. Vic picks up a piece of driftwood and uses it as a sword. He chases me up the rocks until my lungs are on fire and my ears buzz. We come close to the cliff's edge, but I control my fear by purposely turning my back to the sea. My heart is pounding. I'm alive. For a brief moment, I feel perfectly free.

'Come on, time to go home,' Mama calls.

She has changed. Grandma is allowed to take her to the mainland once a week. They buy clothes and makeup and Mama has made herself look beautiful. Her hair has grown out and hangs like a golden wave down her back. Sometimes we hear her wonderful laugh. She isn't allowed to have a phone or a TV, but Father gave her a PlayStation so she can watch movies. He's spent a lot of time in our cottage recently, and he has been kind to her.

This evening, she is radiant. The moonlight gleams in her eyes.

The whole way home, my feet feel lighter. I'm bursting with energy.

When we get home, Father is waiting outside. He looks annoyed. All of a sudden, my mood takes a nosedive.

'I need to talk to your mother, boys. You have no objections, do you?' He's talking to us, but his eyes are on Mama. They sweep over her face, breasts and legs. For the first time I can imagine how a person who isn't her son might see her. She's at least as beautiful as the actresses in movies. And her long red hair makes her special. So even if she is a mother, my mother, I can understand why Father thinks she's attractive.

Father smiles at us, but his gaze is so cold that I don't dare smile back.

He takes hold of Mama's arm and pulls her into the bedroom. More than once, in the past, he has come to Mama's bedroom at night. I've heard voices and mumbling from the other side of the wall. And then other sounds – heavy breathing, moans, bodies moving, the sound of the headboard thumping against the wall. A hoarse scream now and then. But it never seemed dangerous. It almost felt nice. As if they liked each other.

Today, everything feels different.

Maybe he thinks we can't hear him now, but each word reaches us through the half-open door.

'I don't have time for a relationship, and the girls on staff are worthless, so you'll have to do. After all, you've prettied yourself up. A couple times a week, up in the attic.'

The word attic *makes me shudder. I've heard rumours, things I refused to believe. They say Father kept Mama prisoner there.*

Mama's great despair streams from the bedroom. I don't know much about the attic. All I know is that Mama is now speechless and scared. I can feel her panic in every cell in my body. The jovial atmosphere from earlier this evening ebbs out of the house and is replaced by terror.

Vic is watching Mama's PlayStation and isn't listening, but my ears are on high alert.

'I don't want to go there. Can't you leave me alone?' I hear Mama say, faint and reedy.

I take a nervous breath. She has defied him, broken the rules, and now she must be punished. I know what Father is going to do long before I hear the smack of Father's palm against her cheek.

'Quit your whining. That wheedling tone is so *unattractive. Twice a week. We start tonight. Come on! Put on something short and tight.'*

Father walks out without deigning to look at us. I hear Mama's muffled sobs as she changes clothes in the bedroom.

She leaves us alone with a movie and some candy, which is strictly forbidden. Somehow this makes me even sadder. I don't dare to ask when she'll be back. Once she's out the door, I ask Vic instead.

'No idea,' he says. 'They're probably gonna fuck.'

I can't fall asleep; I toss and turn in bed until I drift into a light, dream-filled slumber. I wake to the rumble of a passing thunderstorm. It seems to come and go in just minutes. Through the window I can see the pale light of dawn. I get up and check Mama's room, but her bed is empty. Where is she now? I go to the living room and am dazzled by the sky outside. Beautiful colours shimmer beneath the black thunderclouds. Then the front door opens. A gust of cool air comes in and the light turns on.

Mama stands before me in her fancy dress. Her eyes are red from crying and her lower lip is trembling. She recoils when she sees me. There are red marks on her neck and a purple bruise blooming on her thigh.

I want to comfort her but can't bring myself to move. I lick my lips, which have gone dry.

'Does it hurt, Mama?' I ask gingerly.

'It's not these,' she says, pointing at the marks on her throat. 'I am less important to him than his motorcycles, cars and fucking suits. I'm an object to him, that's what hurts so much.'

Mama has never talked to me like this. I want to wipe away her tears, but I feel so useless and awkward. I quickly glance down at the floor, unable to meet her gaze. All at once I wish Mama could leave here, but then I realize I would miss her, and I wish she could take me with her.

She always goes to the attic on weekday nights, when we're not home. On weekends, she pretends like everything is fine. She spends time with us. Cooking. Making jokes. Wearing long pants and turtlenecks so we won't see anything. But her carefree smile is gone, and deep down in her eyes I see desperation.

Even so, none of this is as terrible as when I run into Father. He comes more and more often to the classroom, or out to the grounds when we're working there.

I do my utmost to avoid his gaze.

At night he hurts Mama; during the day he's the same as usual.

As though nothing has happened.

For the first time, I'm ashamed of him.

17

Sofia sat on the rocks, gazing out at the sea. She had no idea how long she'd been sitting there. For once, time stood still. The air felt frosty as it filled her lungs. The sea was as still as a millpond, aside from a gentle ripple here or there. The clouds had dissipated, the sun was peeking out, and the water slowly shifted from grey to a cool shade of blue. Her attention was caught by a spot way out at sea. Swans or geese bobbing on the surface. The rocks were cold, but she was sitting on her mittens.

It was the day before Christmas Eve. The thought of organizing any sort of Christmas celebration was overwhelming. They had a Christmas tree, of course – the only thing in the house the burglar had spared – but no presents and no holiday food. She should really go shopping, but she didn't have it in her. Secretly she was hoping that Benjamin or Julia would suggest they go to the Christmas banquet at the pension. Their plan was to give Julia money for her present, so she could do something fun with her friends between Christmas and New Year.

Sofia had told Benjamin she was going out to fill up the car. She didn't want to admit she couldn't stand to be in the house anymore and was constantly looking for excuses to get away.

When she searched online that morning, the news of the break-in had popped up everywhere. Lurid headlines about the family in Assmunderöd whose life had been smashed to pieces.

The police didn't have a single lead. What a surprise. To be sure, they had contacted Sofia, because now they wanted her help finding a picture of Santos for the media to publish. At last he was a person of interest. But Sofia had asked Anna to take care of it, and she had agreed immediately.

Benjamin and Sofia had talked themselves hoarse in an attempt to understand what was going on.

'Why would Santos break into our house? What was he after?' Sofia wondered, rubbing her temples. She had a constant, roiling tension headache these days.

'I think he must have been obsessed with you and Julia,' Benjamin said. 'But then the shelter was destroyed by the storm, and you disappeared. He no longer had an outlet for his fixation, so he attacked Julia to take more pictures.'

'Maybe, but what the heck was he looking for in here?'

Benjamin's gaze turned inward, but then he lit up.

'The pictures in the lockbox, of course! He must have been shocked when it went missing. Then he went berserk in our house, trying to find it.'

'That is actually a possibility,' she said.

She had been stalked and harassed before. For years, by Franz. It had certainly made her tougher, but also more fragile. She knew from experience that psychopaths had no limits. That what seemed intolerable now might merely be the start of something even worse.

Their conversation was interrupted by a security company coming by to install alarms and surveillance cameras. Benjamin had worked enthusiastically with them all morning, but Sofia was sceptical. Santos was still lurking out there somewhere, planning his next move. One of the most polite, mildest people she'd ever met had turned into a crazy madman.

After skimming through the articles online, she decided to

go out and sit on the rocks for a while. Anna had gone to the police station. They had postponed their meeting until later that evening on account of the break-in.

Her phone rang, and the screen lit up with an unknown number. She knew who it was right away and cursed herself inwardly for not changing her number.

'Sofia, don't hang up. Just, please, listen to me for a minute.'

She didn't respond. All she could hear was her own breathing, buzzing through the speaker on the phone.

'Are you there?'

'I told you not to contact me.'

'I'm worried about you all, especially Julia. I demand that you allow me to pay for a security company to keep a twenty-four-hour watch over your house. And I intend to hire someone to snoop under the radar and try to trace Santos, with or without your permission.'

'How do you know anything about Santos?'

'I have my sources.'

The last time he'd called her, there had been a flicker of worry in his voice, but nothing he couldn't have faked. This time, he sounded genuinely concerned.

'I won't accept any help from you,' she said.

'Why not?'

'I don't ever want to owe you anything.'

'You won't. I want to protect Julia, you understand that, right? Don't I have any rights at all?'

'No, not a one.'

He transformed his voice, making it soft and ingratiating.

'I feel so disappointed when you act so chilly and standoffish. Once upon a time we worked so well together, you and me. It's important to learn to love the world you live in, and the people in it too. Can't you try to see beyond your own anger and think of what's best for Julia? Don't you think it would do you good to forgive me?'

She couldn't help but smile to herself at his self-satisfied tone; he probably thought he was saying something terribly deep.

'I don't need to forgive you to feel good. I can hate you for the rest of my life and feel perfectly fine, as long as you leave my family alone.'

'Sweetie, you know I can't promise you that. It depends on the test.'

'I'll deal with the test in the new year,' she said. 'Do not contact me before then. And if you call me "sweetie" one more time, you will never hear from me again.'

She hung up without waiting for a response.

The cold had begun to seep through her mittens and jeans. She stood up, nearly slipping on the rock but regaining her balance. Her phone rang again. It was Benjamin.

'We're all set! Now that bastard can forget ever getting in here again.'

'Then I'll head home.'

'Do you want to go shopping?' he asked. 'Look, let's forget about Christmas dinner tomorrow. We'll make one of Julia's favourites instead. And we can Skype your parents with the Christmas tree in the background and pretend we're celebrating a traditional Christmas. Then we'll do nothing all day and watch all the new movies that have come out. On streaming.'

Easy-going, uncomplicated Benjamin.

Sofia started laughing. She felt the knot in her chest loosen a bit.

'That sounds amazing, just what I need. What would I do without you?'

'It's a good question.'

When she arrived home, she immediately noticed the security

company's logo on the gate and the camera on the front of the house. It felt like a big relief.

'Where's Julia?' she asked Benjamin.

'I gave her some cash so she could go Christmas shopping in Stenungsund with her friends. She was overjoyed. The only thing I didn't take care of while you were gone was getting a shotgun.'

He had lit tealights in little lanterns all over and decorated the tree. There was a wonderful aroma of mulled wine wafting from the stove. She had the sudden thought that Benjamin had been almost exaggeratedly kind in recent days, but this was followed by an immediate wave of shame at her inability to accept his love.

Just as she sat down in the living room, she heard a delighted cry from Benjamin.

'Why – what the—'

'What is it?' she called.

'We've got a visitor, look!'

She hurried out of the living room. Through the window she could see a red car parked at the side of the road, and a figure opening the gate. She squinted and recognized him immediately, even though he looked so big in his bulky winter coat.

Simon had returned.

It wasn't until the night Father came and fetched Mama that I realized how simple life had been before that. All the bad things that happened could be traced back to my own shortcomings. If I made a mistake, all I could do was shut my mouth and accept my punishment. I didn't doubt for a second that Father's word was the one and only truth. Life was a constant battle for survival, but it was a battle free of mistrust.

But as soon as I saw the marks on Mama's neck, I began to doubt.

And sometimes, doubt can hurt worse than physical punishment. It wears you down.

Things went so far that I felt ashamed of being ashamed of Father.

I was in a constant state of inner turmoil. Things that had once been invisible to me were suddenly eerily sharp: the barbed wire atop the wall, the faint contours of the city on the other side of the sound. And the light in the guards' booth where eyes constantly watched over us.

I was standing at a crossroads. It was like balancing on a tightrope.

So in some ways, it felt good to simply fall into the abyss when everything came to a head.

ACTIONS AND CONSEQUENCES

It's Saturday. Vic and I have been allowed to come with Mama to shop in the village. The strong scents of early summer fill the air: lilacs, freshly mowed grass, and the sweet smell of soft-serve from the kiosk. Mama woke up with red eyes again. I know she cries herself to sleep at night. The days of carefree laughter are long gone. She's wearing a turtleneck even though it's so warm out.

Neither Vic nor I want to come into the store. The square is crawling with people and lots of boats are moored in the harbour. Mama lets us stay on the square but makes us promise not to move an inch. Vic catches sight of a cute girl sitting on the pier and eating ice cream, so despite our promise he runs over to talk to her. She laughs at something he says. I stay behind, looking at the people and making believe I'm one of them. On school vacation with friends, totally free. No marching or victory songs, no talk of 'consequences'. A long, awesome summer ahead of me, with normal parents who go sailing and grill supper on the rocky shore.

When I turn around, I see Mama standing outside the store and talking to a man. His back is to me; he's wearing jeans and a button-up shirt. Mama is gesticulating wildly. She looks upset. The sea breeze carries a random phrase my way, and I happen to hear it. Can't stand it. *The man takes her wrists as if to calm her down. They walk into the store together. It's some time before Mama comes back. Vic doesn't care. He's sitting close to the girl now, and she's letting him lick her ice cream.*

No one in the whole world can resist Vic.

When Mama comes out of the store with her bags of groceries, something isn't right. She looks nervous but also exhilarated. When we get home to the cottage, she goes to her room and stays there for a while. After that, she's perfectly cheerful. She makes food for us, tells jokes, hugs and kisses us until we're embarrassed.

Later that night, she says she's going to take a walk while we watch a movie. She never does that, but now there's something restless about her, something I don't understand.

Vic likes the movie, but I think too many people die in it. I get up to look for a book, but something in Mama's room catches my attention. I sneak in without Vic noticing. The blinds are down, but the white summer-evening light filters in through the cracks and illuminates parts of the room. I approach Mama's unmade bed, which smells like flowers from her perfume; I run my hand over the duvet cover. Everything is the same as usual in there. Hairbrushes and makeup everywhere.

Then I spot something on the nightstand. A small grey thingamajig, shoved in among books, moisturizer and tissues.

Mama has a phone.

I quickly leave the room. Somewhere deep inside, I know something is about to change. Something I don't really want to know about, even though it has to happen.

That weekend, things are suddenly strange. Mama is on high alert, her voice unusually shrill, her movements jerky; it's clear that she's nervous. It's the next Friday evening. She lets us do whatever we want. When Vic says he wants to go out to the rocks by himself to go crabbing, she says, 'Sure thing!' even though we all know that's strictly forbidden. It's as though she's let go of all boundaries and is living on some completely different plane of existence.

It's late by the time we go to bed. In the middle of the night, I wake to a scraping sound in the living room. Vic is dead asleep and snoring softly under his blankets. I get up and pad into the living room. Mama is standing in the middle of the room. She gasps when she sees me, her eyes wide. She is fully dressed and has a large duffel bag in one hand.

We regard one another breathlessly. The moon is shining on one side of her face. She looks like a marble statue. Slowly she raises her hand and brings a finger to her lips. There's something melancholy in her gaze. In just a few short steps, she has reached the front door. She opens it, turns around, and blows me a kiss.

The door closes silently.

Mama is gone, and I know she's not coming back.

The next day I wake up with an unpleasant feeling in my belly, but I don't say anything to Vic. The sensation fades as I shower, and hope rises in its place. Suddenly I wish so fervently that Mama's escape has succeeded. No more bruises. No sobs from her room.

At last Vic starts whining about breakfast and goes to Mama's room to get her.

'She's gone!' he shrieks.

'Maybe she's taking a walk,' I say.

A believable lie, because she's been doing that a lot recently.

We wait for a few hours, until Vic says something must be wrong and leaves the house. I know where he's going. By the time he returns with Father, I've transformed into a lifeless lump on the sofa. I'm dripping with guilt.

A single glance, and Father has seen right through me. No wheedling, no threats needed. The confession flows out of me between great gasps. Tears sting my eyes, but I force them back. The fury in Father's eyes grows, erasing the border between his irises and pupils and turning his eyes into a seething ocean of rage.

He asks me about the man, but I can't describe him. He was only a man with long legs, a button-down, and a cap. I wait for the slap to come. But it doesn't, and that's almost worse.

Father vanishes out the door.

Soon I hear the sounds of the hunt for Mama. Motorcycles driving back and forth, people shouting, dogs barking.

But inside the cottage, it's quiet. I know Vic wants to kill me. But he doesn't touch me.

The punishment is in Father's hands, and punished I shall be.

Vic cries that he's going to help look for Mama and disappears too. In my loneliness I feel no shame. They haven't found Mama. She's going to make it. I curl up on the sofa. Waiting. Listening. Hoping.

When darkness falls, Father and Vic come for me.

'Get up!' Father barks, his voice so loud I fly from the sofa.

The scent of pine from his clothes hits me and I know that he too has been out on the island, looking for Mama. He doesn't even bother to hide his scorn for me, what he's felt for me since the day I was born. He takes a firm grasp on my upper arm and hauls me along. He's walking so fast that at times I dangle from his grip. Behind us I hear Vic's quick footsteps.

I know where we're going.

A fresh breeze hits us on the heath. Father hasn't said a word. He drags me down the rocks, letting me stumble many times but tugging me up by the arm.

Not until we're standing at the tip of Devil's Rock does he open his mouth. A single word hisses past his pursed lips.

'Freak.'

Then he pushes me.

For one endless, dizzying instant I fall, caught up by a cascade of icy water. I'm pulled down into the greedy depths, sinking, passive and slack.

It strikes me that Father must know we haven't been taught to swim. And if he knows that, does this mean he wants me to die?

I kick at the water and rise to the light above. The panic hits me before I break the surface. I gasp for air too early, and the water rushes into my mouth and nose. The gulp of cold seawater is so huge that my vision goes black. When I break through the surface, I find myself in a confusion of white foam.

I cough, spitting and sputtering out water, catching my breath between coughing attacks and swells washing over me. I can't see the rocks. I wave my arms in senseless fear. My wet clothes are weighing me down. I kick frantically, but all that's beneath me is more water. I'm afraid to kick off my shoes. I take some strokes between waves but see only the endless sea before me. But then I manage to swing around and catch sight of the rocks, just ten metres ahead but so far away. I try to paddle towards them, and a wave comes to my aid. One foot strikes something hard. A couple more strokes and my feet can touch the bottom. I crawl onto a boulder, where I collapse and vomit through my mouth and nose simultaneously.

I lie like that for a long time, the waves licking at my feet. When I look up at Devil's Rock, I see Father's silhouette against the pale sky.

This is the moment I am expected to break down. Crawl up the rocks, fall to my knees before Father, beg and plead for hundreds of hours of penance work, say I will iron his shirts, polish his shoes, kiss his feet – if only he'll forgive me.

But instead I am flooded with an intense wish that Mama has made it out.

18

As Julia got on her moped to head home it began to rain. At first there were only modest little drops, but the clouds above promised a downpour. The damp air found its way under her clothes. It was cold as hell, and she longed for the warmth of home. She found herself yawning hugely, filling her mouth with cold, humid air. Her nights had been restless in recent days. When she tried to sleep, images from the attack played in her mind. She couldn't help it. It always started with the sensation of the man's hands grabbing her, the shock, and then the fear as she felt the knife against her throat. But if she simply remained calm and let the horrible memories pass, they would eventually go away. She knew she was processing a trauma that she had to get out of her system. Every day she searched for the pictures he'd taken of her online, but nothing showed up.

Just as she reached home, the sky opened and a cascade of water drenched her in a matter of seconds. The sight of a red car parked on the edge of the road prompted her to hurry inside, because a faint hope had been sparked inside her. It looked like Simon's car. Of all of Mom and Dad's friends, he was the one she liked best. He had taught her everything from how to dive off the rocks to how to plant her own garden. One time he had helped her save a wounded baby gull. When it was healed, and could fly again, they had released it by the sea and watched it soar off over the bay. Simon lent a bit of magic to everything he touched. She had been awfully sad when he vanished from their lives.

The raindrops ran from her hair into her eyes and mouth as she parked her moped. Little candles flickered in the windows, and she could see the Christmas tree inside. She dashed into the entryway, hung up her sodden jacket, and wrung out her mittens, placing them on the radiator to dry. Her jeans were soaked through too, but she didn't bother to change, just wanted to see everyone.

And there was Simon, sitting on the sofa and looking like his usual self, with that messy blond mop of hair. He smiled with his whole face as he caught sight of her; his kind eyes turned into narrow creases and his crooked front tooth showed. She threw herself at him, burying her face in his sweater and clinging to him for a long time. He even smelled like his usual self, of soil and plants.

'Now the time has come for me to make a confession,' he said once Julia had loosened her grip. 'When I left Sweden, I couldn't stand the thought of not being in touch with you all. So I created a fake Facebook account under the name Maria Simonsson, and used a picture of my mother.'

He smiled slyly and turned to Julia.

'Your mother rejected my request straight away, but your dad isn't so cautious about who he's friends with on Facebook. So I've been keeping an eye on you over the years. I've seen pictures of you, Julia, so I already knew you'd grown up so tall and beautiful.'

Julia plopped down on the sofa beside Simon. Mom started laughing.

'I still don't get why you had to hide away, but you can tell us about that later,' she said.

'How long are you going to be here?' Julia asked.

'For a few months,' he said. 'I'm going to stay at the pension. But right now I'm so jet-lagged that I just want to sleep. There's something I have to take care of here, but I'll tell you about it later. Maybe tomorrow, on Christmas Eve. That is, if you want me here?'

'Of course! But don't you want to stay with us?' Mom asked.

'No, that's okay,' he said. 'I'm going to help out around the pension.'

'Listen, I've got an idea,' Mom said. 'We can have a little reunion for Christmas Eve. Anna's here, and I'm sure she'll want to come. Maybe Matt would like to come too, Julia? If he's not spending the day with his parents?'

'No, they're going to the mountains and he's not going with. He'll be so happy. Can't we invite Ellis too? Oh, Mom, it would be so fun if he came!'

Ellis was another of her parents' friends Julia liked a lot. She knew he'd been Mom's boyfriend once upon a time and had taken revenge online when they broke up. But later on, they became friends. Ellis, like Simon, had lived in California for a while, where he'd gotten rich, spent all his money, and come back to Sweden. These days he lived in some sort of commune outside Gothenburg. He hung out with people Mom said were leftist radicals who hacked websites they thought were capitalistic. But Julia was strictly forbidden from telling anyone so. Ellis had taught Julia almost everything she knew about computers – like, for instance, how to hack into an email account.

It turned out to be the weirdest but nicest Christmas ever. Matt and Simon arrived in the morning. Ellis came by around lunchtime, wearing a long, lined military coat. He had grown a beard that reached all the way to his chest. Julia had come to realize Ellis's brain worked at least twice as fast as other people's. He spoke at a rapid-fire speed, often in fragmented sentences, because he was always thinking of something even more important to add. But if you could manage to follow his train of thought, he was so much fun. And when it came to computers, he was a genius.

Instead of their usual Christmas fare, Simon and Dad made Julia's favourite dishes and then they lazed around watching movies. Ellis immediately took a shine to Matt and showed him things on his tablet. Matt wasn't like the other guys at school, who stared at their phones all day. It always took him ages to reply to a text. But whatever Ellis was showing him, Matt seemed totally fascinated. Julia looked at Simon's pictures from California, which were mostly of a lot of agricultural fields, but it was still fun. At five o'clock, Mom, Dad and Julia put on dressy outfits and Skyped with Grandma and Grandpa in front of the Christmas tree; when they were done they went right back to their loungewear.

Julia felt safe and relaxed. She was surrounded by everyone she liked and was able to take her mind off the terrible things that had happened recently. Simon told them about his time in California. At first he had worked at various farms, but then he began holding lectures for local farmers. After that, it wasn't long before the rumours of those lectures spread to business giants in Silicon Valley.

'And what's next?' Dad asked.

'We'll see. I'd really like to work on climate and sustainability issues,' Simon said. 'But for now I'm going to take it easy for a while.'

★

Later that evening, as they were chatting on the sofa, the topic of Franz Oswald came up and Mom told everyone about his offer to finance the rebuilding of the shelter. Julia's ears pricked up and she thought of her encounter with him.

'In just a few months he's managed to become a superstar again, it's unbelievable,' Mom said. 'He's hanging out with the *elite* elite, can buy whatever he wants, sleep with whoever he wants, and yet he refuses to let go of us.'

'We can always form our own little fan club here,' Dad said, in an attempt to be funny.

Julia watched as Mom shot an annoyed glare his way.

'I've already told you what I think,' Simon said. 'You shouldn't have anything to do with him.'

'I've already decided not to accept his money,' Mom said.

'But maybe he really does want to make good,' Anna said. 'I think this is the chance of a lifetime, to get redress. Just think of what we could do with that money. First of all, though, I think you should demand a public apology. Maybe you could accept the money without meeting him in person?'

'He used to be a manipulative, bullying shithead,' Ellis said. 'I doubt he's changed. Maybe I can snoop around a little and see if I can find anything shady about his operation. I could start by looking at his accounts and assets.'

'You're welcome to,' Mom said. 'But it's operations, plural – he owns half the west coast. The more you can dig up on him, the better. And there's something else, too...'

Mom cut herself off. Her eyes landed on Julia, but she suddenly broke eye contact and looked down at her hands.

'...something I'll tell you a little later,' she went on.

There it was again, that mysterious look. Julia was dead certain it had to do with her.

'What is it, Mom? What aren't you telling me?' she asked.

'Oh, it's complicated. Nothing important. It just has to do with our finances.'

Mom's voice sounded unsteady, and Julia felt a pang of suspicion. Mom was lying. Everyone in the room must have sensed it, because suddenly you could hear a pin drop.

Julia was just about to attack her with more questions, but Simon got there first.

'I'll pay for the shelter,' he said.

'What? What do you mean?'

'That's the real reason I came here. I can stay for a few months while the house is rebuilt. At the same time, I'll help you start up some gardening plots. Maybe a greenhouse and a couple vegetable beds in the spring. I'm sure I can't offer as much cash as Franz, but it'll be enough to rebuild. And don't you refuse to accept my money. I don't know what else to do with it. It's just numbers in my bank account. I really want to do this.'

No one said anything for a moment, dumbstruck. Julia noticed a blush spreading across Mom's cheeks.

'I've taken the liberty of developing some blueprints for the house,' Simon continued. 'The only problem is we'll have to apply for permits, since the rebuild is so large. And that might take time. But maybe you and I can pester the municipal council and get them to handle the matter quickly. After all, it's an urgent situation, isn't it? There are kids who have escaped cults and need a roof over their heads.'

'This is fantastic, Simon!' Mom exclaimed. 'I know I should say we absolutely cannot accept your money and all that. But I'm not going to. It sounds perfect! Obviously we'll pay it all back when we can.'

In that moment, Julia saw Mom transform. She let out a vast sigh of relief and the lustre returned to her face.

But although she was happy for her mother, Julia felt a streak of disappointment. Because now she wondered if this meant she wouldn't get to see Franz Oswald again. She had been hoping Mom would accept his money and imagined Franz dropping by now and then to oversee the construction. And Julia would be there to run into him, as if by chance. Her casual acquaintance with him was far too exciting to end before it even began. Matt was hot in his own way; Julia worshipped him. But a longing for something more had been awakened inside her. She had begun to wonder how an experienced man like Franz kissed, how his hands would feel on her body, whether he might even be able to fall in love with her. He had looked at her so intensely, and each time she thought of that moment she got butterflies low in her belly. Besides, she was tired of Matt always going on about how they had to wait to have sex. She was almost totally sure that Franz wasn't the type who would want to wait once he had her clothes off.

She had been attracted to older men before – a couple of teachers and one of Dad's friends. But each time, before things heated up, she had asked herself: Do I really want to get it on with someone who will have grey hair and a beer belly if I run into him again ten years from now? When it came to Franz, though, the answer was, for the first time, not so clear. She couldn't even picture him with a beer belly, and she was sure grey hair would only suit him.

The only part she couldn't get past was the thought of what Mom and Dad would say. They would never give their blessing. The idea of it made a lump form in her chest, a feeling she associated with lying.

All at once, Julia felt terribly alone. In fact, she'd been feeling that way for a long time. She didn't understand her friends. They smoked and thought they were cool, but they never had anything interesting to talk about. Mostly she hated the way girls were supposed to tell each other absolutely everything. Julia was so tall that she always had to look down on her friends. Sometimes they looked at her like she was a freak. They stared at her chest – those were the breasts of a woman, not a girl. Once, she had been eavesdropping and heard a teacher describe her as 'precocious and too smart for her own good, but easily manipulated'.

She was tired of being young. Shouting to be heard over the thumping music at parties, fending off guys who stank of beer and had hardly reached puberty. Using silly American words when there were perfectly good ones available in Swedish.

And now she felt a wave of longing to talk about all of this with Mom. Mom would listen. But that was also all she could do. Julia knew she had to live her own life. Which meant taking responsibility for her own decisions.

Everyone slept over that night, except for Matt, who was still hesitant to sleep in her bed while her parents were home. Simon and Ellis took the sofas in the living room, and Anna had the guest room. Julia was the last to go to bed, and the house was already dark, gently rocked by the deep breathing of all those who were already asleep.

She cracked her window to let in the cold night air. Resting her head against the chilly and slightly damp windowpane, she gazed out. The rain had ended during the day and now the sky was dark and clear. The lake glittered between the trees. She loved the view from her room. If she was the least bit anxious, all she had to do was look out the window for a while to calm herself down.

She took off her clothes and inspected her body in the mirror while putting on her nightgown. Her gaze caught on her eyes. She thought she saw something new and exciting there. She lay down in bed to think for a while.

Her phone dinged just as she was drifting off to sleep. She propped herself on one elbow and took the phone from her nightstand. It was a text from an unknown number. *I think about you often.* She thought it seemed shady and was just about to block the number when another text arrived.

Lunch in Stenungsund after New Year's? F

She smiled to herself. And here she'd thought her magical powers might have faded.

The Earth's Children prison camp came about entirely on account of me.

The ViaTerra staff had an equivalent program they called Penance. We often saw them running around the property in their red caps, work boots stomping. They had to live in the barn. My Uncle Anders had to stay there for several years.

The kids' version was simply called the Hole.

There was a small shed in a dip beyond the barn, barely ten metres square, full of junk, spiderwebs and mould. The floor was just large enough to squeeze in two sleeping bags, if you shoved the little table up against the wall. Maybe this place got its name because the shed was lower down than the other buildings on the property. It really was a hole, in all aspects of the word.

That was where I was sent after Mama disappeared.

Luckily it was springtime when I was sent to the Hole; in the winter the shed was frigid and draughty. Here I was expected to confront my wickedness and write down all the ways I had betrayed Father. The point was to cast off my shame and free myself from my guilty conscience.

At the same time, I had to dig out the ditch along the property wall, which had filled in over the years. Father said that hard labour would do me good.

There was just one problem. I couldn't be left alone. With Mama on the lam, there was a chance I would try to escape as well.

So Matteo was sent to the Hole to watch over me and report back to Karsten each day. This report was then sent on to Father.

THE HOLE

I'm sitting on a stool at the rickety wooden table and writing down the terrible things I've done to Father. Thoughts count too, even fleeting ones that never really took hold. It could be something as vague as a feeling of unease when Father is nearby.

The stacks of papers grow taller. Pages full of sorrow, covered in my spidery handwriting. Matteo keeps nagging me. There has to be more. If you deny something enough times, you eventually start to feel guilty of it. That's how it goes for me.

Father comes every day. He always shows up when we least expect it. Each time, he takes a sheet of paper from the pile and reads it. He never says a word to me, but the looks he gives me are so full of scorn and hatred that I want to slink under the table and curl up there.

Today his eyes turn grim as he reads. I know exactly what he's seen: the part where I found Mama's phone. He turns to Matteo, who's standing in a corner, stiff as a rod, always at attention when Father is here.

'Have you read this trash?' he asks.

'Yes, boss, I read everything he writes every day,' Matteo replies.

'All right, so what do you think?'

'That what Thor did is horrible and disgusting.'

Father squints at him in distaste.

'And so are the thoughts he has, of course,' Matteo hurries to add.

But Father shakes his head in irritation.

'Some members of your group would look at this in a much more serious light than you do, Matteo. I hope you aren't showing Thor any kindness. People like him only respond to harsh measures.'

I cast my gaze downward and try to look regretful. Now I'm afraid Matteo will change, start being cold to me, maybe even attack me. He has acted tough and unreasonable ever since he was sent to the Hole to guard me. But in his eyes I could see something else. Empathy.

'No, I'm not kind to him at all,' Matteo says, a little too fast.

But Father doesn't seem convinced. I've looked up from the stack of paper now and he nails me with his gaze.

'It's too bad you survived that fall from the cliff,' he says.

At that moment, while our eyes are still locked, I hate him for the first time.

When he leaves the Hole, the tension between Matteo and me is unbearable. I search his face for a flicker of empathy and feel relieved when I see it.

'Do you want to go out and do some hard labour?' he asks.

I nod. The very thought of picking up my pen again makes me feel ill.

A thick layer of clouds has blown in from the sea and hangs, alarmingly heavy, over the manor. It smells like rain. The air is so humid that it feels like I could drown in it.

I work in silence for a few hours. At last it feels as though Matteo's watchful eyes have moved away from me and it's just me and my harsh thoughts. First there is a desolate loneliness, as though a cold north wind is blowing right through me. Then the feeling transforms into a sort of freeing dizziness. My orderly, disciplined life has been torn up by the roots, and between thrusts of the shovel there is time to think.

I'm astounded by the way the seasons come and go in two different worlds, the ones inside and outside our walls. It's incredible that people out there can see the same sun and moon as I do. And then I wonder who I am, who I will become – and who I will never be allowed to be.

It feels as if I'm shaping a new, secret identity for myself.

The sweat trickles down my forehead, stinging my eyes and wetting my lips until they taste like salt. The ditch grows ever deeper. The shovel hurts my hands, which are covered in blisters. One bursts and my palm gets all sticky and nasty. But I keep digging, filled with a growing realization. I've always believed that Father can read my mind, but he can't. He didn't feel my hatred there in the Hole, even though his eyes were boring into my soul. My thoughts are mine alone. I have something he can't take away from me.

Matteo's voice yanks me back to reality far too quickly, but a vague sense of well-being lingers.

'Time to go home and do some more writing,' he says.

When we get back to the Hole, Vic and Didrik are standing outside the door. The sight of them causes all the air to rush out of my lungs.

'There's the little shit!' Didrik cries.

Vic comes up to me and grabs my jacket in both fists. His face is only a few centimetres from mine. He's breathing hard and his eyes are wild; I know just what to expect when he's like this.

'Were you fucking Mama?' he asks.

'What?' At first I think I must have misheard.

'The boss says you were tight with her, so you must have been fucking. And now we're going to knock the truth out of you.'

I think they must be joking. But then I see that peculiar look in their eyes. The boss sent them here. No amount of begging or pleading will save me now.

'I was not!' I shriek in my shrillest, cracking voice, trying to wrench free of Vic's grasp.

But Didrik is behind me now, and he locks my wrists behind my back.

Vic's fist hits my solar plexus so suddenly that the wind is knocked out of me and I collapse onto the ground. Didrik lets go of my arms and I land with a thud. He moves to stand before me, next to Vic, who hauls me back to my feet.

'Say it! You were fucking Mama!'

'But I wasn't!' I whimper. Out of the corner of my eye I see Matteo nearby. Suddenly I hate him just as much as I do Vic and Didrik. They could kill me, and he wouldn't try to stop them.

The next punch hits me in the groin. The pain is incredible; I double over and stagger backwards. Didrik takes a few steps towards me, grabs my throat in one hand, and squeezes. With the other hand he hits me in the stomach.

As Vic tells him to stop I hear a faint clicking sound.

Behind Vic and Didrik, Matteo is holding up something black and oblong, but he quickly sticks it in his pocket.

Vic and Didrik are too wound up to notice what has happened.

But I understand.

Matteo has a mobile phone. And he just used it to take a picture.

19

Sofia was pulled from her slumber by the nagging feeling that something wasn't quite right. The bedroom was full of a dim, grey light. She reached for Benjamin, but her hand landed on the cool sheet. On his side, the covers were crumpled, shoved halfway onto the floor. She could see the indentation his head left in the pillow. The digital alarm clock showed quarter past five.

All at once, she was aware of a presence in the room.

Someone was standing in the dark, watching her. She couldn't say how she knew this, but she did.

She was about to call out for Benjamin but stopped herself at the last second. It wasn't his presence she felt in the room, the smell of his skin, the familiar sound of his breathing. This was a strange, creepy, invasive sort of feeling.

She readied herself to do something – jump out of bed, startle the intruder – but realized she was paralysed with fear, incapable of moving a single muscle. Her eyes adjusted to the darkness and she noticed that the bedroom door was ajar. She listened intently for any sound. There was a faint squeak of a floorboard, and someone took a quick breath. Light, tiptoeing steps moved across the floor and the stairs creaked. Then came the thud of something falling over.

She sat bolt upright in bed, then forced herself to get up. Her heart was pounding at her ribs. In a thin, strange voice she called Benjamin's name; she approached the door and opened it cautiously. The hallway outside looked empty, deserted. The door to Julia's room was closed.

From downstairs came the sound of steps on the parquet floor. She quickly padded down to the living room but paused on the last stair. Why wasn't she calling for help? The house was full of people, but mixed with her fear was a determination to catch the intruder in the act. She looked around the room. The outlines of Simon and Ellis, each asleep on a sofa, were clearly visible. The silhouettes of the furniture were familiar. But she saw something else too, a shadow wobbling, nearly unnoticeably, in the corner. For a few seconds it seemed to hover over the floor, but then it disappeared.

There was a click of a door handle somewhere.

'Stop!' she shouted, but the shadow was gone. She hurried to the entryway, where a cold gust of wind hit her. The front door was half open. She suddenly realized that something was missing. If there had been an intruder in the house, why hadn't she heard Denzel barking furiously? She peered out at the yard, which was deserted, the only light coming from the moon. She hurried to close the door and then walked slowly back to the living room.

The sense of a stranger's presence was gone. The creepy feeling had been replaced by a soft emptiness.

The house was back to normal. Ellis and Simon were still on the couches; the door to the guest room, where Anna was sleeping, was closed. There was no one else there. Now she decided that Benjamin must have taken Denzel out to pee. But why would he have been sneaking around the house? She sat still for a moment, trying to gather her thoughts.

A crash came from the entryway; it was so loud that she jumped. Then there was a scratching sound on the parquet and

Denzel came bounding over and leapt at her. She crouched down to hug him. When she looked up, Benjamin was staring at her.

'What are you doing up?' he whispered.

'What are *you* doing up? You almost scared me to death.'

'I woke up and realized we forgot to take Denzel out. The moon was so beautiful, so we took a walk by the lake.'

'What do you mean? How long have you been gone?'

'Half an hour or so.'

Sofia whimpered.

'Oh my God! I thought it was you I heard. Someone was in the house while you were gone, in our bedroom. Did you see anyone out there?'

'No, not at all, are you sure? Could it have been Julia?'

'Aren't you listening? Someone was here! Someone was watching me while I slept.' She was no longer whispering; her voice was hysterical. Benjamin took her by the shoulders and pulled her close.

'Of course I believe you. That's horrifying.'

But she saw a shadow of doubt in his eyes.

'Benjamin! This is serious! I'm not imagining things. Someone was in the house. Probably Peder Santos. Did you turn on the alarm and the security camera before you went to bed?'

'Shit, no. With all the people here, I forgot.'

'Did you lock the front door when you went out?'

Benjamin shook his head dejectedly.

Simon had sat up on the sofa by now and was rubbing the sleep from his eyes. Ellis was still fast asleep. Sofia turned on a floor lamp and told Simon what had happened.

'Peder Santos is taking a hell of a risk, entering a house full of people,' he said.

'Maybe he didn't know you all were here,' Sofia said. 'If

only you had turned on the camera, Benjamin. We could have caught him.'

Benjamin suggested they call the police, but it seemed unnecessary to drag them out there on Christmas morning. They searched the house to see if anything was missing, but even Sofia's purse was untouched in the bedroom. There wasn't a single trace of the intruder.

After Benjamin turned on the alarm and security camera, and locked all the doors, they decided to go back to bed and continue the discussion later that day.

But Sofia had trouble falling asleep.

Someone had been staring at her while she slept.

Someone was watching them.

It was a few days after New Year's. She and Simon had arrived to mill around outside the municipal building in Henån long before it opened, ready to submit their application for a building permit for the shelter. They were determined to put the pressure on so the matter would be handled swiftly. Sofia told a good sob story.

After they handed their application to the receptionist and had waited for half an hour, a woman came out with a baffled expression on her face.

'But there's already a building permit for the lot in question,' she declared.

'That's impossible,' Sofia said. 'I owned that house. You must have gotten it mixed up with some other property.'

'No, I don't think so,' the woman said, spreading a blueprint across the desk in front of them. 'The person you lease the land from has approved these, and I'm almost positive I saw your signature on it as well.'

At that moment, it dawned on Sofia what had happened.

She didn't even have to look at the drawings; she knew she had seen them before.

'Can you explain to me how Franz Oswald got blueprints approved for my property? Without my own approval? This is insane!' she said.

Her voice had grown so shrill that Simon placed a reassuring hand on her shoulder.

'But I'm sure your signature is right here, somewhere on these papers,' the woman said, looking even more baffled.

She paged through the stack of documents, but to no avail. The desk was a terrible mess, with papers, pens and folders lying every which way. The more they discussed it, the more convoluted the matter seemed to become. They were getting nowhere, and Simon suggested they go home. Mostly because Sofia's enraged voice was causing the staff of the municipal building to dart disapproving looks her way. Simon hated conflict.

Back home, Sofia sent a furious email to Franz, in which she threatened to sue him, among other unpleasant things.

Half an hour later, he called her mobile phone.

'What do you say to a late lunch? I'm at my office in Stenungsund for once. I can explain everything.' He sounded breezy and completely unperturbed.

'Just answer my email. I don't want to talk to you.'

'You will once you realize what I've got to offer. I have a solution to the building permit issue, so you can start right away. Without accepting any money from me. Besides, I have a document for you to send to the publisher that gives my permission to release the book. There's only one minor condition.'

'You and your damn conditions.'

'It's not Julia this time, it has to do with the book itself.'

She had absolutely no desire to see him, but something in his voice suggested that this meeting would be to her advantage.

There didn't seem to be any other solution. She was desperate and frustrated and so royally tired of all the obstacles that stood in the way of construction.

'Don't go!' Simon exclaimed as soon as she relayed what Franz had said. 'Don't you see that he's messing with you? Call him back and tell him you're not coming. Tell him to go fly a kite. Can't we sue him for this?'

'Sure. But then the lot will sit vacant for at least five years. Look, I'm not afraid of him in the least. I'll call you right away if anything goes awry.'

Simon reluctantly gave in. He was muttering in irritation when she left the house.

Rage throbbing in her veins, she sped to Stenungsund. They'd agreed to meet at a high-end restaurant. The lunch crowd had already thinned out by the time she arrived. That, or there weren't many people who could afford to eat there. She was wearing ripped jeans, sneakers, and the biggest button-up she could find in Benjamin's wardrobe. She'd washed off all her makeup.

Franz's eyebrows shot up when he saw her.

'Whoa!' was all he said.

He was already sitting in a booth, wearing a grey suit and white shirt. As he playfully drummed his fingers on the table, she caught a glimpse of cufflinks. Did people even still have those? His usual one-day stubble was gone. She thought his new suit-guy style was boring but realized with a pang of annoyance that it made him even more attractive. He had already ordered a meal for both of them, and the waiter came rushing over with wine as soon as she sat down.

'We're keeping this meeting short,' she said. 'I just want to know how you managed to get a construction permit for a house that I own.'

'But you don't own the property, do you? It's a ground lease.'

'How do you know that?'

'Because I'm the one who owns it. Have you ever heard of a straw owner?'

Sofia was suddenly exhausted.

'What the hell?'

'There's no reason to be upset. I own land all over Orust and Tjörn, under pseudonyms. And I'm not going to stop you from rebuilding the shelter. Why can't you accept my generosity? I only want to help you.'

'I'm sure. But now you've ruined everything. Because I am not taking your money. Simon is paying for the shelter.'

'Yes, I read as much in your delightful email. But it doesn't matter. I'll just sign over the blueprints to you and arrange everything with the building commission. You can use my drawings and get going on the house. If it ends up being too expensive you can hold off on the pool, the barn, and so on. That will be fine, won't it?'

For a while she could only sit there feeling confounded, but then she realized he was right. This would solve everything. Before she could respond, he reached over the table and put his hand over hers. She yanked her hand away.

'In that case I want to buy the property off you,' she said, without even knowing whether Simon had enough money for that. 'I refuse to build a house on a lot that you own.'

'You can buy it for ten kronor. How's that?'

'That's fine. But Simon will be the one to purchase it. I won't accept any charity from you.'

'Shall we discuss the book now?' he asked. 'You're welcome to publish it, but I just want to look over a few things in the manuscript first. Take the part where my shithead of a father stuck clothespins on my dick. I mean, people might start to think

I'm damaged down there, when in fact the opposite is true. It would affect my image.'

The corners of her mouth twitched.

'Yes, that would be a disaster.'

'So if you send me the manuscript I promise to take a quick look. I took the liberty of contacting a couple of publishers and there's a great deal of interest, but maybe you already knew that.'

Here came the sense that she was being drawn into his web once more.

'Now's about the time you're going to demand I do that DNA test, isn't it? Or else there will be no book or blueprints.'

'Not at all! We'll keep the Julia issue totally separate from this. I don't think you want her to hover in this state of uncertainty all her life.'

'She won't.'

'Yes, she will. Unless I tell her the truth.'

As she nearly got her wine down the wrong pipe, he placed his hand over hers again.

'I'm just kidding. What happened to your sense of humour? We used to have fun together, before I ruined everything. You can deal with the Julia stuff at your own pace. Anything else you'd like to know?'

'Why are you suddenly pretending to be so disgustingly nice?'

'I always have been, deep down. Ask Benjamin – he's known me from the very beginning.'

'He hates you.'

'Benjamin dislikes me because I stole his girl. More than once.'

'Come on!'

'It's true. The first time was when we were teenagers on the island. There was this girl he liked, but they ended up on the rocks after I got her pants off. And he was jealous when you worked with me. And then there was that whole thing with Elvira.'

'What do you mean?'

'You didn't know? Benjamin and Elvira were together before you came to ViaTerra. But she was so young that I put a stop to it right away. To be honest, I suppose I wanted her for myself. I'm surprised Benjamin never told you about that.'

'You're lying! Benjamin was never with Elvira.'

'Ask him,' Franz said with a smug smile. 'I'm positive there are things you don't know about Benjamin.'

Sofia ate quickly to get lunch over with. She hardly wanted to admit to herself how delicious the food was. Now and then he looked up at her with an amused expression on his face.

'Even when you're gobbling your food like that, in those clothes, you're still beyond beautiful, Sofia,' he said at last.

She stood up, took her pocketbook from her purse, and placed a five-hundred kronor bill on the table.

'I'm paying for my own lunch. Sign over the building permit and blueprints to me. Simon will handle the purchase of the property. I'll send the manuscript. Don't call me again. Any contact between us will take place over email.'

Franz didn't answer; he merely smiled.

All the way home she thought about what he'd said about Benjamin.

I didn't ask Matteo about the phone. It would be too hard for us to keep a secret like that. Unspoken secrets were safest, in ViaTerra. That way there was nothing concrete.

I don't quite know how long I was in the Hole. It could have been four months, or six. All I know is that the scents of spring and summer had vanished from the earth, replaced by the faint aroma of autumn. The leaves, their green stage complete, began to turn yellow. And it was colder in the shed at night.

When Karsten appeared at the door one day, shouting at me that I was to return to Earth's Children, I thought at first that Father had realized I had nothing more to confess. The daily stack of papers was getting ever flimsier.

But it turned out that the real reason was that they needed more workers. Father's gym was going to be expanded and the heavy work would be done by the staff. I was thrown from my relatively peaceful existence in the Hole into a hectic renovation project. When I arrived, the other children were already so exhausted and stressed out that they hardly reacted to my return. Our little group had grown. When we turned thirteen, in Earth's Children, we were called cadets. Teenagers were easier for Father to recruit than little kids. Their parents didn't feel as guilty sending them away. After all, it was basically like sending them to boarding school. These days, teenagers were lining up to get into

Earth's Children. Our group had grown from eight members to twenty. There was hardly any space between the bunk beds in the dorms. Our classroom had been divided into two sections and was packed. A new teacher, a member of ViaTerra, had been hired.

For the first time in a long time, I was among other people. Even so, I felt detached. I wondered why I felt such loneliness while surrounded by so many others. When I was in the Hole I'd had good reason to feel alone. Now it seemed illogical.

I realized, when I was reunited with my old friends – Hugo, Molly, Sara and Livia – that I had changed. I no longer felt any shame. Something had awakened inside me. All through the hard labour of renovation, where we were constantly surrounded by a cloud of dust and sawdust, a reassuring voice offered solace in my mind.

One day, this will be over.

One day, you will live a real life.

My voice had grown deeper, but it was stuck in limbo – I never knew whether it would sound normal or squeaky when I opened my mouth.

The day I returned to the dorm, I saw my reflection for the first time in a long time. The hard labour had emphasized the muscles of my upper body. Despite my sensitive skin, I was tanned, and it suited me. My hair had grown and fell in copper waves over my shoulders. Red hair had begun to sprout in my armpits, and lower down as well.

There was something new in my eyes.

Determination.

A VOICE FROM THE OTHER SIDE

It's Friday, and I get to spend the weekend with Grandma. We haven't seen each other in so long that her eyes fill with tears when she catches sight of me.

Vic doesn't want to come along. He's taken to speaking about Grandma in a condescending tone. He says she's like the others and calls her an old bitch. Like me, Vic changed during the months I was in the Hole. He moves with the confidence and agility of a grown man. His face has become broader, sharper; his eyebrows have filled in and he has dark fuzz on his chin. Girls' eyes linger on him, even those of the older ones who work at ViaTerra.

As I step into Grandma's cottage I wonder if she's noticed that I'm different, but it doesn't seem so. Instead she takes in the sight of me tenderly and hesitantly, as though there's something she can't quite bring herself to say. All day something goes unsaid between us.

It's early morning, and we're walking to the sea. The heather is in bloom, the landscape gleaming purple and burgundy. The greyish dawn light has softened. The rocky outcroppings are bathed in the rays of a newly risen sun that lends them a sepia tone. We climb down the rocks and collect mussels that have caught in the crevices between boulders. The gulls, shrieking, dive at us again and again. Wispy sea smoke lies on the surface of the water, as if the sky were brushing it. I feel unusually calm. For once, this lovely day isn't being ruined by my anxiety over having to return to Earth's Children after the weekend.

Grandma tells me she tried to send me letters when I was in the Hole, but they were returned.

'I was so worried about you,' she says. 'And here you are, looking as good as ever! You've grown, and you're so tanned. And look at that amazing hair!'

Later, as she cooks mussel soup while I sit at the kitchen table to chat with her, the tension between us returns. Eventually it becomes unbearable.

'What is it you're not saying, Grandma?' I ask.

'There's something I need to show you after dinner,' she mumbles.

'What is it? Show me now!' I say.

'It'll be best if we eat first,' she says with a deep sigh. I see relief in her face. All day she's been brooding about this. It must be something very important.

The soup tastes so good compared to the food we eat in Earth's Children that I manage to ignore the tension between us for a bit. When I offer to do the dishes, she shakes her head.

'No, I'll take care of it later. Let's get this over with first. Have a seat on the sofa and I'll explain.'

She fills me in on what's been going on during my long period in the Hole. Father has been searching obsessively for Mama. When a couple of human-chain searches turned up nothing, he went to the police. Mama was officially labelled a missing person and they wrote about her in the papers. But despite patrols from the police and plenty of tips from the public, she had vanished without a trace.

'The police think the man you saw by the shop was a red herring,' Grandma says. 'That he was just someone she only had a quick chat with. After all, she lived in such seclusion that she took every opportunity to make contact with others. But the man identified himself as soon as he saw her picture in the paper. He hadn't seen her since they met at the store.'

I feel a sinking feeling in my belly; Grandma is acting so serious.

'Eventually they were convinced she was dead. That it was a suicide. They thought she had thrown herself off a cliff and her body had been washed out to sea.'

I steel myself for what she'll say next – they've found Mama's body. I withdraw into a place deep inside my mind. The tears begin to fall. They drip stubbornly onto my pants as I wring my hands so hard my knuckles go white.

'Don't be upset,' Grandma says. 'I have something to show you.'

She stands up, goes to a window, and peers through the gap in the curtains as though she's making sure no one is there outside. A shiver runs down my spine. She takes out her tablet and opens a web browser. I expect to see something terrible. An obituary or an article with the headline 'Woman found dead on Fog Island'.

Instead she shows me an email from a sender with a strange name – it's nothing but numbers.

My darling Thor! *it begins. I gasp.*

I wish I could have written to Vic too, but that would be dangerous for both of you.

I'm sorry I left you.

I didn't see any other way out.

I'm doing fine, but I think about the two of you all the time.

One day we'll be together again.

I love you both so much.

Mama

And that's all. But it's enough to make me start crying even harder, this time in relief. I curl up against Grandma, who holds me close.

'There's no way for me to find out if it's truly from Elvira,' she says. 'But who else would it be from?'

'It's her,' I say with certainty. I recognize Mama's way of expressing herself. Short and sweet.

The tears have stopped falling. I feel totally drained of emotions.

'I probably shouldn't ask you to keep this secret,' Grandma says. 'Especially after everything they've done to you.' She scrunches her face into a sad grimace. 'And if your father finds out I showed you this email, you and I won't be allowed to see each other anymore, and I couldn't bear it.'

'What about the police? Do they think Mama is dead?'

'Yes, they've closed the case for the time being. After all, your grandmother Mona committed suicide. They assumed it might be some kind of hereditary mental illness.'

'But why can't you talk to the police now that you've gotten that email? Couldn't they trace it?'

'Your mother doesn't want to be found, Thor. She trusted that I would show you the email and then keep my mouth shut. I felt that you had to know she's alive. They're going to tell you she's dead. I'm surprised they haven't already.'

I sit there stunned and numb for a while, trying to take it all in. Mama is alive, and she loves me, but I'll probably never see her again. I wonder why no one has told me, but that's the way it goes in ViaTerra. Enemies are as good as dead. You don't speak with them or about them.

I look at Grandma and realize she too has changed since we last saw each other. She doesn't laugh or talk as much now. Carrying secrets is heavy work.

'You can do whatever you like,' she says. 'I'm not going to ask you to lie about this.'

This is the moment of truth. How many secrets can one person bear?

20

Franz kept his promise. Within a few days they had the green light to start rebuilding the shelter. Sofia's relief was so great that it overshadowed everything else, even her fear of Peder Santos and annoyance at Franz.

He'd been right about Benjamin. When she came home from the meeting in Stenungsund she confronted him immediately.

'Did you have a relationship with Elvira?'

'What?' He looked mildly surprised, but his gaze darted away from hers.

'Answer the question.'

'Well… I wouldn't call it a *real* relationship. Where is this coming from?'

'What's a *real* relationship? Stop dodging the question and answer me!'

'Is Franz the one who put this nonsense into your head? When Elvira came to ViaTerra, I was rather fond of her. We held hands, kissed a few times, that's all. Then Franz discovered us and hit the roof. Why are you bringing this up after twenty years?'

'Why didn't you ever tell me?'

'You never asked. Nothing happened between Elvira and me.'

'She was fourteen and you were like twenty-five. It feels wrong.'

'I can't believe you listened to Franz. He's a viper. *I'm* not the one who locked Elvira in the attic and raped her. I forbid you from having any more contact with him.'

Benjamin had raised his voice, which was totally unlike him. He should have simply shrugged, laughed, and said it was so long ago that he hardly remembered. But that wasn't the path he chose, and it rekindled the humiliation she'd felt when Franz told her about him.

'You have no idea how gross it feels for Franz to know about this but not me,' she said. 'As though you're living some sort of double life.'

'I cannot believe that you would listen to him. And then we find out he owns the shelter property. Do you think that's a coincidence? Don't you get it, he's trying to turn you against me!'

'He could never, as long as you don't have a secret past as an axe murderer.'

Now they were laughing together. It was a relief in the midst of all this misery.

Sofia let whatever relationship Benjamin did or did not have with Elvira be. But she'd learned something new about Benjamin after nearly twenty years together. You had to ask him questions to find out the truth. And now she wondered what other questions she should be asking.

Then there was the manuscript. Franz had sent it back to her with notes, and not just a few comments either. The whole document was full of opinions, remarks, and suggestions of how to improve her language. And the worst part was, some of his suggestions were helpful.

She was so annoyed that she put the manuscript aside for a few days. At last she capitulated and took out the sentence about how Franz's father had tortured him as a boy by fastening a clothespin on his penis. But she left in the part about his being kept prisoner in the cellar, naked. After some consideration, she deleted the word 'naked' as well. Then she sent the manuscript back to Franz with a message letting him know she wouldn't be making any further changes, and that she wasn't the least bit interested in his acting as the language police.

The response arrived a week later. He apologized and didn't hesitate to tell her that he'd just returned home – he'd been in Washington, DC to meet with politicians, but wouldn't be travelling again for some time. He said it was fine if she published the book with the few changes she'd made but included the snide comment that any linguistic errors would be caught by a competent publisher anyway.

A wave of relief washed over her. At last. Now people could read the sad story of Sigrid von Bärensten and the reign of terror at the manor on Fog Island. The von Bärensten family's deep, dark secrets would finally see the light of day. She copied Franz's approval and saved it both on her computer and a flash drive. Then she updated the cover letter that had been languishing in a folder forever, adding a line about Franz's approval. She typed in the email address to one of the biggest publishers in the country. Closing her eyes, she took a few deep breaths and hit Send.

Meanwhile, she finally got to spend some time with Simon. Each day, they worked on getting the house rebuilt. They contacted and visited contractors, got offers, and examined the blueprints again. When Sofia asked Simon if he'd known about Elvira and Benjamin's relationship, he only shook his head.

'I think you're asking the wrong questions. You should be asking yourself why Franz is suddenly dredging that old thing up. As long as I've known him, he's had a plan. Considering the amount of attention he's been giving you lately, his latest plan definitely involves you – and that gives me the chills.'

It was Saturday afternoon. They were sitting on the sofa, trying to wind down after a week's hectic hunt for the best construction firm. But now they had settled on one and this weekend they could take it easy. Benjamin had taken Denzel for a long walk. Anna would be coming by later that evening. Julia had gone to Stenungsund with Matt.

'I have to get going on finding some permanent sponsors,' Sofia said.

'I told you, I'll help you out with the money.'

'Still, we need to promote ourselves. I'm sure Ellis can make us a website. We can bring in a whole bunch of grants if we can show we're launching a serious project.'

She wondered if Ellis was even awake. He typically didn't get up until after lunch. Most of the time he would go to bed at four or five in the morning, unable to turn off his brain before then. But when she called, he answered right away, sounding unusually energetic.

'Funny you should call,' he said, before Sofia could tell him why she was calling. 'I've got Julia's boyfriend here, teaching him a bunch about computers. I've never met someone with such natural talent. He's got an amazing way with numbers. I'll be able to teach him to get past most security measures in no time.'

'What?!' Sofia said, surprised. 'Julia said she and Matt were going to Stenungsund. Can I talk to him?'

Matt was quick to reassure Sofia. When the chance came up for Matt to spend a day with Ellis, Julia had decided to go to Stenungsund with a friend instead.

'I think it was Laura,' he said. 'But I'm not sure. It's not always easy to keep track of where Julia's off to.'

Ellis promised to help Sofia with the website, and they chatted for so long she almost forgot to figure out where Julia was. But once Simon left, she grew anxious and called her. Julia answered right away.

'Where are you?'

'Did you call just to ask me that? I told you I was going to Stenungsund.'

'Right, and who are you there with?'

'What's with the interrogation?'

'Matt is with Ellis in Gothenburg.'

'I'm so happy for him! Look, I already knew that. I'm here with other friends. Stop spying on me, I'll be home tonight. You worry too much, Mom. I love you. *Mwah!*' She hung up.

A few hours later, Sofia checked her email to see if there was a response from the publisher, even though she knew they weren't in the office on Saturdays. Just as she was about to log out, an email arrived from an unknown sender.

She opened it and stared at a single sentence, written in red italics. As she read the words, something cold expanded inside her chest.

Julia is lying to you.

21

Julia had decided to show up to the meeting a little late. She waited outside a tall building she'd never noticed on her previous visits to the city. The restaurant looked insanely fancy.

She had taken care to dress up for this meeting. A white blouse with a plunging neckline, a silver leather jacket, and a grey skirt that hit mid-calf but had a slit up to her thigh. High-heeled pumps despite the cold. She wasn't about to look like an idol-worshipping teenager on her first date with Franz Oswald.

If you could call this a date, that is.

When she walked into the restaurant, a waiter approached right away to say that her lunch date had booked a table in a more private area. He showed her up a spiral staircase to a small, dark room and helped her off with her coat, which he hung on a hanger just inside the door.

At first the room appeared to be empty apart from a table with flickering candles. But then a shadow emerged from the dim edges and suddenly Franz Oswald was right in front of her.

'Thanks for coming,' he breathed.

The first time she'd met him, he'd been wearing a suit and tie. Today he was wearing an unbuttoned black blazer over a white T-shirt and black jeans. The jeans were tight and probably would have looked ridiculous on most forty-year-olds, but not Franz Oswald. His legs were muscular and the denim fabric was worn in in a luxury-brand sort of way. He aimed a dismissive wave at the server, who immediately vanished down the spiral stairs. Then he looked her up and down and gave a soft, appreciative whistle.

He placed a light hand on her elbow and showed her to the table, which was decorated with white flowers and candles.

'Why did you want to see me?' she asked as soon as they sat down.

'Isn't it obvious?'

'No, it isn't.'

He observed her in silence, their eyes locked. There was something hypnotic about his gaze. He had just the right mix of humility and confidence.

'It doesn't matter how far away I am, Julia. I could feel your power of attraction from across the globe when I was in Washington,' he said, putting his hand over hers.

She squirmed, uncomfortably aware of the electricity that was building up in the air, and pulled her hand away. All of a sudden, the comfortably cool room felt too hot. She tried to look nonchalant. It was dangerous to let someone with such a huge ego see the effect he had on her.

'The kind of attraction that's between us is exciting – you never know quite where it will lead. While I'm not particularly romantic, I'm passionate in a different way,' he said.

'But what was it you wanted to talk about?'

'What I really want to discuss is your future.'

'I'm not at all concerned about my future,' she said.

'I know. That's what I like about you.'

He spread his napkin over his lap.

'What would you like to eat, by the way?'

'It doesn't matter.'

'Good, we'll let the chef decide.'

He took his phone from the pocket of his blazer and spoke to someone downstairs. Julia found herself fingering the tablecloth. It was annoying that he had put her off balance. She wasn't that type.

'This is like a huge joke,' she said. 'I don't know why I came here.'

'I do. Let me tell you a little about myself first, and then we'll talk about you. I've done things I'm not so proud of, hurt other people and turned quite a few people's lives upside down. But I've never compromised on my goals, not once. My calling is to help people find the right path in life, I've known that since I was thirteen. Do you know what your goal is?'

'No, I have no idea. Right now my goal is to get out of the boring hole of a town I live in and do everything you're not allowed to do when you're sixteen. Meet new, exciting people, take risks, cause scandals. Try everything but drugs, because those kill your brain. The only thing that makes me anxious is the thought of having to decide what I'm going to do with the rest of my life. I don't want to do *one* thing, I want to do everything…'

He gave a loud laugh.

'Exactly! You don't need to worry about the future. You're in the perfect position to do whatever you want. That's why you and I are drawn to one another. You can't find your calling by sitting at a computer and searching for career options. I had to risk my life more than once before I found my purpose. But now I'm going to tell you something about myself I've never revealed to anyone else.'

He cut himself off, because the server had arrived with the food. Warm, butter-fried lobster on toast with avocado salad.

'I'll tell you more once we've eaten,' he said as the server poured them both wine. 'This meal should be enjoyed warm.'

It was exciting that Franz was letting her drink wine even though it wasn't allowed. She felt so grown up. The food was so good that she managed to forget her nervousness for a while. The wine was strong and made her feel warm. Her uncertainty in his presence had faded. She watched him as he cut his toast into tidy bites, which he slowly brought to his mouth.

He looked up at her. His expression was unreadable. Deep down in his gaze, there was a glimmer of amusement.

Just then, her phone rang.

'You'd better answer it,' he said.

She took her purse from the back of her chair and dug around inside until she found her phone.

'It's Mom,' she said.

'Great, time to see how good you are at lying.'

It wasn't hard at all. Her mother knew there was a limit when it came to snooping, a limit Julia always pointed out by hanging up on her. Most of the time, she wasn't ashamed of it. Sure, she loved her parents, but she was certain that breaking free from their anxious protective instincts was a crucial part of her development. Although this time it hurt a little to ignore the call. A lump formed in her throat; mysterious tears sprang to her eyes. It only lasted for a second, and then she was back to normal. But Franz noticed.

'There's nothing wrong with having strong emotions. Don't be ashamed about feeling upset when adults treat you like a child.'

Exactly! That was just it. *You can't pretend to be a child when you aren't one*, Julia thought.

'Mom's cool. She's just a little overprotective.'

'It's probably not always so easy for her.'

'Her life is as easy as a life can possibly be. She knows she can trust me. That's how our relationship works.'

'Sure, and here you are with me, her arch-enemy.'

'She doesn't need to know that.'

'No, she's got a lot going on right now. I hope she can forgive me one day.'

A shadow passed over his face.

'Each time I see your mother, I beg and plead with her to bury the hatchet,' he continued. 'And when she refuses, it feels like my heart is breaking in two.'

'What did you *do* to her?'

'I didn't treat her well. She was an outstanding secretary. My right hand. I should have given her greater freedom. Let her grow. Instead I hemmed her in. I was younger and more controlling back then.'

'Controlling? From what I've heard, you were a straight-up tyrant. Like in North Korea.'

'Yes, that's Sofia's version, but that doesn't mean I wasn't fond of her.'

'Sounds to me like you were in love with her.'

He considered this for a moment.

'Yes, in some ways. It felt like an incredible betrayal when she ran away from ViaTerra. I've never been able to stop thinking about Sofia. You remind me of her. The same wonderful energy.'

He looked sad.

'Come on, let's talk about something else. Tell me about yourself instead,' he said.

The tension between them had abated. He radiated calm and trustworthiness and was easy to talk to. To steer her thoughts away from his physical presence she rattled on about all sorts of things: school, how much she liked Matt, her frustration over living in such a small town. He listened intently. Oh my God, how he listened! As if each sentence she spoke was poetry. As if his whole body heard her, responded to her.

He never interrupted her. He nodded in the right places, affirming what she said. Eventually she found herself sharing the most intimate details of her life, like how hopeless guys her age were at having sex.

Then he reached across the table, cupped her cheek, and followed the line of her jaw with his thumb.

'Forgive me,' he said. 'I didn't mean to interrupt you. But I don't think guys that age understand that sex is about pleasuring your partner. That's how to get the greatest pleasure yourself.'

'I read somewhere that you like to choke your partner during sex.'

He laughed aloud. It was an honest, disarming laugh.

'Definitely not. That's just something the tabloids made up. For me, sex is about accommodating what my partner likes, and after that you can stretch the limits, if you both want to.'

She felt her face flush with heat and decided to guide the conversation away from this topic.

'Anyway, what is it you wanted to tell me? The thing you never told anyone else?' she asked.

He pushed his plate away, picked up his glass, and swirled the wine for a moment before taking a sip.

'Here's the thing. I've spoken before the great leaders of the world, bought things not even one in a thousand of the world's inhabitants can afford, and spent time with the crème de la crème. But what really gets me going is venturing into a forbidden, slightly shameful relationship. Everything else is boring as hell in comparison.'

'You're too old for me,' she couldn't help but say.

'I sure am. That's what makes it so thrilling.'

Somehow she managed to force a smile, even as her legs went numb and all her blood rushed between her legs, where a delightful ache began to pulse. She crossed her legs to counteract the dull pressure, but it didn't help. He noticed and gave a sly smile.

He knows exactly what I'm feeling.

'I think I should go now,' she said.

'Not before you've listened to my proposal. I want to spend a few days with you on Fog Island and show you everything I've created and believe in. A meeting entirely without strings. Maybe in early May, when the island is most beautiful?'

'No way. What would I tell my parents?'

'Can't the leech cover for you?'

Julia bit her lip. This was so exciting; she couldn't help it. The familiar curiosity took over again.

'If you mean Matt, maybe that would work. This isn't something I can decide on here and now. I need to think about it.'

'Of course. I'll give you my private number.'

He took a business card from his pocket and handed it to her. He'd planned this encounter well. The thought of spending two days with him sent a pleasant shiver down her spine.

'Would you like a ride home?' he asked.

'No, I'd better take the bus,' she said, flashing him a grin.

She quickly rose, pushed back her chair, and went to the coatrack. He followed her and helped her on with her coat. He stood so close that she could feel the heat of his body against her back. When she leaned forward a bit to tie the belt he gently brushed the hair from her throat. His lips grazed the back of her neck softly. Matt briefly popped into her mind. His lovely eyes. She knew she should feel guilty, but her feelings for Matt couldn't extinguish the fire Franz's touch had lit in her body.

'See you again soon,' he said. 'It would be amazing if you came to visit me.'

All the way home on the bus, she was lost in a fog of shameful fantasies.

After my conversation with Grandma about Mama I lived a sort of double life.

I absolutely could not risk ending up in the Hole again. There was so much pressure to confess, and I was constantly thinking about Mama. I couldn't risk revealing the truth about her. So I had to obey in every way, and force my eyes to blaze with that fire that was typical of Earth's Children. What's more, I had watchful eyes on me – once a traitor, always under suspicion.

It was Ali-Khan who told me about Mama. She asked me to stay behind after class and explained in a serious voice that my mother was, in all likelihood, dead.

'After all, those who turn against ViaTerra can expect terrible punishment. It must have been her transgressions against your father that drove her to suicide. But now you know. There's no reason to be upset. You've still got your father. He's worth more than a thousand of your mother.'

Tears came to my eyes, but I didn't break down. There was no reason to.

Mama wasn't dead.

In the months that followed, my life was like a play in which I acted the role of Devoted Earth's Children Member by day and sank into forbidden, critical thoughts by night, after lights out in the dorm.

I never stopped loving Father. I just hated who he'd become. I often daydreamed that he would change, come to beg forgiveness for what he'd done to Mama.

But then, suddenly, I got some breathing room. All hard labour was put on hold and we were assembled for a briefing with Father. A new phase of our education would begin. After an intense training period, we would be sent out on assignments to sites on the mainland. These assignments would be so important that they were called 'tasks of honour'.

Almost like little soldiers being sent into battle.

BRIEFING

We wait with bated breath for Father. Ali-Khan has cleaned the whiteboard a number of times, has meticulously laid out markers, and is now darting nervous glances at the wall clock. When Father steps into the classroom, she shrinks, backing silently into a corner.

'There you are!' Father says, sounding exhilarated. 'I'm sorry to make you wait.' He's in a good mood. The tension in the room dissipates. He's carrying a thick folder under his arm, and he places it on Ali-Khan's desk.

'This briefing is more important than anything else on my schedule today. Can you guess why?' he asks, his eyes drifting from face to face.

He avoids mine, but I'm used to that. No one seems to have an answer to his question.

'Because out of everyone who works at ViaTerra, you are the most significant,' he says. 'And without question, the smartest.'

Despite my doubt, my heart swells in my chest. The mood in the classroom has grown so solemn.

'A little bird told me someone has been exploiting you all as labour for a renovation project, but I put a stop to that right away,' he says. 'It's a misuse of resources. Instead, you'll be working with me soon. And that's what we're going to talk about today.'

He picks up a marker and draws a sun with rays at the top of the whiteboard. Then he writes something inside the sun. I squint; I've always found his handwriting hard to read, but then I realize it says 'ViaTerra'. Next he draws a big circle below, and on it a bunch of stick figures reaching their arms for the sun. Above them, he writes 'the world's population'.

'More people than ever are interested in ViaTerra, even though I haven't shown my face in public for some time. In a few years, we're going to launch a big campaign, and then it will look like this. Everyone will want to come here, to Fog Island,' he says, pointing at the stick figures and their outstretched arms. 'But there's one little problem...'

He draws another stick figure holding one of the sun-worshippers by the legs. He fills this figure's face in with black, and then draws horns on top of its head.

'A few individuals, about two per cent of the world's population, have committed horrific crimes. They are terrified that we will disclose them and will do anything to stop us.'

He pauses, gazing out the window for a moment. He's pondering something, but he quickly looks back at the class. He stares at Vic while he continues his monologue.

'For years now I've been working on a plan,' he says. 'Something that will make ViaTerra popular all over the world. Our solutions to society's problems will be praised by the greatest world leaders. And then guys like this one will awaken,' he says, pointing at the stick figure with the horns.

Didrik eagerly raises a hand.

'Are we going to war with those guys?' he asks.

Father gives him an indulgent smile.

'Yes, in a manner of speaking. We can simply call them "enemies". You will be sent on assignments – you'll be my eyes and ears – to keep them under surveillance. In addition, you'll be sent out to watch over people I'm particularly interested in.'

'Will we be working directly with you?' Vic asks.

'Yes, you will. No one else in ViaTerra could guide you through tasks like these.'

'Awesome,' Vic says, sitting up straighter.

'Maybe not so awesome for you,' Father contradicts him. 'People would recognize you. You'll be working in my office.'

Vic is sitting in the front row, as usual, and he turns around to flash me a taunting grin. But it's not mean through and through. A long time ago he realized that I pose no threat to his position of power in ViaTerra. Sometimes he defends me. Maybe it's because in the end, we're still brothers.

'There are some of you I don't trust yet,' Father says, glaring at me. 'But in ViaTerra, we believe everyone deserves a second chance. This education will winnow out all the traitors. It's going to be tough. It's also going to be several months before you're ready.'

He approaches the desk, picks up the folder, and hands it to Ali-Khan.

'This is their material. First they must learn to recite my theses by heart. The theses are the foundation everything else is built on. Then they need to learn to socialize with the others. *So they are able to blend in, out there in the world.'*

Ali-Khan accepts the folder with reverence. She mumbles some polite words. Father turns to us again.

'For each assignment, I will write a program of orders for you to follow. But now I'm getting ahead of myself. We'll start with your studies. I'll come to speak with you each night to make sure you understand all of this.'

When he leaves the room, we remain perfectly silent. Then Vic lets out a hoot of joy and high-fives Didrik. Amidst all this cheer I realize that the worst of my suffering is over. If there's anything I'm good at, it's learning things by heart.

*

Our initiation begins. The hard physical labour is over. Ali-Khan assigns us daily goals for our studies, and no one can go home before they are fulfilled. Each evening Father comes to speak to us, typically just before we're done for the day. His monologues sometimes last for several hours. At times, the sun is peeking through the windows of the classroom before we're allowed to go to bed. It's hard to study when you haven't slept, but no one dares to point this out to Father. When he speaks, his addresses often flow into anecdotes about his life. Stories about his time in prison, so unjust, but the inmates revolted because the prison administration wouldn't allow them to study the theses.

The other children have a hard time learning the theses by heart. There are so many of them. The 'Foundational Theses' and the 'Propositions' that supplement them, and then the 'Existential Theses' Father developed in prison. The latter deal with the laws that govern the universe:

> In the beginning there was an endless fog and from the fog an impenetrable ash fell over the universe.
> From this ash a consciousness awakened.
> Thus there was life.
> Thus there were ideas.
> Thus there was interaction.

It's so abstract. I don't have the faintest clue how to put this to use in real life. But I memorize it all, faster than anyone else. Father comes in one time as I'm reciting in front of the class. I perform gallantly, not a single mistake or hesitation. For the first time, I see a spark of pride in his eyes when he looks at me.

This is how it goes, the education whose goal is to shape us into a cohort that is, by nature, superior to the rest of humanity. Out on this distant island, where Father rules over a kingdom of his own, it's easy to feel omnipotent. Especially when he speaks to our group in his chummy way.

Sometimes I ask myself why we can't be satisfied with what we have, why we must conquer the world. But Father's speeches give me to understand that the unique way we've been raised has made us immensely special. So the world needs us. And if you believe in something hard enough, eventually it will become reality.

We've been assigned a higher rank than the ViaTerra staff. Father gives us more power than them. Sometimes he sends one of us to give one of them a violent upbraiding. We've turned into his messengers.

He calls us 'the Chosen'.

Sometimes he says we're humanity's only hope.

There's no longer any hatred in his eyes when he looks at me.

Even so, I'm incapable of being drawn into the frenzy that spreads through our cohort like wildfire. There's a fissure within me that not even a fiery speech from Father can repair.

On the outside, I give the appearance of participating just like the others. At the same time, my conviction that there's something sinister about all of this only keeps growing.

22

What do you do with a message that has come out of the blue and could mean a hundred different things?

Sofia was aware that Julia sometimes lied. Didn't all teenagers? There were lots of reasonable explanations for the email. Maybe some classmate was jealous of Julia's relationship with Matt, or maybe it was one of Julia's admirers, or was the email from some nutcase who simply wanted to mess with her?

Julia had had her fair share of online harassment. She'd been called a 'slut', a 'bitch', and any number of other names. But it didn't seem to bother her. Mostly, she laughed it off:

'Look what that idiot is saying about me! They're such babies.'

Julia didn't seem interested in gossip or talking shit. Sure, she had girlfriends, but she kept them at a certain distance. Oftentimes she hung out with the guys. She was more independent than most kids her age, but she was also bolder.

At first, Sofia thought she should just ignore the anonymous email, but something about it didn't quite make sense. A jealous teenager wouldn't have settled for just one sentence. She was familiar with the way they spoke and wrote. Long, rambling phrases full of unpleasant adjectives.

Julia is lying to you.

Sofia thought for a moment, then hit 'reply' and wrote:

About what?

Once she'd sent the email she considered telling Benjamin and Julia about it, but decided to wait until she got a response.

Later that evening, when Julia came home, she searched her daughter's gaze for something unspoken, or a smidge of shame, but found nothing of the sort.

'Why are you staring at me like that, Mom?'

'I'm just happy to see you.'

Julia laughed and cocked her head.

'Same here.'

Sofia noticed that Julia was wearing unusually nice clothes. She took off her jacket, which had hidden a white blouse that emphasized her breasts. A long slit in her skirt revealed one leg. Sofia hardly dared to look. Julia's cheeks were rosy, and her eyes sparkled. Sofia thought that Julia had probably never been so beautiful, standing there with her bright red purse slung over her shoulder and her phone in hand. She felt an intense urge to snoop on that phone but knew that was a line she must never cross.

A fleeting intrusive thought of Julia, naked and tied up, invaded her mind. Out of nowhere. She squashed it down and tried to tell herself it was nothing but a random, false image caused by stress. That was all. Nothing to worry about.

'How was Stenungsund?'

'Super fun. Don't start interrogating me.'

'Why are you biting my head off? I'm interested in who you spend time with. And your relationships, too. Why don't you want to talk about that stuff?'

'I'm not like Laura, having cosy mother–daughter time and sharing *everything*. Can't I have a private life? I never interrogate you and Dad about your sex life. Would you like it if I did?'

Sofia didn't know what to say. She simply walked up and embraced her daughter, who, to her joy, hugged back – hard.

And Julia's fresh scent, her breath against her cheek, was all it took to calm her worries.

The next day, she checked and checked for a response from the mysterious sender, but her inbox remained empty.

Each time her phone rang, her heart skipped a beat; she was hoping for a call from the publisher, but instead she heard from Simon and then Anna. Simon was going to Gothenburg on some errand. Anna said she had to go back to Stockholm for a few days and see to her mother; Benjamin was on a job site in Uddevalla.

Which meant Sofia was home alone all day long.

She had snooped in her daughter's room twice before. The first time, she'd thought she smelled pot on Julia, so she searched the room for drugs. The second time, she'd spotted a sex-toy catalogue that had been mailed to Julia, so she'd been looking for porn. But that time, Julia caught her and flew into a rage. Sofia had promised to leave her room alone and had kept that promise ever since.

But now she couldn't stop herself. The room was drawing her in with a powerful force. *It must look like a pigsty in there*, she thought, *and tidying up is never a bad idea*. She brought a dust rag, just in case Julia happened to come home.

The room was dark with the black blinds down. It smelled strongly of Julia's perfume. Sofia raised the blinds and was horrified at the mess. Clothes were strewn everywhere, the whole duvet was on the floor, and lipstick, mascara and compacts were scattered across the bed. Under the military-style requirements of ViaTerra, Sofia had developed a meticulous tidiness that she had never managed to let go of.

She began a systematic search. She looked through drawers, wardrobes, under the bed and the pillows, even as she occasionally wiped away a little dust. In half an hour of searching, she didn't find the slightest hint of anything odd. Just a frightful mess.

Julia had her own en suite bathroom. Sofia steeled herself for the mess she would find there, but the bathroom was surprisingly neat and clean. Everything seemed to be in its place. The shower looked freshly scrubbed.

She caught sight of herself in the mirror. Suspicion didn't suit her. Her eyes looked wild; her skin was pale and the corners of her mouth turned down in a sour grimace. She stared at herself, wondering what kind of person didn't trust her own daughter. She decided to stop digging, but just then she caught sight of something at the top corner of the mirror. It could have been a clamp that held the glass in the frame, but it seemed larger than that and was round. She reached up to grab the object. She was able to twist it and when she pulled it fell into her palm.

Horrified, she stared at the small gadget. No doubt about it: it was a surveillance camera.

Just like the ones at ViaTerra. In every room.

She wanted to bang her forehead on the mirror.

You have been taken for a ride by Franz. What did you expect?

She inspected the camera closely. It didn't look like the ones she remembered from the cult. It was rounder and had a fastener that had clipped it to the mirror. But sure enough, there was a tiny staring eye in the middle. She poked at it and realized that it could swivel.

Her hands began to shake so hard she almost dropped the camera. She stuffed it quickly into the pocket of her cardigan. At first she thought she should call the police, but that felt pointless. She hadn't heard a word from them since she handed over the flash drive with all the photographs, and she doubted they would help her this time. It seemed unnecessary to bother Benjamin in Uddevalla. What could he do from there? She might as well wait until he got home.

When she tried to stand, her legs folded beneath her and she sank onto the lid of the toilet. She looked at her watch. Quarter past two. Ellis must be awake. He'd started to visit more often, and, like Simon, had become part of the family. She took her phone from her pocket. It rang a few times, and when he finally picked up, she burst into tears and couldn't speak.

'Sofia, what's wrong?' he asked. 'Can you try to tell me what's going on?'

At last she managed to describe the camera.

'I'd need to take a look at it,' he said. 'But it sounds like an HD Trackerdome.'

'What's that?'

'The best surveillance camera there is. They've got a huge range, and they're completely wireless. Not only do they stream 24/7, the viewer can turn and move the eye and see the image from all angles. That kind of camera costs a fortune.'

'Is it traceable?'

'Not a chance. Given that you took it down, the connection will have been broken. All I would be able to do is estimate when it was installed, depending on how much charge there is in the battery.'

'Oh, please, come do that. Or should I come to you? I guess I'll have to report this to the police, but I'm sure they won't do a thing. Unlawful surveillance is Franz's specialty, but how did he get a camera into our house? And into Julia's bathroom – Jesus.' She whimpered.

'Okay, I'll be right over. Don't touch the camera in the meantime. I'll try to be there in an hour.'

She paced the living room anxiously as she waited for Ellis. Now and then her eyes were drawn to the tiny staring eye she'd placed on the coffee table. She thought of how Julia liked to pose in front of the mirror and felt so sick that she went to the bathroom, knelt before the toilet, and tried to vomit. When nothing came up, she realized she hadn't had any lunch. As she tried to figure out how all of this was connected, her brain idled. The missing piece of this miserable puzzle had to be somewhere, but she couldn't find it.

When Ellis turned up, he gave her a long hug.

'Yup, that's a Trackerdome,' he said as soon as he laid eyes on the camera.

He'd brought a toolbox and took out a tiny screwdriver, which he used to open the back of the camera. He took out a battery that was smaller than the nail of her pinkie finger and hooked it to a tester.

'The battery's brand new,' he said. 'The camera couldn't have been there for more than a week or so.'

'Are you sure?'

'Totally sure. This camera was just installed.'

'And here I thought the Christmas Eve intruder put it there.'

'Unfortunately, that can't be. That was almost a month ago. Do you think Julia installed it herself? Maybe she's showing off for some guy?'

'That sounds bonkers. Don't people do that sort of thing on their phone or computer?'

'This camera would provide a much clearer image. Amazing angles.'

Sofia thought for a moment. It sounded unlikely, but it wasn't entirely implausible. Julia did have exhibitionist tendencies. But Julia also had Matt, and they seemed crazy about each other. Matt wouldn't be able to afford this kind of camera. And surely there was no way Julia's allowance would go far enough.

'No, I don't think it was Julia,' she said. 'Although, if someone did break into our house, they must have been caught on our security cameras, right? I made Benjamin keep them on around the clock ever since the incident on Christmas Eve.'

At that moment, Julia walked into the room. Judging by her curious gaze, she'd heard part of their conversation. The only option was to tell her everything.

If Julia had anything to do with the camera, she hid it well.

'What the hell were you doing in my room?' she snapped at first, but before Sofia had time to supply any lies about cleaning in there, Julia started to cry.

'Oh, gross,' she said over and over as Sofia held her and rubbed her back.

Together they looked through the footage from their security camera. The tape was still rolling when Benjamin arrived home that evening. There wasn't a single stranger to be found – aside from their family, only Anna, Simon, Matt, Ellis, and Sofia's friend Maggie had been inside the house.

'I guess we have to rethink this,' Benjamin said. 'There's just not a trace of any of Franz's spies in these images.'

For the first time, Sofia had the feeling that someone close to her was hiding a nasty secret.

Our education took longer than expected. Not only did we have to learn the theses, we had to learn the arts of public speaking, dressing fashionably, and having conversations, all with the intent of blending in with the others.

And then there were Father's orations on the disasters that befell ViaTerra. These could comprise anything from a blogger who wrote nonsense about him to a guest getting food poisoning. And once he got started, he could lament for hours. We had become his confidantes.

But none of these disasters shook us as much as the one that involved Elisa.

She joined our cohort a little later than most and was the daughter of one of Father's most devoted followers. All the girls in Earth's Children were cute, each in their own way. But Elisa wasn't just cute, she was adorable. With the sweet face of a little girl and the developed body of a woman, she landed like a bomb among us. Her long blonde hair swinging across her back as she walked – everything about her was beautiful. She moved with such confidence, like a woman on her way somewhere. Everything about her was sensual, her laughter, looks, and movements. Like the rest of us, she wore a uniform, but she didn't wear a bra under her T-shirt, and you could see a hint of her nipples.

Us guys were crazy about her. Even me – I wasn't all that interested in sex, but masturbation and wet dreams became part of my daily life from the moment I saw Elisa. I knew she was unattainable, but my fantasies about her made me long for the darkness under my covers each night.

She was the cause of a nervous restlessness in our classroom. The guys were suddenly so full of testosterone that we could hardly sit still. Our laughter was shriller. As soon as Elisa was in our vicinity, we were on tenterhooks.

I remember the first time Father saw her. He had come in to give one of his speeches and she was in the front row. His face didn't change at all, but I'll never forget the look in his eyes. It wasn't that lascivious, bewitched look that the guys cast after her. It was the look of a predator that had just laid eyes on its quarry.

Father approached Elisa slowly. He sometimes interrupted his monologues to ask her simple questions; he would praise her answers. And hold her gaze a little too long. Now and then he would lean over her shoulder and pretend to look at what she was writing as he brazenly stared at her breasts.

Given his position of power and his charisma, he immediately caught her interest. She absorbed his attention like a sponge, pouting her lips when she knew he was looking and smiling coquettishly. She would do that dainty hair-twirling thing. But I noticed that she was a little afraid of him. And Father was in no rush.

So someone beat him to it.

Really, it should have been Vic who got Elisa on her back first, but it was Didrik. He was older than us, and his power of attraction was more than Vic could compete with.

You could see Didrik and Elisa on breaks and after school, intertwined, making out shamelessly. It was almost like the beginning of a mating dance.

From the start, I knew it would end in disaster.

I wake early and notice that Didrik's bed is empty. I mean to go back to sleep, but my curiosity gets the better of me. I know who he snuck out to see. When I gaze around the dorm, I think I see Vic staring at me from his bed, but when I take another look his eyes are closed. I get dressed unnoticed and sneak out.

It's spring again. The sun has barely risen over the horizon and the pale light makes the lawn shine as though each blade were luminous. A faint breeze blows in from the sea. The water in the pond has taken on a pale pink shimmer. It's so beautiful that I almost forget why I'm there. I crouch on the grass in front of a lone narcissus that has sprouted in the lawn. A hundred tiny dewdrops rest on its petals. They're so tiny and light, but still the flower bows to me.

For a moment, my thoughts are carried away by the recurring daydream of being in another place and living a different life. But then I hear steps behind me and startle. I turn around to find Vic on his way to the manor house. He doesn't seem to notice me. I sit still until he's out of sight.

Just then, I hear strange noises from the Hole, which is uninhabited for the time being. Sighs and moans. I quickly move across the lawn and hope the guard won't spot me. There's a small window in the back of the shed. You can stand in a grove of trees and peer in without being visible from the guards' booth.

At first I hardly believe my eyes. Elisa and Didrik are lying naked on the floor atop a pile of clothing, right where my sleeping bag used to be. Elisa is on her back with her hair fanned out. Her eyes are closed. A couple of sunbeams have made their way through the window and shine on her white breasts. Her legs are in the air, and Didrik is pushing them back as he thrusts into her. They move together like one being.

The hoarse, primitive sounds emanating from them wake an intense feeling inside me. I can't stop staring. Their tandem motions are so lovely. Ever since Elisa turned up on the island, I've had sex with her so many times in my fantasies. The pressure against my pants becomes unbearable, and I'm just about to slip a hand down there when I'm interrupted by the sound of a motorcycle. I think it's the guard at first, but when I glance over my shoulder I see it's Father. It seems so improbable. Father always sleeps in late. What's more, he's on his way here, to the Hole. But then I know who's behind this.

Quickly, silently, I retreat into the bushes and hide behind a tree.

I hear the sound of the motorcycle braking, the kickstand coming down, steps so close that I almost piss myself in fear.

I can see Father now, in front of the Hole. He opens the door and sees them. I expect him to shout, fly into a rage, but he only watches them for a moment with a look of amusement.

'Come out here, you little shit,' he says in a frosty voice.

Didrik comes out, holding a pair of underpants over his willy. The blow comes so fast I hardly comprehend what's happening. Suddenly Didrik is on his back on the ground. He whimpers and snuffles like a little kid.

'It would have been one thing if you were fucking her properly, but that looked terrible,' Father says. 'You stay here.'

Elisa's face pops up in the doorway. She blinks in confusion at the light.

'And you, my lovely, have truly made it through your first few weeks here marvellously,' Father says, his voice dripping with sarcasm. 'Get dressed and report to my office. Seems you haven't realized who's the boss around here.'

I take a few steps back, hunkering down, trying to make myself invisible. Father doesn't see me. He's already back on the motorcycle; he starts it and takes off.

From my hiding place I watch the confusion that ensues. Didrik stands up, dizzy, his face full of tears. Elisa comes out, hastily dressed and terrified.

'Obey him!' Didrik says. 'You have to obey him right now.'

Elisa nods and starts for the manor house. Didrik goes into the shed.

I know he'll be staying there for a while, and I hope I won't have to be the one to watch over him.

I quickly sneak back to the dorm. The room rests in a mild sunny haze. Everyone is asleep except for Vic, who shoots me a triumphant look. Quiet as a mouse, I take off my clothes and crawl into bed.

The next day, Didrik and Elisa's seats are empty. Karsten comes to inform us that Didrik has been relegated to the Hole, but he can't yet say why. Hugo is sent to guard Didrik, and I give a sigh of relief.

For two weeks, Elisa's seat remains empty. No one dares to ask where she is. We don't even dare to talk about it. When she shows up again, everything about her has changed. She looks like she just woke up in the middle of a hurricane, totally destroyed. She gathers her things from the classroom, doesn't speak to us, and vanishes from ViaTerra the same day. We never see her again.

After this turmoil, Father's secretary presents us with a new policy. There's already a ViaTerra rule against having sex unless you live together, but this policy spells everything out clearly. Over the coming days, we must learn to recite the words by heart. I don't think I'll ever forget them.

POLICY CONCERNING SEXUAL RELATIONS IN VIATERRA

ViaTerra is an elite group and accordingly we must always strive for strong ethics and moral standards. These are the rules concerning sexual relations in ViaTerra and they are applicable to all staff as well as cadets in Earth's Children.

1. ViaTerra staff are prohibited from having sex with one another if they are not married.
2. Women reside in their own dormitories which men may not enter, and vice versa.
3. The staff are prohibited from having sexual relations with guests.

4. No heavy petting is permitted among staff who are not married.

Masturbation is a pathetic pursuit and a distraction from the greater purpose of ViaTerra. Organizations that permit promiscuous behaviour always fall apart. If you would like to prevent ViaTerra from fulfilling its goals, break these rules.

And then we'll know what you're trying to do.

Franz Oswald von Bärensten
Founder

I feel demoralized when I read the policy. In recent days, I've been caught in a haze of sexual lust. Every day my groin feels tight and I get hard down there. There's no controlling it. It might happen when Sara goes to the whiteboard to solve a math problem and her skirt slips up to reveal her thighs. Or when Livia bends down and I catch a glimpse of her panties. I start to feel nervous when I'm around girls. They smell so good; they have those round bottoms and small breasts. The worst part isn't what happens to my body, but what goes on in my brain. I start to have intrusive thoughts about going into the girls' dorm 'by mistake' and catching a glimpse of one naked. I constantly fantasize about having sex for real. Now nothing can come of this until I get married. Get married? It sounds so unreal. Sometimes I dream about a girl and wake to an explosion in my crotch, which makes me feel both fantastic and ashamed.

But worst of all are my critical thoughts about Father. I know what he did to Mama. I can only imagine what he did to Elisa. It seems unbelievable that he wrote a policy that keeps us from having sex. Our sex ed. The way he looks at the girls. I can't make it make sense. Are these rules only for us underlings? As a leader, maybe a person has the right to do whatever he likes. Maybe that's true out in the real world, too.

23

The call from the publisher came a few days after Sofia's discovery of the surveillance camera in Julia's bathroom. The woman on the line said they liked her manuscript and wanted to meet with her as soon as possible.

The knowledge that the book would finally be released made life bearable again.

She had handed the camera over to the police, who had come to search the house for more cameras but found nothing. The officer managing the case suggested that Julia had installed the camera herself. He said there didn't seem to be any other explanation, assuming no one else in the family had wanted to keep her under observation. This disgusting dig prompted Sofia to forget about the police and solve the mystery on her own.

Her driving force nowadays was all her terrible suspicions.

Maybe it *was* Julia who put up the camera. In recent days, Sofia had seen something new in her daughter's eyes, a dreamy look that hadn't been there before. Sofia found her staring into space sometimes. And then there was the email, which she'd never gotten a response to. Even so, she couldn't bring herself to pester Julia; that would lead nowhere. Instead she found reasons to chat with her as often as she could, trying to give Julia an opportunity to open up.

Sofia thought about Ellis. He had started spending time with them again just before the camera showed up, and Ellis had done some awfully perverted things back in the day. But the idea that he could be working for Franz was unthinkable. She quickly ruled out Simon, Benjamin and Anna. They had no reason to look at Julia naked. Sofia's friend Maggie had also turned up right around the same time as the camera. She worked at the library, and they'd once been in the same book club. Maggie had been rather pushy when they ran into each other. But Sofia couldn't help smiling at the thought of Maggie, a librarian on Orust for the past twenty years, sneaking around their house putting up cameras. It was a bizarre thought. And Peder Santos hadn't been there and couldn't have installed the camera.

At last she decided to look the truth in the eye. It had to be Matt and Julia. She decided to have a one-on-one talk with Matt as soon as she got the chance.

A few days later, Sofia was on the train to Stockholm for a meeting with her publisher. Something as simple as this – sitting alone on a train while the barren winter landscape flew by outside – was liberating. She had developed an uncomfortable amount of paranoia inside the house, always on the lookout for cameras or intruders, or something even worse. She really needed to get away for a while.

The meeting with the publisher, an enthusiastic young woman named Louise Ringvall, went well. They signed the contract and discussed the release schedule and marketing plan for the book. There was just one thing they couldn't agree on.

'Listen,' Louise said. 'How would you feel about doing a couple of media appearances alongside Franz Oswald? He's always a crowd-puller, after all.'

'I wouldn't be comfortable with that,' Sofia said, with no hesitation whatsoever.

'I got the impression that you two were pretty close these days.'

'No, we sure aren't. I don't want anything to do with him.'

Louise frowned in concern.

'Well, think about it before you make up your mind. It would increase sales considerably.'

Sofia promised to consider it; she didn't want to seem media shy in front of Louise. But she already knew she would never agree to appear with Franz on TV.

Still, when the meeting was over, she was exhilarated. Her life was turning around. Her book would finally come out, and it would probably sell a decent number of copies. And the rebuilding of the shelter had begun. She was surrounded by friends. Besides, it would soon be spring.

Benjamin picked her up at the train station. When they arrived home and she opened the front door, everything was different. The house felt like its old self again, free of cameras and intruders. It was as though all the misery had aired out while she was away. All at once, she was sure a new period of her life had begun.

The next day, Louise Ringvall called early in the morning.

'I just wanted to let you know you should watch *Morning Hour* today,' she said. 'It starts at nine. Franz Oswald is a guest.'

'I'm not all that interested in his goings-on.'

'No, I understand that, but I heard from a reliable source that he's going to mention your book.'

All the good energy Sofia had just regained faded a little.

'What? How can he do that? It hasn't even come out yet.'

'He can basically say whatever he wants in an interview like this. Don't worry. I'm sure it will be positive.'

Sofia hung up and called for Benjamin, who was working from home that day, and they decided to watch the program together.

Sure enough, Franz was a guest on *Morning Hour.* There

he was, wearing all blue – his suit, shirt and tie were different shades – sporting a confident look, and manspreading all over the sofa. The host, star reporter Sandra Malik, was about to interview him.

First there was some small talk. Sofia noticed that Sandra Malik's eyes went a little dewy when she looked at Franz.

'What does it take for you to leave your comfort zone?' she asked.

'I don't have a comfort zone, I always feel secure.'

'But what drives you? Where do you get your energy?'

Franz leaned towards Sandra Malik, and there was that blinding smile.

'Making new connections with interesting people. There's nothing I enjoy better than a new, captivating relationship. And I don't mean only with women, I mean with people in general.'

'Really? Rumour has it you've never had a serious relationship with a woman.'

'But it's not true. There was somebody, a long time ago. She was very special, but she…' He paused as if to collect himself. 'That is, things didn't end well between us. Now my focus is almost entirely on ViaTerra. There's no room for a long-term relationship in my life.'

He turned to one of the cameras. 'It takes a lot of devotion to ViaTerra to tolerate me. That's what I work on, night and day.'

And with that, he will have recruited a hundred new members, Sofia thought. *Why am I even watching this?*

'But now I want to discuss something more important,' Franz said, picking up a stack of papers from the coffee table. 'This!'

She knew immediately that it was a manuscript. *Her manuscript.*

'I've begun a collaboration with a competent author called Sofia Bauman. She has written an excellent book about my family history. *The Family on Fog Island*, it's called. It's a tragic story that begins with a fire at the manor house where I was born, where ViaTerra is headquartered these days. But despite all the tragedies, the book proves that something good can always be born out of evil. We got right back up again the second time the manor house burned, too, and now we're stronger than ever.'

Franz went on and on about ViaTerra's successes, but Sandra Malik didn't seem particularly keen on advertising ViaTerra's teachings on TV and quickly steered the conversation elsewhere. Franz was polite about it. He listened intently when she spoke, even more intently than was necessary. Sofia looked at the clock and realized that the program would be over soon, so she turned off the TV.

Benjamin hadn't said a word.

At first, Sofia was speechless and simply stared straight ahead.

'You don't think... he wasn't talking about you, was he? That relationship,' Benjamin said at last.

'Oh, lay off. We didn't have a *relationship.* That's just a sob story he always squeezes in to make sure the stupid women watching believe they have a chance. How can he talk about my book like that? Without permission from me or the publisher?'

'Are you surprised?'

'Yeah, actually, I am. It's disgusting how he twists everything to his advantage. He's at least as perverse as his father and grandfather before him, in the book. Now he's a damn rockstar. I have to break off contact with him entirely.'

'Sure, you can say that, and I've been saying you should do that all along, but it doesn't seem like it will be that simple now. Although maybe you could sneak a chapter about the rape into the book.'

'That would only end in a legal battle, and I don't want to drag Julia into this. There has to be some other way to make him stop. I'll just have to call him and give him what-for.'

'Go for it, but don't get angry. He gets off on it. Don't get caught up in his smooth talk. Just tell him you want to handle the release of the book on your own.'

She pondered her book project for a long time. Why was it so important to her; why couldn't she just put it aside? No matter what she did, it seemed like Franz always swooped in and hogged all the attention. But people could think whatever they wanted – this book wasn't about Franz, it was about the women. Some stubborn part of her refused to give up. The book was redress for all the women Franz and his forefathers had enacted violence upon.

She held off on calling him for a few hours, and then he didn't answer his phone. She forced herself to leave a polite message on his voicemail.

When he called back a few hours later, he sounded annoyed.

'What do you want?'

She recognized that tone of voice immediately. He was upset about something else entirely and would take it out on her if she made a misstep.

'I want you to stop talking about my book and let me handle the release.'

'Did you really think you could publish a book about *my* family without any participation on my end?'

The humiliation of having to maintain a calm tone was starting to eat at her. This was just like being back in his office. Fawning to put him in a good mood.

'Yeah, I did. I don't need your help.'

'Did you know that true success comes from humility? It wouldn't hurt you to be a little more humble, Sofia. For God's sake, put your old demons aside. Are you capable of that?'

'I can sell my book on my own.'

'Look, there is not a single publisher that's not on the verge of bankruptcy these days. Were you planning to leave the marketing to them?'

'I'm planning to work with my publisher to sell as many copies as I can. Just like any other author.'

'That sounds awfully boring. Do you remember my grandmother's last words in the family history? She wrote that she was going to give it to me. That she trusted me to spread her story. I will sell hundreds of thousands of books for you, Sofia. There's nothing you can do about it.'

The bitter irony in the fact that the bastard who had tormented her for so long was now telling her off swept away her forced politeness.

'Shut up and listen to me!' she shouted. 'Stop trying to control my life and drop anything that has to do with my book. Do not contact me again. Ever!'

This time, he was the one who hung up.

Later that night, finding herself unable to let go of her irritation at Franz, she called Ellis.

'I need your help – I'm desperate, and I think you're the only one who can help me.'

'What do you need?'

'I want you to dig through Franz's business dealings. Go deep, use whatever illegal methods it takes. I'll pay.'

'Oh, you don't have to give me any money. Of course I'll help you out.'

'There has to be something unsavoury I can use to make him leave me alone.'

'So you're declaring war?'

'Yes, this is war,' she said, and she realized the words made her feel better.

24

Julia's birthday was fast approaching, but her family didn't celebrate birthdays the traditional way, with cake and parties. Instead, they usually made a day trip somewhere to do something fun. This year, though, Julia didn't feel like it. A very different kind of trip was calling her name – the one Franz had suggested. The one to Fog Island.

She thought of him often. It was her last semester of compulsory school. She really ought to be focusing on her work. Instead, she used her upcoming graduation as an excuse to hang out in her room and read about Franz online. She watched all of his live webcasts and TV interviews. She really wasn't all that interested in his philosophy, but she found him fascinating to look at. That bright voice and intense gaze. You just had to believe whatever he said. He radiated honesty.

Some nights, she made up excuses not to see Matt, which made her feel guilty.

Never before had she been so incapable of controlling her emotions.

Never before had she felt so affected by another person.

She wondered if Franz Oswald had hypnotic powers. She was constantly recalling parts of their date. Remembering the moment he pulled out her chair and a lock of hair fell over his forehead. Why did that image keep popping up over and over? She never dreamed about romantic stuff. It was all about sex.

Be careful what you wish for, Mom liked to say in a teasing voice.

It was so pathetic to listen to Mom talking about Franz, all that never-ending whining. Mom, who had once been an incurable optimist, had started to take a pessimistic view of life. She would hit the roof if she found out about Julia's meeting with Franz. So Julia had no choice but to lie. Mom was smarter than most, totally resistant to flattery, and not very easy to fool.

But the same was not true of Dad.

Suddenly something happened to put Julia's mind on another track. Matt disappeared. One week before her birthday, he waved her over after school and said he was going to be travelling for a while. When she asked him where he was going, and how long he'd be gone, he answered evasively.

'What do you mean? You know where you're going, right?'

'It's something my parents planned, I don't know more about it.'

'Will you be back for my birthday?'

'I can't make any promises.'

'Well, will you come back at all?'

'I hope so.'

He looked strange. Not nearly as easy-going as he usually was. He seemed serious and concerned. No matter how much she pushed, he wouldn't give her any real answers. He said he would text and call as often as he could, but he couldn't even promise that much.

In the following days, she missed Matt so much she stopped thinking about Franz entirely. She was almost sure that Matt's disappearance was punishment for her lying to him.

In school, she functioned on autopilot. She almost stopped

eating and had trouble sleeping at night. Several times a day she would call and text Matt. But there wasn't a single response.

Eventually she decided to talk to the headmaster, who would say nothing beyond that Matt was dealing with some important family matters for an undetermined amount of time.

She wasn't in love with Matt, was she? The whole time they were together she had been sure he was just a fun way to pass the time. But now that he was gone, she missed him so much she was going crazy.

When Matt had been gone for five days, a message arrived. She had her inbox open; there was a chime and at the top she saw the name *Matt Larsen*. She hesitated a moment before opening the email.

Coming back soon.

That was all.

She hit 'reply' and wrote a long email to chew him out for not being in touch and to accuse him of all sorts of things. Then she deleted it all and wrote, 'When?'

No response arrived that day. The silence prompted suspicion inside her. What did she really know about Matt? He almost never talked about his family. He often said he wanted to make it on his own and only spent time with them when it was necessary. And now they were suddenly more important than she was?

The next day was a Friday, the day before her birthday. The family was going to Gothenburg for the whole day and would stay at a hotel. Julia had felt positive Matt wouldn't show up, and she tried to convince herself she didn't care. But in reality, it felt like the saddest birthday ever.

When she got home from school, his car was parked outside her house. He must have spotted her through the window, because he came out to the yard to greet her. Even though she could tell his eyes were full of guilt, she decided to yell at him.

'I'm sorry, my mom was super sick!' he said before she could open her mouth.

'Why didn't you say anything?'

'She made me promise not to talk about it. She's feeling better now.'

A quick shadow passed over his face. Maybe it was concern, or maybe it was something he wasn't telling her. But he did seem genuinely sad. She wondered if he was lying, but for the moment it didn't matter. She had gotten her explanation.

It turned out to be a good birthday after all. After a day in Gothenburg with her family, she and Matt were the only ones to stay overnight. Mom said they had to get home to work, but Julia knew they wanted to give her some time alone with Matt.

As soon as they walked into their hotel room, they tore each other's clothes off. They had sex on the floor, on the bed, on the sofa, and in the shower, totally insane and full of throbbing, insatiable lust.

Later, once they'd caught their breath, they lay beside each other on the huge bed and she fell asleep with her head on his shoulder.

When she woke up, daylight was peeking through the blinds. She was a little sore down there but felt perfectly content and at ease. Matt's face rested on the pillow beside her. She moved so close that she could feel his shallow breathing against her cheek. Her heart constricted with love and gratitude that he had made it so good for her.

After that weekend, everything felt normal again. Matt was back. They saw each other each night and she could focus on her schoolwork again. She had decided that what she felt for Franz was a passing fancy. The feelings she had for Matt were real. Maybe even long-lasting.

But late one night, Franz called.

She had just crawled into bed. Her phone rang and she saw his number on the screen. She almost fell to pieces. Guilty feelings towards Matt washed over her, but she couldn't stop herself from answering.

'I was thinking about how your neck felt against my lips,' Franz began the call.

She couldn't produce a sound.

'I've figured out how we can spend a few days together this spring. Maybe in early May,' he continued.

'Okay...' she said hesitantly.

Silence settled between them. It was so protracted that it felt as if he had disappeared.

'Are you there?'

'Yes, I'm sorry,' he said. 'Sometimes it takes my breath away to think about you. There was such a strong attraction between us when we met. That's how I remember it. Am I wrong?'

'No, I suppose not,' Julia said quickly.

'Do you want to come see me on the island?'

Another pause before she could respond.

'I don't think it's right. And I like Matt so much.'

'One doesn't rule out the other. And he never needs to know. Say yes, Julia. I know you feel the same, that this is something we have to do. Or else we'll never stop thinking about each other.'

Julia's body felt warm. Her heart began to pound. She did want to do this, even if it was forbidden – or maybe for that very reason.

'Okay.'

'Good. I'll send you an email later. It will come from an unknown sender.'

'How can you be so sure I won't tell my parents about this?'

'You're welcome to, but if you do our chances of meeting are probably zero. I have to go now. Keep an eye out for my email.'

She stared into space for a long time after the call. The pattern on her wallpaper faded; it was like she was gazing into a spotty fog. Eventually she realized she was squeezing her phone so tight her hand hurt.

In Earth's Children, when we turned sixteen, we were expected to work as staff in ViaTerra. This rule, instituted by Father, immediately became a headache for him. His relationship with the ViaTerra staff had hit rock bottom. He gave them funny nicknames and joked about them whenever he was in a decent mood. On his bad days, he would fling so many curses about them that he nearly frothed at the mouth.

Time and again he complained that the staff were his greatest burden. Worse than all the media scandals, more time-consuming than his research and lectures. We could see from our section of the property that the number of people in Penance was growing. The faces of those sent there were pale, haggard and grim. They seemed to exist in a state of anxiety, or actual fear for some of them. I wondered what they'd done to deserve it.

But Father thought Earth's Children was fantastic. Accordingly, he didn't want us to mix with the staff. His solution was to create a brand-new unit for us in ViaTerra.

It all happened in the span of one day.

This was always the way of it, when Father made a decision. Everything had to happen now, *as fast as possible.*

He sent everyone who worked in the staff unit of ViaTerra to Penance. In the directive he sent out it said that he was still the only one on the whole property who upheld ethical norms.

At the same time, everyone over sixteen in Earth's Children was moved to the staff unit's empty offices.

Vic and I were still fifteen, but we got to come along anyway.

We were given new uniforms, the same as the ViaTerra staff, but with a special emblem: a large, gold V and T, embroidered on a black background.

With our new haircuts, pressed uniforms, freshly polished shoes, and Father's complete confidence, we felt mildly euphoric.

Father came by to give a short speech that evening.

'Now we will discuss fraternizing with the enemy,' he began. 'The moment you participate in the ViaTerra staff's indolence, or listen to their damn whining, you have become one of them. If you sit beside them in the cafeteria, accept gum from them, or take a single drag from their cigarettes when they're sneaking a smoke, you automatically become a loser, just like them. And if you let them get away with having bad breath or body odour, you will soon be just as slovenly as they are. Never offer them a kind look. Always speak to them coldly. Never mix with them. They are worse than the others, *because I once trusted them and they betrayed me.'*

Here he paused and, for some reason, fixed his eyes on me. I mustered my most innocent expression, and he turned to Vic.

'Believe me – they will fawn over you, flatter you, and try to ingratiate themselves with you. This is all on purpose. But you won't fall for their brown-nosing. From this moment on, you are my messengers. Everything they do to you is done to me. Everything they say to you is said to me. You are my eyes and ears. You will enforce my rules and enact my directives. Never forget that.'

I stepped into this new role with great hesitation. But I couldn't bear the thought of the alternative, which was being sent off to Penance with the shattered ViaTerra staff.

So I decided to adapt as best I could.

Since the blow of all sex being forbidden, a terrible thought had gone round and round in my head.

This is your life. This is how it's going to be until you die.

25

It was the end of February, and each morning they awoke to the sound of rain. Sometimes there was a heavy, sleety snowfall that never stuck on the ground. Sofia longed for the sun to return. It was tedious to watch the construction workers trudging around in the mud and slush. But the construction was going as planned, slowly but surely.

When she wasn't at the worksite, she kept herself busy with the book. An editor at the publishing house was working on her manuscript and Sofia was in touch with her daily.

Late one afternoon, while she was home alone and waiting for an email from the editor, a different email turned up instead. She had almost forgotten about the anonymous message regarding Julia. But now she received a response. It was written in the same red italics as the first email.

She has dangerous connections, was all it said.

That particular feeling came over again. It crawled over her skin like a shudder. *I know the person who wrote this*, she thought, and all at once she was sure it was true. She didn't know how she could be so certain, but she was. It felt like the sender was there in the room with her, an invisible but palpable presence. The creepy-crawly feeling had spread to her neck. She hunched her shoulders in an attempt to shake off the feeling and clicked on 'reply'.

With who? That was all, and she sent off the email.

Answer me now, she thought, *just give me one clue*. But her inbox remained empty all evening.

She knew she needed to have a serious talk with Julia, but she'd learned a few things about sixteen-year-old girls. They were caught between two different worlds. They still hadn't entered the adult world, yet they had left the world where you believe your parents are superheroes and feel certain everything will work out as soon as you have a good cry in your mother's arms. Although Julia gave the impression of being tough and independent, that gap between worlds made her fragile. Moreover, she longed for drama and excitement. If life wouldn't deliver it to her, she would search it out herself. And the hormones rushing through Julia's body were more powerful than a thousand admonitions.

She wasn't shy in the least and could blurt out the most shocking things. So if she was lying about something, she must have a good reason. It had to be something she didn't think Sofia or Benjamin could handle hearing. Or something she believed would flat-out hurt them. And if Julia thought something might hurt her parents, there was nothing she couldn't keep a secret.

As Sofia sat at her laptop, once again waiting for a response to her email, she made up her mind. She would put the screws on Julia, tell her about the email and really squeeze the truth out of her. But if she didn't get anywhere with that, she wouldn't hesitate to snoop on her daughter's phone.

The ringing of her own mobile woke her from her reverie. It was Ellis.

'Hey, I did some digging, like you asked me to,' he said. 'I've been rooting through Franz's finances, but I couldn't find anything of note. He's totally loaded, but we knew that already. ViaTerra is very much in the black and he had that inheritance from his dad. He's got a ton of cash stashed abroad, but what capitalist pig doesn't, these days? I did find one thing that might be of interest, though. Have you heard of something called Earth's Children?'

'Kind of. It's some sort of school Franz runs for the children of his followers. He gave us a tour while we were on the island. Just empty buildings – he'd sent the kids off somewhere.'

'Interesting. I found a blog post from a girl called Elisa Bonelli. It's long since deleted, and it was written a couple years ago, but the internet is forever, if you know where to look. In any case, this girl said she was with Earth's Children for a month but was sent home. She claimed Franz locked her into the manor house attic for three days and raped her. He did any number of horrifying things to her.'

Sofia disappeared in thought for a moment. The word 'rape' brought on a stream of unpleasant memories. This fit in all too well with her own experiences.

'Are you there, Sofia?'

'Yes, sorry, this is a bit of a shock. It sounds just like Franz. How old is the girl?'

'She was fifteen when it happened. Why do you think she took down the post?'

'If her parents are members of ViaTerra they might have made her. Or else Franz bribed her. Do you think you can find a phone number or email address so I can contact her?'

'Definitely. I've got her email. I'll send it your way along with a copy of the blog post, so you can read it for yourself.'

'This is good, Ellis. If it's true, we've got something concrete to accuse Franz of. Thanks for being so amazing.'

'It was nothing. This is a good start, and I'll keep looking.'

*

As Sofia read the blog post, she was flooded with both disgust and triumph. Elisa Bonelli wrote that her parents had sent her to Earth's Children after she had a hard time adjusting at school. They had been sure the strict atmosphere on the island would do her good. But then Franz found her having sex with another student. He ordered her to his office, took her to the attic, and had sex with her himself. The description of what Franz had done to her was full of disturbing details. He had tied her up, forced himself on her, and eventually choked her while raping her. Three days later he said he was tired of her. She had been sent to the ethics unit, where she was forced to sign a non-disclosure agreement promising not to speak out about Franz or Earth's Children. A few weeks after that, she was sent home.

Sofia searched online for Elisa Bonelli and found lots of hits, but most of them were about her parents. The Bonellis were wealthy and influential. The father had a position in the lower ranks of government and the mother owned a law firm. There was a picture of them with Franz as they accepted a statuette, some sort of recognition that they were elite members of the cult. There was also an interview with the father in which he mentioned how much the ViaTerra philosophy had helped him attain his goals in life.

The more she searched, the more certain she felt that there would be no point in contacting the Bonelli parents. But writing directly to Elisa was worth a shot. There were pictures of her online. She was strikingly beautiful, exactly Franz's type.

Sofia composed a short email to Elisa in which she introduced herself as an author, gave a brief description of the book, and said she was working on a follow-up and was interested in Earth's Children. Would Elisa consider speaking with her?

She wondered if the email would bounce back – teenagers seemed to change email addresses at the drop of a hat these days – but it didn't. She resumed her online search, so elated at the thought that she might be about to uncover something major that she hardly noticed when darkness fell. She searched Franz's name too and was immediately faced with the news that in some mind-boggling fashion he had managed to gain access to a political summit about climate change in Brussels, and that great strides had been made there. She was struck by the thought of what might happen if Franz decided to pursue a career in politics. People would almost certainly vote for him. Suddenly she was shivering so hard that she had to go get a cardigan.

Only later did she realize that Benjamin and Julia should have been home a long time ago. When she called them, Benjamin said he was stuck in a meeting in Gothenburg and was considering staying overnight. Julia was with Matt and promised to be home in an hour. Sofia felt an irresistible desire to talk to someone about Elisa Bonelli, so she called Simon, and then Anna, and told them everything. Simon encouraged her to keep snooping. Anna was more hesitant and thought it sounded risky. She felt that the girl might have read about Franz's trial, the one involving Elvira, and made the whole thing up for attention. After all, there were plenty of young girls who idolized him. Most of the time Sofia trusted Anna's judgement, but this time it felt like she was being too dismissive. It was unlike her. Still, Anna's argument made Sofia feel even more certain that Elisa's story was true. This was the very reason Franz was able to get away with so much. Women worshipped him and 'obviously made things up'. He was always alone with them during these assaults. It was always their word against his.

It was past ten o'clock before she wrapped up with Anna. The doorbell rang. She assumed Julia had forgotten her key. When she stood up to open the door, she noticed how quiet it was in the house. Somewhere in the distance an engine started, but otherwise she didn't hear a thing. When she turned the key in the lock, she was suddenly on high alert. The wind grabbed hold of the door, which slipped out of her hands and flew wide open.

It took a moment for her to recognize the man standing outside. He had changed. His bulky winter coat made him look larger. He had grown a beard and was wearing a cap on his head.

But damned if it wasn't Peder Santos.

It's hard to write about the next part I have to tell.

Because you're not going to like this.

Not one bit.

Even so, I hope you will still write to me, even if you send nothing but a string of curse words.

I'm not asking for your forgiveness. The important thing is for you to understand how everything turned out the way it did.

What it was that drove us to the cliffs on that terrible day.

And how our lives came to be intertwined.

It started with a top-secret meeting behind closed doors.

ON SECRET ASSIGNMENT

I'm roused from sleep by impatient pounding on the door, and shrill cries.

'Vic, Thor and Didrik! Vic, Thor and Didrik!' Again and again, like a broken record.

I recognize Madde's voice straight away. The women don't have access to the men's dorms, which is why she's shouting outside ours.

Didrik, who has returned from the Hole, bounces out of bed and reaches the door first, but he doesn't open it. He likes messing with Madde.

The door flies open and hits Didrik in the forehead with a bang. Madde pays no attention when he howls in pain.

'Vic, Thor and Didrik, the boss wants to see you,' she says. 'Hurry it up, he said immediately*!'*

She turns on the light and we stagger around, putting on our uniforms. Curious eyes watch us from the other bunks. When the boss calls you to a meeting in the middle of the night, it's always something big. If luck isn't on your side, you won't be back to the dorm for some time.

When we step into Father's office, the room is barely lit. For a moment I can't see him, but then I spot a shadow behind the desk. He's staring through the picture window and into the darkness outside. His eyes are on the sea, the waves rolling in in tight, white lines. I know he hears us when we come in, but he doesn't make any move to welcome us. Instead he takes a step closer to the window. He strokes his chin thoughtfully.

'You can wait outside, Didrik,' he says at last, his back still facing us. I figure this is probably for the best, given the goose egg that's appearing on Didrik's forehead.

'Sit down, boys,' Father says to us.

Father's office is like a spaceship. White walls, screens everywhere. Computers, stereo systems and printers. There are no pictures on the walls, and not even a decorative plant. It's so quiet that you become aware of your own breathing. So sterile that you notice even the faintest whiff of sweat your body is producing.

Madde, who has shooed Didrik out, stands uncertainly by the door.

'You can go too,' Father says to her. 'But turn on the light.'

Now it's just Father, Vic and me. He looks at us, letting his gaze move back and forth. Vic-Thor. Vic-Thor. He mutters something inaudible, then takes a seat at the enormous desk. There must be two metres between him and us. I try to interpret the expression on his face. He's not angry. There is some amusement in his eyes. He even seems a bit self-conscious, which has never happened before.

'There's something I need to tell you, boys.'

He gives us the long version of the story. Explaining his ethical and moral values. How he has managed to build up a fierce intolerance for sexual entanglements in ViaTerra. An organization in which people sleep together at random will eventually go under. It creates too much tension in the air and people can't think clearly. He speaks to us the same way he crafts a policy. Sometimes he pauses to make sure we're following along. Then he tells us about a woman who worked at ViaTerra a long time ago. She was very special, irresistible – no, he truly couldn't resist her, and now he has a suspicion.

There might be a child.

Vic and I startle in unison.

This is thrilling, exciting. A child. The fact that Father is being so open with us, even hinting that he might have a weakness.

'I want to know more about her, this girl,' he says. 'Without her or her parents finding out. I'm curious to know whether she's my daughter or not. That's something I will look into, but first I want some information about her. This is where you come in, Thor.'

'What about me?' Vic interrupts, before he can help himself.

Father isn't angry. He smiles and shakes his head in amusement.

'You would attract too much attention. Girls fall for you on the spot, don't they? But you, Thor, you're pretty average-looking.'

Average is fine. Better than ugly, a failure, incompetent. I can settle for being average. My pent-up hatred for Father recedes a bit. He suddenly seems so human, sitting there and telling us about his shortcomings.

'I want some pictures of her. To get an idea of what kind of person she is. Who she spends time with. What her habits are. You must try to form an understanding of her, discreetly, and then report back to me. Without her noticing you.'

He opens a folder on the desk.

'I have all the information right here. Where her school is, the places kids hang out nearby.' He pages through the documents. 'It won't be a long trip, it's basically right across the bay.'

'How old is she?' Vic asks.

'Thirteen or fourteen,' Father replies.

'But why can't someone else—' I ask hesitantly.

'Because you will look at her a very different way. Not like a private eye simply doing a job. I think you'll be more curious. You will form an understanding of the sort of person she is. Besides, you're young and can blend into her social circles without sticking out.'

He turns to Vic.

'You're here because you have just as much a right to know as Thor does.'

'But why did you ask Didrik to come?' Vic asks.

'He's going to keep an eye on Thor so he doesn't get any ideas in his head out there in so-called freedom. Didrik will make sure you fulfil my directives, Thor. You're never allowed to go on assignments alone, you know that.'

I nod, dejected, but I still feel some hope.

'But Didrik can't know the reason. That she might be my daughter. Understood?'

I muster my courage.

'What's going to happen to her in the long run, though?'

'That depends on the information you obtain. If she's a boring, spoiled brat I want nothing to do with her. I'm meticulous about the people I elect to surround myself with, and you two should be too.'

I swallow and wonder how it's even possible to choose the people around you in ViaTerra.

'Two or three days, that's all it will take. You can stay at a hotel.'

A hotel. The very word makes me shiver in anticipation. Staying at a hotel, far from the island, out in the real world. Eating real food. Maybe even a hamburger, if I can get Didrik to go along with it.

Father takes a sheet of paper from the folder and places it before me. It's a printout from the internet, a blurry photo, possibly enlarged from a class picture. A girl with long hair stares into the camera with a defiant, scornful gaze. The corners of her mouth are slightly turned down. It's clear she doesn't want to be photographed. But despite her grim expression, you can tell she's beautiful.

The girl in the photograph is you.

But I don't know that yet.

26

Sofia's first impulse, to run away from Peder Santos and hide, vanished when she looked into his sad eyes.

'I'm sorry to bother you so late,' he said. 'I've been at the police station all day, and then I tried to call, but the line was busy. I won't be able to sleep until you and I have talked. May I come in?'

Sofia let him in. Her intuition told her that the man in front of her was light years from posing any sort of threat.

She showed Santos into the living room, where he gingerly took a seat in an easy chair. He looked tired and worn out. He was scruffy and his eyelids looked heavy, probably on account of a lack of sleep.

'I've been meaning to get in touch,' he said, 'but my whole life has turned upside down. My mother was dying, in Portugal. I found out right before the storm hit, and I told one of the substitutes at the shelter that I had to go home. I'm sure he forgot to mention it to you – the storm hit, and you had other things to worry about.'

He took off his cap and thumbed it nervously.

'Then I forgot all about it, because my mother died, and then there was the funeral. When I saw online that I was wanted back here in Sweden, I was terrified, so I held off getting in touch. I didn't have anything to do with the terrible things that have happened to your family. I was with my father the whole time.'

'I believe you,' Sofia said. 'It's just that you vanished at exactly the time it all started. We got suspicious.'

'Yes, it's all so strange,' he said. 'And I apologize for lying about my address. But I didn't have a residence permit…' He looked like he was about to cry. 'I'm going to apply for one now, though,' he rushed to add.

'Of course you had to go. I'm so sorry about your mother.'

'The police questioned me about some pictures someone took of you. It wasn't me. But people were always taking photos on their phones around the shelter.'

'These were taken on an SLR camera. They were in a metal box in your shed.'

Peder was startled.

'I saw that box. It was on a shelf in the tool shed. I'm not the only one who stored things there, you know.'

'Was anyone in there often?'

He considered the question.

'No, not that I recall. I was almost always in the yard or inside the house.'

Once again, he looked despondent.

'It's okay,' she said. 'I know you aren't the one behind all this.'

'I liked working at the shelter, but I suppose there's no chance I'll get my job back, is there? You must think I'm so unreliable, to disappear like that.'

He wrung his hands anxiously.

'Of course you can have your job back, once the house is finished,' she said. 'Talk to Anna, and she'll take care of everything. But you'll have to get your residence permit in order first, of course.'

Peder Santos gave a sigh of relief.

He left the house soon after.

Now there were no suspects at all in the increasingly hopeless case.

The next day, she was supposed to meet Simon and Anna at the construction site. Just as she was getting into her car, her phone rang. It was Louise Ringvall from the publishing house.

'Get a load of this!' she chirped. 'I just had a call from Carmen Gardell, Franz Oswald's head of PR. Do you know her?'

Sofia had a sinking feeling.

'I know of her. What did she want?'

'They had a fantastic idea! Franz Oswald has offered to hold a release party for your book, at the manor house, right where all the action takes place! He promises there will be a guided tour of the estate. They're going to invite a bunch of celebrities, and—'

'You'll have to excuse me,' Sofia interrupted, 'but it feels as though Franz Oswald is taking over the whole release of my book. I don't like it.'

'But you have to recognize what an opportunity this is! You'll sell hundreds of books there, and the news of the book will spread through celebrity circles. I know it's difficult, but can't you try to keep your personal feelings out of it? For the sake of the book?'

Sofia felt like an idiot; she was tongue-tied.

'We took for granted that you would take advantage of your acquaintance with him when we decided to publish this book,' Louise went on. 'He's a great resource.'

'The book is about how his forefathers abused and raped women. He is exactly the same. That's the issue,' Sofia said.

Louise didn't say anything for a moment.

'But I thought… Didn't that happen almost twenty years ago? From what I understand, that girl was mentally unstable and committed suicide a long time ago. Isn't that the woman he had children with? They lived together afterwards. How do you know she wasn't making the whole thing up?'

Sofia resisted the urge to hang up on Louise. She emphasized that she had no intention of having her release party on Fog Island. They ended the call.

Now she was so enraged that she could hardly think clearly. She let herself consider the possibility of forgetting about the book, of getting out of all this. But she had once made a silent promise to Sigrid von Bärensten that she would bring her tragic story to light.

She called Franz, got his voicemail, and left a message:

'Leave me, my family, and the book alone, or else I will take action.'

She didn't have the slightest idea what that action might be, but still.

For the rest of the day, she had to repress the idea of that stupid release party. With the foundation laid, the construction of the shelter was rapidly moving forward. All traces of the storm on the property were erased. The house was growing; it was like it had always been part of its surroundings. It clearly belonged there.

That night, she went out to eat with Benjamin, Anna and Simon. All day she avoided her phone, which she had turned off and stashed in a pocket of her purse.

When she opened her inbox, she saw that she'd received a response from Elisa Bonelli. Her heart skipped a beat. Elisa wrote that she wasn't at liberty to talk about what had happened at ViaTerra; she had signed an NDA. Would Sofia be willing to talk to her on condition of anonymity? She had included a phone number, which Sofia dialled immediately despite the late hour.

Elisa Bonelli was still hesitant to agree to a meeting. She whispered into the phone and sounded uncertain, but Sofia managed to convince her to meet the next day – in Gothenburg, where Elisa lived.

'It would be a relief to talk about it,' Elisa said at last. 'But you have to promise not to tell anyone else what I say.'

When Sofia got to the café where they would meet, she spotted Elisa immediately. A single glance, and she just knew everything Elisa had written was true. Not only was she beautiful, she had a radiance that overshadowed everyone else in the crowded café. Honey-blonde hair. Big eyes with long eyelashes. She was thin, with large breasts. Just Franz's type.

They ordered a whole carafe of coffee. Elisa glanced around nervously.

'You're not recording this, right? You really, really can't. If my parents found out I was talking to you… They've said from the start that I was making it all up. When I wrote that blog post, oh my God, they were convinced I was only doing it for attention. There were no marks, no proof.'

Once Sofia had promised not to spread Elisa's story any further, Elisa began to talk, her voice a half whisper. The beginning of the tale was what Sofia had read in the blog post, but then the descriptions grew more detailed.

'The first time, it was okay. You have to understand, I was crazy about him. I had hoped I would be the one to hook him, but it ended up the other way around.'

She dropped her head into her hands for a moment.

'He saw me having sex with another guy from Earth's Children. He caught us in the act, it was so embarrassing. We were a little crazy, really going at it. Franz took me to the attic and said that what we had been doing was amateurish. That there were ways to prolong the pleasure, and he would show me. He made it good for me that first time. He was thoughtful, almost passionate. But then, the second time, it was like he had lost interest.'

'What do you mean?'

'Like, you know, he couldn't get it up.'

'What?'

'For real. And then he was furious, as if it was my fault. He tied me up and choked me, and when I got scared he was suddenly hard as a fucking baton. It went on like that for two days. Then he kept me prisoner in a room for a few weeks, with a guard. Probably so the bruises would fade.'

She paused to collect herself.

'Even so, when I got home I told my parents what had happened and wrote that blog post, but they were so mad at me. They're elite members of ViaTerra. Soon Franz called them to a meeting out on Fog Island and when they came back they were convinced I was a pathological liar and I had hallucinated the whole thing.'

Tears trickled down her cheeks.

'That was over two years ago now, and I still have nightmares almost every night. Guys aren't much fun anymore. It's like I've lost that spark. I don't give a shit about what happened to me anymore, but I don't want it to happen to anyone else. That's why I agreed to talk to you.'

Sofia had covered Elisa's hand with her own without really realizing it.

'Look, Elisa, there was this one thing you said. A pig who needs to abuse a woman in order to get it up… wouldn't you say that makes him…'

'Impotent!' Elisa blurted.

They looked at each other in astonishment.

'Exactly!' Sofia said. 'Isn't that just it?'

Out of nowhere, an old memory from ViaTerra popped into her mind. They were meant to be planning how to make life hard for a journalist who had written unfavourably about Franz. He was in a meeting with the director of ethics and Sofia had stuck around, as usual. You were never allowed to go to bed before Franz.

If you take two stories, or more, and mix them together, the result is both an absolute truth and a complete lie, Franz had said. *It's confusing, and extremely effective.*

Sofia turned to Elisa, who was twisting a lock of her hair and staring vacantly into space.

'Listen, I think I've thought of a way to help you without using your name or even your whole story,' Sofia said.

By the time they went their separate ways, the carafe of coffee was empty and it was getting dark. But they had a plan, and it made Sofia excited and nervous all at once. She would write a story that was based on Elisa's tale, but which included details about Franz from her own unpleasant experiences with him.

When she got home, Benjamin was at the kitchen island, making something that smelled very garlicky. She snuck up to him and gave him a long hug from behind. At first she was going to tell him about her plan, but she decided to wait until she'd made that phone call. There was always the chance Benjamin would try to talk her out of it.

She tossed her purse and car keys on the coffee table, sank into an easy chair, and dialled Ellis's number.

'I need your help again!' she said, almost before he picked up.

'Anything. I like digging up dirt on Franz Oswald.'

'I'm going to write an anonymous blog post for a women's shelter website. I don't know which one yet. You have to help me make it go viral. And once that's done, the post will spread on its own.'

'Is it about Franz?'

'Who else?'

'Look, I don't want to kill your enthusiasm, but that won't have any effect on him. He's totally immune to all the rumours that spread about him.'

'Not this one,' she said confidently. 'This one, he's going to take seriously.'

27

Just when Julia thought the day couldn't get any worse, she saw the news online.

It had been raining all afternoon, a constant downpour that Julia watched angrily from her classroom. At times the raindrops were the size of hailstones. There wasn't even the tiniest crack in the heavy, steel-grey clouds that hung over the school. The chances this rain would stop were zero. She was supposed to go on an outing with Matt, but this had put an end to it. Class dragged on.

When she got home, Mom basically threw herself at Julia like a hyena on the hunt. Julia knew right away that a long interrogation awaited her. She desperately looked around the house for someone else, but it was empty.

Mom had been looking secretive over the past few days. She had gone from being stressed and pessimistic to suddenly in a good mood. There was no exasperating her now. The objects Julia strewed about, her occasionally provocative clothing, always coming home past curfew – none of this was bothering Mom at the moment. All of a sudden she was frighteningly vivacious and efficient.

And when Julia got home on this day, Mom had that piercing look.

'I just wanted to talk a little, come have a seat,' she said, patting the cushion beside her on the sofa.

But the cheerfulness in her voice didn't sound genuine. This was going to be a cross-examination.

'What did you want to talk about?'

'Just some small talk, is all.'

She is nowhere near as good at lying as I am, Julia thought. *The second she gets me on that sofa, the probing questions will rain down on me.*

Julia slowly sat down at a comfortable distance, but Mom moved closer.

'What is it you're not telling me?' she asked, pinning her gaze on Julia.

'What?'

'I got this email.'

Julia felt her body tense. She grabbed at the fabric of the sofa.

'What email?'

'It said you were lying to me.'

Julia was flooded with relief and let out a laugh. Mom still believed all the crap people wrote online.

'That's not news, is it? I always have done.'

'It said you had dangerous connections.'

'What does that even mean, Mom, "connections"? This is crazy!'

'Look me in the eyes and tell me you're not involved in anything dangerous. Some kind of criminal gang, drug abuse, what do I know?'

She turned to look at her mother. It was perfectly simple to meet her gaze. She didn't even have to try to muster up an innocent look.

'I'm so not interested in drugs or criminal gangs.'

She pouted stubbornly and held her mother's gaze without blinking once.

'Come on, Julia. Who would send me something like that?'

'Some jealous idiot, how should I know?'

'I can tell that there's something you're not telling me.'

'Fine. I had sex with Matt. More than once.'

Mom's eyes went wide.

'Unprotected?'

'No, you're the one who got me the pill, or did you forget?'

Their eyes were locked. Julia refused to look away. She saw Mom relax a bit, back down from this battle just a smidge. Julia immediately turned this to her advantage.

'I know you've been worried about me ever since the attack, and I get it. But even so, I want to have a private life, without you snooping around. You didn't use to be like this. You used to trust me.'

Mom leaned back on the sofa, rested her head on the edge, and gazed at the ceiling.

'I still trust you, sweetie. But you're growing up too fast. I can't handle it. Now, be honest. Were you and Matt the ones who installed that camera in your bathroom?'

'No.'

'Okay. I believe you. Is there anything else you're not telling me?'

'There's tons of stuff I'm not telling you, but you have to learn to accept it.'

Just then, Dad came home and Julia was saved, at least temporarily. She didn't say much during dinner, instead recalling her conversation with Mom, and she realized that she actually hadn't lied at all. It was just that Mom was asking the wrong questions.

After dinner, as they were relaxing on the sofa, everything felt like it was back to normal. Julia decided to go to her room and surf the internet. When she was halfway up the stairs, she heard Mom's phone ring. She crouched down on the step, immediately curious. She could see Mom down there, flashing Dad a triumphant smile and placing the phone on the coffee table before she answered on speaker.

At first, Julia didn't recognize Franz's voice, which was transformed by rage. He immediately began shouting so loudly the speaker crackled. She couldn't make out his words. His roaring voice echoed through the room like thunder. Mom just sat there, staring at the phone with a grin on her face. The angry vibrations seemed to cause the phone to jump around on the coffee table, but maybe that was just an illusion. He shouted until he was hoarse, and ended with some kind of threat:

'I will crush you,' was what it sounded like.

Not until he was quiet did Mom pick up the phone and hold it close to her face.

'Nice to hear your true self again after all these years,' she said. 'I think you should be able to get psychological help for that little problem of yours.'

Someone hung up – whether it was Mom or Franz, Julia couldn't tell.

The house was quiet now, so quiet that the creak of her weight on the stairs was audible. She shrank back, trying to make herself invisible, and snuck to her room. Something inside her sensed that the conversation Mom and Dad were about to have wasn't something she needed to eavesdrop on. She was sure she would be able to find some clue about Franz's meltdown online.

But she didn't even have to put in the effort to search for it, because Laura had already texted her a link to an article. *Look at this!*

A wave of nausea came over her as soon as she read the headline.

Anonymous woman's warning:

FRANZ OSWALD IS VIOLENT AND IMPOTENT

It was a short article, an interview with a twenty-one-year-old woman who had decided to speak out about an assault that had taken place a few years earlier. She had met Franz at a lecture and been charmed. He'd invited her to come to Fog Island for a free course on ViaTerra and almost immediately made sexual advances. But the sex had turned out to be a disappointment. He hadn't been able to have an erection and took out his frustration on her. Not until he had tied her up and assaulted her was he able to have intercourse. Afterwards he broke down and told her a tragic tale from his childhood: his father had injured him by using a clothespin 'down there' when he was little.

'I'm not after retribution,' the woman said in the end. 'I just want to warn others. But wouldn't you say a man who must resort to violence against a woman to get an erection is in fact impotent?'

After just one search online Julia realized that the story had gone viral. The certainty that her mother was the one behind it made her feel ill. She suddenly wished she'd asked Mom about Franz when they were on the sofa, but it would only have made her suspicious.

Suddenly the thought of a trip to Fog Island wasn't at all tempting. Who wanted to hang out with a violent nutter, especially one who was impotent besides? Even so, there was still a tiny flame of hope burning inside her. It wasn't as if everything you read online was true. Maybe this attack on Franz had come from some bitter girl he'd dumped.

She sent him a text.

I'm not coming to Fog Island, as you might have guessed.

He responded almost immediately.

Welcome to my world full of idol-worshipping liars. Listen to what I have to say on TV tomorrow.

Franz wasted no time speaking out against the article. The very next night he showed up on a talk show. Prime time and everything. Mom and Dad must have known, because they had the TV on. The interview was ostensibly about a book Franz had written called *Earth's Power and Your Future*, which would be coming out in the spring. The woman interviewing him made some small talk about the book before going on the offensive.

'You must realize that people are upset. First the trial twenty years ago, and now this – which seems to have happened recently. Have you assaulted women in the past?'

Franz shook his head slowly. His nostrils flared for an instant.

'I feel sorry for that woman, whoever she is. You must understand I have never done anything with a woman that she hasn't wanted to happen. It would never occur to me to turn to violence in a sexual relationship. That stuff is for cowards and runs counter to the principles of ViaTerra.'

'Are you claiming that this woman is lying?'

'No, just that she has an active imagination. This is nothing new. Unfortunately, I've had to learn to live with it. But it hurts just as much each time.'

Was there a hint of frustration in his voice or was Julia imagining it?

The journalist changed tack and seemed to be after sordid details now.

'Information has also surfaced that you were seriously injured and traumatized after an assault with a clothespin when you were a child. Would you like to comment on that? It must have been a horrific experience.'

Now Franz laughed aloud, slightly too shrilly. He became unexpectedly private and tried to make light of her question to avoid it.

'There was no injury. Everything down there is just fine. In perfect working order.'

The mood in the studio lightened. But Julia noticed a bit of tension in Franz's face. He ran his hands through his hair again and again, and when he rested them in his lap she noticed that his pinkie finger was trembling.

His ego had taken a serious blow.

Mom and Dad exchanged knowing glances on the sofa and smiled at Franz's distress. Julia felt her sweet, shameful dreams turn to dust. All that remained was a vast disappointment.

Just then, Mom's phone rang.

As Mom listened, her face became grim and her eyes went wide. She didn't say anything to the person who called, just mumbled in horror.

After she hung up, she looked at Dad.

'Someone tried to set the shelter on fire,' she said. 'The police caught them in the act, but they got away.'

Mom began to cry.

Julia crawled into her arms and held her.

We were carefully prepared for our assignment.

There were haircuts to be had, new clothes to be tried on, all so we would blend in.

Didrik sometimes went home to spend time with his parents, but I had never been off the island without being under the watchful eye of an adult. So Didrik would be like a guide for me 'out there in the world'.

We studied maps and directions and were shown pictures of you and your family. I took an extra long look at the photo of your mother. You were so alike. There was an unusual resoluteness in her eyes. 'Irresistible,' Father had said, and I understood what he meant now.

Father told us a little about you. You lived on Orust. Your mother had been a member of ViaTerra, but then there was some sort of misunderstanding. You were two years younger than Vic and me, and I thought that was a little weird, that we were here on the island when you came into the world. That you could be my half-sister. I wanted to ask more about your mother and what had happened, but I didn't want to risk setting off Father's hair-trigger temper.

We were given phones (I can still recall the pleasant shiver that went through me the first time I held mine in my hand) that were equipped with GPS so we could find our way anywhere. The phones had cameras, too. And we were given our own debit cards. Didrik knew how to use them, but to me they were pure science fiction.

We would also have a rental car. Didrik had just gotten his driver's licence.

Father did one last run-through before we headed out.

'As they say, it's do or die,' he began. 'That's how you must approach each of your assignments. They are missions to attain the goals of ViaTerra.'

This 'do or die' notion didn't really seem applicable to our assignment, but I nodded eagerly. Anything for Father to let me go, anything to get away from the island.

'"Better dead than incompetent," that's another of my favourite mottos,' he said. 'Do you think that sounds brutal? If so, you don't understand the purpose of everything we do here.'

He had written down an agenda with steps for us to follow. It was highly detailed. Everything from 'Take the ferry to the mainland' to 'Find a hiding place behind X's school so you can watch her.' You see, we referred to you as X. Your name must never be spoken aloud, not even by me and Didrik.

As we were on our way across the sound, on this sunny spring day, it felt like this would be the easiest task I had ever performed.

But that was before I saw you for the first time.

CONFESSIONS OF A SPY

The sun has found a crack in the clouds and is shining down on our little hideaway. We're crouched down in a grove of trees on a small rise looking over the schoolyard. Your schoolyard.

We wait impatiently for break time to arrive. For you to come out.

Didrik is worried that we won't recognize you, but I don't doubt it for a second. I already know there's something about you that is unmistakable.

My whole being is full of a new sensation of freedom, and it makes me feel weightless. I've felt this way ever since I left the island.

The tiniest, everyday details take on so much meaning: the TV at the hotel, which we've already watched in secret. The candy in the fridge. People walking down the street, so aimless and carefree. I saw one boy eating ice cream on a bench with his mother and was astounded that this was even possible. That a person could be allowed to be so lazy.

But now we're in the grove of trees with our phones at the ready, waiting for you to come out.

The school is bigger than I had imagined, much larger than our school at Earth's Children. The bell rings and kids stream into the schoolyard. It's a little scary, being so close. We can hear their feet hit the asphalt. I feel the breeze as they sail by in their wild games.

'Is that her?' Didrik whispers, pointing at a girl with long brown hair.

'Nope,' I whisper back. 'Definitely not.'

Just then I catch sight of you. You're in the middle of the schoolyard, talking to a group of boys. You're almost a head taller than them. Your face is towards us. The gentle breeze carries your pealing laughter to our hiding spot. At first glance, you remind me of a foal that has grown a little too quickly. The way you sway on long legs. The mane of hair draped over your shoulders, falling all the way to your waist.

You're the most beautiful person I've ever seen.

You're everything I've never been allowed to be.

I don't get the same feeling as I do with the girls in Earth's Children; instead it's more like an incredible tenderness, the way you'd feel about a baby bird that has fallen from its nest. It's impossible to say why, but you don't feel like a sister. I'm drawn to you in a way I can't explain.

I forget all about taking pictures until I hear the faint clicking of Didrik's phone.

'Wow, now there's a girl you could—' he whispers, but I cut him off with a jab to the side. We take a bunch of pictures. We watch you pedal your bike home in a frenzy after school. We sneak around outside your house and take pictures of you lying in the grass and sunning yourself. When you get up, I can't take my eyes off your bare, cinnamon-tanned

shoulders. Your dog almost exposes us – he catches our scent and starts barking. I break a stick from your garden hedge, stick it in my pocket, and smell it when Didrik isn't looking. Your bike is carelessly tossed on the road in front of the house. I right it, letting my hands linger on the handlebars just so I can touch something you've touched. That evening, we get in the car and follow you at a safe distance when you leave the house. We take pictures from the road as you hang around a gas station with your friends. The next night, we trail you as you go swimming in the sea with a guy. We watch you pull off your dress. Glimpse your naked body, your breasts, which are already round and large. Didrik wants to take pictures, but I say it's too dark.

We're invisible, clever, and excited by our secret assignment.

In the evenings, we compose long messages to Father on our phones. We give him detailed descriptions of what you do. We send tons of pictures.

Father always answers immediately. The same response.

'Well done, guys! Carry on!' he writes in English, and that makes us feel grown up and important.

Not once do you sense something is wrong when we show up in your life like shadows.

You never turn around when you hear a rustle in the bushes or when we happen to get too close in the car.

You don't seem to have time to react, always so engrossed in whatever you're doing in the moment.

You are more there *than your friends are. More present.*

It seems to me you shouldn't be living in this hole of a town. It seems too small for you. Sometimes I feel like you're a ticking time bomb.

An uncomfortable feeling slowly grows inside me. It starts to feel wrong that we're intruding on your life.

On the third and final day of our assignment, you bike to the library. We follow in the car, staying way behind. Sometimes we pull off on the edge of the road to put some distance between us. Once we nearly lose you. When we arrive, I ask Didrik to wait in the car. I tell him I want to take a close-up shot, and it will be too obvious if we both go in.

I spot you in a reading nook with a book open on your lap. You seem fully absorbed in your reading, leaning forward with your hair falling over the book and onto your legs, all around you.

We're alone in the room. I stand perfectly still, watching you. It's so quiet that I think I can hear your soft breathing. I'm standing so close that I could take a few steps towards you, reach out my hand, and touch your hair. I quickly decide not to take the picture after all, because you would notice right away.

Just as I'm about to turn around and leave, you look up from the book and stare blankly ahead. Something in that book has made you think. Suddenly, unexpectedly, you turn your head.

Our eyes meet.

My heart does a cartwheel in my chest.

I feel the heat radiating off you across the abyss between us.

Time stands still. I can't take my eyes off you. I have to tear my body from this spot, as though I had grown roots; I have to force it to turn around.

My head down, I walk through the dim library and out into the sun.

I feel your eyes on me the whole time.

28

On the same day the police called to tell her about the arson attempt at the shelter, Sofia and Benjamin called an emergency meeting. Anna and Simon came as fast as they could. Ellis stayed home, but he was waiting by the phone in case they needed his help. In the end they decided to take turns staking out the site from a car each night. There didn't seem to be any other solution.

The long, sleepless nights created friction between the friends. It was a rare thing, for there to be a crisis in their friendship, but now they couldn't agree on anything. Benjamin said they should hire a security firm instead, but Sofia didn't even want to entertain the thought of that extra cost. Anna thought it was the police's job. She had started working part-time at the pension and said the nights spent at the site were about to break her. Simon was the only one who didn't complain. He said he liked to listen to music and let his thoughts wander in the dark of the car.

When Sofia told the police it had to be Franz behind the fire, they ignored her. Once again she was told she might need help sorting through her old traumas. After all, there was nothing to link Franz or even anyone in his circles to the harassment.

An unpleasant feeling grew inside her, a hunch that the future was going to be unpredictable and awful. That was what you could expect when you stoked Franz's ire. Even so, she didn't regret the blog post. The sweet taste of revenge lingered.

But then life took an unexpected turn. It was an early March afternoon. Sofia, Benjamin and Simon were chatting. For once the topic wasn't Franz or the shelter. Instead, Simon was entertaining them with anecdotes from his time in California.

Sofia needed to stretch her legs and went to the window. The yard was shrouded in mist; the excessive rain had been replaced by a tenacious morning fog that wouldn't let up until evening.

When a patrol car turned into their driveway, she suspected the worst. Someone had kidnapped Julia. The shelter had burned down. Something had happened to her parents. She didn't recognize the two officers who climbed out of the car: a young woman with dark skin and an older, grey-haired man. As she let them in, she felt even more panicky. They looked so serious. Benjamin and Simon automatically rose from the sofa. The female officer introduced herself as Victoria Heyman. Her colleague was called Antonio Beijer and was with the crimes division in Gothenburg.

'Don't worry,' Victoria said as she saw the fear on Sofia's face. 'We come bearing both good and bad news, but mostly good.'

As soon as they sat down, Victoria began to speak. She said she was the one who had come across the person trying to burn down the shelter. She had decided to dig deeper into the case, even though it wasn't assigned to her unit. Antonio Beijer was a former colleague of hers in Gothenburg. He'd helped her lift fingerprints from the lighter they'd found at the scene, and they had gotten a hit in the criminal database right away. Indeed, they had arrested the suspect.

Sofia held her breath – Victoria's face told her that even more shocking news was on the way.

'He has confessed that he tried to set the fire, and also that he attacked your daughter,' she said, letting the words sink in for a moment. 'His name is Viggo Sankt Petrus – although his last name is really Pettersson. Sankt Petrus is a name he took because he's part of a free-church group called God's Way.'

Simon gasped.

'What? That's the same group my parents are part of. They're totally nuts.'

'Why us, though?' Benjamin asked in horror.

'It has to do with your work,' Victoria said, turning to Sofia. 'He has a daughter who defected from God's Path when she was eighteen. Helena Pettersson, do you remember her?'

Sofia did remember Helena. She had fled God's Way and hidden at the shelter for two years. Her rabid, evangelical father had come by to look for her more than once. Sofia remembered a short man with cruel, bulging eyes. Ironically enough, Peder Santos was the one who had dealt with him. Viggo Pettersson had shouted and made any manner of threats, including burning down the shelter. Santos had eventually filed a police report, and after that he left them alone. So she'd thought. As for Helena, Sofia hadn't heard from her since the storm.

'When the shelter was destroyed in the storm, Helena travelled to a secret location,' Victoria went on. 'She's actually living under a protected identity. Sofia, Viggo has got it into his head that it's your fault Helena turned against him. What he did to Julia was some sort of revenge against you. It sounds crazy, but that's the truth of the matter.'

'But why did he take pictures of Julia?' Benjamin asked.

Victoria took a laptop from her backpack.

'I need to show you something unpleasant now,' she said. 'Is Julia home?'

She looked around the room anxiously.

'No, she's at school.'

'Good, because I don't want her to see this. And I don't think it's a good idea for your friend to see it either.' She glanced at Simon. 'These are nude images of your daughter.'

Simon moved to the opposite corner of the sofa.

Victoria went to a website with a large cross in either corner and an image of the crucifixion in the middle. *The only true way of God*, it read across the top. She typed in a password she had written on a scrap of paper and before them was a new page that read *Atonement* in large type. The background image was a horrible Hieronymus Bosch painting of people being tortured in hell.

'This is a site that only a select group of God's Way members have access to. Mostly older men. We had to hack our way in,' Victoria said. 'This is the page with your daughter,' she went on, clicking an icon.

A HARLOT'S DAUGHTER, read the banner. Beneath this text was a collection of pictures of Julia, naked and bound in vulnerable positions, licking her lips, spreading her legs. The worst part was that the photographs had been taken in such a way that it all looked voluntary. Sofia's lunch turned in her stomach. Benjamin brought his palms to his cheeks and swayed nervously back and forth on the sofa. He couldn't say a word.

'I'm sorry you have to see this,' Victoria said. 'It's meant to portray some sort of divine retribution. These men take the law into their own hands. Viggo Pettersson writes that you ruined his daughter's life and this is his revenge. It's insane. In any case, he's in jail now.'

'I hope you find everyone who logged in and looked at these pictures,' Benjamin said.

'We'll do our best,' Antonio promised.

'Was he the one who took pictures of me at the shelter and broke in here those two times?' Sofia asked.

'He hasn't confessed to any of that yet,' said Antonio. 'But it certainly seems likely. We've only just started untangling this mess. Your daughter isn't the only one who's been subjected to this sort of violation. We've found more cases like this, attacks on girls who have been tied up and photographed nude. Their pictures are here as well, but I would prefer not to show you.'

'I don't want to see them anyway,' Sofia said. 'What's going to happen to Viggo now, though?'

'He's already been accused of additional counts of harassment; there are a lot of reports filed against him. And he's in the criminal database. For assault. Since this has to do with assault on minors, we won't be releasing him for a while. I hope this helps you sleep better at night,' Victoria said, smiling for the first time.

'I knew there was something sick about that cult,' Simon said. 'I hope my father isn't involved.'

But Sofia hardly heard him. Tears of relief poured down her cheeks. She rested her head on Benjamin's chest. He put an arm around her shoulders.

'We'll be in touch when we know more,' Victoria said, standing up.

'Thank you for taking this so seriously,' Sofia said. 'I hope someone will take down that site.'

'Definitely. We just wanted to show you first. I drove by once last summer and I remember how wonderful that shelter was. Just wanted to help out a little.'

Once the officers were gone, the house was silent. Sofia felt a little ashamed that it hadn't occurred to her the harassment was linked to her job. Of course other cults would consider her an enemy too. But she'd been so certain that Franz was behind all the bad things that happened in her life.

At last she decided it didn't matter. Franz was a rapist and people like Elisa Bonelli had the right to redress. Besides, he'd almost hijacked her book release and that was still an infuriating thorn in her side.

'Poor Julia,' Benjamin exclaimed at last. 'It's so disgusting that those old bastards looked at those pictures. I want to go to the jail and smack down that Sankt Petrus.'

'We don't have to tell Julia, do we?' Sofia said anxiously.

'Yes, we do. She can handle it. She'll be relieved to know the truth, you'll see.'

Sofia called to tell Anna all about it; she was staking out the shelter for the moment.

'Just come here instead,' Sofia said. 'Benjamin's going to make something yummy.'

It turned out to be a lovely evening. Their discord was gone and the mood was cheerful. They made plans for the future, but above all they enjoyed one another's company, as well as the fact that the threat hanging over them was gone.

Julia took the terrible revelation well, exactly as Benjamin had expected. She cried a little, but mostly out of relief. Then she asked about the pictures, how much of her body they had shown.

'Basically all of it,' Sofia said. 'But they're going to take that website down now. No one will ever see them again, I promise.'

Julia considered this for a moment and wiped her tears.

'Oh, it's only a naked body. And I really have nothing to be ashamed of.'

★

The next day, the papers were full of lurid headlines about the perverted cult that dealt in child pornography and violence against young girls. Four men were in custody.

Late that night, a messenger came to their door to deliver an enormous bouquet from Franz Oswald. Tucked among lilies, orchids and peonies, his favourite flowers, was a greeting card.

Sofia,
I forgive you for suspecting me.
I forgive you for spreading lies about me.
I hope you can forgive me one day.

All the way back across the sound on the ferry, I thought about you. Not the way you think about a girl you have a crush on, but more like a symbol of something beautiful and unattainable.

I started worrying about what Father was going to do with the pictures. I knew how he tended to react, he was never impulsive aside from when he was extremely angry. He always had some plan that extended far into the future, and now I wondered what part you were going to play in it.

A couple of the photos on my phone were ones I hadn't sent him. In one of them, you were lying on your lawn. Your blouse had slipped up and one of your breasts was visible. The other picture had been taken from behind. You were bending down to pick something up and your skirt was so short that your panties were showing.

I had convinced myself I didn't know why I hadn't sent these particular photos. But I did know. Somewhere deep inside I knew how Father would react to them.

So I hurriedly deleted them before Didrik could catch on.

As the distance between the ferry and the island shrank, I became aware of a new tension in my chest. It was a dull ache that made me want to jump overboard and disappear into the waves. I was ashamed. For once it wasn't aimed inwardly: it wasn't about my ugliness, clumsiness, or inadequacy. I was ashamed of how what we had done might be viewed through your eyes.

*

When we returned to ViaTerra, we were whisked to our office in the manor house by an impatient Karsten. There we wrote a detailed summary of our assignment and handed over the memory cards containing the photographs. It had to be fast, because a new disaster had just happened, and it demanded our attention.

Elisa, the sex bomb, had spread lies about Father.

REVELATIONS AND LIES

We are gathered in the Earth's Children classroom. Karsten is going to address us, and I will soon understand why. This is far too sensitive for Father to speak of himself.

Karsten looks grave and severe. He begins by reminding us of Elisa, the horrible girl who was here some time ago. The one who had to be sent home because she couldn't live up to the high standards of ViaTerra. It was the boss himself who was forced to send her away. Good thing he has the ability to uncover liars with a single glance. He had quickly realized Elisa was here to ruin everything and sleep around with all the guys.

Karsten nails Didrik with his gaze as he continues. I watch from the corner of my eye as Didrik shrinks in the chair beside mine.

Yes, Elisa was a leech who tried to latch onto Father. Promiscuous as hell, as we surely noticed. Yet none of us did a thing about it. As usual, we forced the boss to act as executioner, and that wasn't right. But now we have a chance to put everything to rights. Elisa has written a blog post in which she spreads lies about Father and ViaTerra. 'You remember how she was, don't you?' he says. 'The lies she told! She lied about everything. I'm sure you all have something to say about that. Some good examples. And you will share them, on camera, one by one. This will be useful when Elisa's parents come to speak with the boss. They have the right to know that their daughter is a calculating little bitch.'

I remember Elisa's beautiful eyes, the glimpse of her breasts beneath her T-shirt, and the strong scent of her perfume, but I don't remember her ever lying to me.

I tentatively raise my hand.

'I don't really think she ever lied to me. So what should I say?'

A sharp, cruel gleam appears in Karsten's eyes.

'In that case I suppose you'll have to use your imagination. Hell, I'm sure she lied about something. You will *help out with this, Thor, I don't give a single shit whether you like it or not.'*

The room falls silent. I feel everyone's eyes on me. The traitor who doesn't want to back up the boss. If I speak up now, the trust Father has gained in me will go up in smoke. But at the same time, I feel fury well inside me.

Thanks to my little adventure on the mainland, I've begun to understand that this is far from normal.

Karsten approaches me. An angry vein pulses on his forehead. He's livid now. An uninvited image pops into my head: I stand up and smack him one, right in the face. I think of how good that would feel. But instead I respond, hissing as though my jaw were wired shut.

'I understand.'

I remember that Elisa once mentioned her father was super rich. And later she said he was the richest person in Sweden, but of course that isn't the same thing. Isn't there a pretty big difference between 'rich' and 'richest in Sweden'? When I manage to produce this speculation, Karsten is full of zeal.

'Exactly! Sometimes it can be difficult to remember the lies. She was so ingratiating and convincing. That's a good start, Thor. I'm sure you can all think of similar examples. Let's get going!'

In a small room behind the classroom, they have set up a video camera. We are supposed to sit on a chair, introduce ourselves, say how long we've been in Earth's Children, and then recount our experiences with Elisa. We must not get too carried away. It's fine if we say something nice about her as well. For instance, we could say: 'Elisa was kind sometimes, but she once told me her father was the richest person in Sweden.' Karsten coaches us. We keep it up until late into the night. Father has to approve all these clips before we're allowed to go to bed. Once everyone has been filmed, we sit around the classroom, waiting anxiously.

But Father isn't satisfied. We have to be filmed again, this time to explain what we think of him. Give examples of how he has helped us. Preferably little anecdotes about something kind he has done for us personally.

'With fire in your eyes,' Karsten says. 'Think of how much you admire the boss. Talk about all the good he does here.'

So we speak before the camera. We suppress our yawns and put on carefree, devoted expressions as best we can.

At last, Karsten returns from Father's office and gives us a thumbs up.

A few days later, we're called to an assembly in the classroom. Karsten proudly shares that things went well with Elisa's parents, thanks to our stories. Elisa will receive psychological help, and everything will work out. Father sends his greetings and thanks us for our help.

That night, I think of what it would feel like to jump from Old Nick and simply disappear. My grandmother took her own life, and Mama wanted to, and now I wonder if this feeling, of simply wanting to die, is something I inherited.

Something has changed.

A line has been crossed.

I have done something that can't be undone.

Without wishing to do so, I have betrayed two girls I genuinely liked.

29

The flowers from Franz were the inciting incident in Simon's outburst. Sofia had left them in the entryway, half inside and half outside the house, and that was the whole issue.

They were supposed to be going to Gothenburg. Simon hadn't left Orust since his arrival, and Sofia wanted to treat him to a day in the city to thank him for his help. Moreover, Simon had mentioned in passing that he would be unreachable for a few days later in the week. That he was going to meet someone. And now Sofia suspected that Simon's mysterious girlfriend was going to show up soon. He was unbearably tight-lipped when it came to her, and Sofia thought a little change of scenery might make him open up.

She saw his car pulling into the driveway, but when he didn't come inside, she went to the entryway. There he was, muttering to himself in front of the flowers, with the card from Franz in his hand.

'Why aren't these flowers in the trash?' he asked when he noticed her.

'What do you mean?'

'Why didn't you throw them away?'

His voice was calm and controlled, but there was an ominous vibe underneath that veneer.

'I was going to toss them, but it was raining—'

'It hasn't fucking rained in days.'

Sofia hesitated just for a moment, but that was all it took.

'You think everything's going to work out, don't you? That he's not the one behind all the shit going on around here?' he shouted.

The strength of his voice made her recoil. She tried to defuse the situation with a tentative smile, but he didn't seem to notice.

'I never said that. Stop this, Simon! You're scaring me.'

'No, you're scaring *me* with your naïve approach. He is totally fixated on you and has been ever since he first laid eyes on you. But you can't see it, because you are equally fixated on him!'

'I am not!'

'Yes you are, you refuse to let go. You were much smarter when we first met, you know that? Back then you saw right through him.'

'I still do. Stop being so angry.'

He looked at her, his eyes squinting. She could almost see the colour of his cheeks darkening.

It struck her that she had only ever seen Simon this angry once before. That was twenty years ago, when Franz beat him up in front of the ViaTerra staff. If Franz's cronies hadn't been holding Simon still, Franz would have been toast. Now Simon was equally furious with her, but she had no idea why.

'Look, come inside, why are you just standing there?' Sofia tried again to defuse the situation.

'I think I'll go back home.'

'Come on! Over some flowers?'

'Yes, as a matter of fact. I give up. I came back to Sweden to get you away from him, but it seems like that's an impossible task.'

'It is not. I haven't spoken to him in ages. It was only the book—'

'For Christ's sake, Sofia! Get out while you still can! And anyway, there's a chapter missing from that book. The one about what Franz did to you.'

Fury welled up inside her.

'I work every single day to get over that! I am not ready to write about it, can you respect that? And then there's Julia. And how he could be her biological father.'

'Okay, so what? What does it matter? Does that make him her dad? Sure, I bet he'd be such a great parent to her. You're so naïve, Sofia.'

'I am not!'

'Yes, you are. Completely unpredictable. Have you ever, in all your life, sat down to really think through a single decision you've made? Or do you intend to continue acting on impulse all the time? Because if so, the future looks grim for you and your family.'

She turned away from him. Tears burned behind her eyelids. She didn't understand what had gotten into Simon, but most of all she was devastated to think he was angry with her. She felt humiliated and pathetic, the same way she used to feel when Franz chewed her out in the office.

'Please, don't yell at me like that. It makes me feel afraid of you.'

She saw the anger drain out of him. He put his palm to his forehead and shook his head.

'I'm sorry, Sofia. It's just that I know things you don't. That's the problem,' he said.

'Then tell me!'

'No, I can't tell you yet. Look, it's best if we don't see each other for a while. I'll be in touch,' he said, turning to leave.

She didn't even want to mention their trip to Gothenburg, which suddenly seemed incredibly far away. She just wanted Simon to be his usual self again.

'Please, don't leave it like this. Tell me what you know,' she tried.

He turned around. His expression was no longer one of anger; instead, it was full of tender sympathy.

That was almost worse.

'Someone has to make you see. Benjamin would let you jump off a bridge if you made up your mind to. Franz is like a virus. Each time you treat him like a regular person, a piece of you dies. Think about that. I'll be in touch,' he said, and he was out the door.

She watched him walk across the lawn to his car. His stride was jerky, annoyed, not his usual lumbering style at all. As his car disappeared down the road, she stared crestfallen after it. All at once she was aware of the drooping bouquet; she picked it up and slipped her feet into a pair of clogs.

The sky had been grey all day, but now the clouds looked unusually black, heavy with rain. There was a dull rumble of thunder in the distance. Just as she shoved the flowers into the trash bin, the sky opened and it began to pour rain; she might as well have been standing under a waterfall. She dashed for the house through a curtain of water, drenched and cold.

When she came inside, she shivered in the entryway for a moment.

'There it is, that fucking rain,' she muttered to herself.

She changed clothes. For a long time she stood in the living room, staring outside and listening to the patter of rain on the roof and the slosh of water through the downspouts. All the colours faded until the landscape was a shade of dark grey. Thunder rumbled in the distance, but the clouds were too thick to see any lightning.

She spent the whole day alone in the house. Whether she tried to read or surf the internet, she couldn't settle in. She was still trying to absorb Simon's words: *There's a chapter missing from that book.* Why hadn't she written it? Simon had hit a sore spot, that moment when she put the period on the last sentence in the manuscript and knew that something was missing. That must be why the book had languished on her computer for so many years. And now people would never know the truth. But there was Julia to think of. No one wanted a rapist for a father.

As she sat on the sofa, staring into space, she came to a decision. She would go on a trip with Julia as soon as possible. She would take her someplace nice and tell her everything. The decision made her tremble with relief.

Outside the window, the sky was clearing. In the distance, a blackbird was trilling. Life felt a little brighter, but what if she couldn't make peace with Simon?

When Benjamin got home, she told him about Simon's outburst. Benjamin just laughed.

'I agree with him, actually. Everything was much better before Franz turned up again. I don't want him anywhere near you or Julia.'

But when Sofia suggested that she tell Julia everything, Benjamin was hesitant.

'Shouldn't we do the DNA test first? We'll take some hair from her brush. That way there's a chance we don't have to tell her anything.'

'I'm tired of lying to her. It only makes a bigger mess of it all.'

'Well, just tell her, then, if it feels right. She can decide for herself if she wants to do the test.'

Sofia tried to call Simon more than once but only got his voicemail. She left a few messages begging him to call, but the next day she still hadn't heard from him. Now Sofia was getting worried that he was so upset he had returned to the United States. Not an hour passed in which she didn't think about him, and even when he wasn't on her mind he was behind the aching lump in her throat. One afternoon, as she pulled up to the shelter, she missed him so much she decided to go to the pension and pick him up.

The receptionist at the pension said Simon had checked out that morning.

The next day, Benjamin was travelling for work, Anna was scheduled to work at the pension, and Julia was at school. The thought of being alone in the house, and the knowledge that Louise Ringvall might call at any moment to nag about the book, made her decide to leave her phone at home and go out to the sea. She packed lunch in her backpack and loaded a new book onto her tablet. Then, on with her jeans, sneakers and a windbreaker. As she walked out the door, she stopped to take a breath of the fresh air. It was the sort of bright, clear morning where you could make out each tree and bush around the lake. The sky was streaked with high, thin clouds. The sun glittered on the frost that had settled overnight. Crocuses, brought to life by the rain and sunshine, shone brightly in the flowerbeds. According to the calendar, it was still winter, but spring had come in a hurry, bringing more comfortable temperatures.

When Sofia glanced at the road, she spotted Simon's car pulling off not far from the house. She froze and held her breath until she saw him climbing out of the driver's seat. But then the door to the passenger seat opened and a woman stepped out. She was wearing a winter coat, jeans and knee-length boots, and she had a cap and sunglasses. Sofia couldn't make out her features. But there was something familiar about her long, red hair.

Simon put an arm around the woman's shoulders and aimed her towards the house. They stopped when they caught sight of Sofia. It wasn't until the woman's lips curled and she scrunched up her nose in a familiar expression that Sofia realized it was Elvira.

No one in ViaTerra knew anything about computers. Father was the only one who had one. But now that he had to conquer the internet, he was full of grand plans that couldn't wait. Honestly, he was not particularly interested in the internet, except for when he could use it to spread his teachings. Since the early days of ViaTerra he'd had one employee whose only job was to compile everything that was written about him and ViaTerra in the media. But now he needed someone who could build and launch websites and activate social media accounts. He hired a computer expert from the mainland called Bella Svahnberg. But it was important for some ViaTerra staff to receive training as well.

Matteo and I were selected.

Not only was Bella Svahnberg a computer genius, she was smart and extroverted, a real PR type. Father was sold from their first meeting. Bella radiated glamour and was uniquely delightful. Her hair was short and dyed blonde. Her eyebrows were meticulously plucked and filled in with black eyebrow pencil. Her somewhat forced smile and red lips revealed pale pink gums. Her nails, which were painted black, were so long I never understood how she could type on a keyboard.

Although Bella was unpleasant on occasion, and liked to take credit for everything, she opened a whole new world to me.

Matteo, Bella Svahnberg and I are sitting in Father's office, waiting for him. Bella has been trying to interrogate us about Father. It seems she hasn't figured out that we don't discuss his private life in ViaTerra.

When Father enters, he doesn't sit down; instead he stands by the window and stares out at the sea. None of us says anything, not even Bella.

At last he stops in front of the big bookcase that takes up an entire wall. From day one he has maintained a collection of newspaper clippings and printouts from the internet with all the positive things that have been written about him. Since he's been out of the public eye for several years, not much has been added to the collection recently. But he takes out one of the binders and holds it up to us triumphantly.

'This collection will increase tenfold within a few months, once we've gotten this project off the ground,' he says. 'That's the goal.'

He sits down at his desk, still contemplative. He hasn't fixed his gaze on any of us yet.

'I don't know much about the internet,' he says with a crooked smile. 'But I know the image I want to project there.'

Bella opens her mouth to say something, but he holds up one hand.

'Let me talk, and then you may ask questions. Our website should look slick, but most importantly it must give the impression that we care. Think "first-class aid organization", and it will turn out great. It's all about results. There should be statistics – Jesus, do people ever love statistics! We'll give them scary numbers that show how climate change is destroying the earth. And then some more positive statistics that prove we're doing something about it. How many followers we have, all our charity projects, how ViaTerra is growing exponentially. But I don't want any of those boring bar graphs. Better to use line charts that show constant improvement, straight up, like rockets ending in fantastic fireworks. It needs to be sensational. And we need testimonials from celebrities and spiritual leaders from around the world. Celebrities especially, people love them.'

Bella raises her hand. Father stops talking and nods at her, annoyed.

'How will we obtain these testimonies? Should we reach out to some celebrities?'

'No, there's no need. Plenty of famous people have gone through the ViaTerra program. Everything they say in their sessions is recorded. You can simply look through the archives of those who are still well-liked and find nice things they said. Easy as pie.'

'What about the spiritual leaders?'

'Those, we might need to contact. Talk to Carmen. She can call around to a few of them and coax some praise out of them. She's good at that. Anything else you'd like to know?'

'Yes – how will we produce all these statistics? After all, ViaTerra hasn't accomplished much recently,' Bella says with a gulp.

At first I'm afraid Father will be angry – he looks so stern – but then he smiles. Nothing is as lovely as Father's smile. It softens his face and makes little wrinkles appear around his watchful eyes. At the same time, there's nothing as frightening as when that smile fades. But this time it grows into a laugh.

'Statistics! What the fuck do people know about statistics? Have you seen all the numbers the media throw around these days? All you have to do is estimate, throw something together that looks good. You're good at that kind of thing, aren't you, Bella?'

He stands up and takes a few steps towards her.

'I trust your judgement. Here at ViaTerra, we're not in the business of limiting folks. Just do what it takes.'

Bella seems to appreciate being given free rein, because she smiles so broadly her gums glisten.

'But there's something else I want done,' Father says. 'Now that we're going to be all over the internet, it's going to awaken the ire of the riff-raff that hate us. So we need to develop methods to eliminate them. Perhaps a group of devoted followers who can write negative posts about the haters, with fake accounts and all that. Anyway, that's up to you. Use your imagination, Bella!'

★

All of this is a little unreal to me. I still find the internet to be a complete abstraction. But all that matters is that I'm going to get to work with computers.

That evening, I talk to Matteo outside the dorms. We're too excited to sleep and have snuck out. That's when I ask him about the phone. I've never forgotten the picture he took the time Didrik and Vic beat me up. I can't see Matteo's face in the darkness; I can only hear his sharp breath.

'You aren't going to tell anyone, are you? I just took a few pictures, I don't even know what I'm going to do with them. They might be useful to have. Like, in the future, someday.'

'Where do you hide the phone?'

'With my underwear, no one looks there.'

I feel a pleasant shiver. Matteo does forbidden things. Which means he has forbidden thoughts, just like me. Immediately we become allies. Not the way you do when you have a common interest, but because we each know the other thinks and feels the same way.

Bella isn't easy to work with. She's impatient and clearly tries to act like 'one of the guys'. She likes to tell dirty jokes, and we're not used to that.

But she teaches us exciting things. A totally new language full of words like 'gigabytes', 'SEO', 'platforms' and 'tags'. We work for a few months – finding images and texts and doing the graphic design. Although it's dark in the office and the light of the computer screens hurts my eyes, I enjoy the work.

Until one terrible day.

Father comes into our little office with Vic in tow. Vic has become Father's constant shadow. The plan is for him to lead ViaTerra sometime in the future.

At first I think Father has come to talk to Bella, but he approaches

Matteo. As if on command we all stand up, but Father waves his hand dismissively.

'Sit down. I'm actually here to see you, Matteo,' he says.

He turns to Bella.

'I heard you're almost finished?'

'That's right,' she says. 'A couple months max, and we can take it public.'

'Do you think you can manage with just Thor for these last months?'

I'm so nervous my mouth is itchy.

Bella nods.

'I'm sure that will be fine. Thor is a good worker.'

Father looks Matteo up and down. His hair, his face, his torso, which has grown strong even though we spend so much time at computers. Then he nods.

'Do you like girls, Matteo?' he asks.

'Yes, boss,' Matteo says, looking uncomfortable.

'You're going to be sent on a longer assignment. All by yourself. Do you think you can handle that?'

'Yes, boss, definitely!'

'Great. It's about time you taste a little pussy, and it's not just any pussy.'

I have no idea what's going on, but Matteo seems to know because he's blushing. Vic's whole face is one big grin. Father notices.

'Life isn't all sex, Vic,' he says sternly. But then he turns to me.

'But it's pretty close, right, Thor?'

He winks teasingly and starts laughing. Father has two different laughs. One is a rough, restrained chuckle, and one is a loud, shrill guffaw that can be mean, but is still infectious. This laugh sounds mostly mean.

My face stings and I look at the floor, because I can't bring myself to meet his piercing gaze.

Deep inside I know what this is all about.

And now I realize that I've almost been waiting for it to happen.

'It's best you come with me to my office now, Matteo. You're leaving tomorrow,' Father says.

Matteo stands up so fast he bangs his legs on the desk.

They start to head to the hall but stop in the doorway.

Father's voice echoes through the room. Certain sentences spear me right through.

Play hard to get at first. Like a teenage crush. Hold off a few months with the sex, the young girls like that. All to make sure you're together a long time. Call me once a week.

In that moment, I hate Matteo. I hate him even more than I hate Father.

DEATH COMES TO VIATERRA

A few days later, something happens to deepen my hostility. I lose my faith in ViaTerra. To have faith is to trust something, even though you're not sure it's true. I realize that now.

As usual, I'm working late into the night, but I haven't heard Father and Vic leave the building yet. I'm thoroughly absorbed in some software I'm expected to learn to use. My concentration is broken by an explosion – it sounds like thunder and lightning at the same time. The windowpanes rattle. The power goes out, and the room is plunged into darkness.

I'm not terribly frightened. I just assume lightning struck something.

I get up and look out the window. The courtyard is murky. There's not a single light glowing on the property. Buildings and trees appear as grey shadows in all the black. I hear people running on the stairs, doors flying open, and then I see Vic, flashlight in hand. Father is behind him. Never before have I seen him so shaken. His eyes are wide, his features twisted. He has his phone in his hand.

'Stay here! Do not come out under any circumstances!' he shouts, and then they vanish.

We have an intercom system with speakers in every building, and it runs on a backup generator. Soon I hear one of the guards. We're under orders to stay indoors.

I stand with my nose pressed to the glass and stare out. The guards, Father and Vic are standing by the access manhole that leads to the power station that provides our electricity. We have been warned umpteen times against going there. Karsten used to warn us off by telling us about the incredible amount of power that runs through the lines, and what would happen if you touched them. You would be charred bacon in an instant. *Those were his exact words.*

Now I hear sirens, and soon the area is surrounded by ambulances, fire trucks, police cars and rescue services. My heart starts to pound like a captive bird. Something terrible has happened. I'm too far away to see what's going on, but there are figures going down the manhole now – and something is brought back up. Karsten, Ali-Khan and Father are talking to two police officers. But the ambulance doesn't speed off. No one seems to be in a rush. There's a resignation to the way they're all talking and gesturing. A horrid sense of hopelessness floats through the windowpane and trickles into me.

I stand petrified at the window until the door opens and Vic comes in.

'You can go to bed now,' he says.

'What happened?' I ask breathlessly.

'It's Charlotte. She tried to rescue a squirrel that crawled into the manhole. It fell onto the lines. Look, you don't want to see it, she turned into a lump of coal, and—'

Charlotte is a thirteen-year-old girl in Earth's Children. Shy, sweet and a little uncertain.

'Stop talking that way!' I cut him off.

I'm struck numb by what he told me. My tongue has swelled in my mouth. I can hardly speak.

'In the middle of the night?' I ask, full of mistrust.

'Yes, someone in the dorms said she was talking about the squirrel,' he says.

The lie hangs in the air between us.

This idiocy neither of us believes.

I liked Charlotte. It was totally innocent. Maybe a few times I brushed against her arm, inhaled the scent of her hair, or gazed at her longingly. And I saw the anguish in her eyes. Transient, passing, overshadowed by her trained-in smile – but I saw it.

'She never would have climbed down that manhole,' I insist.

'No, that's exactly what she did,' Vic snaps. 'And that's the important thing. It was an accident. The guards have been sent to Penance, because security around here sucks. That's exactly what the boss said.'

When I go to the dorm, the stench washes over me. It's not just the smell of burned meat, it's something more disgusting: the smell of rotten death.

I don't sleep at all that night.

Obsessed with thoughts of Charlotte, the images from the manhole, the horrid odour and the lies – especially the lies – I lie there with my eyes wide open, staring at the ceiling.

As I write this, I still don't understand how nothing came of this incident. How did they manage to fool the police and the authorities? The girl's parents? Even thinking about it still hurts.

Writing this so you can read it makes me feel sick with shame. Why am I even doing it? Maybe because we later found out that Charlotte had written a suicide letter, and Karsten tore it up.

30

Simon dashed up to Sofia, who was standing on the steps, and clapped a hand over her mouth.

'Is anyone else home?'

Sofia shook her head in confusion.

'Good. No one can know that Elvira is here, not even Benjamin, yet. If it gets out, Franz will dispatch a goddamn army to find her, do you understand?'

Sofia nodded and removed his hand from her mouth.

Elvira took off her sunglasses, revealing those fairy-tale eyes, and flashed a smile big enough to show her dimples. She looked rather surprised, perhaps a bit shaken to see Sofia again. When she took a step closer to hug Sofia, Simon stood between them.

'Let's save that for later. We need to get into the house. Fast!'

Once in the entryway, Sofia hugged Elvira, then held her away to take a good look at her. When they'd last seen each other, Elvira was fifteen and enormously pregnant. In many ways she had still been a child then, but now she was a grown woman. Her face had filled out and was no longer so pale; she had a waist and larger breasts; all of this made her even more beautiful. When she took off her cap, her hair was a wild, blazing halo around her head.

'You have no idea how often I think about you, Sofia,' she said. 'Do you remember the last time we saw each other? You said I could live in your apartment with the babies, as long as I didn't go back to ViaTerra. Just think how different things would be if had listened to you back then.'

Sofia urged them to sit down as she hurried to the kitchen to put on some coffee. She noticed that her hands were trembling slightly. How did this all fit together? She had thought Elvira was on Fog Island with her twins. But now she recalled Vic's strange reaction when Sofia inquired about Elvira.

When she got back to the living room, Simon and Elvira were sitting close together on the sofa. Elvira held tight to Simon's hand. It felt so strange to see them together. She wondered if they were an item. Elvira must be in her early thirties, and Simon was over forty, but that wasn't so unusual. Even so, the thought of them as a couple seemed odd.

'You have to tell her, now, Elvira,' Simon said. 'Start at the beginning. I want Sofia to hear it all.'

So Elvira told the tale. She had been unhappy from the moment she returned to ViaTerra to give birth to Franz's children. The thought of the money she would get was a big temptation, and she had convinced herself she could leave the property as soon as the babies were born. But Franz had put a stop to that. Instead she quickly became a prisoner behind the walls, just like the rest of the staff. When the babies were born, she hadn't felt true motherly love for them at first.

'God, I was so young, I had no idea how to take care of a baby, much less two! And there was no one to show me how, either. Even when the boys got older, I had a hard time being a mother to them. Most of the time it felt like they were my rambunctious little brothers. Of course I loved them, but I don't think I was meant to become a parent so early. It didn't seem real. And they were so different. Thor was cautious and quiet. Vic always looked sort of angry, and he screamed all the time as a baby. If he'd had teeth I'm sure he would have bitten me. But their grandmother Karin came to visit now and then.'

'Karin Johansson? Franz's mother?' Sofia cut in. She had met Karin a long time ago and liked her.

'That's right. She helped me out so much. She taught me to cook and got permission from Franz to take me to the mainland sometimes. The kids loved her. But everything changed when they started attending that school of Franz's. Oh, God, they were always coming home with bruises, sunburn, and big blisters on their hands. They were building some sort of stone wall. But the worst part was that they weren't allowed to tell me anything about school. I sometimes heard Thor crying himself to sleep at night. Eventually I felt so claustrophobic – mentally ill, really. When I tried to ask Franz about the school, he brushed me off. The kids had to be toughened up. He wasn't about to let them turn out like their vapid mother.'

The air in the room felt thick and hard to breathe. Elvira was reliving these terrible memories, Sofia could tell.

'Sometimes when he came to the cottage, he flew into a rage because he thought I was neglecting the boys. He would be furious. But sometimes he came at night and wanted to have sex. He could be so tender. It was almost like we were a family. It really would have been better if he was cruel all the time. I never knew what to expect, I always had to be on guard.'

She paused and her gaze turned inward.

'It was when he decided to use me like a toy in the attic that it got really horrible. He was like a different person up there, aggressive and rough. Simon told me his forefathers used to torture women up there. It was like he was taking after them.'

She stared at the glass of the coffee table. Not once had she looked up at Sofia. She had taken her hand out of Simon's to pick nervously at the fabric of the sofa.

'Torturing me was like an old habit he couldn't quit. I decided not to fight it; I could deal with a few nights here and there, for the boys' sake. He used a leather strap as a noose sometimes. Thor saw the marks on my neck. I could see that he was suffering. Vic was indifferent, but Thor would notice the tiniest change in my mood. He was so damn smart. When he was thirteen, I discovered that his vocabulary was a lot bigger than mine. I don't know how, since all they learned in that stupid cult school was the theses. That was when I realized I would be an idiot for the rest of my life unless I escaped—' The words caught in her throat.

'A couple of times, I ran into Simon in the shop in the village. That was before we fled to the United States. We started talking, and I told him everything. Eventually he made me see that I couldn't stay. That Thor and Vic had nothing to gain from a terrified, abused mother. He gave me a phone so we could plan our escape. When he helped me jump over the wall, my heart was pounding so hard I thought it would burst. I hid at Simon's for a long time, until everyone was sure I was dead. That was when we went to California. But I never stopped thinking about the boys, and I wonder who they've become now that Franz has sole custody of them.'

'How could you even bring Elvira here after everything that's happened?' Sofia asked, looking reproachfully at Simon.

'Because I begged him to,' Elvira said. 'I just need to see the boys again. I've felt so horribly guilty for abandoning them.'

'But how did you manage to get to the United States?' Sofia asked. 'Didn't they look for you?'

'Simon arranged a new passport for me. My name is Elly Ahlstedt now. You'll never guess who helped him.'

Sofia knew right away.

'Oh. It was Ellis, wasn't it?'

Elvira nodded. Sofia felt surprised and a little disappointed that Ellis had never told her this. They could have trusted her. And she was a little mad at Simon, who had never breathed a word about it all. Now here she was, a fool, in the middle of this cursed merry-go-round Franz had set into motion.

'I actually met Vic last winter,' Sofia said. 'Only briefly. He drove us from the ferry to ViaTerra. You know, we were there for a short visit. Maybe Simon told you.'

'Really? How was Vic?' Elvira asked eagerly.

For the first time, she looked Sofia in the eyes as she spoke.

'The spitting image of Franz. Confident, tough, and too attractive for his own good.'

'That doesn't surprise me, that's exactly the way I remember him. Did you see Thor?'

'No, sorry to say.'

Elvira sighed in disappointment.

'Look, there's something else Simon wants me to tell you,' she said. 'You know how Franz is, totally unpredictable, and sometimes he would come to the cottage just to chat. He would be nice as anything. He talked about you sometimes, Sofia.'

'Oh? What did he say? That he was going to squash me like a bug?'

'Not at all. He never said anything negative about you to me. Maybe that's hard to believe, but it's true. He always said the same thing. That you two would "find your way back to each other". He said that more than once. As if you had been married and separated. It sounded completely nuts. He said over and over that you were the only one who understood the depth of his theses.'

Sofia was struck by a memory so real she mentally vanished from the room. It was from her last, terrible day on the island, after Franz raped her. He had held her down from behind. *You're beautiful, Sofia, you know that? Not as tight as a fourteen-year-old, but still beautiful. And while we're on the subject, you have a delightful ass.* She relived the feeling of the weight of his ribcage against her back. The sense that she would never manage to shake him off. Her throat constricted with repressed tears.

'What do we do now, Simon?' she asked, her voice trembling.

'Yes, it seems complicated, doesn't it?' he said. 'But really, we all have the same goal. Elvira wants to see her sons again. You want to be free of Franz. Benjamin and I just want to protect the both of you. We have to figure out how to bring Franz's empire down for good. Elvira could speak out publicly, of course, I'm sure the media would drool over her story. But that would only end the same way as your last attack on him. He can bounce back from almost anything.'

'Then how are we supposed to get him?'

'We'll use every resource we can think of. Ellis, of course. Maybe we can enlist Magnus Strid, that journalist who helped us when you first ran away, Sofia. Are you still in touch with him?'

'No, but I can probably get hold of him.'

'Good. We're just going to have to call a meeting and come up with a watertight plan. And I have some media contacts in the US. We have to make this a worldwide scandal, you know? His networks extend all over the world. But I don't know who here in Sweden I can still trust. Can you vouch for Benjamin, Ellis and Anna?'

'Absolutely,' she said, without a second's hesitation. 'But I'd prefer to leave Julia out of all of this.'

'Of course. Well, okay then. All we have to do is call everyone to a meeting,' Simon said.

He leaned back on the sofa and looked like his normal self again, for the first time in a long time.

Totally at ease.

31

Julia was well aware of everything that was up, you'd better believe it. That massive bouquet had come by messenger, and Mom had sighed in annoyance and carried it out to the entryway. But she hadn't thrown it in the garbage right away. Julia saw the card that accompanied the bouquet and thought it was a lovely message. Could an evil person, a rapist, really write such a thing?

There was only one troubling issue Julia needed to figure out. Elisa Bonelli. After the article about Franz, Julia had snooped on Mom's phone. It wasn't the first time, but she only did it in emergencies. And this was an emergency, because the email from Franz was still sitting unanswered in Julia's inbox. The one about her trip to Fog Island.

Elisa Bonelli's email to Mom was there on Mom's phone. Since the news about Franz had turned up just a few days after the email, the rest was easy to figure out. After searching all the social networks where Elisa Bonelli appeared to be active, Julia had formed a clear picture of her. She was the type that thrived on attention but always pretended to be so disgustingly self-effacing. Her posts were full of comments that began with 'Brag warning!' and 'I will totally burst if I don't talk about this…' So stuck-up, the kind of person who got high on attention. The opposite of Julia, who didn't care one bit what people thought of her.

And that turned out to be the crucial insight. A man like Franz Oswald would never find a girl like Elisa attractive.

Which meant Elisa Bonelli was a liar.

Franz hadn't contacted Julia since he sent the email, hadn't made a single attempt to influence her decision. That made him even more desirable in her eyes. He obviously didn't need to work to get girls.

She had heard Simon and Mom talking about him in lowered voices again. Some kind of meeting. How did they have the gall? She was smart enough not to show any interest, because Mom would only get suspicious.

When those rumours about Franz began to spread, Julia had been struck by doubt; it buzzed in her mind like angry bees. But as soon as she decided that Elisa Bonelli was lying, her thoughts took a different turn. Now she felt the temptation, once more, to visit Fog Island. She always got absent-minded when she couldn't make a decision. She would become clumsy, drop things, run into people. Her friends at school thought she was nervous ahead of their national exams. What naïve children. But that was just the air in Henån, and you had no choice but to breathe it in.

The more she thought about it, and she thought about it a lot, the more she realized she could not let this opportunity go to waste. The regret and disappointment would suffocate her. She would finish compulsory school, die of boredom over summer vacation, and then start at a new tedious school.

It was such a mystery, becoming so ridiculously attracted to someone. To think that it could happen with someone you didn't even know. The excitement of being chosen that way. She felt it in parts of her body she didn't even know existed.

She read the email from him again. Exact dates and times.

Train and ferry tickets attached. Short and concise, even businesslike, if it hadn't been for the last sentence:

Pack: 1) short, see-through negligees 2) fishnet stockings 3) thongs

The balls on him. What if Mom read this? Just think. But she could always bring her Dita von Teese costume.

As she stared at the final line, a sudden, hot current of sexual desire bolted through her.

She began to compose a response to his email.

I'll come.

Too short.

I'll come, on one condition.

Hell, what condition?

I won't be bringing any of those underthings, but I'm coming.

That sounded ridiculous.

No matter what she wrote, it was all wrong. She imagined Franz Oswald opening the email, frowning, and thinking he'd never read something so childish. That he'd better worm out of any encounter with that schoolgirl.

She decided to chat with Matt before she answered the email and see if he could cover for her. He sounded mildly irritated when he picked up the phone. When she pointed it out, he said he had a headache. He'd never said that before. But when she asked him to cover for her for a few days during the Ascension Day holiday, he was so agreeable that she felt suspicious. She told him she was going to visit a friend in Gothenburg Mom and Dad didn't like, and he didn't ask any more questions.

'I'm supposed to see my parents then anyway,' he said. 'So that's fine.'

He didn't like visiting his parents, she knew. But you wouldn't have guessed from his voice. He sounded totally unbothered.

'Can we say we're going to Gothenburg to visit a friend of yours?' she asked.

'Sure.'

'What's the friend's name, in case they ask?'

'Make something up. Send me a text.'

She felt a pang of guilt that she had lied to Matt, but it was only a brief adventure, and then everything would go back to normal between them again. She knew that what she was planning to do was crazy, risky, and totally reckless, but wasn't that the whole point? All she needed now was one last lifeline. If there was trouble out there on Fog Island, no one would know where she was. Her clever lies would make it impossible to trace her.

Then she had an idea. She checked the dates in the email Franz had sent. She would be back home on the Monday after Ascension. There was a way you could schedule texts on your phone; you could write something ahead of time but have it sent on a specific date. Sometimes she used that function to send herself reminders. She composed a message to be sent to Matt. She couldn't send it to her parents; it would give them too much of a shock.

I'm on Fog Island. Something is wrong, she wrote. She scheduled the text to be sent a few hours after her planned return. Just in case. But it would never have to be sent, she would make it home in time.

Now there was only one more step. Accepting Franz's invitation without sounding too easy. She decided to call him, get him to beg a little. It was nine-thirty. She wondered what a man like Franz would be up to at nine-thirty at night. Working, maybe. Or seeing another woman. She hadn't added his name to her contacts. Instead, his number was labelled 'Library', a number Mom would never think to investigate more closely.

He answered after the first ring.

'Hi, Julia! What's on your mind?'

'I could go public with this email you sent,' she said. 'I mean, the part about the underwear.'

'I doubt that would have much effect, aside from increasing sales of thongs.'

'Okay, fine. But anyway, I want to talk about that trip. Is this a bad time?'

'Not at all. I'm in the gym, doing a spinning session.'

She had the quick mental image of his chest, his six-pack covered in beads of sweat.

'Doesn't it bother you, going behind my mom's back, after you sent her those flowers?' she asked.

'I'm not going behind her back. She never asked. Has she asked you anything about me?'

'No, not exactly.'

'There you go.'

'Fine, I'll come. Do you promise not to choke me with a leather strap?'

He sighed so hard the line crackled.

'You know there are people who live in the same boring shithole town all their lives and then die there in some smelly nursing home? You'll never be that kind of person, Julia.'

'You didn't answer my question.'

'I told you, I don't do that kind of thing.'

'Good, because I will *not* want to. Will you be with me the whole time?'

'No, but I will spend as much time with you as I can. I want to show you the island. The most beautiful spots. You'll be staying in a house that's a little out of the way. It wouldn't be right for the guests to see you. So young and beautiful. They might get the wrong impression.'

'How will I find my way there?'

'Someone will come meet you at the ferry.'

'Sounds good.'

'I already can't wait.'

'Me neither.'

Her mouth had gone horribly dry.

When she lay back on her bed and took it all in, it really felt as if she was about to pass out with desire.

After the tragedy in the manhole, I moved through the days as if in a fog. I had become skilled at what I was doing, and Bella was always happy with me. Father was mildly impressed with my work, but the joy I took in it was gone.

When I was younger and in school, I was always initially shy and uncertain about everything. I was afraid of being asked a question in the classroom. Sometimes I would stutter when I answered, always afraid the other children would tease me. But eventually I came to realize I had an unusually easy time learning things. It was a gift I had inherited from Father, whereas Vic had inherited his looks, charisma, and all that. When I was nine or ten, I started taking advantage of this ability. I answered questions quickly, sometimes with a tone suggesting that anyone who didn't understand was a little slow. I sometimes challenged Ali-Khan with responses that put her off balance. If there was anything I made use of to survive Earth's Children, it was my ability to learn quickly.

The same went for computer programming. It only took a few weeks for me to learn things not even Bella Svahnberg could manage. All summer we worked in a dark room, where the only light came from the computer screens. On the inside I was restless, but I still took pride in my work.

That autumn was when the storm came. The whole staff, and all the visiting guests, lay crowded together in the basement as it hit the island. It sounded like a massive, endless freight train as it roared over the property. But after the fire, the manor house had been rebuilt to be hurricane-proof. And somehow, miraculously, the school and annexes and cottage where we'd lived with Mama survived. Even the newly built auditorium still triumphantly raised its glass cupola to the sky once the storm had passed. Father held a lecture the day after the storm. He said that the highest power of all, Mother Earth, had protected us. We were the chosen ones. We were the ones who would pick up the pieces after the disaster and save the world. Everyone thought it was so beautiful; some people cried.

Over a couple of sleepless days and nights, we launched it all: our new platforms, websites, databases and ViaTerra's social media presence. At last we collapsed into deep sleep before the computers.

That winter, Bella and I worked on maintenance and improvements. But I never stopped thinking about you. Father's betrayal. Matteo's secret assignment. I was most afraid that he would hurt you. All of this was constantly smouldering inside me, until the day something enormous happened.

I got to see you again.

It happened during the big ViaTerra summit, the one to which the Pope himself lent his approval. Preparations of the property took several weeks. The whole staff had to help out. According to Father, this was the biggest thing that had ever happened, so we abandoned our jobs and pitched in wherever needed. I was assigned a role as server. I strolled around the auditorium, overwhelmed by the crowds and pompous speeches.

You were standing with Matteo in the middle of the space. You had come together; Matteo pretended not to know anyone. He acted as if he were visiting ViaTerra for the first time and appeared to be your bodyguard. Among thousands of people, I spotted you immediately. I came closer, until you collided with my cheese tray. Matteo shot me a look of warning and quickly pulled you away from me. But I lingered in a corner, watching you. You had become even more beautiful. The light you radiated illuminated the whole gathering.

For one magnificent second, our eyes met. I knew you felt it too. That connection.

Everything changed that night. The simmering doubt I had carried within me for so long turned into hatred. Father's presence wound my nerves as tight as bowstrings. But my fear had vanished.

I truly longed for those strings to snap.

EVERYTHING COMES TO A HEAD

I wake up and my skin is already crawling. There is no one else in the dorm; Bella and I are working the night shift. She likes working at night. The likelihood of Father popping in to admire her work is greater then. He always works late.

Out on the property, the sun is already high in the sky. The scent of damp earth rises from the ground. A gentle breeze makes the bare trees sway. I feel like I ought to be enjoying the beautiful day, but my brain seems to have gone numb. Bella's not in the office. I recall that she was going to the mainland on some errand. Just as I take a seat at my computer, I hear the door open.

That's when I make up my mind. Before I've even seen them, before I know why they're there. I simply make a decision.

It's Father, with Vic in tow.

'Aha, here's our little boy,' says Father. 'Industrious as usual. Do you have anything new to show me, Thor?'

My tongue feels like sandpaper against the roof of my mouth.

'Not since last night, boss,' I mutter hoarsely.

Vic goes to stand by the computer screen. His eyes glitter with arrogant scorn. There's something about their attitudes, they're like little boys out to pick a fight, mess with the first likely victim they come across.

'Shouldn't you stand when I enter?' Father asks, but just as I make a move to do so, his hands press me back down.

'Listen, Thor, that girl... Don't look so surprised, you know who I'm talking about. It turns out she's really hot.'

I bolt to my feet and find myself eye to eye with him.

'That's disgusting,' I say. Quietly at first, almost in a whisper.

'What did you say?'

'It's disgusting, the way you talk about her.' Loudly now.

It takes Father a few seconds to register my words and realize he heard me right the first time. My fists clench, open, clench again.

'Oh, you think so, do you? Well, in that case, you don't understand a goddamn thing,' he hisses through clenched teeth.

Vic has already taken out his phone to call someone.

I know who. The guards.

Then something strange happens: the corners of my mouth turn up in the beginnings of a smile I can't repress. I'm nervous and can't control my reactions. Why is this happening right now?

'What? You think this is funny?' bellows Vic, who has finished his phone call.

I don't respond, my whole body is tense and numb all at once. And there is Father, legs planted wide before me. His hand comes up but stops halfway. It looks like he's aiming a gun at me. It would only take a second for him to fall upon me, this large, heavy man, furious that I have contradicted him. I have defied him and his authority. Therefore I must be punished. He is going to hurt me, I know it. By this point, I am paralysed with fear. I must not start crying. Must not piss myself.

He is giving off a strange smell, something almost animalistic. Hatred is reflected in his face, not only for me but also for people like me – skinny, awkward, reedy-voiced. I wait for the slap I know is coming, but instead he lowers his hand and starts to speak in an odd, monotone voice.

He has battled all his life to build up everything we have, he says. When he was much younger, his eyes were opened to the true nature of human beings: they are egotistical, fake, like mice biting each other to death when they're stuck in an overcrowded cage. He set out on a long journey to discover the meaning of life, and in so doing risked his own life, more than once. Yes, he was only thirteen, but what does that matter? He has been an adult as far back as he can remember.

His heavy hand drops onto my shoulder.

'And you know what I realized in the end, Thor? Out in the world, the real *world, no one knows a fucking thing.'*

He takes a step closer; his monologue continues. All of this made him curious about the meaning of life. But there were no answers to the question out there *so he had to search for the answers inside himself. He did that, and he built up all of this. He throws his arms out and his hand nearly hits me in the face. And no matter how much he toils, working himself to the bone, people like me – Satan's rats – throw obstacles in his way. Little besserwissers, know-it-alls, fucking vermin crawling all over everything.*

And there it is: the slap. He hits me so hard that my ears ring; I stagger backwards and crash into the computer screen.

I've always known this moment would arrive. I swore I wouldn't cry. For Christ's sake, don't cry!

When the guards come, I initially make the mistake of trying to get away. I resist like a panicked animal, but within a few seconds they've got me on the floor. They twist my arms behind my back, like cops, and it hurts so much I cry out. They're heavy, violent, pressing me into the floor until I can hardly breathe.

'Shut up and lie still! Don't move, you fucking little cunt!' one of them screams.

They drag me across the floor and then haul me to my feet. Out in the courtyard they pull me along so fast I fall, scraping my knees and gasping for breath. But I don't cry. I will not fucking cry.

*

Penance is full, but that's not where I'm going. Benny will guard me day and night.

'Make that little shit work. The filthiest jobs. See if you can find any clogged drains anywhere.' Father's last words to me.

I sleep in the barn, under all the names carved there so long ago. When I see the scrawling letters I get a lump in my throat and realize I'm not a child any longer. It's dirty in the stall; it's full of dust bunnies and the dried corpses of insects. It's cold and draughty at night even though it's early spring. But I curl up in my sleeping bag. And when I think about that moment in the auditorium when I caught sight of you and our eyes met, it's easier to sleep. I long to see you so much it hurts. I dream of being with you in some parallel universe. I often pray to God, who I don't believe in, for you to hear my thoughts and warnings.

I spend my days digging a sewer behind the stable. Benny watches me like a hawk. But one day he doesn't show up. At first I am baffled, but then Madde arrives, sent by Father, to inform me that they have neither the time nor the desire to waste staff on guarding me. All the work I did with Bella has to be reviewed because I am an enemy to the group and can't be trusted. From now on, I have to manage on my own.

The sewer work is soon done. I start to think of other jobs to do. I clean the stable, sort through the tools there; I even wash the windows, which are covered in decades' worth of spiderwebs and filth. The cows have just been let out to pasture for the season, but I clean their stalls and the chicken coops. Once the stable is clean I find a small, overgrown garden behind the house and clear away the weeds. Under the mess are daffodils, which start to bloom while I'm working there.

I find a flashlight and a couple of dusty, stained mystery novels someone left in a cleaning closet. But when I reach in farther, my hand runs into a thicker book. It's stained too, and its pages are yellowed; its cover is about to fall off. East of Eden. *I read it every night before I fall asleep. It lets me vanish into a world far away from the island.*

All these words. So smoothly woven together. Once I've finished it, I start over from the beginning. I can't get enough of this book.

The only person I ever see is Benny, who drops off my food once a day.

Sometimes I catch a glimpse of someone going by on a motorcycle; sometimes the guards or Madde or Father walk past, but they don't even glance in my direction.

Soon I have no idea how long I've been here. There is a shower at the back of the stable where I wash, but I have no razor or mirror. I can feel that my chin is becoming covered in downy fuzz.

I always wake up early. Each morning I watch the sun rise and fill the sky with magnificent shades of red. It's so lovely when the rays hit the floating morning mist and transform it into a shimmering blanket that shrouds the property.

Each morning I am astounded that I never noticed this before.

My small, meaningless, routine days make me happy.

When they come to get me, I know I can never return to my work at ViaTerra.

32

Sofia had lost touch with Magnus Strid over ten years ago. Sometimes she happened across a piece he had written; once in a while he showed up on a news program. Magnus had been the one to convince Sofia to speak out when she escaped from ViaTerra. He had written a number of articles about her. In her first years out, they had spoken often, but then they drifted apart.

At first it seemed as if she would never get hold of him. He must have moved fifteen times and now lived in a secret location with an unlisted number. She called the newspapers he used to work for, but they refused to give her his contact information. Just when she was about to give up, he called.

'Sofia Troublemaker Bauman! I heard you were looking for me. Is that really you?'

His voice sounded gruffer than she recalled, as though he had continued to smoke two packs a day.

'Yes, it's me. You're so hard to get hold of! Are you under witness protection or something?'

'No, I just need some peace and quiet.'

'It's good to hear your voice again,' she said. 'That voice I could always depend on.'

'Same to you. And that, I assume, means you want my help with something?'

'Exactly. Just like in the good old days. We can either meet up somewhere, or else turn this into a long conversation.'

'I've got all the time in the world.'

Sofia told him the whole story from the beginning – about the storm, how Franz had attained star status again (which Magnus was, of course, aware of already), and about the attacks, the break-ins, and the book.

Then she paused to ask if a person could be taken to court for a crime committed fifteen years ago. When Magnus laughed and asked if she'd murdered someone, she told him about the rape and how she'd set the fire at ViaTerra. And, last of all, she told him the truth about Julia. That she didn't know who Julia's father was.

When she was finished talking, he didn't say anything for a long time.

'You aren't going to go to the police about this, are you?' Sofia asked, suddenly frightened.

'Hell no, I just have to process it all,' he said. 'What a bastard. But I think you did the right thing, setting the manor on fire instead of reporting him. As usual it would have been your word against his, and he has an incredible talent for worming his way out of stuff. You know he doesn't have any rights at all when it comes to your daughter, don't you? Maybe it doesn't matter who her biological father is. What do you and Benjamin think?'

'We love her no matter what, obviously, but we're not sure what to think. Maybe she has the right to know. But we want absolutely nothing to do with him, that's for certain.'

'There you go. Just give him a big fat finger and tell him to stay away from you.'

'Well, that's easy to say, but he has a penchant for popping up in our lives in the creepiest ways.'

'It really is incredible. After all these years. But I'm sure you didn't call me just to reveal all of this and hear my opinion, did you?'

Sofia took a deep breath.

'No, I called to ask for help inciting the media scandal of the century.'

Magnus didn't take much convincing. His interest was especially piqued when Sofia told him about Elvira and her sons, and Earth's Children. They decided to meet up in Gothenburg, the better to keep Julia out of the loop.

In her eagerness to contact everyone and arrange the meeting, Sofia almost forgot she'd never told Anna about the rape. She wondered if they even needed Anna at the meeting, if she would bring anything to the table. But if there had been anyone Sofia could count on in recent years, it was Anna. She had supported Sofia through good times and bad; they could talk about anything. Except what had happened in the cellar at ViaTerra fifteen years ago. That was a secret Simon, Benjamin and Sofia had decided never to reveal. But now Ellis and Magnus knew, and Anna would never violate Sofia's trust.

Sofia drove to the pension to pick Anna up when her workday was over. They went out to the sea and sat on the rocks. Sofia told her all about the terrible week of being held prisoner in the cellar, the rape, the fire. At last she told her that Elvira had come back.

When she was finished, Anna turned her face away, towards the sea. The thick fog that had scattered earlier that day had returned and visibility was terrible. The damp air had settled over them like a cold, wet blanket. When Anna turned to look at Sofia again, she was crying. Tears trickled down her wet cheeks.

'What is it, Anna?'

'Why didn't you ever tell me this? It's terrible. Are you serious? Did he really do that?'

'You don't believe me?'

'Of course I do. It's just a lot to take in.'

Sofia had the sudden, fleeting feeling that something wasn't quite right. She felt afraid without knowing why. But then Anna took her hand.

'I'm shocked. Jesus, how awful. Poor you. How have you been able to carry this around for so long?'

Sofia swiped her wet bangs out of her eyes.

'I just put it all out of my mind. Didn't want to talk about it. But I can't do that anymore, you know?'

'Are you sure Julia is his?'

'His or Benjamin's. The whole thing was so stupid. I had gone off the pill because I promised Benjamin I'd be faithful while I was in the US. Like, I hadn't foreseen that Franz would kidnap me the minute I got home.'

'But didn't you have a relationship with a guy over there?'

'Yes, but I'm sure Julia isn't his. We used condoms. And the dates wouldn't match. I've counted the days at least a thousand times. Franz raped me just as I was ovulating. Unbelievable, right? My usual bad luck. And then I hurried to have sex with Benjamin. For some weird reason I thought it would help.'

'Why didn't you ever check, though? It would have been so easy.'

'It's much harder than you'd think. The idea that it could be true was unbearable. It still is. We repressed the idea so successfully that we eventually almost forgot our suspicions. But the question right now is, do you want to help me?'

Anna leaned forward and took hold of Sofia in an awkward attempt to hug her. The rocks were slippery and dangerous, and Sofia slid backwards on her butt and nearly fell into the sea. One of her shoes ended up in the water. She started laughing as Anna helped her up. But Anna still looked sad.

'Of course I'll help you. I always have, no matter what,' she said.

They drove home in silence. All the while, Anna gazed out the window. The fog had enveloped everything; Sofia had to drive at a snail's pace the whole way. Clearly Anna had taken Sofia's tale awfully hard, but later that evening the mood between them was back to normal.

A few days later, Sofia, Benjamin, Anna, Simon and Elvira crowded into Sofia's little car and drove to Gothenburg. Ellis and Magnus would meet them there.

When they arrived at the café where they'd planned to meet, Magnus was already waiting for them. Sofia didn't recognize him at first. He used to look like a lumbering bear, flabby and unkempt, his clothes buttoned oddly, coffee stains everywhere, and days of stubble. Apparently he had changed his style, because his beer belly was gone, and he was in good shape, sporting a short haircut, a smooth chin, and a blazer.

'I hardly recognize you. What happened?' Sofia asked as she embraced him.

'I received a death sentence from a doctor who said I'd kick it before sixty if I didn't get my ass in gear,' he said, chagrined. 'I stopped smoking and started working out and all that. Sucks, but I do actually feel better.'

Just then, Ellis arrived, and they sat down in the relatively empty café.

They told Magnus the whole story, one by one. He listened patiently with his eyes half-closed. Sometimes his eyelids drooped so much that Sofia thought he had fallen asleep. But when they were finished, he quickly sat up straight and began to speak.

'All I can say is, *damn*. But here's the thing. It's incredibly easy for Franz to recover from one little media scandal. He can deny a rumour, get someone to speak out on his behalf, blackmail people, all that. He's a showman, an actor. It's almost like he gets off on brushing off scandals, minimizing them. But if the bomb drops in different media all over the world at the same time, and if the news is sensational, that's how we get him. The fact that children are involved will make it spread like wildfire. It's gruesome.'

He paused, twisting a napkin between his fingers, and glanced up with a look of concern on his face.

'Unfortunately, the truth is that people are tired of Franz's sex scandals. It doesn't matter what kind of shit he does – he somehow always turns it around, just as he did with you, Elvira. There's always a hell of a lot of chatter, but once the case makes it to court all the air goes out of it. Sure, he spent time in prison, but now he's made a comeback and become an environmental saint. In some incredible way, it's always the women who end up the losers, who have to live with the scars. It's the same old tune: "They went along with it." I think we have to focus on the children this time. Dig more into that. If it's true that he's created some sort of Hitler Youth movement out there on Fog Island, we can sink him. In this fucking society, it's fine to harm a woman, if you claim she was in on it, but not a child, you see?'

'Sure, but how do we learn more about this school?' Sofia asked.

'We have to get someone who attended it to speak out,' Magnus said. 'Best of all would be one of the children.'

'In our dreams,' said Sofia.

'Don't say that. I'd be willing to bet they're not all as brainwashed as you think. How old are your sons now, Elvira?'

'They recently turned eighteen.'

'Then he can't stop them from speaking out. I think you have to try to get in touch with them somehow.'

'Not Vic,' Elvira blurted. 'He worships his father, he would never turn on him.'

'Or he's already turned out exactly like Franz,' Benjamin added. 'He definitely works close beside him. Power corrupts.'

'Bullshit,' Ellis said. 'Any bastard who seizes power is already corrupt. And we just let them do their thing. But I'm sure you're right, his son is a Franz Oswald clone.'

'Maybe Thor will be brave enough to speak out,' Elvira suggested. 'I was in touch with his grandmother a few years ago. Over email. But then it became too risky.'

'Start with the grandmother, then,' Magnus said. 'Contact her again.'

He turned to Ellis.

'And you – I want you to hack every one of Franz's websites, platforms and social media accounts so we have access to them when we drop this bomb. Instead of only spreading the news the usual way – through articles, news broadcasts, and so forth – I think we should also make use of his vast network when we go public. He hosts a video chat each night. Figure out how we can hack that and tell his followers what a bastard he is.'

Ellis nodded eagerly. He had taken on that look he always got when he was on the trail of something juicy. 'Yes, and I'll set up an encrypted link online so we can communicate securely. I'll do it tonight,' he said.

'As soon as we have something more concrete, I'll get in touch with some media contacts in the US,' Simon said.

''And I'll contact all the journalists I know, and that's a heck of a lot,' Magnus said. 'We have to release the news of this scandal all over the world simultaneously. Can you set up a secure link between the journalists and our server, Ellis? One that can't be hacked?'

Ellis nodded.

'What about me?' Sofia asked. 'What do you want me to do?'

'Back out of your contract with the publisher,' Magnus said. 'Think up a good excuse. Then you can write that final chapter of the book, because as soon as this hell breaks loose, all the publishers in Sweden will want to release the book, and foreign publishers too, for that matter. Then you can sign a new contract, without Franz's involvement.'

Anna, who hadn't said much, leaned forward and gently squeezed Sofia's hand.

'Look, I can handle the shelter so you can focus on the book. I promise I'll stop by every day and check in on the construction.'

'I will write the articles and contact every newspaper and news service I've ever worked for once we're ready,' Magnus said. 'I want to start by interviewing you, Elvira, and sharing your story. We can do the interview over the phone.'

Elvira nodded.

'Anything to help me get in contact with Thor and Vic again.'

They looked at each other in silence for a moment.

'Well, we've got a plan,' said Benjamin, whose main contribution had been to listen wide-eyed to Magnus.

'Sure, and what are you going to contribute, Benjamin?' asked a mildly irritated Ellis.

'Keep earning money and make sure nothing happens to my lovely ladies,' he said, putting his arm around Sofia.

'You haven't changed. Just as gullible and a little lazy too, if I may say so,' Magnus said, shaking his head in amusement.

'You should find out who put that money into Julia's account, that might be a lead.'

For a whole day after the meeting, Sofia felt hopeful, even though it turned out getting out of her book contract was trickier than she'd expected. But once she explained that her conscience was heavy on account of further revelations about Franz, things she simply had to include in the book, the publishers relented. Sofia got the feeling that the last thing they wanted was to be dragged into a lawsuit with him.

A few days later, in the middle of the night, a phone call came in from Simon. He was renting a house farther inland with Elvira. Simon's typical phone manner was painfully slow, but now his words came quickly, in fits and starts.

'It's Elvira... she's at the hospital... those bastards... Jesus Christ...'

Sofia's spine began to tingle with misgivings.

'Simon, what's going on?'

'She was just taking out the trash...'

Simon was seriously shaken up and didn't seem to be able to produce coherent sentences. Sofia didn't say anything for a moment to let him collect his thoughts. As she stood there with the phone pressed to her ear, her head began to buzz as if someone had released a swarm of bees. Her heart beat double time.

'This car came by, it ran right into her,' came Simon's voice through the hum. 'On the most deserted road in the area. Late at night. They had been waiting there, with the headlights off. If she hadn't reacted so quickly, leapt out of the way, she probably wouldn't have made it. She's got a broken toe and a sprained wrist. I don't know what to do. I don't even know where we should go.'

He whimpered.

'That's terrifying!' Sofia exclaimed. 'Did they catch whoever did it?'

'No, the police say it was a hit and run, but I'm positive it had to be attempted murder. It was a matter of seconds. Hell, I heard the crash, it sounded so awful, and then Elvira, screaming… out of her mind… and the car starting again.'

'I'll come straight to the hospital.'

'No, you don't have to come. They're going to discharge her tomorrow morning.'

'Come straight to our house after that. Don't even stop by your place to pick up clothes. You can borrow everything from us.'

'It doesn't feel safe. It has to be Franz, out to get Elvira. He knows where you live.'

That was when Sofia decided to put Benjamin to work for real.

'I'm going to make Benjamin turn our house into the safest place on Orust, I promise. Guards, alarms, the whole nine yards. Our house is going to become a fortress.'

Her voice had risen half an octave.

At first, the shock made her so numb that she didn't feel any fear, but then came the notion that she was probably next in line. Or Benjamin.

Or Julia.

33

That night, when Julia saw Matt, he was acting strange. He seemed scattered. His gaze kept wandering away from hers, which wasn't like him. He had a couple days' worth of stubble and had been wearing the same clothes three days in a row.

There was a chilliness to him, a kind of self-discipline that closed her out. She felt itchy all over when he was like that. Not to mention upset. But when he realized how she was feeling, he reached over and cupped her cheek.

'Hey! Are you okay?'

'Of course,' she said, but her voice trembled. She was surprisingly moved by his touch.

He pulled her close. His leather jacket was open and she smelled his familiar scent. She rested her head against his chest and let her hands fall to his hips. She felt a little lonely. Being with Matt wasn't quite as exciting as usual, but there were still strong feelings between them. He knew exactly what she liked. They had become delightfully familiar with one another's bodies. He went home at eleven, and Julia fell asleep soon after.

The insistent ringtone of her phone woke her in the night. There wasn't even a hint of dawn outside. She glanced at the clock – five-thirty. It should have been getting light out, but the damn fog must be blocking the sun. The trees moved in the breeze; a few leaves fluttered past the window. She searched the room for her phone and found it in her purse. When she saw Matt's name on the screen, the hair on the back of her neck stood up. He was never awake this early.

'Matt!' she said before he could speak.

His voice was low and hardly audible on the other end.

'I'm going away.'

'Yeah, I know. You told me that. Why are you calling so early?'

'Listen to me carefully. I'm leaving this morning. I can't tell you everything, but you have to believe me.'

There was an urgent note in his soft voice that made her shut up and listen.

'I've been involved in something horrible. I can't stay here. You'll find out all about it later, but right now you will have to trust me. I love you *so much*, Julia. And you can't go on that trip over Ascension. Listen to me, you have to promise not to go.'

She didn't know what to think. Her mind was a total blank.

'Why not? What's going on? I don't understand.'

'I can't tell you yet, it's too dangerous. Promise me not to go. I know where you're going. Please, promise me.'

'Okay,' she said, an empty promise. Could he know that she was going to see Franz? But how?

'Is it another girl?' she asked. 'If that's it, it doesn't matter.'

'No, of course not, just listen. First I have to find a good place to hide out, and then I'll get a pay-as-you-go phone that can't be traced, and after that I can call you and tell you everything. I promise. Until then, you have to trust me. Please, Julia, trust me right now.'

She heard a quiet sniffle on the phone and it dawned on her that he was crying. She felt awkward and unsure, totally off balance.

'Are you upset? Please, if you're sad, come over here.'

He didn't respond. The sniffles had turned into muffled sobs.

'Hey! Tell me what's going on. Why are you crying?'

She had a panicky thought that he might try to take his own life and feverishly racked her brains for something to say. This was all so unlike Matt. It was starting to feel like a nightmare. She tried to make her voice calm and authoritative, to break through the thick wall of sorrow he had built between them.

'Tell me about this terrible thing you did, I can take it.'

'The worst part isn't what I did, it's that you'll never forgive me,' he said. His voice sounded so strange that for an instant she wondered if some crazy person had got hold of Matt's phone and dialled her number. But it had to be Matt. With that special way of drawing out certain words.

'Are you going to go to jail?'

'Probably.'

'Did you kill someone?'

'No! Jesus.'

'Then I'll forgive you, as long as you tell me. I'll come visit you in jail.'

He laughed. It sounded like a hiccup between his sobs. For a long time, he didn't say anything, and then his voice sounded almost normal again.

'I wrote to tell the headmaster I'm going to Germany. He's not going to like that, and my parents are going to lose their minds, so I'm positive folks at the school are going to ask you about me. Please don't tell them I called. Just tell them I sent you a text and told you I was going away.'

'Okay, then you should send a text for me to show them. And if I don't hear from you right after Ascension I'll call the police.'

'No! Don't!' He sounded like his normal self again.

'Then you have to call me before then.'

'Okay, I will. And Julia…'

'Yes?'

'Whatever they say about me, I am totally in love with you. I always have been. You're my favourite person in the world.'

And then he was gone. And although she immediately dialled his number and left a voicemail demanding he call her back, she knew he wouldn't.

Now she could see the dawn light outside her window, faint and cold. She lay perfectly still in bed, listening for sounds in the house. But all she could hear was the grim whistle of the wind outside, as chilly as the morning sky. She got out of bed and went to the window. A couple of last year's leaves rustled across the lawn, as if they were in a rush to get somewhere. It reminded her of the storm, of the feeling she'd had right before it hit.

Her phone alerted her to an incoming text as she stood there. *Going to Germany for a few weeks. I'll be in touch. M.* So uninspired that she felt angry with him.

She couldn't seem to move as she stared at the dull text. This was serious. He wasn't coming back. Was this her punishment for lying to him about Franz? Her lower lip trembled. She felt so empty inside. Slowly, moving like a sleepwalker, she went back to bed and crawled under the covers. At first she couldn't sleep. She tried to come up with some terrible thing Matt might have done. Maybe he had stolen something. He did wear nice, expensive clothes. She'd read online about a recent armed robbery in Uddevalla. But that didn't seem quite like Matt's style. She couldn't imagine his wonderful eyes staring angrily from behind a balaclava. After she'd ruled out all the possibilities, each worse than the last, she drifted off into an uneasy, dream-filled sleep.

The very next day, she was called to the headmaster's office. He said it seemed Matt had taken a trip somewhere, which was puzzling, to say the least. Matt had always been so conscientious – in fact, he was the best student teacher they'd ever had. And now this. Did Julia know further details about what he was up to?

Julia showed the headmaster her text.

'That's all I know,' she said. 'I tried to call him, but he isn't picking up.'

As she stared into the headmaster's concerned eyes, she was once again impressed with herself for lying so readily.

She showed the text to Mom too, but Mom didn't seem concerned in the least. She had other things to worry about. Elvira and Simon had moved into their house after the accident. Mom had gone a bit hysterical and made Dad hire a security company. Now there were guards posted at their house around the clock.

When Julia showed her mother the text, Mom just smiled and ruffled her hair.

'Oh, I'm sure he just took a trip with some friends to get away for a while. All that means is that he likes you so much he can hardly stand it. Guys can be like that – and so can girls, for that matter. When he comes back he'll be full of regret and he'll tell you he loves you, you'll see.'

Mom – so smart, yet so hopelessly naïve.

Julia didn't know quite what to think about this all happening at once – Matt's disappearance, the terrible thing that happened to Elvira, and her upcoming adventure on Fog Island. She was a little scared, but also excited. Her monotonous, humdrum life in Henån had taken an exhilarating turn. There was no way to know what would happen next. These days things were happening in real life instead of on her computer screen, and she had one of the starring roles. Things might go south; maybe this trip could even turn out to be kind of disturbing. But whatever happened, it would be something different.

And she knew one thing for certain.

Life in Henån wasn't the least bit boring anymore.

When they came to get me, I was on my knees weeding my little garden plot. Dandelions and nettles had shot up in just a few days.

I had woken with the feeling that there was something special about this day. I didn't have a calendar, no way to keep track of time aside from the sun, and yet I realized, as I lay staring at the ceiling of the stall, that it was my birthday. I don't know why I was so certain of it. Maybe it was my biological clock. As I enjoyed a deep and peaceful slumber, I had turned eighteen. We didn't celebrate birthdays in ViaTerra; they were nothing special. Even so, this day felt important.

The sun was high in the sky when I heard the motorcycles. There were two of them – a bad sign. As their roar approached, I was positive they were coming for me. But I didn't stand up, didn't turn around, just knelt there pulling up the intruders in my lovely plot of blooming daffodils.

Although I heard the engines quit, the kickstands fall, the steps behind me, I kept puttering in the soil.

'Thor, the boss wants to see you in his office immediately.' It was Madde.

'There's some problem with the computers, something only you can fix,' said Sten, the guard. I was sure he had come along to take control in case I decided to put up a fight.

I could see their feet now. Madde's pumps were scraping nervously at the grass and Sten's work boots stomped on one of my daffodils.

'Get out of my garden,' I said.

'What? Didn't you hear us? The boss wants to see you,' said Sten.

'I want you to stop stepping on my flowers,' I said.

Madde snickered.

'Stop being ridiculous! We are here on the boss's orders. He wants to see you. Come on!'

'But I don't want to see him. Tell him he can come here if he has something to say to me.'

Madde gasped.

'Get the fuck up, go take a shower and put on clean clothes. You are coming with us!' Sten shouted.

But I didn't obey.

After half an hour of fruitless wheedling and nagging, they left. But I knew they would be back. With reinforcements.

I calculated that it would take about an hour for them to report to Father, decide what to do with me, and set their plan in motion. So I went into the stables and showered, put on clean clothes, and sat outside to wait.

Four guys showed up. The very strongest ones, with Didrik leading the charge.

I stood up and followed them willingly. Not because I was afraid, but because it seemed more practical than being dragged across the property.

It turned out I was to be taken to the cafeteria.

The whole staff of ViaTerra and Earth's Children were waiting for me there.

CASH TO EASE THE PAIN

There's a chair in the centre of the room; that's where I'm supposed to sit. The staff sit facing me, just like when Father holds his lectures. But this time I'm the one they're staring at. Didrik pushes me into the chair, although it's not necessary. I'm not planning to resist, not even against what I know will come later.

We wait in silence. The hands of the clock creep forward. My palms are sweaty, but I'm not scared, not yet.

When Father comes in, he doesn't look at me. Instead he starts a conversation with the staff as he paces in front of them. Questions that are easy to answer, that's the idea. This is a warm-up of sorts, a prelude to my punishment. He fixes his gaze on people at random and poses questions to them.

'Here is Thor. He hasn't done a damn thing while you've all been working your asses off. He's just been lying around sunning himself. What do you think about that, Benny?'

'It's horrible, boss. Awful.'

'It took a hell of a long time to go through all his work with the computers. All his mistakes and carelessness, it was pure sabotage. Do you think that's fair, Didrik?'

'No, not at all, boss.'

'And what do the rest of you think, as you see him staring at me with such spite?'

A dissatisfied murmur rises from the staff.

'Do you know what he said when I called him to my office? I wanted to help him, you see, give him a second chance. Do you know what he said to that?'

'No, boss,' they reply in unison.

'He thought I should be the one to come see him. Go to the pathetic flowerbeds he planted. Interrupt my work and go out there to weed with him.'

The staff gasp in horror.

I am filled with equal parts hatred and pity. They are so desperate to make a good impression on Father, blissfully unaware that one day it will be their turn to be in my position.

'No, I'm not exaggerating! It's true, isn't it, Thor?'

My face is getting warm.

He hasn't turned around yet, hasn't met my gaze.

'That's true, boss,' I mumble.

'The world is at our feet. Politicians, spiritual leaders, celebrities, powerful people in every country – they all sing our praises. ViaTerra is on everyone's lips. They have come to realize that we have the answers. We have never been so popular. But Thor thinks I should be weeding flowerbeds.'

He turns around to look at me. I have no idea how I look, but the expression on my face triggers something inside him, an explosion in the depth of his pupils. I have been waiting for this. The rage in his eyes, like glowing magma.

He won't be able to control himself.

So kill me, then, *I think.* Here I am, a rat, vermin, the betrayer, the parasite. Crush every bone in my body. You'll still have one son who worships you.

In his darkest, hoarsest voice, he says my name.

He presses his palm to my chest and forces me back until the chair almost tips over.

'Look me in the eye, Thor.'

I turn my face away.

Even so, I can see what's happening from the corner of my eye.

His clenched fists. His leg, pulling back before the kick strikes me, sending me and the chair toppling backwards so my head hits the floor with a thud. His body falling over me, heavy as a boulder, his fingers digging into my throat, and eventually, the stars in my eyelids when all the air is gone. It hurts so much that my legs jerk, but I don't kick, don't windmill my arms; I just lie there waiting for him to drain all the oxygen from my lungs.

Squeeze harder. Get it over with. 'Better dead than incompetent.' After all, that's your favourite motto.

The silence in the room is worse than my panic over not breathing.

Everyone remains respectfully quiet as the life trickles out of me down on the floor. Father's face, twisted with fury, so recently hovering above me, has vanished. All that's left is flickering static, explosions blinding me.

He quickly rolls off me. At first I don't realize he's gone, because the pain encircling my throat is still there; I can still feel the weight of his body, but he's sitting beside me, panting. It's so hard to breathe. It feels like a bird is caught inside my ribcage, flapping its wings wildly to get out.

Father's eyes are suddenly confused. As though he doesn't know where he is, what he's done. He looks around and discovers the staff. It's like he's once again aware of their presence. And the fact that they saw the whole thing. That he crossed a line. His bewilderment lingers for just an instant, but then he gets up and heads for the door.

The guards fly from their chairs, lunging for me to haul me away, but then Father turns and holds up a hand.

'Leave him be,' he says, and then he's out the door.

I lie on my back for a moment, staring at the ceiling. I realize that I really can breathe, even though there's a faint rattle coming from my lungs. I observe a cobweb near the ceiling; it moves in the gentle draught that arose when Father closed the door. Then I become aware of the silence in the room. Ripples of shock bounce off the walls. Did that really just happen? What do we do now? I sit up. The staff aren't glaring at me with their usual murderous gazes. They might even look a little frightened.

When Father returns, he has collected himself. He has smoothed his wrinkled clothing; he is standing erect, having recovered his authoritative presence. The staff hurry to stand. He gestures at them to sit down again and goes to the podium. And here I am on the floor, like a fool.

Father asks everyone who is or has been part of Earth's Children to stand.

Everyone does, except me.

'You are the ones I am most proud of in this group,' he says, sounding

melancholy. 'I value your loyalty more than anything. You are the future of ViaTerra, never forget that.'

Then he turns around to look at me.

'You too, Thor. Forgive me. I truly want you to forgive me. I forgive you for everything.'

And when he asks for my forgiveness, it sounds so genuine, so lovely, that I almost feel grateful that he strangled me. But only almost, because he must have some ulterior motive.

'Take a seat, Thor. All is forgiven. Go ahead and sit with the others.'

I do. It feels like I have no choice. As though I have depleted my time as a victim on the floor.

'You should know that I did something for you last fall, those of you who are in Earth's Children,' he says. 'I deposited money in your bank accounts, a rather large sum. For your future. If you ever feel like I have hurt you, or someone else, in any way…'

There are scattered gasps here and there. He raises his hand.

'No, let me finish. I know you don't feel that way right now. But you never know what turn life may take. You will always have something to fall back on, I've made sure of that. There now. You can all return to your work. I've said what I wanted to say.'

He leaves the room first. The boss is always the first one to leave the room. Then the staff filter out. I stay until everyone else is gone. I feel the pain in my throat again, the blood pulsing powerfully through my carotid artery. And now I wonder what to do – just go back to my garden, perhaps? That's what I want to do, anyway.

And then it occurs to me that this is the strangest thing I've ever heard. Depositing money into the accounts of people you have hurt, or intend to hurt.

34

The truth. Why was it so damn hard to write down the truth? For the hundredth time she erased the first line on the page. She stared at the blank document.

The cursor blinked. She was getting nowhere with her writing, and she knew why. Writing about the rape hadn't been as difficult as she'd expected. For fifteen years she had been processing her memories of it. She had partially gotten them out of her system. But writing about the arson was a totally different story.

'You're a goddamn coward,' she muttered to herself. It was as if their crimes were superglue, pasting her fate to Franz's forever. He had hurt her, but she had committed a crime. The game of cat-and-mouse would continue.

She had done her research. Arson carried a prison sentence of two to eight years. Its statute of limitations was fifteen years. There were certain exceptions that carried a life sentence. Cases of arson that put the lives of many in danger, or fires set in dense areas or on sites of particular cultural relevance. In those instances, the statute of limitations was twenty-five years. But she doubted what she had done fell under those rubrics. Which meant she could no longer be held accountable. So what the heck was her problem? Shame washed over her the moment her fingers touched the keys.

*

She had asked Benjamin for advice, suggesting that perhaps it was best for their family if she didn't mention the arson. But he just told her it was up to her. Simon, on the other hand, was sure she would be praised for her actions once the truth about Franz was out.

Her thoughts were drawn to the day they'd sat at the police station, lying so convincingly and so credibly that Franz had almost gone down. It had felt like the right thing to do at the time. She had been so consumed by her hatred for Franz, had laughed inwardly at how he'd provided her with a watertight alibi. He had been hoisted by his own petard. But now she wondered if her life would have been different if she'd told the truth that day.

The officer who'd questioned them was called Titus Berg. He'd had a stern look about him, a penetrating gaze. But after the interrogation he had been as kind as anything. He was a man who seemed to take his work very seriously. He'd done his very best to bring Franz down.

She turned to gaze out the window, letting her thoughts wander until they stubbornly returned to that interrogation. Mattias had sat right next to her and lied. And how they lied! She remembered Titus Berg's shrewd gaze. His large hands on the desk. Just as she recalled those hands, an idea came to her.

Titus Berg was almost as hard to get hold of as Magnus Strid. He was over eighty now, and long since retired. The Gothenburg police refused to give out his contact information. But eventually she reached a more cooperative receptionist at a smaller police station he'd once worked at. It turned out that Titus Berg lived on Orust these days, not far at all from Sofia and Benjamin's house. Since she was feeling restless and unable to write, she decided to take a chance. It was a beautiful day, and she needed to get out in the fresh air.

Simon and Elvira were still asleep. Elvira had been interviewed by Magnus into the wee hours. Benjamin was working in his office, and Julia was at school. She told Benjamin she was going down to the sea for a while. He was absorbed in something on his computer and only muttered in response.

Titus Berg lived farther inland. The last stretch was a narrow gravel road that crunched under her tyres and kicked up pebbles at the car. The GPS led her to the end of the road. She parked and almost stepped into a ditch as she climbed out.

The house was red with white trim and perched on a little hill. A small stream burbled across the property, and wood anemones crowded in the grass. It was idyllic.

And there he sat, in front of the house, as though he had been waiting for her.

She opened the gate and stepped cautiously onto the property. The sun hurt her eyes; she shaded them with her hand and squinted up at him. Yes, that was Titus Berg, all right. The same broad shoulders and beard, those familiar features.

In a few quick steps she was up the hill and standing before him.

'I apologize for showing up uninvited. Do you remember me?'

He looked up at her with a frown, but then there was a flash of recognition in his eyes.

'Oh, that's right, you were part of that cult. What brings you here?'

'May I sit down?'

'Go right ahead!' He nodded at a wooden chair beside his own. There was a rickety coffee table between the chairs.

'Well, I have a confession,' she said once she was seated.

'I don't hear many of those these days,' he muttered.

She could see now that he had aged. His hair was entirely white. His skin was tanned, furrowed, and thick as leather. His narrowed eyes had sunk deeper into their sockets. But he still radiated an aura of stubborn cheerfulness.

'Well, start from the beginning, then,' he said. 'I remember that case as though it was yesterday, you know. It was my very last case before retirement.'

'I'm sorry to say, you're not going to like what I'm about to tell you.'

'No, I had assumed as much. My stomach is already turning.'

He was a good listener, although he sometimes grunted, raised his eyebrows, and shook his head. Only once did he interrupt her.

'And here you were so convincing. There was no evidence against you. Your alibis were watertight. Imagine that...'

As she spoke, her perspective changed; she could almost view what had happened through Titus Berg's eyes. The tangle of lies. The actual crimes – a kidnapping, a rape, and an arson – that were never solved. All because Sofia was obsessed with getting revenge on Franz. When she was finished, she took a quick breath and hurried to add:

'I was so full of hate for him. It didn't even feel wrong, you know? I thought that I was taking justice into my own hands. That I had no other choice. It's only recently that I began to feel guilty over it. I'm trying to work through it all in this book I'm writing. It's based on Franz's family history, and I want to show how evil can be passed down, how history can repeat itself. And I want my daughter to know the truth.'

Titus Berg's features had hardened as she told her tale. In fact, his gaze looked furious now.

'I never managed to get Franz Oswald convicted for that arson, as you know,' he said bitterly. 'I really would have liked to solve that case before I retired, and I was beyond disappointed when he got off scot-free.'

'I'm sorry. I truly hope you can forgive me,' she said. 'If you want to report this to the police, that's obviously fine.'

'I think you should do that yourself. I'm sure the statute of limitations has run out. No one will dig any farther, they've got too much on their plates these days. But I guarantee it will soothe your guilty conscience.'

'Then that's what I'll do,' she said. 'But I don't regret setting fire to the manor house. If I had to go through that nightmarish week again, I would still do it. But I would probably tell you the truth when I was questioned later on.'

He began to chuckle.

'Jesus! Didn't you all have me fooled! Well, I suppose I have no choice but to forgive you. After everything you've been through. Even so, the police ought to know, you really should tell them.'

He no longer looked angry.

'What's she like, your daughter?' he asked.

'She's... well, she's wonderful.'

'You're doing the right thing, keeping her away from Franz Oswald,' he said. 'I remember the interrogation with him, when he became so cruel. He's one of the most unpleasant people I've ever questioned. An honest-to-God bully.'

'Okay,' she said, relieved that he was being so understanding.

'I'm going to go inside and put on some coffee, and once we've drunk it you can go home and finish that book,' he said, shaking his head.

Before she left his house, he enveloped her hand in his large, warm fist.

'Get him good this time. Don't let him slip away. If you put him away, your sins will be forgiven, I promise you that.'

She drove home slowly, with the windows open. The rays of the sun warmed her, and birds chirped ardently in the trees. Spring had come streaming in like a powerful tide. The cold, frigid air had been driven away and the wind had lost its bite. Lawns were still full of puddles from the many downpours. The light was a pale veil draping the earth. The clouds were wispy, white, and wild. There wouldn't be any rain today.

She stopped the car in a lovely spot next to a grove of trees to call Benjamin and tell him about her meeting with Titus Berg.

'I'm proud of you,' was all he said. 'So proud.'

They decided to go out to eat that evening. Recently they had spent most of their time hanging around the house. But they could always ask a security guard to come along. Simon and Elvira really needed to get out.

When she arrived back home she checked the mailbox out of habit, although they seldom got any mail these days.

There was a white envelope at the bottom. Even before she picked it up, she had misgivings. It looked so formal, with a handwritten address – it wasn't an advertisement.

When she turned it over and saw the sender – his name and address, neatly printed in embossed silver letters – her hands began to tremble. She was positive he was up to some new tricks. Maybe he was going to sue her. She hurried to the front door, stuck the key in the lock, and heard the beep of the alarm before she disarmed it. She raised her hand in greeting to the guard on the lawn. Quickly she retreated to the kitchen to slit open the envelope with a knife from the island. There were two documents inside. The first was a handwritten letter on cream stationery.

I managed to obtain a few strands of hair from your sweet daughter on my own. I really did want to do this with your knowledge, the right way, but as you know I'm impatient by nature. Franz.

That was all.

The other piece of paper was a printout of some official-looking document. She read it carefully, inspecting it from all angles. She read it once more as dizziness overtook her and her legs threatened to collapse beneath her. The document wasn't hard to understand. It was the results of a DNA test.

Franz Oswald was not Julia's biological father.

Initially I decided I would refuse to go back to work on the computers.

I had realized why they needed me. As ViaTerra grew in popularity, Bella Svahnberg had become wrapped up in some PR-related tasks Father assigned her. And there were some software functions that only I understood. The alternative, hiring someone from the mainland, was out of the question for Father. He had an ulterior motive with everything he did, and this time it was all about keeping me under surveillance. And it was when I began to suspect this that an idea came to me. That I could keep him *under surveillance at the same time.*

The computers were installed in a room immediately adjacent to Father's office. That's where I would work, so that he or Vic could check in on me occasionally.

There was a new tension between Father and me. He avoided eye contact with me sometimes. He hadn't picked on me since almost strangling me in the cafeteria; he kept his distance when he came in to check my work. But I knew his mood could change in a flash. That another eruption was always lurking beneath the surface. But he seemed to have stopped letting me get to him.

Instead, Vic started to get on his nerves.

EVERYTHING FALLS INTO PLACE

It's one in the morning. I'm listening to Father's voice, a roar behind the closed doors of his office. He's castigating Vic. It's a frequent occurrence these days. His voice is increasingly shrill. I hear the bang of something being thrown at the wall.

Then there's silence for a moment. I listen for more sounds. Secretly, I'm waiting for them to go to bed so I can snoop in Father's office. Tonight's the night I've decided to try to hack his computer.

The door of my little room opens and Father enters. For once, he's alone.

I pretend not to notice him; I stare at the screen and type rapidly at the keys. He is next to my desk now.

'Shouldn't you at least stand up when I come in?' he says with a sigh.

I stand up and realize that I'm almost as tall as he is.

'What is going on with you? What is it you think I'm so wrong in doing? Out with it. I'm listening.'

There's a hint of resignation in his voice. But I'm not going to let myself get caught in this trap. I know this kindness of his can turn into rage in a split second.

'It's nothing,' I say sullenly.

'Fine, then maybe you can do something about your brother, the incompetent fuckwad who's trying to sabotage everything I want done these days. He is beyond hope.'

'What do you want me to do?' I ask. I purposely leave out the word 'boss'.

'I'm going to have a visitor,' he says. 'You already know who she is. You see, Vic is jealous. He doesn't want to admit it, but he's been out of his mind ever since he found out she's coming. He seems to think I should spent the rest of my life in celibacy. I've actually been thinking of making use of my Russian contacts and sending him to a gulag there. In the Siberian tundra. What do you think of that?'

'I don't know.'

'Haven't I made sure you two have everything you need? I've given you the best jobs, protected you from all the crap that happens in the world. But Vic will never be satisfied, always after that sickly sweet

fatherly love. I'm just waiting for him to ask me to buy him a fishing rod so we can go fishing from the cliffs…'

'You said she was your daughter,' I blurt. Mostly to interrupt his unpleasant harangue about Vic.

He makes a sound between a grunt and an ahem and fixes his eyes on me.

'Yes, but she isn't. I've known for a long time. Thanks to your former best pal Matteo.'

'Who is she, then?'

'Someone I'd like to get to know. Are you interrogating me now? I'm speaking to you, Thor. This is a conversation between boss and subordinate, in case you had missed that? And, boss, for Christ's sake. Call me boss when you speak to me.'

'Yes, boss. I understand, boss.'

'In any case, I want you to keep an eye on Vic.' He glances at the closed door. 'Report back to me if he does or says anything suspicious. And he is to have nothing to do with the girl. Matteo was supposed to be here to keep a discreet eye on her, but that bastard has gone up in smoke. I'll keep her under watch myself, but you'll have to pick her up at the ferry. I don't trust the guards. She needs someone sweet and innocent, like you.'

Father laughs and places a hand on my shoulder.

'Have you looked in the mirror recently? You look like one of those Botticelli angels. That's exactly the welcome I want her to have. And for crying out loud, don't go cutting that hair.'

Sweat breaks out on my palms, and my mouth is dry again. For a brief moment, Father's face is a blur before me.

'She'll stay in your old cottage while she's here. Just for a few days.'

'I don't have a driver's licence. I've never driven a car.'

'Well, I guess you'd better learn. Ask Karsten, he'll show you. You're a quick study. Are there any other problems you'd like me to solve for you?'

'No, boss. But I do have a question.'

'Oh, hell. Let me guess. You want to know if I stocked the toilet paper and vacuumed the cottage. In that case, the answer is no, because you are to make sure the household unit does that.'

'No, I want to know if you're going to hurt her.'

He laughs. Loudly, shrilly, creepily.

'No, Thor. She's not the kind of girl you want to hurt. She's something special. In a class of her own. And that's why your pathetic brother is so jealous. Can you just shut up now and accept your orders?'

'Yes, boss. I'll take care of it.'

'Good. I suppose there's a little of me in you after all, when you get right down to it. You are capable of independent thought. I like that about you. Are you going home now?'

'No, I need to keep working for a bit.'

'Okay,' he says with a loud yawn. 'You do that. See you tomorrow.'

There's a look of genuineness in his eyes. As though he is seeing me for the first time. The person I am, the person I could become. But I know these moments are as scarce as they are fleeting. I'm sure he'll be back to his usual self tomorrow.

I hear his steps fade away as he goes downstairs to his room. The door opens again. I ignore it and stare at the computer screen until my eyes hurt. I steel myself for the questions I'm sure Vic is about hurl at me.

'What did he say to you?'

'Nothing much. He wants me to make sure the cottage gets cleaned, that's all.'

'A whore is going to stay there, did you know that? A little slut who's younger than we are, and he plans to fuck her. In our house. What do you think of that?'

'I don't know. Go to bed. I don't have time to talk about this right now. I've got work I need to finish.'

Vic slaps the computer monitor, hard, and for a moment I think it's broken. I bolt to my feet on reflex and look at him. In all the years I've known him, he's never been so wrecked. Vic, the hottest guy on the island. The spitting image of Father. Younger, more vivacious. Now he looks like a bad caricature. His hair is standing on end. His eyes bulge from their sockets. His lower lip is trembling, and I'm afraid he's going to burst into tears.

'Don't worry, Vic,' I say in my most soothing voice. 'No one can replace you. Father knows that.'

Then Vic does something astounding. Something that still hurts me to recall.

He embraces me. He stumbles over my chair a little, which makes him lean harder into me. I hug him back, awkward and clumsy.

'I'm sorry I used to be mean to you sometimes,' he mumbles. 'I guess I was afraid Father would figure out that you're smarter than me. You're the best, Thor.'

He trudges out of the room and closes the door behind him.

I wait for a long time, until I'm sure he's gone to bed. Then I turn off my computer and turn on the overhead light. I send up a silent prayer that Vic, in his shattered state, has forgotten to lock the door to Father's office, and he has.

I had been prepared to hack into Father's computer, crack his password, but there's no need. He's left his email open, and all I have to do is search through it. I immediately find an email Matteo sent some time ago. His email address is so transparent that I have to laugh: mattan@hushmail.com. *The message is cryptic but creepy enough to make the hair on the back of my neck stand up.* Tracker successfully installed. *And there's a link – I click on it. A webcast of a bathroom. There's no one there, but I immediately know whose bathroom it is. My discomfort has given way to overwhelming nausea. I search Father's sent messages. There are emails to business contacts I don't understand, and there are cocky little greetings to celebrities and politicians. And then there's the email to you.*

Pack: 1) short, see-through negligees 2) fishnet stockings 3) thongs.

When I read that line, everything becomes clear. I have been caught up in a rolling snowball, like an avalanche or tsunami, something I had no chance of stopping.

But if I play my cards right and pretend to be that sweet Botticelli angel, there is still a chance I can save you.

35

It was harder to lie to Edwin Björk than to Mom and Dad. Julia had told her parents she was visiting a friend in Gothenburg. She had given them a fake address and a made-up phone number. They were acting so odd these days, often engaged in whispered conversations with Elvira and Simon that ended abruptly whenever Julia was in their vicinity. What's more, the house was under heavy surveillance around the clock, and it felt increasingly like some sort of institution.

But Julia hadn't expected Edwin Björk to recognize her on the ferry. His sharp eyes almost made her blow her cover.

'Why, hello there, Julia! What are you off to do on the island, all by yourself?'

'I found it so interesting, last time I was here,' she said. 'All those stories and legends you hear about this place, you know…'

She paused, fumbling for something believable to add.

'I'm going to write about Fog Island in an essay. For school.'

'I see. And what are you going to do there, in a practical sense?'

'Walk around and look at everything. Devil's Rock, the heath, the cliffs. Take pictures and stuff. I'm going to stay at the pension,' she said, hoping he wouldn't try to check in on her there. She felt slightly ashamed that she could so easily transform herself into a skilled and unscrupulous liar.

'And you have your mother's permission to do this?'

'Of course. I'm sixteen now, almost an adult.'

'I almost forgot,' he said with a smile. 'Time sure does fly.'

'And I was wondering if you could tell me that ghost story,' she added. 'The one about the countess who haunts the manor.'

It was a perfect distraction, because he was happy to. Mom had told her that Björk was the one who knew the island and its mysteries best. All the way to the island he regaled her with the tale of all the terrible things that had befallen the family at the manor house.

Franz had said that someone would pick her up on the square adjacent to the harbour. She was a little disappointed that he wasn't going to come get her himself, but in some ways this made it even more ceremonial. Her own chauffeur!

This time, there was no fog shrouding the sound between the island and the mainland. The sea air was markedly fresher than in the harbour – it was saltier, cooler, and carried a whiff of sunshine. The wind, which came in gusts, made the surface of the sea look like broken glass, each shard reflecting the weak rays of the spring sun. The vast, glittering water reached in all directions to the horizon. It was so beautiful that her mind was occasionally swallowed by the sea, and Björk's voice faded to a dull murmur.

'I heard your mother wrote a book about all that,' he said at last. 'Isn't it coming out this fall?'

'No, she chickened out. She says there's more to write about.'

'I see – I wonder what that could be?' he said, stroking his chin thoughtfully.

Just then, it was time to dock, and she moved to stand at the stern of the ferry, where passengers disembarked.

★

The square had been crowded with people last time she visited, but today it was almost deserted. There was a woman sitting by the fountain with a stroller, but otherwise Julia was the only one there. But then she caught sight of someone on the other side of the square: a guy standing next to a gleaming black car. As she approached him, she thought he looked familiar, but she couldn't remember where she'd seen him. He was backlit by the sun, and his longish hair gleamed like copper. His eyes were a clear, icy blue, but they looked kind. His face was rosy, as if the blood pulsed just beneath the surface. His cheeks and nose were covered in freckles. Cute lips – and now he was smiling self-consciously, as though he owed her an apology. And he did, actually, because now she remembered that they'd met before. That hair! No one else she knew had hair that colour.

'You almost dumped a tray of cheese on my head!' she exclaimed.

'Yes, I'm sorry,' he said, ashamed. 'It was when you were here for the conference.'

Then another faraway memory came to her. Those lovely eyes. She had stared into them before.

'Hold on! You were at our library too! That's why I recognized you at the party. What were you doing at our library?'

'It's a long story. Is it okay if I tell you later?'

'Were you spying on me?' she asked.

'Something like that. I promise I'll tell you everything later.'

'But who are you?'

'I'm Thor,' he said, offering his hand. It was warm and felt good in her own hand, which had nearly frozen solid on the ferry over. He gave her a hesitant smile and clung to her hand just a little too long.

'I'm here to pick you up. Franz Oswald is my father.'

'Really? You don't look anything like him.'

But now she could see a hint of similarity in the straight bridge of his nose and wide jaw. His muscular arms and upright posture. She knew Franz had sons who were twins, she'd read about it online. But there were no pictures of them there. In some interview or another Franz had said that he 'wanted to spare his sons the media circus and allow them to live a normal life'.

All at once, she felt cheap in front of Thor. The fact that Franz had sent his son, who was older than her, made her feel keenly aware that what she was planning to do was far from normal. *It's sick*, she thought, *but it's just like Franz*. Then again, why should she care? If she wanted to be normal, she would be hanging around the gas station in Henån right now, bored half to death. She thought about the silky undergarments in her bag and immediately felt exhilarated again.

Thor led her to the black station wagon, which looked new. The inside smelled like leather and plastic. As soon as he turned the key, the car took a violent leap forward.

'Oh, I'm sorry, I forgot to put it in neutral,' he muttered, embarrassed.

When he hit the clutch and turned the key again, the engine howled like a sawmill.

'You're hitting the gas too hard,' Julia said, giggling.

He collected himself and managed to back out of the parking spot, but he nearly hit a pole and had to brake so hard that they were thrown forward in their seats and the engine died. Julia started laughing, and he joined in. Soon enough they were howling with laughter.

'Do you even have a licence?' she managed to say at last.

'A licence? Are you kidding?' he said. 'This is only the third time I've ever driven a car.'

Eventually he managed to guide the car onto the road, but

he wouldn't go any faster than a crawl. To her amusement, he was so nervous that beads of sweat sprang out on his forehead. She looked out the window and saw how beautiful it was. The sun was sparkling. The cliffs plunged to the sea at the edge of the road. But it was hard to tear her eyes from Thor, who was piloting the car with stubborn determination. There was something special about him, something lovely. She figured if Franz had a son like this, he couldn't be all that dangerous.

Just before they arrived at the enormous iron gate, he stopped the car.

'I'm going to take you to the house where you're going to stay,' Thor said. 'But before we drive through this gate, there's something I want to say.'

'Okay, what is it?'

'My father can be charming and all, but he has a terrible temper, and I know he's not always nice to the girls he meets. Are you sure you want to keep going? Because if you don't want to, I will drive you to the pension in the village so you can get the morning ferry home.'

'Nice to the girls.' What a strange thing to say about your own father, she thought. She could feel the corners of her mouth twitching; it was almost laughable.

'No, I want to meet him,' she said. 'Nice guys aren't really my thing, you know? I know what I'm getting myself into.'

'That's too bad. Or you and I could go somewhere,' he joked.

'Thanks, but I'm really here to see him.'

She wondered if Thor was upset because she was so young. But when he turned to look at her again, there was a flicker of worry in his eyes.

'Is there something sick going on in there? Or, like orgies?'

'No, nothing like that, but when it comes to Father I know he was rough with my mother. She was afraid of him.'

She wondered why this didn't concern her. Why she wasn't afraid of Franz. But she wasn't.

'Has anything like that happened recently?'

'Not that I know of. Father spends most of his time working. I haven't seen him with any women for a while. There was one young girl who was here. We were told she spread lies about him. But I don't know for sure what they did together.'

A prickle of doubt hit her. But she had come so far and wanted this so much. Franz wasn't dangerous, she could just feel it.

'I want to do it. Drive through the gate!'

He fixed his eyes on her; his gaze was full of resignation. But even so he looked angry, as though a battle were being waged inside him. At last he let out a long sigh and said:

'I figured as much. But I still want to give you something, in case you need help.' He took a small gadget from the pocket of his blazer. 'Most of us in ViaTerra don't have mobile phones, but this is a pager. All you have to do is press this button here. It's linked directly to mine. Please, use it if something happens.'

She stared at the little doodad, which looked like a mobile phone but with fewer buttons.

'Okay… I guess I can do that,' she said. *As if*, she thought to herself. She didn't need his help, she could take care of herself.

His pale blue eyes seemed so intensely fixed on her. She wasn't sure he was the kind of guy that could turn her on, but his smile and his touch as he pressed the pager into her palm took her breath away. She tucked the gadget into her pocket and looked up at the gate. Angels and devils hung on the sides and in the middle was a large keyhole. There was a booth built into the wall. The guard inside raised a hand in greeting and the gate opened with a sorrowful creak.

The property spread before them, with the manor house in the middle. The sky had turned a pale shade of blue and she could make out a crescent moon, although it was hardly visible in the daylight. Something twisted in her heart and she took a sharp breath. She thought of Mom, working here on frigid nights. Being forced to sleep in the stable. Escaping over the electric fence. But Julia wasn't like Mom. She was her own person. She formed the words silently. *I'm sorry, Mom. I have to do this. I love you so, so much.*

Thor drove through the courtyard and past the manor house, up to a small, white cottage that was secluded in a grove of trees. The lights were on inside. They got out of the car at the same time, and she felt a sudden urge to hug him. She could feel the knobs of his spine through his blazer. They quickly backed away from one another as if they had gotten too close, too fast.

'You can go inside,' he said. 'The door's open. I'm sure Father will come by soon.'

As she touched the handle, the door glided open and a large room with white walls and a tile oven came into view. She whirled around and saw that Thor had gotten back in the car. She didn't go inside until she heard the engine starting and coughing, and then the sound of the car tyres crunching on the gravel of the courtyard.

The floorboards creaked gently as she stepped inside. The air in the cottage was slightly musty, as though no one had lived there for a long time, but otherwise it was clean and tidy. The thought came to her like a lightning bolt as she stood there.

What am I doing here? What have I gotten myself into?

It was the gate, first creaking so eerily and then closing so firmly behind them. The knowledge that she was surrounded by a high wall with barbed wire on top. She had never experienced that before.

The floor was polished wood, the furniture beige with colourful throw pillows. In one corner of the room was a pair of wicker chairs in front of a large fireplace. A vase of white flowers stood on the coffee table. She walked over to smell them and roamed about the house, looking around like a curious child. Besides the living room, there were two bedrooms and a bathroom. Although it was neat and clean, it was clear that someone had once lived there. Scuffs on the woodwork, a wall with dark spots that had been painted over but not very well. A ceiling fan spread a monotonous hum through the room. The fridge was full of food and several bottles of wine.

She went out on the deck. The sky had turned deep azure; the crescent moon was clearly visible through the tops of the pines by now. High above the trees hovered a raptor, hunting for something to eat. In the distance she heard the roar of the sea. The chilly spring air made her shiver and go back into the house.

One room had twin beds, and the other had a double. She unpacked her clothes in the room with the double bed, hanging her coat in the wardrobe and smoothing her short dress. The everyday clothes went in a bureau and the flimsy negligees were stashed under the pillow. She put the bag with her makeup and other toiletries in the bathroom. She washed her armpits and between her legs with soap and stared at her reflection in the mirror for a while. Her eyes seemed unnaturally large; her gaze was shining and wild.

Just then, she heard a door opening.

Her throat constricted; she seemed incapable of going to the front hall to greet him. She simply waited breathlessly in front of the mirror. From the corner of her eye she saw the outline of him approaching from behind. When his face popped up beside hers in the mirror, she jumped. He looked so serious, his eyes hard. She was gripped by a sudden urge to run away. But then she felt his hands on her shoulders, pulling her backwards until her back was pressed to his chest. The scent of his aftershave and the heat of his body hit her at the same time. The lust and desire in his eyes looked like nothing she'd seen in other guys, like Matt, for instance. *He's doing something dirty to me in his mind,* she thought, and all at once she felt uncertain in front of him and licked her lips nervously.

He was wearing a pale blue cotton shirt that was open at the neck. A dark blue tie hung carelessly, half knotted around his collar, as though he had been in a rush to see her. His lips were so chilly against the back of her neck that she shuddered involuntarily. She tried to pull away, but his grip on her shoulders tightened. Her heart began to pound.

There was an electrical charge in the air, like just before a thunderstorm.

'You came,' he whispered. 'You're finally here.'

36

Once Sofia recovered from the shock of Franz's letter, she noticed two things: the DNA results had been issued last winter, two weeks after she and Benjamin visited Fog Island, and there was something else in the envelope – a small plastic bag containing some long, dark strands of hair. Her relief and joy were immediately tempered with suspicion. She wondered how she could be sure this wasn't a forgery.

But the strangest part, what really made her uneasy, was that he had sent this to her. Why hadn't he simply let them agonize? That would have been more his style. He always had some clever ulterior motive in whatever he did. Always. And when she thought about that, she felt a strange desire to bicker with him. Force him to reveal that ulterior motive.

At first, Benjamin wouldn't hear of double-checking the test. He had danced around the house, flashing victory signs and letting out whoops of joy when he read the document. Eventually Sofia had to shush him, because Julia was upstairs in her room.

'It seems fishy that he's known for so long,' she protested. 'And you know what's even weirder? How the heck did he get his hands on Julia's hair? And who does he think he is, doing this behind our backs?'

'Well, she did go to that conference on Fog Island. She

sheds hair wherever she goes. I'm sure he just wanted to keep us guessing. Why do you have to ruin this with all your suspicion? Don't you know how happy I am?'

Benjamin was so overjoyed that he couldn't sleep that night. Sofia woke up at four in the morning and noticed that his side of the bed was empty. She found him down by the lake with Denzel, staring at nothing with a strange smile on his face.

But Sofia kept pestering him; she wanted to be one hundred per cent sure. So she suggested they send a few more strands of hair to the same company, this time with hair from Benjamin. Make them confirm that the two of them were a match. The company was happy to oblige. Sofia was astounded at how simple it was – and it was so ridiculous that they hadn't done it themselves. She felt a pang of guilt as she collected a wad of hair from Julia's hairbrush, but there was no helping it. The truth had to come out.

They got the results within days.

Benjamin's hair was a match. Julia was his daughter.

Now Sofia, too, was so euphoric that she gave Julia permission to stay with a friend in Gothenburg for a few days. After all, it was a long weekend and Julia was out of danger. What's more, it was convenient to have her out of the house while they were working on their secret plan.

Her friends had varied reactions to the news about Julia. Anna seemed as relieved as Benjamin and Sofia. Ellis said it was great, but that it didn't matter – he liked Julia just the way she was. Simon, though, was enraged that Franz had sent in the test himself.

'He has no right to interfere in your private life that way. We should ask why he sent you the results when he did. I promise you, he has something up his sleeve.'

'Maybe,' Benjamin said idly. 'But really, he did us a favour.

Now he won't have anything to hold over us when we enact our plan.'

And Simon could only agree.

It was around this time that Ellis made a breathless call to Sofia.

'I found something! Since Benjamin is such a slacker, I tracked down that big deposit to Julia's account myself. It came from that finance firm Franz owns in Stenungsund, Stone Equity. But we can't go public with this yet. The way I got hold of the information isn't exactly legal, as you may have guessed. I have to talk to Magnus first and figure out a plan.'

Sofia's skin crawled with uneasiness. Of course, that deposit had come in last fall, before Franz knew the truth about Julia. Presumably he was no longer interested in harassing them, now that he knew Julia wasn't his daughter. Why would he be? She asked Ellis to hold on while she called Benjamin from their landline to update him. He was in the car, almost home, and blew his top.

'I'll send that money right back to one of Franz's accounts,' he said. 'Julia is not going to take his money.'

Sofia thought about the strands of hair again. She decided to compare the date of Julia's school trip to Fog Island with the date on the DNA test. Why hadn't she thought of that before? Then she remembered that Ellis was still on her mobile phone.

'Sorry to make you wait. Did you find anything else?'

'The creep who attacked Julia is a dead end. I can't find any connection to Franz. Viggo Sankt Petrus must have been acting of his own accord. What a sick coincidence.'

Sofia muttered in response. Her mind was still on the two dates.

'And, get this! Magnus just emailed the interview he did with Elvira. It's incredible. It's going to be a bombshell, as soon as we're ready to set this all in motion. And by the way, I've got full control of the ViaTerra websites. Whoever set them up must be a real amateur. They didn't worry about security in the least.'

Sofia thanked him and ended the call.

She took the DNA results from the locked drawer where she kept it and got out a calendar.

Julia had been on Fog Island two days *after* the test was completed.

Her head began to pound. How on earth had Franz gotten hold of Julia's hair?

She heard Benjamin coming through the door and shouted so loudly for him that he came dashing in with his coat still on. When she told him about the dates, his face contracted into a thoughtful grimace, but then he shrugged.

'There could be something wrong with the date,' he suggested.

It was the shrug that triggered Sofia. She picked up a book from the kitchen island and hurled it at Benjamin. The edge hit him in the chest, and he stepped back in fear.

'Ow! Why are you so mad?'

'I am so sick of your bullshit. He got some of her hair, don't you get it? How did he do that? Why is he doing this? Why can't he just get his disgusting tentacles out of our lives?'

Benjamin grabbed an apple from the fruit bowl and took a big bite. She went up to him, yanked it from his hand, tossed it in the sink, and turned on the garbage disposal. The apple sounded like it was shrieking in pain.

'Sofia, quit it! Why are you acting this way?'

'Because you're not taking this seriously.'

'I'm just trying to stay positive. Julia is *our* daughter, isn't that enough?'

'She always has been.'

'I know. Come here, honey,' he said, opening his arms. He always did this. When he couldn't deal with her outbursts, he became tender. He looked honestly distressed. She moved closer to him.

'I'm sorry if I seemed like I don't care, but I don't think it's that weird. He's got spies everywhere. It wouldn't surprise me if he made someone shadow Julia when he thought she was his daughter. After all, he's been all over us like a leech. Hopefully that's all in the past now. Has he even tried to talk to you about her since last winter?'

'No, I don't think so.'

'See? Stop worrying. Try to focus on the positives.'

'You always believe the best about everyone. I'm so worried about her. Just think of what happened to Elvira. Someone actually tried to kill her.'

'Or scare her off speaking out. If whoever was driving that car really wanted to kill her, I'm sure he would have done it.'

'I'm still worried about Julia.'

'So call her then!'

When Julia didn't pick up, Sofia sent a text. She got a response right away.

Everything's fine. Gothenburg is sick. She attached a picture of herself lying on a pink pillow, a pout on her lips.

Sofia's pulse slowed. Maybe it was good for Julia to get away for a bit.

On the same day Julia was supposed to come home, the police showed up. Benjamin was out on a job site and Julia was supposed to take the bus straight to school.

When Sofia peered out the peephole and saw the man in uniform, her heart flew into her throat. Instinctively she thought it must have to do with Julia. She hadn't been in touch for almost twenty-four hours. Sofia hurried to open the door. The officer gave a friendly smile.

'I just wanted to drop this off,' he said, holding out a metal box she recognized immediately. 'We didn't find any link to Viggo Sankt Petrus, but as you may know he's still in custody awaiting trial. I happened to be in the neighbourhood and thought you might want this. We found fingerprints on it, but unfortunately there was no match in the criminal registry.'

As soon as the officer left, Sofia decided to look at all the photographs that had been taken of her. Maybe she would find a clue there. She had finished writing the chapter about the fire and was planning to let it rest and read through it later.

She placed the box on the sofa next to her laptop and inserted the flash drives into the computer one by one. It was creepy to look at the pictures again, especially the ones where she was undressing or scantily clad. She tried to figure out where the photographer had been hiding. Some of the photos had been taken from just outside the window; others, from a grove of trees on a small rise above the shelter. The photographer must have been standing far away, because some of the images were zoomed in so far they were blurry.

They had been taken over a period of several years, that was the creepy part. It was as if this person had been with them constantly, and had decided to photograph her regularly. Whoever had taken these knew her routines. She inserted the very last flash drive. The images on screen this time looked different, seemed to have been taken with a mobile phone. These weren't images of Sofia, they were various landscapes on Orust, a picture from a restaurant, a glass of wine on the rocks at sunset.

She felt her eyes widen as she looked at the screen, but her field of vision shrank into a tunnel and focused on the last two pictures. The world around her began to spin, except for the pictures, which took on a surreal clarity. They were of a naked man who apparently didn't want his picture taken and was holding a hand up towards the camera, embarrassed. There was a glimpse of a drooping penis resting on a scrotum; a blanket wound around one leg. The lace pillow she knew so well.

That delightful grin.

Benjamin, in their bed.

I have met you. Sunned myself in the warmth of your eyes. Held your chilly hand. Listened to your infectious laugh. Felt your soft breasts against my skinny ribcage. Inhaled your floral scent. And now I know I have to save you, but I don't know how.

I gaze out the window. The cottage has a cosy glow. The certainty that Father is in there with you makes my chest ache. I can't stop thinking about what happened when I got back from picking you up. His eyes. His eagerness. How quickly he was out the door.

He was at the picture window, looking out. When he heard me, he whirled around. His shirt was unbuttoned at the throat and his tie was in a sloppy, loose knot. His eyes were strange, greedy. His mouth was half open, his teeth shining white. I couldn't help but think of a piranha's rapacious jaws.

'She's in the cottage,' I said grimly.

When he stepped toward me, his scent hit me. Extra aftershave today. For you.

'What do you think of her, Thor?' he asked.

'I don't know.'

'Then you're either a fag or you need glasses.'

'She's pretty, I guess.'

'That's not it, kiddo. The world is full of boring, pretty girls. She is something special. I'm sure you noticed.'

I muttered something incomprehensible. When I placed the car key on his desk, I felt a vague sense of relief to be getting rid of it.

'You're not jealous of her, like your pathetic brother, are you?'

'No, not at all, boss.'

I looked around and realized Vic wasn't there.

Father noticed my wandering gaze.

'He's taken over your flowerbeds. I couldn't stand another minute of him. Maybe you should go over there and give him some tips on weeding.'

At first I thought he was serious, but then he shook his head.

'No, you stay here. I might need you. Look around, listen, do you hear how quiet it is? So peaceful!'

It occurred to me that Madde's desk was also empty.

'She was moved to a job as dishwasher in the kitchen,' he said. 'There is no one around here who can take the heat in my office. Am I really that difficult to work with?'

He looked proud, not depressed in the least about this fact.

'I don't know, boss.'

'Maybe I should try having you here,' he said, but when he saw my horrified face he tousled my hair.

'Back to Julia. Is it possible you are jealous of me?'

His gaze was penetrating. He wasn't about to give up.

'Maybe,' I said.

He barked a hoarse laugh.

'I knew it. But nothing's going to come of it. She must have liked you. And me, for sending an angel to pick her up. How did driving go?'

'Not great.'

He burst into laughter.

'There, there. Now get to work, you've got your computers to take care of.'

He waved his hand dismissively, suddenly impatient.

I knew why. He was in a hurry. To see you.

Once he was out of sight, I tried to get to work, but my body was too restless.

And now, here I am – nervous, jumpy, totally incapable of thinking about anything but you. I sit down. Take a deep breath. Try to calm myself. It doesn't help.

But then something strange happens. Images from my life parade through my mind.

The rocks, the gulls, the cottage, Mama, the classroom, the dorm, the pigsty, the stall, the Hole, and, finally, my little flowerbed.

That's when I realize that only the truth can save you, and that there is only one person in the whole world who can save me.

I wait for a long time, until it's dark out. Again and again I peer out the window at the courtyard. The staff rush back and forth like ants whose anthill has been disturbed. This is going to be easy. Everyone seems so stressed out, so absorbed in whatever it is the boss wants them to do.

My plan takes shape in my mind. Walk along the wall to the stable, get the ladder, put it up where the trees hide the wall, and jump. Run through the forest as fast as you can.

The cottage glows welcomingly as I sneak by. The breeze strokes the long shadows of the trees and I have become one with them. I hear your burbling laughter inside, and then Father's, lower and hoarser. My hearing is enhanced, so sharp I can hear the hum of electricity running through the barbed wire. A crackle of warning. I burn. Watch out for me!

When I pass the small gate near the back of the property, I decide I should test it in case it's open. It's always locked, I know, but even so I try its handle.

At first I think I'm dreaming.

The gate opens wide.

All I have to do is walk out into freedom.

37

Franz spun Julia around and took in the sight of her. She liked it when he did that. No one had ever looked at her that way. She didn't want him to stop. Suddenly she thought of Matt and felt ashamed, but not ashamed enough to end this. If this was a sin, then she was incurably infected with the sin-virus. His fingertips slipped lightly across her bare shoulders. The touch sent jolts of electricity down her arms. There was something mischievous about him, something almost childish.

She had mentally prepared herself to go straight to sex. That was what was so titillating – not knowing. Anything could happen. But instead he let go of her and backed away.

'Food is on its way. You must be hungry. Come on, let's go sit down.'

He led her to the kitchen table and patted a chair.

'I'm sure you like sea trout, right? They're in season. It was caught right here off the coast.'

She had no idea what made sea trout so special but nodded obligingly.

There was a knock at the door. Franz quickly stood up to open it for a woman in a housekeeping uniform who pulled in a serving cart on wheels. The woman set the table and served the food with downcast eyes and occasionally trembling fingers. Julia felt embarrassed by her presence but Franz just shook his head in amusement and sent her away the moment the food was on the table.

'Why was she like that?' Julia asked as soon as the woman was gone.

'She's just nervous around me. That happens to a lot of people around here. But not you.'

He leaned towards her and gently touched her wrist, giving her butterflies. His other hand stroked her cheek and moved down her throat, his fingers stopping in the cleft between her breasts. A jolt of pleasure ran from her arms to her breasts and down between her legs, and she had to squirm in her chair. Now that amazing fury began to simmer in her body, the feeling that could only be appeased by sex. She fantasized about how it would be, with him. A slow, almost torturous rise towards orgasm. Where you don't even know who you are towards the end, or whether it's day or night. But he didn't seem to be in any rush.

Just as when they met in Stenungsund, she found it easy to talk to him. He was interested in everything she had to say. She had never met someone who seemed so interested in *her*, who had listened so intently. He nodded in all the right places and never interrupted. He was never impatient or bored. She told him things she'd never told anyone else. How, one night, she let her fingers slip under the covers while thinking of him. At that, he gave her a dangerous smile.

He told her about some select parts of his life. Mostly anecdotes from when he was in prison, because he could tell she thought that was exciting. Eventually he fell silent and regarded her for a long time. He reached across the table and took her hand.

'There is a reason you and I are sitting here right now, out of all the moments in eternity,' he said gravely.

What on earth could she say to that?

He pushed his empty plate aside, then got up and pulled her to her feet. When he took her in his arms – his big, broad-shouldered, masculine embrace – it struck her that he was as old as her father. But her desire to do forbidden things was much stronger than the voice of warning in the back of her mind. *If Mom knew about this…*

She let herself be rocked, for a while, by the motion of his body, his firm chest. He slowly unbuttoned her dress, all the way to her waist. This was exactly why she had put on this outfit – all the buttons. He gently pushed the cups of her bra out of the way and placed his hands over her breasts. He let them linger there, his thumbs against her nipples, as he bent down to kiss her neck. She reached her arms over her head, thrusting her chest out to give him better access. He pushed against her so hard that she almost lost her balance and took a step backward. He was hard; she could feel it through the light fabric of her dress. But out of nowhere he stopped, readjusted her bra, pulled her dress back over her shoulders, and started buttoning her up. She was so surprised that she couldn't make a sound.

'Do you understand what's happening between us? There are people who never get to experience this,' he said.

'Then why did you stop?' she asked.

'I want you to suffer a little, you see? Just like I am. Feel.'

He took her hand and placed it on the front of his pants. She didn't dare to squeeze him; she let her hand rest on his big, hard bulge as she wondered if it was even going to be possible to get him inside.

'And also I like to test the limits of my self-control,' he said. 'I get off on it, you know.'

She suspected there was more to it. Some hesitation. Something he didn't want to say.

'Why did you invite me here, really?'

'It's a little complicated, but mostly it's because I'm crazy about you. Tomorrow, you and I will have a look around the island. Then, at night, I'll make you feel good in a way all those little boys can only dream of, I promise.'

'Why wait until then?' she asked, her voice soft and flirty.

'I already told you. Things have to happen in the right place, at the right time. Tomorrow night is the right time. I have to do some work now. Help yourself to anything here. There's a phone to the housekeeping unit if you need anything. They'll come pick this up soon.' He gestured at the table.

When he saw the disappointment in her eyes, he put a finger under her chin and tilted her face towards his own.

'Don't forget, I'm the seducer here. You can trust me.'

'We'll see.'

He cocked his head and squinted at her.

'Aren't you afraid of me?'

She wasn't. In his little universe, where the world seemed far away and nothing was concrete, she felt safe.

'Not at all. Why should I be?'

'I could hurt you.'

'You won't.'

He suddenly looked confused.

'How can you be so sure?'

'You can just tell that kind of thing. Nothing you do to me could be worse than dying of boredom in the shithole town where I live.'

'You're a firecracker, Julia. Now go to bed. I'll come pick you up early tomorrow morning.'

After he left, she realized it was eleven o'clock. Despite the annoying tingle between her legs, she was tired. She went to the bathroom and showered. As she got out, she heard someone clearing the table, and then the clatter of the serving cart being pulled out the door.

She left the bedroom window cracked so she could hear the waves on the rocks. She crawled into bed naked. So much for the negligees. Quickly but peacefully she drifted off, rocked by the quiet rhythm of the sea.

Breakfast was already on the table when she went to the kitchen in the morning. There was so much to choose from that she lost her appetite and simply chowed down some yoghurt and cornflakes. She dressed in jeans, a wool sweater and boots and decided not to bother with makeup. If hiking was what he wanted to do, then she would look natural. Just as she was pulling on her boots, she heard a shrill whistle outside. Franz was on the lawn, dressed in the kind of ridiculously expensive outdoor gear that made him look like a walking Fjällräven ad. The whole property was shrouded in a thick fog, yet the light was blinding.

'Hurry up,' he said, waving eagerly. 'I'm going to show you where it all began.'

She followed him to a small gate in the wall. He took a key from his pocket and muttered in irritation when he realized the gate was already open. But he didn't lock it behind him; instead he started laughing.

'It's funny, actually! All these industrious little ants running around here and thinking they can't get out.'

As they walked through the forest and out to the heath, he didn't hold her hand or put his arm around her shoulders. It was almost as if he had transformed into a guide, enthusiastically pointing out all the sights and sharing little anecdotes.

'This has to be the most beautiful heath in Sweden. You should see the colours in the fall. I once ran through here wearing only my underwear, when I was fleeing the shack where I lived. And look there! Do you see the cliff hanging over the sea? That's Devil's Rock. That's where I jumped in.'

She was delighted to finally get to see the notorious cliff. The view was so beautiful that she simply stood staring. He had to tug at her arm to get her moving again. Devil's Rock hung over the sea like a diving board. Her father had been forced to jump off it in a storm, she'd heard. He almost hadn't survived. Jesus.

When they reached the tip, he herded her ahead of him so she was facing the sea with his hands on her shoulders.

'This is where I made the life-changing decision. Jump, risk my life, and leave it all behind, or chicken out and get stuck in the shithole they call a village, which, by the way, is even more revolting than where you grew up. I was thirteen and had to make it on my own. When I got out in the world, I realized no one knew the meaning of life, so I had to find it inside myself. That's the kind of person you have to be, Julia.'

'You forced my father to jump from here, right?'

'Yes, but he deserved it. And he was fine. He survived, and now he's got you! I brought your mother here once too, when there was a hell of a gale.'

'What? She never told me that. Why did you do that?'

'Sometimes she turned into my worst nightmare. Let's just say she deserved it too. She'll tell you all about it one day, I'm sure.'

'Do you ever think about your father?'

He turned to look at her.

'What do you know about him?'

'That he tortured you when you were little. I read about it somewhere.'

'That's true. The absolute scum of the earth. He came from a dark place. I sent him back.'

'What about your mother?'

'She betrayed me when I needed her the most. Now she lives in a shitty little cottage, which I'll show you later. But first, there's something else.'

He led her away from Devil's Rock, taking her hand and helping her down some steeply sloping boulders. Out of the blue a big cave opened before them. It was so large that she could have stood up straight inside it. He sat down just inside its mouth and she sank down beside him.

'In here is where I made the plans that have travelled all over the world today. This is where I thought up the theses. This cave was my special place, the only place I could think clearly.'

His gaze had taken on a melancholy cast.

'We could crawl in and light a fire, and watch the fog scatter, but I would rather show you the cottage instead.'

'What cottage?'

'The disgusting place I grew up, it's a terrible slum. It will give you a fresh perspective on ViaTerra.'

He walked ahead of her through the heather and into the forest, where he hurried down a narrow path, going so fast she could hardly keep up. They had to climb over fallen trees left behind by the storm. Eventually his back vanished from sight and she had to call out to him to slow down. The forest opened and they found themselves in a clearing. He took her hand and led her to a gap in the trees. Before them was a red cottage. In the middle of the forest. There was even a garden with flowerbeds in bloom. She made a move to walk closer, but he stopped her.

'Don't. The bitch still lives in there.'

'What bitch?'

'My mother. If it weren't for the boys, I wouldn't concern myself with her. But they have the right to see their grandmother. And she has taught them some useful things.' He shook his head. 'Anyway, this is where I grew up. We didn't even have a washing machine. My room was about the size of a closet. Jesus, was it ever cold in the winter. Compare this to ViaTerra, Julia. Imagine what my life would have been like if I stayed here.'

'I think the cottage is cute.'

'Fine. But you wouldn't think so if you had to live there. I refused to live such an uninspired life. And now I have created a movement that spans the globe. Just let that sink in.'

'Why are you telling me all this?'

'Who else would I tell?'

'Well, maybe the millions of people who listen to you?'

'Yes, it's incredible, isn't it? But everyone knows there's something wrong with them. And everyone is searching for the one truth that can explain everything.'

'So why don't you tell them about this in your video chats?'

'They would never understand the depth of it all. And there's something more. Listen carefully now. In this country, people think they have the right to have an opinion about everything. From fucking childless women who think they're experts in child-rearing, to the psychologists fleecing people in their claustrophobic offices. People complain when the world doesn't wipe their asses for them. They have some idiotic opinion about everything. Sometimes you just have to take off the kid gloves, Julia, no matter what people think. Now and then you have to hurt someone for the sake of justice. Either you live and die in a shitty hovel like this, or you stop caring about what people think and help yourself to what life has to offer. I know you are going to hear terrible things about me. But never forget that I refused to lead a meaningless life.'

He believes all this, she says. *He honestly believes what he's saying.* She thought he looked a little strange, maybe slightly insane. He hadn't made eye contact with her while he was speaking; his gaze darted around. She felt a little scared and slipped her hand into his. He squeezed it, didn't push her away, and then she felt safe again. All the way home to her cottage, he held her hand tight. He helped her over the fallen trees.

'Now you've got something to think about this afternoon,' he said when they arrived. 'Unfortunately I have to do some work, play host for a silly celebrity who's visiting. But tonight you and I will have dinner together, and drink some wine the likes of which you've never tasted before.'

He followed her into the cottage and lingered in the front hall as though there was something he was trying to remember.

'Did you bring thongs?'

'I'm wearing one now.'

'And what else?'

'Want me to show you?'

He nodded and gestured at her to go get it.

She hurried into the bedroom and grabbed the see-through negligee she had tucked under the pillow. The super hot one, which lifted her breasts and didn't leave anything to the imagination. He whistled appreciatively when she held it up for him to see.

'Wear that tonight during dinner. Just that, and the thong,' he said with a brazen smile.

She paced restlessly around the cottage all afternoon, checking to see if she had any new emails or texts, answering one from Mom. *Everything's fine. Gothenburg is sick.* The reception was bad indoors, so she sat on the deck to surf the internet but went back inside when she couldn't concentrate. An eerie silence had settled over the house. She opened the deck door to let in sounds from outside, but it was too windy and cold now. She wanted to light a fire in the fireplace, but there was no firewood.

By five o'clock she was getting ready. She took a long bubble bath. There was a little rubber duck on the edge of the bathtub, faded and scuffed. So had kids lived here once upon a time? Maybe it was Thor and his twin brother.

She shaved meticulously. Her hair went in a high ponytail, which she braided to expose the back of her neck. On with the negligee and thong and on top of that a thick robe that was hanging in the bathroom. She put on makeup. Layers of mascara, eyeliner and matte pink lipstick.

Around six, a girl came from the kitchen, bringing food and a message from Franz that he would be late. Julia had no appetite; she was feeling anxious. What if he didn't come at all?

She was supposed to go home the next day. What a pain, if she had to go back without sleeping with him.

It was almost nine o'clock when he opened the door. She was half-watching TV, wearing only the negligee and thong. At first she pretended not to hear him; she didn't want it to be obvious how eagerly she had been waiting.

'I'm sorry!' he said immediately. 'It was practically impossible to shake off that celebrity chick. Can you forgive me, Julia?'

She heard him uncorking the wine at the sink and taking glasses from the kitchen cabinets.

He was wearing jeans and a T-shirt under a denim jacket, which he tossed over the back of a chair. This outfit made him look younger.

'You're so cute when you pout like that,' he said. 'Come here, you've never tasted wine like this.'

She reluctantly got up. His eyes immediately fastened on her body, sweeping over her breasts and down to her thighs. He didn't say anything for a moment. A strategic pause.

'Perfection,' he whispered.

She went over to him and took the glass of wine from his

hand. Still mildly grumpy, but the compliment had softened her a bit.

From the very first sip, the dry wine spread through her body like hot lava. She wasn't used to drinking; she only ever had a glass on special occasions. She felt warm and tingly all at once. It felt like a kick of adrenaline that had nothing to do with stress or fear, only happiness.

'What kind of wine is this?'

'Something that will help you relax and enhance your experience.'

Now she was scared.

'You're not going to drug me, are you? You are absolutely not allowed to do that.'

'No, this is a natural substance. But at least as effective.'

'Why do I need it?'

'You have to be completely relaxed. I'm going to make it good for you. From now on, you're going to do exactly as I say, understand?' There was something stern in his hoarse voice. Sexily stern, not dangerously so.

'Now drink up. Empty that glass in one gulp.'

At first she felt nothing, except for an acidic sensation in her stomach, but then came that feeling again, like warm rays spreading down her nerves. He came over to stand behind her and pressed against her back. He pulled down one strap of her negligee and bit her shoulder playfully. When he kissed the back of her neck, it radiated to her breasts and belly and between her legs, as if he'd touched all of those places simultaneously. It was like a layer of her was peeled away, and what was left was smouldering. Then came his chilly fingers on the insides of her thighs, finding their way up, slowly, and giving her goosebumps.

She tried to turn around, but he stopped her.

'Hold still. Don't move a muscle. You are entirely under my power. How does it feel?'

'Exciting,' she said, noticing that she had slurred a little bit.

Now his hands were all over her body: breasts, belly, back and butt. Her knees felt strangely weak and gave way unexpectedly, but he caught her and placed her on the sofa. As though through a mist she watched him pull the negligee over her head and move his hands to her thong, which he drew down her legs. He lay on top of her, pressing her into the soft cushions. His heart was pounding so hard against her chest that it felt like it was trying to force its way inside her.

The wine had made her so sleepy. Her thoughts floated slowly through her brain, thoughts as light as wispy clouds. Her eyelids were heavy; she tried to squint but could hardly move them.

'Why do I feel like this?' she whispered.

'It's just the wine. Focus on how it feels when I touch you.'

Her body was heavy and slack, but at the same time she was alert and awake, as though she had forgotten to turn off her consciousness. She seemed to be floating high above herself, looking down. Her legs fell open. The sensation between them was heightened, and her nipples were rock-hard. She felt an intense longing for him to touch her again, anywhere. Cool, wet lips pressed against her belly. His hands were everywhere all at once. He pinched her nipples, sending a sharp jolt down to her stomach. His breath was warm on the insides of her thighs. Her thoughts were so slow now that she couldn't make sense of them anymore. But her body was tense, casting side to side. Her nerves felt like electrical wires. She heard a hoarse whimper and realized it had come from her lips. Her skin was too sensitive and felt like it might burst at any moment. She wanted to push him away, find room to breathe, but her arms were heavy and wouldn't obey. A tight, tingling sensation between her legs, pulsing in her groin.

It was impossible to say how long it lasted; there was no time, only his fingers, tongue, lips, and heavy breathing, which came in spurts against her body. Her muscles tensed. There was a far-off scream, as if from inside a tunnel. She knew that was her. Everything went still. He bent down and kissed her gently, tenderly, on the lips.

When he stood up, a thought forced its way through her fluffy brain, sharp as a knife.

He was still fully dressed.

Then she slipped into a deep darkness, smooth as a warm bath.

38

Rage simmered in Sofia's veins, nearly blinding her, and she had to stop the car on the edge of the road on her way to the pension.

Control yourself. You will hurt her if you don't get it together.

She found Anna right away; she was sweeping the dining room. A couple of other employees were cleaning too. When Anna turned around and caught sight of Sofia, she knew. It must have been something in Sofia's eyes, or the vibes coming off her, because Anna's eyes went wide and she took a quick step backwards. Sofia went up to her and shook the flash drive in her face.

'Where can we talk in private?'

'Oh, hi there, Sofia! Of course we can talk, I just need to put this away first,' Anna said, holding up the broom. Her voice was shrill with forced cheerfulness, and she interrupted herself with a nervous giggle.

'Let's go to the office,' she said, casting an anxious glance at the other staff members, but no one else seemed to have noticed Sofia.

As they walked down the hallway, Anna babbled nervously and breathlessly, but Sofia didn't register a word of it. She was squeezing the flash drive so hard that her palm hurt. Anna opened the door to a small storage room.

'You'd better explain yourself fast, before I kill you,' Sofia said once Anna had closed the door. They were standing eye to eye in the messy, crowded space.

'It's not as terrible as you think.'

'Spare me the bullshit. I refuse to drag this out, so start talking, because I have other stuff to take care of.'

She moved closer to Anna, who backed into a corner stacked high with boxes.

'We only did it twice. It was a year and a half ago, when you were at a conference, the one in Gothenburg. But Benjamin wanted to stop. Nothing happened after that, I swear.'

'To hell with Benjamin. I want to know who you sent the pictures to.'

'You already know that,' Anna said snootily.

Sofia's hand darted out to catch Anna's hair, and she pulled so hard that Anna howled in pain. Tears sprang to her eyes and her lower lip trembled.

'Fine! Let go! I'll tell you,' she whimpered. 'Franz contacted me right before we started the shelter. He invited me out on a date. He said it was about time we made up. It was exciting. Everyone thought he was in hiding, developing more theses, but he still made the time to see me. Then he took me to ViaTerra, and... you know how he is, it's so hard to say no to him...' The words caught in her throat.

'It was just the once. He didn't have time for a relationship, but he wanted to stay in touch. He made me believe we would see more of each other eventually. We talked on the phone sometimes. Then he suggested I help you with the shelter. He said you deserved all the help you could get. It seemed like he really cared.'

Anna was speaking in fits and starts. She unconsciously

pressed farther and farther back among the boxes. Her eyes were downcast. Tiny beads of sweat sprang out on her forehead.

'And when he mentioned he wanted some pictures of you, that didn't seem so strange. He said he wanted to see what you looked like, that he was curious. And then he wanted more, and he started putting money in my account, and I really needed money right then, and eventually it was all one big mess, I completely lost control...'

Anna started to cry. Ugly, hoarse sobs that shook her body. Her pitiful behaviour only made Sofia angrier.

'Pull yourself together! Why did you keep the pictures on those flash drives?'

'I couldn't leave them on the computer. But Franz told me to keep them. He thought they were good, he said I was a great photographer. Phone pictures wouldn't cut it. He even sent me an SLR camera, a really expensive one. We had to make sure you didn't realize anyone was taking pictures. He was planning to make them into a collage at some point.'

The very thought of such a collage forced Sofia's mind away from the cramped closet, and the hatred she felt for Anna shifted to Franz.

'How can you live with yourself, Anna?'

'I can't. You have to realize I never wanted to take the pictures. I felt jealous that Franz was so fixated on you. I wanted him for my own. But I couldn't resist him when he asked me to do it.'

'Does Benjamin know you were in contact with Franz?'

'No way! Those last pictures – I don't know why I put them in the box. Everything I sent to Franz was supposed to be kept there, a flash drive for every set of pictures. But those last ones were my own private photos. I sent them anyway. I was trying to impress Franz, show him I could seduce Benjamin as easy as pie. I guess I wanted to make him jealous.'

Suddenly she doubled over and started crying again. Sofia grabbed her shoulders and shook her roughly. Even though Anna was taller and more sturdily built than Sofia, she must have felt Sofia's rage, smelled the uncontrolled wrath, because she was trembling in fear. She collapsed into a heap on the floor and wept. Sofia crouched down, lifted her face, and slapped her hard. Anna's eyes widened in shock.

'I've had enough of this disgusting self-pity. You broke into our house while were at the party, and then you snuck into our room on Christmas Eve and scared the shit out of me. You are disgusting, you fucking traitor.'

'I'm sorry, I was desperate. I didn't have time to search the whole upstairs that first time, because you came home. It was the pictures of Benjamin I was after. I knew you would figure it all out if you saw them.'

'Did you tell Franz that Elvira came to us?'

Anna's chin sank to her chest; she wrapped her arms around her knees, rocking and whimpering like an animal.

'Answer me!'

'What do you think? It was unbelievable that she was back – I thought she was dead! I don't know how I ended up so desperate. I thought that if I helped him with all this, he would understand that we belonged together. I've never managed to get him out of my system.'

She hiccoughed a few times. The tears and snot formed a nasty goop that dripped down her chin. Sofia grabbed her by the jacket and shoved her back so hard that the boxes at the top of the pile fell down. The edge of one hit Anna in the forehead, but she hardly reacted. She just startled and stared blankly ahead.

'Write down all the shit you've done for him and turn yourself in to the police, or I'll do it for you.'

Anna muttered.

'Give me your phone.'

'What?'

'Your fucking phone, give it here!'

Anna dug in her jacket pocket, took out her phone, and handed it to Sofia.

'So you don't get it into your head to call him.'

'No, I promise...'

The mark on Anna's forehead had blossomed into an angry purple bruise. Sofia's rage cooled and instead she felt a vast disgust towards Anna. She wondered how she ever could have thought she was beautiful, how she could even stand to be near her. She was ugly, disgustingly ugly, with those fake, bloodshot eyes and snot all over her face.

The sun was still high in the sky, gilding the hazy spring air, as Sofia drove home. It was unbelievable and unfair for it to be so beautiful out just as her life went to pieces. The tears began to fall. The road before her went blurry, but she slowed down and stubbornly drove on, full of an inhuman strength.

She drove all the way up to the house. Then she took Denzel out to pee in the yard, but kept her shoes and coat on when she went back inside. She went to their bedroom and took out a suitcase, haphazardly tossing a bunch of clothes inside. When she went into the bathroom to get her toothbrush, she realized her hands were trembling. In the mirror over the sink she caught sight of her own eyes, which were unnaturally large and looked like twin black holes. She hauled the suitcase to Julia's room. There were already clothes and underwear strewn across the floor; she gathered them up and tossed them into the suitcase. Lacking the strength to carry it, she let it bounce down the stairs.

She no longer felt present; it was like she was outside her body. She wasn't even angry, just beside herself, as if this were a terrible nightmare. Grabbing a canvas bag from the kitchen island, she went into Benjamin's office. It was so dark and quiet in there, the smell of Benjamin – safe and a little boyish – hung in the air and pulled her back to the present moment. She sniffled. Nausea welled up from her stomach, and she wanted to throw up on his desk. She unplugged his laptop and put it in the canvas bag. On his bookcase she found the two binders where he kept his work documents and bookkeeping records and took those too. She noticed he'd left his tablet at home, so she added that.

Before she left the house, she gave Denzel food and water. She petted him gently and kissed him on the head.

She drove slowly and single-mindedly. It had to be *that* spot, on the rocks where she and Benjamin liked to sit and watch the sun go down. She parked the car and left everything but the canvas bag. She gingerly climbed across the rocks to the flat boulder where they'd sat together so many times. She moved to the very edge and almost lost her footing as she pulled the laptop from the bag. It made a splash when it hit the water. It sank sideways, like a shimmering shark fin. Tiny bubbles rose to the surface, and then it was swallowed by the sea. The binders didn't want to sink at first, so she got them wet and held them down until they were drawn into the water. Last of all, she tossed in Anna's phone. Once it was out of sight, it felt like it had dragged her heart with it into the depths.

The air rose from the sea, forcing its way into her nose and mouth and filling her lungs. A gentle breeze made ripples on the surface.

She quickly stood up and returned to the car. For a long time, she simply sat there.

Then she took out her phone and called her mother, who didn't pick up. She left a voicemail: 'Julia and I are coming to visit tonight. Miss you.' Brief and cheerful, to keep from alarming Mom, with her overly sensitive nerves. She glanced at her watch. Quarter past two. Julia would be done with school soon.

When she reached the school building, she felt restless, and there was an aching heaviness in her belly. She decided to go inside to wait for Julia. In the corridor she ran into the headmaster, who greeted her heartily and effusively.

'It's so great to see you! How can I help you?'

'I'm here to pick up Julia. She's been out of town, and she was going to take the bus straight here today.'

A perplexed expression fell across the headmaster's face.

'But... she's not here.'

'What do you mean?'

'I'm actually the one who took the call, from Franz Oswald, you know, the spiritual leader. He said that Julia was delayed. It seems she had decided to write an essay about their operations there and was going to interview him today. A school project, of sorts. He was so pleasant. He said she'll be back tomorrow, as usual. I assumed you knew. We're quite proud that she was given such an opportunity.'

Everything went perfectly silent. All Sofia could hear was her pulse, like a ticking time bomb. And then she exploded.

'What is wrong with you? He is *dangerous*! Why didn't you contact me? Jesus Christ, Julia is a minor!'

The headmaster was about to place a calming hand on her shoulder, but Sofia had already spun around and run out the door.

I dash down the path. The wet grass licks at my calves. I jump fallen trees, catch my breath, and run on. My lungs are burning; they feel tight in my chest. Although I have walked this path countless times, I'm worried I will take a wrong turn onto some small side path and get lost in the forest.

When I reach the clearing by the cottage I stop. Here, far away from the lights of the manor, I have a clear view of the night sky and its millions of stars. The half-moon is bright. Here, everything is still. The mild air carries the sweet smell of pine needles and pitch. I steady myself against a knotty tree trunk that is battling the ivy for survival. I hold tight to the trunk and lean back until it feels like I'm floating up to the sky. But then a wispy cloud blows in and rips apart the moonlight.

What will I tell Grandma? Where will I start? Will she believe me? I haven't even figured out how she could help me; I only know that she always has before.

The cottage is dark but I'm sure she's at home. I can feel the warmth of her trickling out into the chilly night.

She opens the door, her hair a mess, half asleep, but all she says when she sees me is:

'Why, hello, Thor! How nice to see you. Come in.'

As if it weren't late at night. As if it's perfectly normal to find me standing here out of breath, the legs of my trousers all wet. Her scent and warm embrace as she hugs me is so familiar that I let out a sob.

'I'll put on some tea. See if you can get the fire going.'

I can. By the time she returns with steaming mugs, the fire is crackling cosily.

'I'm not going back to ViaTerra,' I say once we've sat down.

'What do you mean?'

'There's something I have to tell you. Quite a bit, actually.'

'Well, go ahead then. I'm listening.'

Our eyes meet. She has been waiting for this. She knew it was coming. She is ashamed of all the times she didn't ask about our bruises, our calloused hands, our eyelids heavy with sleep deprivation.

Throughout my tale, the shame grows in her eyes. She doesn't say 'Oh, how terrible!' or 'Why didn't you tell me this before?' Because she already knows, and maybe she even imagined something worse – if that's possible.

Eventually I take pity on her and tell her it's not her fault. But now I need her help. There are still children at the school. There is a girl with Father.

She's a tough lady, Grandma; she doesn't cry, but I can tell she's on the verge. For a long time, she is lost in thought. I don't disturb her, because I know she's deep in a line of reasoning that can't be broken.

'Do you have proof?' she says at last.

'Proof? Don't you believe me?'

'Of course I do, honey. But if we go to the police, it will be your word against that of your father and all the children, and they're terrified of him.'

I consider this for a moment.

'There is someone,' I say. 'Matteo, from Earth's Children. He took pictures. Father sent him on an assignment to keep this girl under surveillance. A few days ago, Father said Matteo has gone up in smoke. That's exactly how he put it. But how can I get in touch with him?'

Grandma sighs.

'We'll figure this out, I promise. But first you need to sleep. You look absolutely wrecked. Sleep as long as you like. I hope no one will miss you up there, because I'm sure they would come looking here.'

'I don't think Father will notice I'm gone,' I say. 'He fired everyone who worked in the office. And he's busy with that girl.'

When I bring up 'that girl', Grandma shudders.

She brings me a pillow and blanket and then retires to her little bedroom. I stretch out on the sofa. The last few coals glow in the woodstove. I notice how totally beat I am. All those sleepless nights seem to have piled on top of me, crushing me with their incredible weight. I don't wake up until Grandma rouses me.

'Thor, you've been asleep for twelve hours. I was worried. You're not sick, are you?'

I sit up on the sofa and rub the sleep from my eyes. It takes a moment for me to remember why I'm here. My plan.

'Grandma, we have to go to the police.'

'Don't you think your father will hush it up, that you'll only be making things even worse for yourself?'

'It can't get any worse.'

'Are you sure about this?'

I well up with fury at being challenged like this. She has ignored everything. She's been sitting here in her little cottage and hoping everything would work out. Settling for the moments she got to spend with us. And now I realize how it was possible for this to happen. Children have vivid imaginations. They make things up. *There's no concrete evidence, nothing you can touch. A child's words are easy to explain away if you can't handle the truth.*

'Come on, I want to show you something,' I say, going to the entryway and putting on my shoes.

'Where are we going?'

'To ViaTerra. There's something I need to show you there.'

'But we can't just march in there, can we? You said you didn't want to go back.'

'The back gate is open. Come on.'

'But if your father—'

'Are you afraid of him? You never used to be. I remember the first time you visited us. You were tough as nails. Why are you so chicken now?'

'I'm not afraid of him. I'm afraid of losing you two.'

'You basically already have.'

We walk the path through the forest. I take the lead, moving so fast that she can hardly keep up. She doesn't say anything, just follows me breathlessly. I imagine that if Father spots us he will kill me. And maybe that's just as well. If Grandma is watching when he beats me to death, she'll take what I've told her seriously.

The gate is still open. It's afternoon, and the courtyard is full of activity. Staff are running back and forth. Guests are enjoying coffee outside the annexes.

'We'll pretend nothing is out of the ordinary,' I say to Grandma. 'That way no one will notice us.'

We quickly move across the courtyard toward the barn, as though we have some important task to see to there. None of the staff seem to bother about us. Their vacant eyes look right through us.

The barn is empty. The door creaks as I open it. The sun is shining through the windows, illuminating the dust dancing across the floor. I take Grandma's hand and lead her to the stall. There's a sleeping bag there, probably Vic's.

'We slept in the pigsty,' I say. 'That was our punishment for disobeying. But we carved our names in this stall here.'

Grandma's baffled eyes sweep across the wall.

'We started the tradition when we saw this name,' I say, pointing. 'We thought she was a spirit who would protect us when we were scared of the dark.'

'Sofia…' Grandma whispers, running her fingers over the name. 'It's Sofia.'

Only then does she truly see the other names. Her eyes take in the crooked letters. The attempts left by those who couldn't even write. Backwards letters. Misspelled names. Names that were never finished. She touches them with her fingers, stroking them as if to assure herself they're real.

For a moment so brief it almost doesn't exist, our eyes meet. Even so, it's sufficient for me to understand that she believes me.

Then she falls to her knees. Her face crumples and she covers her eyes with her hands. I can't see her tears, only the shaking of her back.

It's as though she's forgotten I'm there. She hurriedly takes her phone from the pocket of her jacket and dials a short number. She speaks breathlessly and at length, in an authoritative voice I've never heard her use before.

'This is not the sort of matter where you come in to file a report!' she says angrily. 'Don't you understand? This is serious!'

She snaps and snarls until she has made herself clear, and suddenly her voice is calm again.

Once she has hung up, she reaches for me and takes my hand.

'The police have been notified,' she says. 'Time to go to the cottage and wait.'

39

Sofia stared through the windshield, unaware of the world outside. Paralysed. Her ears were buzzing. Her eyes were wide open, yet she was blind. She wanted to open the window; it was scorching inside the car. But she couldn't manage. She wanted to fasten her seat belt. But she couldn't even do that. She was incapable of moving. Her insides were in such turmoil that she couldn't breathe.

This isn't happening.

This can't be happening.

There has been some misunderstanding.

Julia will be here soon, knocking cheerfully on the window.

'What are you doing here, Mom?'

But the schoolyard was deserted, the car felt empty, and her heart was completely hollow.

Panic spread through her body as though she had been injected with it. She slammed her fists into the steering wheel until her knuckles ached. Although she collected herself enough to pick up her phone for the call she knew she had to make, the phone slipped from her hand and thumped to the floor. By the time she picked it up again, it seemed to have speed-dialled him, because his number was on the screen.

With no prelude she began shouting. Curses, swear words,

obscenities. At first he said nothing, but she could hear him breathing. Heavily, the way he did when he was excited.

'Are you finished? Because if so, you should listen carefully if you ever want to see Julia again.'

'Don't hurt her! I beg you!'

'I won't, if you come here and take her place. You will strip for me, get down on all fours, kiss my feet, spread your legs, and beg for it. Tonight you will be my devoted slave. I have been longing for this for fifteen years, Sofia.'

'What have you done to Julia? Please, don't frighten her!'

She gave a sob as she thought of Julia's intense fear of the dark. And he had no way of knowing about it.

'I wouldn't dream of it. Julia worships me. She isn't the hysterical type like you are.'

She whimpered and dropped her phone again; it fell into her lap. When she brought it back to her ear, all she could hear was his breathing.

'Please, let her go. This is between you and me. Don't bring Julia into it.'

'Nothing will happen to her as long as you come here. But if I see a single cop on the ferry, and believe me, I've got eyes everywhere, or if I see a helicopter fly over the island, Julia will disappear. And I'm good at making people disappear. It's astounding how many teenage girls show up at our gate asking to meet me. Some of them simply lose their minds when I don't respond to their propositions. It's so easy to get lost on the island. The rocks are slippery. There's quite a gale today.'

'Stop it! Stop it!' she shrieked. 'I'll come, just don't hurt her. How can I be sure you'll let her go if I come there?'

'You have my word.'

'And I'm supposed to trust that? How can you attack a sixteen-year-old girl? How do you sleep at night? How sick *are* you?'

He heaved a sigh.

'You have no choice but to trust me. Now get going.'

She tried to put on a calmer, more authoritative voice.

'Do the right thing. Let her go and we won't breathe a word, I promise. You don't want to take this risk. Think of your good reputation, all over the world. Think of all the success you've had with ViaTerra.'

He laughed so hard the line crackled.

'Oh, sweetie. I'm happy to risk it all just to grab your delightful ass again. You like it from behind best of all, don't you? Haven't you figured out what turns me on by now?'

'Is this about revenge? Hand Julia over unharmed and I will shoot myself in the head.'

'That would be unfortunate. It's not revenge, Sofia, it's obsession. I have thought about you every day for the last fifteen years.'

'You can't deal with the fact that I rejected you. You crave attention. You have to be in the limelight. It's about time you take responsibility for all you've done, Franz.'

'That's enough!' he snapped. 'You will come here. Best hurry so you don't miss the ferry.'

Distract him. Get him away from Julia.

'Okay, I'll come.'

'Lovely to hear. And listen, maybe we should take this opportunity to go ahead and have that baby we never made together.'

'You perverted bastard!'

She suddenly found herself staring at the words 'call ended' on the screen. Right away she tried to call Julia, although she knew she wouldn't answer. She left a breathless message: 'Julia, don't be scared, I'm coming to get you.' Maybe Julia would hear the notification of the voicemail arriving.

The drive passed in a fog of anguish. Her mind was racing, but her focus had been obliterated. She nearly skidded off the road a time or two. Her good sense told her to stop the car and call the police, but her instincts warned her in a tone cold as ice: *He will kill her.*

The beautiful landscape passing by was blurry and distorted, coated in a dirty yellow film. She realized she hadn't used the bathroom since that morning; her bladder was about to burst. But she simply stopped at the edge of the road, peed in the ditch, and totally ignored the passing cars. She was on her way back to the car when the first attack of vomiting hit her. And then another, as she leaned against a skinny birch tree. Once she'd emptied her stomach it felt like she had also expelled all her emotions. But she stubbornly started the car again and drove onward, frantically racking her brain for solutions. A way to free Julia. Someone she could call. But it was like wandering around in a labyrinth full of dead ends. She didn't dare take any risks. He would hurt Julia, he'd said so himself. That was a promise he would keep; she was sure of it.

Her phone rang. She had set it on the passenger seat with the screen visible. Ellis. He could wait. The phone dinged; he'd left a message. He called again. Another message. Nothing Ellis had to say could be important right now. If she picked up the phone, she would drive off the road.

She reached the ferry twenty minutes before departure.

A text arrived from Franz. A close-up of Julia's rosy face, fast asleep. Her mouth was half open, the covers drawn up to her neck.

Have to distract him, get him away from her.

She called him.

'Thanks for the picture. How do I know Julia will be there when I arrive?' She tried to make her voice sound normal, but it was hard. Every system of her body was out of order.

'You can see her. Presumably she will be sleeping heavily.'

'Please don't drug her. This isn't her fault – leave her alone.'

'I can't make any promises. She's totally crazy about me, you know. She's the one who won't leave *me* alone.'

Keep him talking. Keep him away from Julia.

'There's something else I want to know, before I get on the ferry.'

'Are you at the ferry now?'

'Yes, in the parking lot.'

'Out with it.'

'Why now? It's been years. Why do you have to ruin our lives now?'

'You've got it all backwards, as usual. You think I vanished from your life, but I never did. I've always been there, in one way or another. Now get on the boat before my patience wears thin.'

'You sent the DNA test so we wouldn't say anything to Julia. She never would have come to the island if she thought you were her father.'

'Exactly.'

'How does it feel, being so cruel?'

'Better than you can imagine.'

He hung up again.

She put down the phone and squeezed the wheel so hard that her knuckles went white. It was a beautiful day. The sunlight was intense, but it was only May; this was a deceptive sun that stung her eyes. The surface of the sea moved slowly, as though it were breathing. Parents strolled here and there, pushing strollers. Kids with ice cream cones; pigeons and crows. It was so upsetting to see all these happy families when she had lost her own. At least she couldn't hear their eager voices from inside the car. According to the radio, this would be the warmest day of spring so far. She turned off the radio, hardly aware that it had been on in the first place.

Her phone screen lit up, flashing Ellis's name. She glanced at the time. Fifteen minutes until the ferry would depart. Best to get Ellis out of the way.

'I can't talk right now. I promise I'll call tonight,' she said, before he could say a word.

'This can't wait. Are you driving? You know what, I don't give a shit if you are. Listen up, this is life or death.'

'Be quick, there's something I have to take care of.'

'Julia's boyfriend, Matt, is here.'

'Great, she's been worried about him.'

'But his name isn't Matt Larsen – it's *Matteo* Larsen and he's one of those ViaTerra kids. Franz sent him to spy on Julia. Matt has been sending pictures of Julia to Franz. He put up the camera in her bathroom.'

'What the hell are you going on about?'

'Sofia, it's true. You're *not* driving, are you? If you are, pull over. I have to tell you this.'

'I'm not driving. But what are you saying? Matt was sent by Franz?'

'I'm sorry to say he was. But he got fed up and is hiding out at my place now. I'm choosing to believe him – he says he wants to try to make everything right. Is Julia in Gothenburg?'

'Yes, why do you ask?'

'Matteo received an email from her that says she's in danger. Shit, Sofia. It seems she's on Fog Island with Franz. They've been in touch ever since that conference, having lunch together and talking on the phone. And now she won't pick up when Matteo calls.'

Sofia whimpered.

'I know, I'm taking care of it right now. Please, can I just call you back in a few hours?'

'Sure, but listen! Matteo got disillusioned, he's totally besotted with Julia. And he's got pictures, Jesus, Sofia, these pictures! Of all the awful shit that goes down at that Nazi school. You have no idea. They dump ice water on five-year-olds while they're sleeping. Brainwashing, threats and beatings. And Franz was behind it all. Jesus Christ, Sofia, it's horrific. But Matt has decided to speak out about Franz. He's on our side now. He wants to help us.'

Sofia didn't even have the wherewithal to be shocked; her brain couldn't process more information. But then she noticed a gum wrapper Julia had crumpled and tossed in the storage box of the car door. For a moment she pictured Julia sitting beside her and chewing loudly, and she began to cry.

Have to distract Franz. Get him away from her.

'Listen, Ellis. There's something I have to take care of. I'll be in touch tonight. In the meantime, I need you to spread all our material, all the evidence, in every way you can think of, everywhere you can. Get hold of Magnus.'

'I already am. I couldn't wait. And I talked to Magnus – he's contacting reporters all over. This is going to go viral in no time. It's going to be huge, Sofia!'

'Good. Make it even bigger,' she said with a sob.

'Do you need help? You're not trying to deal with Franz on your own, are you? If Julia's with him, you have to go to the police.'

'Just trust me. I'll be in touch.'

'Should I call Benjamin too?'

'No, not Benjamin! Listen. Simon can help you. Benjamin is a bastard. He fucked Anna, and she's Franz's spy. I don't have time to explain, but whatever you do, don't say a word to Anna. I have to go.'

She noticed a text come in from Benjamin. *Where are you? Call me!* She turned off her phone and stashed it in her purse.

She stayed in her car on the trip over to the island, wondering if Edwin Björk was there, whether he'd seen Julia, but Björk's brother was piloting the ferry that day.

Sofia felt powerless; she couldn't feel her body any longer, aside from her upset stomach. Her fingertips felt numb. Her brain was full of five thousand things and nothing all at once. But there was one thought that kept returning and growing stronger. There was a small general store in the village on the island. Surely they would have a knife. Maybe she would have time to slip out of the car and run into the store before Franz saw her. Any knife would do, even a kitchen knife.

And when they reached the island, and she drove the car over the ramp, she was almost sure this was the only way to end the nightmare.

It was the right thing to do. The only option, consequences be damned.

40

Julia struggled to open her eyes, but she was blinded; she opened them more slowly and squinted into the light. She tried to stretch out her legs, but they were too heavy. Her bare feet with their pink toenails stuck out over the edge of the bed. She could move her arms a bit, and tried to stretch them out, but only got halfway. One of her breasts was peeking out from beneath the covers. The sun had found its way through a window and was warming her body. Her skin was damp and warm. The room was stuffy, and she was sweating under the heavy blankets. A lone fly buzzed angrily, hitting the windowpane again and again. She had a strange feeling in her abdomen, as though she had to pee. The pressure was like pins and needles between her legs. When had she last used the bathroom?

Slowly she became aware of another person in the room.

Someone observing her at close range.

She saw the shape of him between her eyelashes, his shadow falling over her. Her gaze sharpened. He was freshly shaved and showered, with wet hair. He had a sexy grin on his lips and aimed a teasing look at her.

She rubbed the sleep from her swollen eyes.

A jolt went through her body, a warning.

She shouldn't be there.

'I forgot to set the alarm on my phone. Fuck! I missed the ferry,' she exclaimed.

'You don't have to go to school today. I've taken care of it,' he said, placing a hand on her arm.

'What do you mean?'

'Your headmaster knows you're here interviewing me. He's very proud of you, as you can imagine.'

She was bewildered.

'"Oh, what an honour for our school!"' he imitated the headmaster. 'He said you were a very *promising* student.'

Julia felt a bit put out. She hadn't planned this, but now she laughed because it was almost funny. The headmaster's comment, and the fact that she was lying here, naked in Franz Oswald's bed.

'How long was I asleep?'

'A long time. It's late afternoon.'

'What about Mom?'

'She knows you're here too.'

Despite his light tone, there was something that didn't add up. Something had changed between them, she noticed now. There was something that needed to be said, but he simply sat on the edge of the bed, looking at her.

'What aren't you telling me?' she asked. But he didn't respond.

She lost patience and tried to sit up, but something pulled at her ankle. She tried to yank her leg away, but pain sliced at her ankle.

He placed his hands on her shoulders, bent down, and kissed her forehead.

'You need to trust me now. There are a few things your mother and I need to work out. Unfortunately, you'll have to stay here a little longer. None of this is your fault, it's important that you know that.'

Now she could see that something was odd about his smile.

'What's on my foot?'

'It's just a leather strap. I'll take it off later.'

She knew this was the moment she should panic. Scream, try to get loose, beg and cry. But her experience with the attack not so long ago had taught her something about panic. It was a worthless reaction that didn't change a thing, except maybe to trigger the attacker. Too much panic – as in, hysteria – typically led to being silenced one way or another.

What's more, she realized, to her own astonishment, she really wasn't afraid of him. Yes, there was something odd about his gaze, but whatever it was it didn't seem to have to do with her.

He bit his lip. He seemed nervous. She had never seen him like that before.

'I thought you liked me,' she said. 'Did you only invite me here to lure Mom in?'

'Yes, that's how it started, but feelings change all the time. I like you more than you could know. This isn't the way I wanted it to be, but everything will work out fine once I talk to your mother.'

'I need to pee.'

'Of course.'

He pulled down the covers. She saw that the leather strap around her ankle had a chain, latch, and lock. He took out a key and opened the lock. Just like that! Now all she had to do was convince him to let her go.

But as soon as her feet hit the floor her head began to spin and she nearly fell headlong. Immediately he was there to catch her. Her legs trembled uncontrollably.

'That'll pass in a few hours,' he said with an apologetic smile.

He led her to the bathroom, helped her to the toilet, and left, closing the door behind him. Once she had peed she grabbed the sink and pulled herself up. She found that there was some steadiness in her legs after all. There was an unpleasant metallic taste in her mouth, so she brushed her teeth to get rid of it. It occurred to her that she could lock herself in, but then she realized there was no key.

Just then, he opened the door. He took her by the arm and led her back to bed. When she sat down, the room began to spin again. He handed her a glass of water from the nightstand.

'Drink this, it'll help.'

She drank greedily, suddenly aware of how thirsty she was. He gently pushed her back into bed and reattached the ankle cuff.

'Get some sleep now. Everything's going to be fine, you'll see.'

'I'm not tired. It's only when I stand up. Where's Mom?'

'On her way. To confront me.'

'You promised not to hurt me.'

'And I won't. I'm sorry you got dragged into this, but I don't regret the time we had together. I never will.'

'You didn't mention that you planned to drug me and chain me up to a bed.'

'Didn't I make it good for you yesterday?'

His voice was calm, but it was missing some of its warmth.

'Sure, but if you hurt Mom, you hurt me. You know that, right?'

'She's tough, your mother. She can bounce back from just about anything.'

'I don't get why you're so mad at her. She's super nice.'

'It's not about being nice, Julia,' he said, shaking his head slowly. 'A ViaTerra employee must be humble and obedient, and grin and bear it when necessary. Your mother wasn't able to do that, despite her vast potential.'

'If that's what it takes, I could never work here.'

'No, I suppose not,' he said with a sigh. He took a lock of her hair and twirled it. 'I did everything in my power to make sure you had a nice visit here. But now it's about Sofia, and that's a different matter entirely. I apologize if I've upset you. That was never my intention.'

'What was your intention, then?'

'It's not something that can be explained, not when you're driven by such powerful forces as I am.'

She realized that his gaze had come to rest on her breasts and was sliding down her thighs. Although she understood that he had changed, that perhaps he was even a threat to her life, that wonderful, sinful feeling streamed through her body again. She wondered if she could take advantage of the fact that he seemed attracted to her. Get him to take off that fucking ankle cuff.

'You didn't go all the way,' she said.

'That was for your sake. You were so beautiful. Almost like a porcelain doll. Are you disappointed?'

'Yeah, actually. After all your bragging. It almost makes me wonder if those rumours are true. I mean, that you can't get it up.'

Suddenly a black shadow crossed Franz's eyes.

'You little witch,' he whispered, grabbing her throat. His hands were cool and dry and his grip was firm. His gaze was hard, but she wasn't afraid. He was breathing heavily, as though he'd just been running. But she simply looked up at him indifferently, and he lost focus.

Really, she had been expecting this. The punishment for her lies. All Mom's warnings that had gone in one ear and out the other. *Never respond to propositions from older men, they're all perverts, and never take a ride from a stranger.*

Even so, she couldn't fear him. He simply didn't seem

frightening. Her lack of fear was so obvious that it surprised her. To her delight, it seemed to knock him off balance.

Now she realized that he was insane, somehow. Under some delusion that made him want to take revenge on the world because he had never found the answers to his questions about the meaning of life. Everything and everyone must be 'conquered', but she didn't have the least interest in fighting his madness. Yesterday he had listened to her. He hadn't been at all judgemental. Maybe she could make him listen again. There was a peculiar peacefulness in her mind. And whatever it was he had drugged her with had put her restless body into a more relaxed state.

He took his hands from her throat and tenderly ran them down her sides.

Just then, there was a knock at the front door. It was cautious at first.

'Boss, are you there?' came a voice.

'Go to hell,' he muttered.

Then a firmer rap.

'Boss! Something happened!' the voice called.

Franz stood up and rushed out of the bedroom. She heard the front door open.

'What is the meaning of this?' he shouted.

'Sir, I think you had better come to your office, sir... something is happening... all the newspapers, and online... Matteo...'

All she heard were mumbling voices, and at last his voice, roaring:

'That goddamn fucking piece of shit!'

He didn't come back into the house; instead, she heard the door slam. And there she lay in her damn ankle cuff. She tried in vain to get loose, but ended up pounding her fists on the blanket in a rage before she gave up and lay still.

He would be back, of course he would. With any luck, it would be before he got his claws into Mom.

Julia sat up; when she looked out the window she realized it was early evening. The sun was shining mildly through the trees instead of beating down on the roof. She thought of Mom, of her lovely eyes and wonderful laugh. Then she thought about Dad and felt like a little girl again. His large but gentle hands. His wide embrace, which she could crawl into whenever she wanted. The way he always smelled clean, even when he was sweaty. And the way he would wink at her whenever Mom got all hysterical. It occurred to her that she hadn't thought about him since she got to the island. Maybe it was because he was such a fixture in her life, always present, like a calming current through her body.

The dress she'd been wearing the day before was in a messy pile beside the bed. She reached down, caught it, and pulled it on. It had gotten chilly in the cottage. No bra or underwear within reach. Her sense of time quickly disappeared. She lay there for an hour, or maybe two.

Her heart began to pound when she heard the door open. Franz came in and stood before the bed. His fists were clenched. She could see in his eyes that something had happened; they had lost their razor-sharp focus. A vein pulsed on his forehead. When he relaxed his hands, she noticed that his little finger was trembling. He seemed broken. Some of his authority had vanished.

He approached the foot of the bed and unlocked the ankle restraint.

'You can go now. Sofia is at the ferry.'

She was so astounded that she couldn't move at first.

'Didn't you hear me? Julia, you have to hurry.'

She sat up in the bed. Although she didn't know why, her lip began to tremble as though she was about to burst into tears. She knew she should be angry with him for keeping her tied up, but she was so tired and confused. For the first time in a long time, she felt weak and uncertain.

He came up to her, sat on the edge of the bed, and took her face in his hands.

'Sweetheart, go. It's not a good idea for you to be here right now.'

She grabbed his hands and pulled them away from her face, observing them.

'Why is your little finger trembling?'

'It is not. Now go, before I change my mind.'

He stood up as if to leave, but then he turned around and looked into her eyes.

'There's something I want you to remember, Julia, can you do that? For me.'

'What is it?'

'The thing is, I'm not very good at regretting things, or apologizing, I hardly ever do. And all the whining that people get up to, it gets on my nerves. Principles and morals, all that. But there's one thing I want you to remember. Can you do that?'

'I already said.'

She thought he looked very strange. Eyes darting. A crooked, creepy smile. His forehead was sweaty.

'What we had together was more potent and more sensuous than any carnal sensation. That's all I want you to remember.'

'Those were some fancy words, but I'll try,' she said.

He laughed, but it was a kind laugh, not creepy at all.

Then he turned on his heel and left the cottage without looking back.

With a tug, she got her legs out of bed and placed her feet on the floor. She was stronger than she had been a few hours ago. The room wasn't spinning; her nausea was gone. She still felt tongue-tied, as though there was something she hadn't been able to say to him. She wanted to call Mom right away, but she couldn't find her purse, where she'd left her phone. After searching in vain for a while, she decided to forget about it. He must have taken it. Now she had to find Mom, and fast. Franz was crazy. Although he didn't seem to want to hurt Julia herself, she had the uneasy feeling that he wouldn't treat Mom so kindly. In the entryway, she put on her jacket and sneakers. When she stuck her hand in her jacket pocket she found the pager Thor had given her. She thought about leaving it in the cottage, but she didn't want to break the lovely connection she'd had with him.

Chilly air hit her as she opened the front door. A gust of wind tossed her hair backwards. Steely grey clouds towered over the manor. Employees were running back and forth across the courtyard, but they didn't seem to notice her. There was something hysterical about the way they were moving.

She was still too wobbly to run, but she walked hastily and a bit unsteadily to the gate. The muscles in her legs were totally beat. The forest scent hit her as she stepped out, to the other side of the wall. She knew she had to find the main road, but the path branched in different directions. Best to take the one that ran alongside the wall.

She had only one thought in her head: find Mom.

She heard something snap in the forest. She stopped, taking a quick breath. Immediately she was on guard. An animal? Were there moose on the island? The steps came closer. Large strides, breaking heather twigs and sticks. She tried to gather her wits, to listen and figure out where the sound was coming from.

Just then, he popped up in front of her.

For an instant she thought it was Franz, but then she realized he was younger, ganglier, and slimmer.

In a few steps he had reached her, and he grabbed her by the hair.

She stuck her hand into her pocket and pressed the button on the pager.

Now she was scared. Scared for her life.

41

Sofia drove the car off the ferry and parked by the square. She kept an eye out for one of Franz's cars, but she didn't see anything that remotely resembled his usual flashy rides. She took out her phone to call him, but just then a text arrived. *Got held up. Wait there.*

Perfect. She got out of the car. Her legs were trembling uncontrollably. She was sweating, even though it wasn't warm out anymore. Demonic clouds were towering on the horizon; a storm was on its way in across the strait. But through a crack in the clouds, the last rays of sunshine lapped at the surface of the sea. A raw breeze swept in across the water and slipped under her clothes. She crossed the square to the general store, which was just about to close.

'Please, this will only take a minute,' she said to the clerk. 'We're going to grill out on the island this evening and I forgot to bring a knife.' Her voice sounded shrill and artificial.

The clerk aimed a baffled gaze and a vacant smile at her.

'It's going to be bad weather. Not great for grilling.' He gestured at the sky outside.

'Oh, I didn't notice,' she lied. 'But I still need a knife. I guess we'll have to eat indoors. Can you help me?'

He showed her a small paring knife, the only one they had. She decided it would have to do. In her confusion she forgot to ask for a bag and left the store with knife in hand. Its sharp blade reflected the low sunbeams and hurt her eyes. Quickly she stashed the knife in her purse. She thought of how the clerk would remember her. *That flighty woman who said she was going to grill out in the middle of a storm. I had no idea…*

She sat in the car to wait and noticed she had received several texts. She clicked on one from Benjamin first. *Where are you two? Please, call me. PLEASE.* A guilty conscience. Too late now. Then another text from him, sent fifteen minutes after the first. *Is Julia with Franz? Where are you? Answer me now or I will go to Fog Island!* Apparently he had spoken to Julia's headmaster. Benjamin hadn't listened to her when she was worried that Franz was back, and he had allowed that snake Anna into their beautiful bedroom because he couldn't keep it in his pants. Her silence was only the beginning of the punishment that awaited him.

There were also several texts from Ellis, including links. She opened the first one and was exhilarated to see the pictures that popped up on her screen. They were blurry, had definitely been taken by someone who hardly knew how to use a phone camera. Even so, there could be no doubt about what they depicted. A large, sturdy boy holding another boy still so a third boy could hit him. A boy forced to the edge of a cliff, looking terrified. A man with a chokehold on a youngster. An underexposed picture of a sleeping bag in a dim room. Children hauling stones by a large wall. A close-up of a hand with massive blisters. She was so disgusted at the sight that she couldn't bring herself to keep scrolling. She heard her own voice as if through a fog.

Oh, my God, my God.

The rest of the links led to articles online. The headlines were not kind to Franz's so-called school.

Children Endure Forced Labour on Fog Island

Gulag-like Conditions at Fog Island School

ViaTerra Cult School – A Modern-Day Internment Camp

Child of ViaTerra School of Horrors Speaks Out

Franz Oswald's Reign of Terror over Children

There were even statements from a few celebrities, former followers, who were now distancing themselves from Franz and his methods, and denouncing the organization.

It was all happening at once; it was too fast and too much. And in the midst of this nightmare there was Julia, and Sofia no longer dared to hope she could put everything to rights. She just hoped she could get Franz to hurry. With any luck he would be coming alone. Once again she dialled Julia's number, but there was no answer. Just Julia's cheerful, teasing voice:

'Hi Mom, since you're the only one who leaves me voicemails let me assure you that everything is fine. I'll call later.'

She leaned against the wheel and let the adrenaline flow through her body, bringing a fist to her forehead in an attempt to hold back tears. *I can cry,* she thought, *I can press my face to this filthy car window and bawl my eyes out at this hopeless situation. But if I start crying now I will never stop.*

She felt an intense desire to hear Simon's reassuring voice, so she called him.

He picked up immediately.

'Sofia, where are you?'

'Where are *you*?'

'Elvira and I are with Benjamin. We're beside ourselves with worry. You're not on Fog Island, are you?'

'Yeah, I am. But listen up, Simon, because I can't talk long. Benjamin fucked Anna in our bedroom. Anna has been spying for Franz for years. She is totally in love with him. We have been taken for a ride. Don't trust them – call Ellis and Magnus instead. Benjamin didn't mention any of this, did he?'

She heard Simon's gasp, but his voice remained calm as he spoke.

'No, he didn't. But right now we're worried about you and Julia. Can you tell me what is going on?' He almost sounded like someone taking calls on a crisis line.

'There's no point. There's nothing you can do anyway.'

'Sofia, listen to me. I understand that Benjamin was an ass. I promise I will beat the shit out of him as soon as possible, but first I just want to get you and Julia home.'

'Franz has got her. I'm going to do something terrible, Simon, I'm going to…' The words caught in her throat. Tears welled up and dripped into her lap.

'Sofia, don't do anything rash! The news about the kids has leaked everywhere. We spoke to the police. Franz's mother had already contacted them. They're coming on the next ferry, the one early tomorrow morning.'

'That will be too late. They still won't manage to put an end to all this crap. Just promise me one thing before I hang up—'

'Don't hang up!'

'I have to. Promise you'll come visit me. Wherever I end up. Do you promise?' she asked, her voice thick.

Simon's voice was smooth as silk when he replied.

'I would visit you even if you moved to Mars. But right now you have to think through this before you make any snap decisions. Should we ask the police to send a helicopter?'

'No! No helicopters! He's got Julia! Don't you hear what I'm saying? You have to trust me. I'll call later. If I can.'

She hung up. His name came up on the screen as he tried to call back; then came the ding as he left a voice message. But Simon couldn't help her now. Not this time.

There was no holding back her tears anymore. She pressed her hands to her forehead as the tears fell and everything went blurry. The trees swayed in the wind; the sea looked cold and cruel. She thought of the times Julia had a bad dream and came into their bedroom in the middle of the night, wearing her threadbare nightgown. How it felt to hug her then. Julia's warm breath against her neck. Almost grown, yet so small in Sofia's arms. How she still smelled like a child.

It was incredible to think that it was just this morning she had found those pictures of Benjamin. It had been a perfectly ordinary day. Was it even possible for your whole life to go to pieces so quickly? But really, this hell had been ongoing for twenty years. They thought they were living a nice, quiet life, but a snake had been coiled in the wings. You don't feed a python that winds around your body. You don't lie there passively, waiting for it to suffocate you. There is only one thing to do in that situation. A thought came to her like a wave crashing on the rocks.

There is only one way to put an end to this nightmare.

She picked up the knife and cautiously ran her finger down its sharp blade. Straight into the heart, and then a deep slice through the belly. She had seen it on TV. It wasn't survivable. But it had to be fast. He had reflexes like lightning. She had once seen him drop a glass of water and catch it mid-air. Without spilling a drop.

She gazed out at the parking lot. No sign of Franz. She checked her texts and incoming calls. He hadn't tried to contact her. She called his number. No answer. Now she began to suspect this was part of his evil plan. Get Julia out of the way first, then her. She sent him a text. *Where are you? Don't hurt Julia!* She waited a moment. Still no response. He must be livid about all the revelations that had turned up online. She started the car and drove along the coastal road to the turn-off for ViaTerra and parked the car there. Better to walk the last bit on foot and show up before the guards could warn Franz. She made sure the knife was in her purse and got out of the car.

Dusk had begun to fall over the island. A pale half-moon rushed out from behind wispy clouds. The sea lapped and sighed anxiously as it struck the rocks. She hung her purse over her shoulder and set off for the manor at ViaTerra.

The silence in the cottage is broken by the shrill beep of my pager. It's clipped to my belt, but I don't bother to look at it. I know immediately that it's you, and you need help. And now I can hear a shriek from the heath. Loud and piercing.

Grandma has gone to the village to buy groceries. She has made me promise not to go anywhere.

All day I've been pacing the cottage. Worrying about everything. Father doesn't seem to have noticed I'm gone. What is he doing to you?

But now I leap from the sofa and hurry to the entryway. I put on my sneakers and jacket. Outside, I stand still for a moment to listen. At first all I can hear is the dry rustling of leaves in the wind, but then there's another shriek, once again from the heath.

I set off through the forest, hurrying down the paths, scratching myself on thickets and twigs that scrape my face and get caught in my hair. I run as fast as I can until the forest ends and I emerge onto the heath.

Vic has hauled you all the way to the slope that leads to Devil's Rock. He's dragging you, on your back, across the barren terrain as you bellow, kick, and try to yank your arms from his grasp. I run across the heath, trying to catch up, but by the time I get there he is already heading up the rocks to Old Nick. When he catches sight of me, and I meet his cruel gaze, a cold hand squeezes my heart. He is so much stronger than I am. I am no match for him. And if he knocks me out of the equation, there's no one else to save you. I have to plead with him, break through his insanity.

I shout in the most powerful voice I can muster: 'Vic, stop! Let her go!'

But he keeps dragging you towards Old Nick. The rock reaches over the sea, its nose nudging the clouds that have closed in from across the sound.

I cry, 'Not there!' but Vic doesn't listen. I can see you struggling, so close to getting him off balance, but he throws his elbow around your throat. You gurgle and spit, then go limp in his arms. He lays you on the grassy patch just before the rocks take over, plunging to the sea.

'Are you going to help me or what?' he calls to me. 'We'll throw her over and then we'll be rid of her. Don't look so horrified. No one will ever know.'

My legs will no longer bear me. I fall to my knees on the slope and bawl at him to stop, but he only stares at me, bold and defiant.

My head is pounding. Something wants out. The pounding turns into something else, something worse and more stubborn. Like a chainsaw biting its way through my frozen brain.

I shout the only words that will come to me:

'Father is going to be furious!'

And as I say those words, I realize they're true.

Vic stares at me, his mouth agape, looking panicked. The momentary delight I feel to have reached him transforms into horror as I realize he has spotted something behind me. I don't have to turn around; I know who it is. The shadow falls across my body like an eclipse. All at once I'm in the midst of something dark and forbidding. The sound of the sea and the wind has faded. The air feels different, sharper and colder.

I meet Vic's gaze. For a second, our eyes are locked. Something passes between us, an awareness.

That life will never be the same again.

'Let her go!' I hear Father say behind me, brusque and adamant.

Vic stares at Father in terror. But the fear in his eyes quickly turns to rage.

'If you want this whore so bad, come get her!' he shouts.

I start to climb up to Old Nick. Father's panting breaths reach my ears as he follows. I'm the first to come to the shelf of the cliff. I dash up to Vic and try to grab him, but he quickly drops you and shoves me aside, enraged.

And at that moment, as I lose my footing and nearly fall and glimpse the sea far below, I am sure these are my last moments on Earth. The wind has caught me and is about to carry me to a certain death.

But then I feel something around my ankle – your hand. You yank and I fall, but I don't hit the rocks. I land on your belly. Vic has a hold on your arms again and is trying to drag you to the precipice. I press my whole weight against your body, but Vic manages to pull us a little bit closer to the edge.

Suddenly Father is standing above us, his legs planted wide.

'Let her go this instant, Vic!' he roars. 'There's no need for you to take revenge on me, because others already have.'

I crawl away from you, between his legs. There's a flicker in which I observe something strange about Father. Although he is furious, there's something missing. His unbearable obstinacy. It's as though I'm seeing his bare face for the first time. He looks at you. He looks at you tenderly.

Vic stares at Father, livid. He is absolutely seething.

'You care more about that little slut than about me!' he wails. His chin is trembling. It looks like he's about to burst into tears.

Father takes a step towards him. Vic backs away, dragging you with him; the two of you are dangerously close to the edge now. I grab your feet, but he's got your wrists in an iron grip and is pulling so hard that you howl in pain.

'Everything has gone to hell, do you hear me?!' Father shouts. 'There is no more ViaTerra! There is nothing for you to take over!

That was all you wanted, wasn't it? So you might as well stop sucking up to me. But you are not going to drag her down with you, so LET HER GO!'

Vic goes totally mad. He lets go of your wrists and throws himself at Father. He punches him, aiming for his chest and face. But Father is so much stronger. He blocks the blows and shoves Vic away until he's staggering backwards. Vic is only a few steps from the cliff's edge now.

'No! Watch out!' I cry, but no one pays any attention to me.

Vic throws himself on top of Father again. I have never seen such rage as what's pouring out of him now. He roars and pounds one fist straight into Father's ribcage, but Father thrusts him off – and it all happens so fast that it's like it isn't real.

The last thing I see is Vic's wide, bulging eyes; I see him take a breath, his hands trying to grab the air, his arms windmilling, and he falls backwards like a lifeless doll and is swallowed by the dim evening sky. I wait for the scream, but all I hear is a loud thud and a horrific crunching sound that breaks through the howling of the wind.

And here's what I learn later: it only takes a split second for his skull to be crushed and his spine to be broken; in under ten seconds, his heart stops beating. But there, on the cliff, I know that Vic is gone the very instant he falls over the edge. A jolt of grief slices through my body before he's even hit the rocks below.

Father simply stands there. He sways oddly in the wind, reeling as though he's about to fall too. I throw myself forward, grab his legs, and pull him back. He feels stiff as a mannequin. He takes a few steps away from the edge, turns around, and staggers off, out of sight.

And now I notice you, hyperventilating on the ground. Your dress is torn to shreds, your hair is a mess, your eyes are wide. You're covered in scrapes: your arms, your knees, your face. Blood trickles from a wound on your forehead.

My mind is a total blank. The sound of my pounding heart drowns out the wind. For one bewildering second I have no idea where I am.

This is like the most terrifying scene in a horror movie. Vic is gone. The wound in my heart is deeper than I can stand. I sob, vomit into the grass, and then I feel your chilly hand on my forehead. It feels like Mama's hand, when I was little and got sick. You don't say a word as you brush the hair out of my eyes.

I turn around and see Father sitting on a rock. He is motionless except for his hair fluttering in the breeze. I get to my feet and approach him.

'It was an accident, you were saving Julia,' I say, placing a tentative hand on his shoulder. But he doesn't hear me. His eyelids are heavy, like those of a toad. His body seems frozen to the rock he's sitting on. He offers me an eerie smile that's really more of a grimace. Time and again he mutters something strange. It sounds like a foreign language. But then he falls silent and stares straight ahead, as if he's in a trance. His jaw is clenched. His eyes are bits of coal in that uncannily pale face. His hands tremble uncontrollably, but the rest of his body seems paralysed.

All the life has drained from him, leaving nothing but a shell. No matter how much I hate him, I have always admired his fiery aura, pulsing with life. But now it's gone.

I take his hand, squeeze it, try to reach him. But his hand jumps and trembles as he stares vacantly. He doesn't seem to realize I'm there. The air around him is heavy and hard to breathe. He's somewhere else entirely, locked in a dark room with no doors or windows, a prisoner in his own madness.

If this were a scene from a horror movie, maybe he would have come to life and said something cruel. But he doesn't, because this is real life, and it hurts so much I whimper.

I look at him, this father whom I never stopped loving, whose reign of terror has kept me awake at night in fear, who has slapped me for daring to question him, and I know that he has ceased to exist.

You come over to us, bend down to touch his cheek.

'He's had a stroke or something. Jesus, this is terrible. I don't have

a phone, what do we do?' you moan. 'And that other guy—' You make a move towards the cliff, but I take your arm.

'There's nothing we can do for Vic. Please, don't look down there!' I beg.

You start to hyperventilate again, shaking uncontrollably. Suddenly you're in my arms. You cling to me and press yourself against my chest. You sob so hard I think my heart is going to break, and I hold you, rock you, stroke your hair. I resist the impulse to pull free and run. Run away from the miserable howl of the wind. Away from everything that hurts so much. Your sweet scent is calming; I bury my face in your hair. We stand like that, as one, until your sobs ease.

Father hasn't moved a muscle. He looks like a scarecrow keeping watch over the sea.

I gaze at our surroundings.

The heavy clouds over the sound have lifted. The storm has fizzled out before reaching the island.

The wind has begun to abate.

The heath is nearly shrouded in darkness.

I can see the stars, scattered like glitter in the gaps between the clouds.

Below us, restless waves lap at the rocks.

I can see someone standing on the slope.

The silhouette of a woman becomes clear against the heather.

She gazes up at us and calls your name.

42

Sofia had barricaded the door with chairs and closed all the windows. Benjamin had a key. And she knew he would come.

While the police questioned them, as they each held one of Julia's hands, Sofia had avoided his gaze. And once the interrogation was over, she had ordered him never to show his face in their house again.

'Text me your new address and I'll send the divorce papers,' she had said, right in front of Julia, and she was truly ashamed of herself. Even so, she took her daughter's hand and pulled her out to the car. Julia had protested, but there was no helping it. It was time for them to start a new life, surrounded only by people they could trust.

There was something about Julia's attitude that suggested she wasn't quite taking this situation seriously. In fact, there was something about Julia's demeanour in general that wasn't quite right. She wasn't acting like a victim who had just escaped the grip of a psychopath by the skin of her teeth. On the surface she seemed tough, unaffected. It was like she assumed everything would be fine and refused to let it get to her. But Sofia knew better. She would deal with Julia the moment they got some peace and quiet.

She knew Benjamin would come. It was only a matter of time. And indeed, that very evening he showed up in front of their house. First he knocked tentatively on the door. Rang the doorbell. Called out cheerfully.

'Sofia! It's me!' And then, a little more gravely: 'Look, I think we need to talk.'

When she didn't answer the door, he stood outside the living room window and started shouting for her. Initially, there were declarations of love.

I love you, Sofia! I've always loved you!

I can't live without you!

You're the only one, don't you know that?

Think of Julia. Julia, are you in there? Daddy loves you, sweetheart!

As twilight settled over the yard, his cries grew increasingly desperate.

I'll do anything, just let me in!

Can't we talk about this? Please? Please!

I will stay out here until I starve to death. I would rather die than live without you.

But once darkness had fallen, his desperation turned to rage.

You ruined all my stuff. I can't even work anymore. What you did is illegal, you know that?

I'm calling a locksmith. I own this house, you know!

Let me the fuck in!

You cheated on me too!

That was the point at which she wanted to shout back. *That was before Julia. Before we were a family. Which you ruined!* But it was true that she had cheated. And Benjamin had taken her back without any complaint at all. Because that was the kind of person he was. A forgiving one.

Julia seemed amused by all the drama. She curled up on the sofa with her tablet and giggled at some of his commentary.

'You're going to let him in eventually, right, Mom? Aren't you?' she asked nervously.

Sofia only grunted in response. But then she saw Benjamin's boyish, freckled face, nose pressed to the windowpane, and couldn't help but laugh.

'He looks like a giant pig,' Julia said from the sofa.

By the time Sofia opened the door, it was nearly midnight. She stood off to the side a bit so he wouldn't get the idea that he could hug her. Julia rushed over and threw herself into his arms, but Sofia turned her back on him and went to the kitchen. It was actually the very first thing he'd said that made her want to let him back into their lives. She had always loved him too, ever since the first day they met on Fog Island.

It took three days before she sat near him on the sofa again. Four days before she let him touch her. And a whole week before she said she forgave him. It was time to move on. To focus on helping Julia get through the trauma – or, rather, make her realize she had experienced trauma in the first place. They had to do this together, help each other out, as a family.

Sofia tried to get Julia to open up and talk about the feelings she'd had while Franz was keeping her prisoner. But she stubbornly refused to admit she had been frightened.

'I understand *now* that he was violent and dangerous, after all the stuff you've told me. Well, and after everything that's come out about his horrible school. I *never* would have gone there if I'd known all that. But he was never like that to me. In fact, he was pretty nice. So there's nothing to work through there,' she maintained.

'Julia, he is a terrible, evil rapist and murderer. Evil can take many forms, and sometimes it's hard to spot it in an attractive man. He has ruined so many lives, you have no idea.'

'I get that. But he actually *saved* my life. And now he's turned into a nutcase at a mental hospital, so why should we even care?'

'But, honey, you went through something horrible.'

'I was never scared. So why do I have to work through it? Do you know what scares me? The future. Having to slave away at some boring-ass job. That's what I'm afraid of. Can I go to therapy for *that*?'

'Of course. As soon as you've worked through what happened on the island.'

'The only part I still think about is that moment when Vic fell, and the sound when he hit the rocks. Jesus, it was so awful. I've been having nightmares about it.'

Sofia nodded encouragingly.

'That's a great starting point. I'll make you an appointment with a psychologist, someone I know...'

'Fine. I'll go. But don't expect me to obsess over what happened with Franz. I've turned the page on that. He got what was coming to him, and I don't want to talk about him anymore.'

Sofia, too, had had nightmares since the night she went out to Fog Island.

When she had reached the guard booth at ViaTerra, she was breathless and hysterical. She was prepared to use her knife, but Franz was nowhere to be seen. The guard had shooed her off, saying that Franz was unavailable. But when she insisted that Franz had invited her to a meeting, the guard told her he had left the property on foot.

She knew instinctively where he had gone. She set off for the heath. At first, when she arrived, she saw nothing. All she could hear was the wind and the sea. The rocks were dark and threatening and the sea frothed anxiously. But then the moon found an opening in the clouds and she could make out the silhouettes of two people at Old Nick. She thought it was Franz, about to push Julia over the edge. She shouted Julia's name. The response came from a voice she didn't recognize.

'Please, help us! Up here!'

And as she climbed up those damned rocks, so slippery and treacherous in the dark, she stumbled more than once, scraped her hands, and ripped a hole in her jeans.

She nearly fainted at the sight of Julia, with blood trickling down her face and her clothes torn, clinging to a young man Sofia had never seen before. She would come to see this image in her nightmares for years. And there, on a rock, sat Franz – petrified, staring at the sea.

She was so caught up in what she'd planned to do that she thrust her hand in her purse to find the knife. But it would have been like stabbing a corpse, because she quickly realized Franz had, for all intents and purposes, left this world.

Julia detached herself from the young man's embrace and threw her arms around Sofia's neck. They held each other tight, unwilling to let go for a long time.

'Mom, someone fell. We're too scared to look. Please, can you go see if he's down there?'

Sofia hesitantly approached the edge of the cliff and spotted the body, a black shadow on the boulders below. Arms and legs were bent around the body at strange angles, as if he had tried to fly in his final moment. Blood had spread across the rock like the tentacles of a squid.

'Don't come over here!' she called to Julia and Thor. 'We have to call the police.'

The police arrived in a helicopter that night and took them to the hospital. A pair of paramedics loaded Franz in first and gave him oxygen. Sofia hardly registered what was happening to him. She couldn't care less. She had Julia. Sofia burrowed her nose into Julia's hair and held her hand.

She had no intention of letting go.

They floated high, high above the cliffs, until Fog Island

became a tiny dot fading in the dark. So much had happened in such a short time that her head was about to explode. But she clung to a comforting thought.

Julia is alive, and everything is going to be okay.

Ever since that night, Sofia had felt like the worst mother ever. Thankfully, Julia's adventures with Franz had escaped the media's hungry maw. They were still chewing over the scandalous details of the children on Fog Island. The official story was that Julia had gone to the island to meet Vic, who became violent and tried to shove her off the cliff. Franz had saved her. A tragic accident. The headmaster at Julia's school was the only one there who knew the true story, and he had promised to keep it quiet. Sofia's lust for revenge was as good as gone. What was the point of taking revenge on a man who was incapacitated, who could do nothing but stare with the vacant eyes of a fish?

And now there was just one last hurdle. Making Julia see that she really needed psychological help. Sofia couldn't forgive herself for letting Julia dupe her so easily. That she had let her travel alone even after those warning emails (which had turned out to come from Matteo).

But Benjamin had no patience for Sofia's self-accusatory ramblings.

'Don't play the guilt card now. She is the person she is. And she's wonderful,' he said. 'In just two years she'll be eighteen, and what can we do then? All we can do is hope she learned something from this horrible experience.'

A few weeks later, they all reunited in their house: Elvira, Simon, Magnus, Ellis and Matteo. Sofia hadn't heard from Anna since the confrontation at the pension. The police had confirmed that Anna had turned herself in. She would be questioned as part of the case against Franz Oswald.

Elvira and Simon would help Sofia with the shelter for the time being. Thor hadn't come to this meeting, which Sofia found strange. She would have loved to see him again. But Elvira said he was still on the island, working on some important project on his computer. What it was, she didn't know. He seemed to be totally absorbed in it and hardly registered her presence.

It was summer now. It wasn't a beautiful day; the sky was almost completely overcast. But it was a mild evening with a gentle breeze. They sat in the garden, chatting until it was so dark they could hardly see each other's faces. The tealights flickered. Moths fluttered against the light next to the front door.

Ellis noticed that Julia kept glaring at Matteo.

'You can stare at him all you want, Julia,' he said. 'But it's thanks to him and Thor that we managed to bring down Franz's reign of terror. I'm sure he's not proud of what he did to you. But he did what he was raised to do. And he broke away in the end, didn't he?'

Julia's grumpy face burst into a smile.

'Here I thought that I was a world champion liar, but apparently Matteo is a born con artist,' she said. She went over to Matteo and ruffled his hair. Sofia noticed the longing glances he cast after Julia – glances that weren't yet being returned.

Julia's thoughts were elsewhere, on something Sofia hadn't yet managed to wheedle out of her.

'What are you going to do now, Simon?' Benjamin asked. 'Move back to California?'

'No, I have other plans,' Simon said with a secretive smile.

'Tell us!' Sofia said eagerly.

'I'm sure you'll all think I'm nuts, but I've been thinking of buying the pension on Fog Island.'

'What?' Sofia exclaimed. 'Why would you do that? You're famous in the US, you could get any job you wanted there. You're not going back to *that place*, are you?'

'I don't think being famous suits me,' he said. 'I've always wanted to create something that could serve as a model for eco-friendly operations. You know – the kind of thing Franz was always going on about, but which he only ever used for marketing purposes. I want to do it for real. Inga Hermansson who owns the pension there is almost eighty now. She'd be happy to sell it to me.'

'But why do you want to live out there? Won't it remind you of ViaTerra?'

'Franz Oswald doesn't own Fog Island, and he never will. I think it's the most beautiful place on earth, and I'd love to live and work there.'

Sofia's gaze shifted from Simon to Elvira, who nodded in agreement. It was clear that she worshipped Simon. Sofia hoped Thor would too, that they could become a new little family.

When Elvira had arrived that evening, it was clear she had been crying. Sofia knew it was about Vic. It must be hell for her, finding and losing a son like that. She had been so close, but she would never see him again. Later that night, Elvira's eyes welled over with tears. She had gone to the bathroom and stayed there for a long time.

'What are you going to do now, Sofia?' Simon asked.

'The shelter will reopen this fall. It's going to be a full house. I already have a waiting list of defectors.'

'Then I'll write an article about you,' Magnus suggested. 'A follow-up about kids who find their way back to real life after being in a cult. And, speaking of that. Does anyone know what's going on out on the island these days?'

'Yes, I actually do have some info,' Matteo said. 'I talked to Thor and my parents yesterday. They used to be members, although by now, obviously, they've left. ViaTerra has been closed by the authorities, and it seems to be for good this time. I mean, it would take a whole heap of permits to restart operations, and they can dream on. Thor's grandma, Karin, is managing the property now.'

'How are the children?'

'I'm still in touch with most of them. I guess we're all a little shaken up. But we're getting psychological help. Didrik is the only one who still thinks Franz was God. Which is pretty sick, considering what Franz did to him. But I'm sure he'll come around eventually.'

'I expect so too,' Magnus said. 'It really is such a beautiful old manor. One day maybe it can be used for something positive.'

'Thor's going to move into Karin's apartment, the one she kept in Gothenburg,' Elvira said. 'He's going to finish school and wants to make it on his own for a while. He talks about you a lot, Julia.'

Sofia noticed a faint blush on Julia's cheeks, and she was flooded with gratitude towards Thor for saving her daughter's life.

It had grown chilly out. They went into the house and kept talking late into the night, until the first rays of dawn turned the sky a pale grey.

A few weeks later, Julia came dashing down the stairs, out of breath, her eyes alight. She seemed euphoric – and yet her cheeks were stained with tears. Sofia was cooking, for once, but Julia pulled her away from the stove.

'Mom, get this! I got an email from Thor. Well, actually, it's a whole book. You have no idea! He writes so beautifully!'

'That's wonderful! What's it about?'

'I can't tell you now, while you're cooking. And I'm not done reading it yet. But it's the saddest thing I've ever read, and also the most beautiful. We're going to meet up. On Fog Island.'

Sofia slammed the saucepan on the kitchen island, but all she could manage to say was 'Not on your—' before Julia clapped a hand over her mouth.

'Listen to me, Mom, before you react. I know you've had it rough. And I know you're trying to protect me from all the evil there is in the world. But it's honestly not dangerous on Fog Island anymore. It's so pretty there. We're going to go to the place where it happened again. Try to put it behind us. It'll be part of my therapy. It's time for you to start living in the present, Mom. The nightmare is over, don't you get it? Now, I'm going to go answer Thor's email and tell him I'm coming.'

She let go of Sofia's mouth and galloped up the stairs like a frisky foal.

The house was quiet. Calm and perfectly still.

Sofia stood in the kitchen, staring straight ahead for a moment. She thought about Thor, who had written about his experiences for Julia, and then she thought of her own manuscript, which still sat unfinished in a folder on her computer. One day, the time would be right to take it out again. Maybe it would bring her closure.

It struck her that this had all started with the storm.

In its aftermath, everything that had once been hidden rose to the surface.

The storm had revealed their secrets; it had turned out that her family and friends were held together by an invisible web of lies.

Then something else occurred to her. Maybe the storm hadn't brought only chaos and destruction. Maybe, in fact, it was a good thing that it had come, that it had swept through their lives, tearing up evil by the roots – so that eventually, they could move on with their real lives.

43

The nursing assistant was tired. It had been a long shift – a lot of lifting and carrying, and the small of her back ached mercilessly. Her joints throbbed with constant pain.

Her work at the psychiatric hospital took its toll on her. She was far too young for this chronic back pain and these achy joints. Even so, she couldn't bring herself to quit. She didn't understand why she felt so tied to this place. There was never a word of appreciation from her surly boss; she never received thanks for her efforts. Maybe it was the illusion that she was making a difference that kept her there. It was nice when she could counter a bit of the madness in a patient's eyes with her calm manner or bring temporary relief to someone's shattered mind.

She went to check on the patients in the common room one last time. The sun was shining through the picture window, pooling in a golden path on the floor. The room was quiet. A little too quiet. Some patients were dozing in easy chairs after lunch. Others were reading or staring into space.

Her eyes were drawn to the man in a wheelchair by the window.

Franz Oswald, the former cult leader.

His back was straight and stiff as he stared at the lawn outside. The unit manager had decided it was good for him to sit there, his eyes facing the world. Maybe something would turn up and capture his interest. So now they put him there each morning, and he stayed until bedtime.

It wasn't that long ago that she had admired Franz Oswald. She had watched his video chats online and thought he was the most attractive man she'd ever seen. And so charismatic. But now he just sat there staring. His eyes seemed to be watching something only he could see. But there was no life in his pupils, just a creepy hollowness.

She was overcome by an unexpected wave of tenderness and melancholy, the way you feel after something terrible and permanent has happened in your life. Such a good-looking man, world-famous, turned into a vegetable. It was only a matter of time. During her time at the hospital, she had observed the slow, cruel process that broke down a body that only ever sat still. Muscles atrophied; skin lost its lustre. Healthy people had turned to living corpses right before her eyes.

This would happen to Franz Oswald as well.

He seemed so lonely and abandoned. He hadn't had any visitors, which perhaps wasn't that surprising given everything the media wrote about him these days. Descriptions of his 'ruthlessness' were everywhere, and while she could believe he'd had a temper, the man in the wheelchair didn't seem ruthless in the least – only pathetic and abandoned. But then, this morning, his son had stopped by. A lovely boy with a cloud of curly red hair. He didn't look anything like his father. But it was clear to see that he cared, although he'd seemed a bit awkward as he sat beside his fossilized father.

She had lingered in the room during the visit, eavesdropping out of curiosity. But the son had only said a few words to Franz, and his voice was so faint she couldn't make out the words.

She approached the window and bent down over Franz so

she could see his face, which was partly illuminated by the sun. She shifted the wheelchair a little, to get the sun out of his eyes. Then she leaned against the back of the wheelchair and brought her lips close to his ear.

'Come back to the world. Maybe it won't be as terrible as you think,' she whispered, but she immediately felt ridiculous and turned around to make sure the other patients hadn't heard her.

But everything was just as usual in the room: quiet, aside from a chess piece moving as one patient played a match against himself.

When she turned back around to look at Franz, she saw a single tear rolling down his cheek. She knew that there were some moments when he was unable to control the blinking of his eyes. She quickly wiped the tear with her finger, although it was forbidden for aides to touch the patients that way.

Her shoes squeaked on the linoleum floor as she walked away. When she reached the door, she turned around one last time.

That was when it happened.

For the briefest of moments, he turned around and looked at her. She thought she was seeing things. And in that instant she froze, as though someone had driven an axe into her nerve centre.

She knew it was her imagination, a side effect of all the overtime. Yet that moment felt more real than life itself.

She looked back at him once more, just to make sure. Everything was normal. He was simply sitting there and staring out the window. It's wild, the things your brain can make you see.

God, do I ever need a vacation, she thought as she sighed in resignation and left the room.

Epilogue

There's more I want to write to you about, now that we've met again. The end of the story. When light conquered darkness. And with these last lines, I bring the account of my life to a close. It's a little like closing the door on the past and throwing a new door wide open, to face the future.

So bombastic, I'm sure you're thinking, but you know how I am.

I stand outside the hospital where Father is and stare up at hundreds of tiny, sad windows. It seems to me he must feel lonely in there. Grandma offered to come with me, but I wanted to make this journey on my own. I hesitate at the door. What is the point of my being here, really? But then I remember what I told myself over these past few days: I need to see him; I won't let myself be controlled by fear any longer. And then I walk inside.

The hospital staff are kind. A female aide shows me to the room where Father is. Her eyes fill with sympathy when I tell her whom I'm visiting. The air in the room is so close. Lunch has been served, and the odour of food hangs in the air like a flimsy veil. It feels strange to see Father in a wheelchair. I approach him, and the aide pulls over a chair so I can sit down.

He's staring out the window. His once lovely eyes are clouded and dull as granite. His little finger has stopped trembling. His skin is pale, his tan gone. The expression on his face is grim, his jaw clenched, but his bloodless lips are slack. There's a tic in his left eye, but otherwise his face is motionless. Despite this stiffness, he's so fragile. His breath smells faintly of metal. If only he knew. Always so concerned with smelling good. At first he feels like a different person, but no, it's him. You can't flee from yourself; he is trapped somewhere deep inside his madness. I think of all the things he is incapable of now. His beloved spinning sessions, giving passionate lectures to his followers, fraternizing with celebrities, riding around on his motorcycle and ruling ViaTerra. I feel a bit of schadenfreude, but I'm not ashamed.

But then a memory hits me. I recall the only time he picked me up to hold me in his arms and tell me he loved me. All at once the room is blurry and I must turn away, look out the window. I sit beside him in silence for a long time, holding his slack hand and stroking his palm with my thumb. Initially it's like touching a doll, but then I discover the warmth in his hands; I place my thumb to his wrist and feel the pulse beating there, faint but steady.

All at once I know what I want to say to him.

'Listen, Father… these days I'm allowed to surf the internet as much as I like. And do you know what? Yesterday I read about something called "karma". It seems to me the law of karma is more powerful than all the theses we had to learn at ViaTerra.'

A shadow seems to fall over his eyes. But I'm sure it's just my imagination.

The aide approaches us to say that Father's psychiatrist has time to see me now, so I leave the room. Outside of it, the air is immediately fresher. Then I remember the aftershave, so I take it out of my bag and hand it to the aide.

'He liked this scent, so, I mean, if you have time…'

'You're so sweet,' she says with a smile. 'I'll make sure we use it.'

The psychiatrist is a young woman who squints curiously at me over round glasses. She seems to have a permanent smile on her lips, as though the corners of her mouth are suspended by clothespins. Being forced to smile at strangers makes me nervous, so I simply nod and take a seat facing her.

'Hello, Thor. Would you like to hear about how your father is doing?'

'I just want to know what's wrong with him,' I reply.

'When he was brought into the emergency department, his blood pressure was very high. The doctors there believe he had a minor stroke, something called a TIA. That's when a blood clot blocks a blood vessel in the brain but it gets better after a while. They took some images of his brain later, and there is no physical damage, yet he is in a state we call a dissociative stupor. That means he is nearly incapable of purposeful movement and hardly reacts to stimuli, but he isn't unconscious – as I'm sure you could see. His consciousness may or may not be reduced. You can tell by his breathing and the reaction in his eyes that he's awake. He can also control certain muscles – he can chew and swallow, for instance, if he is fed. If we put him on the toilet, he can control his bladder and bowels,' she says, and then she cuts herself off. 'Goodness, you don't need to know that.'

Now I'm annoyed.

'You know nothing about my relationship with my father. I am only here to find out what's going to happen with him.'

She gives me an apologetic smile and fiddles with a folder on the desk in front of her.

'I don't want to give you false hope. His condition hasn't improved since he arrived here. It may be permanent. And if he does get better, it's unlikely he'll be the same person he was. I just want to be straight with you, Thor. If he were to recover completely, against all odds, we would be forced to turn him over to the police so he can be held accountable for the allegations against him. We never give up hope about our patients here, but we are realistic, and the chances aren't good.'

'Do you know why this happened to him?'

'It seems that his stroke was the catalyst. Why he hasn't recovered, we don't know. But it could have to do with the trauma he went through.

A combination of the media scandal and the tragic incident at the cliff, when your brother died.'

'That's not what broke him,' I mutter.

'Excuse me?'

'Oh, nothing.'

But my mind completes the thought. Father could have recovered from any worldwide scandal, no matter how big. He could have recovered from Vic's death. He never cared about a close, loving relationship with his sons anyway. It took something totally different to break him so completely. His love for a sixteen-year-old girl. It must have terrified him.

I say goodbye to the psychiatrist and tell her I'll be moving to Gothenburg soon and will try to visit now and then. I can tell she feels sorry for me, but I don't feel sorry for myself at all. Because now I get to see you, and the thought makes my heart flutter in my chest.

When I get to the ferry and don't spot you right away, I feel anguished at the thought that you might have changed your mind. But then I see you, perched on a fence with your legs dangling. You call my name and I walk over and take your hands. You're bursting with life. Your pale, radiant skin, your mischievous eyes, your lovely lips bowed into a smile. If I look at you for too long, I eventually have no idea where I am.

On the ferry across the sound, you talk nonstop. I like listening to your voice. You ask about Father – how he's doing, how I'm doing, everything. But then you fall silent and watch me solemnly.

'What a hell of a life you've lived. Thanks for writing it all down and sending it to me,' you say. 'You're such a good writer. Where did you learn that?'

'Oh, I just have an easy time picking up words.'

'I think you should write a book, like one of those tell-all biographies about your dad, and become a millionaire.'

'Maybe I will. Who knows?'

'After I finished reading it, I wanted to hate your dad. I wanted

to hate him so much. But then I wondered if he changed in the end. Do you think he did?'

I think about that for a moment.

'Well, something happened to him, anyway.'

I put an arm around your shoulder. You rest your head against my chest.

'Jesus, think of all the stuff you weren't allowed to do. Have you ever even had sex?'

I shake my head self-consciously.

'Maybe you'd like to try it out? I mean, I think it would be nice.'

You're so cute that I have to laugh.

'No, that's okay. I'm sure all that will happen in time. Right now, it feels good just to sit here and hold you.'

'Let me know if you change your mind.'

'You like sex, huh?'

'I love sex! But when you're sixteen and you say that, people think you're totally nuts, or that your parents are nuts. Or both.'

Time flies, and suddenly we're there. I lock my bag up in a locker at the ferry station. We'll be riding back together on the evening ferry. Today I'm moving into Grandma's apartment in Gothenburg. I'm going to explore the city, study online, and catch up with compulsory school. Then, in the fall, I can start upper secondary school. I'll be older than everyone else, but that doesn't matter. And I'm going to get my driver's licence – for real this time.

You ask if I want to stop by ViaTerra, but I say no, there's nothing to see there. So we go straight to the heath, head out to the cliffs.

It'll be some time before the heather is in bloom, but there's already a faint pink shimmer from the millions of tiny buds just waiting to blossom.

We climb up the rocks, all the way to Old Nick, and stop at the little slope where it all happened. You take my hand and squeeze it hard.

'Think how it might have ended,' you whisper, 'if you and Franz hadn't come.'

And no matter how much I try to repress the image, I see Vic's face as he fell. He looked surprised, not afraid. Maybe he didn't know what was going to happen until he hit the rocks. It must have been over so fast that there was no time for him to suffer.

'And just think if you hadn't grabbed my legs,' I say.

'But I did. Come on, let's go sit down. This is something I read about online. If we don't say a word, and we take deep breaths and let the terrible memories float up to the sky, we will eventually be in the moment.'

'But what do we achieve by doing that?'

'Presence!'

The word hangs in the air. Simple, beautiful.

'Who knows?' you say then. 'Maybe it's all bullshit. But can't we try?'

We sit down on the rocks, so close I can feel your breath on my neck. I quickly lose all sense of time and vanish into a mental void. Not until the air feels chillier do I become aware of my surroundings once more. But then something strange happens. The darkness of that terrible night, and the eerie howling of the wind, which I didn't even know I had carried inside me – they shrink away, turn to dust, and scatter. All that's left is the endless sea and sky.

You release a heavy sigh.

'There, that feels better, doesn't it?'

It does, actually. It almost seems like magic. The vast sky seems to open above us. The future is this moment. Everything that will happen originates here and now. I don't believe I've ever felt so free. In the end, it turned out to be a wonderful day.

You pick up your phone and take a picture of the sea, and then one of me.

'Next time I'm freaking out about some tiny thing, right before

I melt down, I'll look at this picture,' you say. 'I'll think of how silly my problems are compared to everything you've been through. And of how wonderful you are!'

The air has grown cold. Thin clouds block the once blazing sun. It hangs before us, pale and round as a wheel of cheese. The lighthouse reaches for the sky out on its islet. Decades of salty air have scoured away most of its white paint; today it's the same shade of grey as the clouds. The breeze is gentle; the waves lap gently at the rocks. The open water looks like glass, but then – slowly – a light mist rises from the deep, hovering and dancing and stroking the surface.

'Look, sea smoke!' I exclaim. 'I've never seen sea smoke in the summer before. It only comes in the autumn and winter.'

'I've seen it on the lake at home,' you say. 'But where does it come from?'

I'm thrilled; when it comes to nature here on the island I'm something of an expert. Thanks to Grandma.

'Sea smoke is fog that arises when cold air moves over warm water,' I explain. 'The evaporation of the water makes it seem to smoke. It can rise as high as fifteen metres above the surface.'

'It's awfully pretty,' you say, taking my hand. I feel a soft, pulsing rhythm all through my body.

We sit still for a while and watch the sea smoke spread and grow like a living being dancing on the sea.

You're the one to break the silence.

'"More potent and more sensuous than any carnal sensation,"' you say. 'What do you think that means?'

'I don't know. Where did you hear it?'

'Your dad said it. That was the last thing he said to me.'

'He liked to toss around deep sayings. He was always doing it.'

'Yeah, but it seemed like he meant it.'

'Too bad you can't ask him now,' I say.

'I think he felt lonely. I do too, sometimes.'

'My father? Hardly.'

'No, he did. When you're that lonely, eventually it turns you mean.'

I feel annoyed at you for bringing him up, but I also understand. You can listen to people's opinions forever, but you can only judge something based on your own experiences. If you persist in talking about him, though, I'm going to speak my mind. That he got what he deserved.

'Do you hate him?' you ask.

'Sometimes. But other times I fantasize that he'll get better, serve his time in prison for all the horrible things he's done, and come back as a normal dad. Isn't that sick?'

'Not at all. Everyone needs a dad. I love my dad.'

You don't say anything for so long that I almost wonder if you've fallen asleep. But then you turn to look at me.

'What do you think? Are we a couple of those cult kids?'

'I am, for sure. But not you. I don't think so.'

'Don't be so sure. I think the fact that my parents were so entangled in it had more of an effect on me than I realized. Their past was always with us, this terrible thing you weren't allowed to talk about. Mom was so secretive. But what's going to happen to us now?'

'I guess we'll have to learn from what we've been through. I want to become a teacher, I think. Help other kids.'

All at once, I feel solemn. Sitting here with you and discussing the future feels so wonderful.

'But listen. What I really think is that I have a bunch of stuff I'm not even aware of imprinted in my brain,' I say. 'And that people are going to think I'm strange sometimes. I guess it will take a while to become normal.'

You make a face, smiling and frowning at the same time.

'Who wants to be normal? It's normal for my friends to smoke weed and get drunk on the weekends. And act like little kids. Who wants that?'

'Yeah, you're right. Maybe there's some sort of middle road,' I say.

'What if it's as simple as knowing that life is a highway ahead of us. And there's a lot of detours you could take, but at your own risk,' you say.

I think about that for a moment. But it seems too random.

'Or else we leave traces around us with everything we do,' I suggest. 'Every day, we have a choice between right and wrong. Eventually our environment reflects our actions.'

'You read that somewhere, but it sounds nice,' you say. 'Now we have to hurry, or we'll miss the ferry.'

Banks of fog hover before us on our way to the village. The gravel crunches beneath our feet. Outside ViaTerra, I feel the desolation reaching for me with its claws and trying to drag me back. But then I remember that we intend to live in the present moment, and it's easy to do with you walking by my side. I put an arm around your shoulders. I feel brave and nuzzle my nose under your mane of hair, taking in your fresh scent.

When we leave the island, the air is humid and the sea smoke floats before the ferry. Behind us, the façade of the manor house stands out against an iron grey sky, getting farther and farther away until it vanishes into the fog.

A note on events and characters

All characters and events in this book are fictitious. Franz Oswald, Fog Island, and ViaTerra are products of my imagination. Even so, in writing all my books I am inspired by true events from the twenty-five years I spent as a member of a cult.

Acknowledgements

Now it's time for me to say goodbye to Fog Island and devote myself to other literary adventures and challenges.

Thanks to everyone who has helped and encouraged me as I wrote the trilogy about the cult on Fog Island:

Dan, my beloved husband and very first reader. You make it difficult to regret those twenty-five stolen years. Without them, I never would have met you.

My parents, Olle and Ella Westam, who never gave up hope of being reunited with me.

My son John, his wife Noha, and my grandchildren. I'm sorry, John. I can never apologize enough that you were forced to grow up in a cult.

My brother Kristoffer and his wife Isabella, eager readers who are happy to share opinions.

My wonderful extended family: my cousins and their children; my aunts and uncles. Thank you for all the ways you have contributed to my books. Everything from computer knowledge to test reading and knowledge about children. Special thanks to my cousin Martin Larsson for your help on this third book.

My publisher, Karin Linge Nordh, for helping me make this book so much better with your comments and suggestions.

My editor, Lisa Jonasdotter Nilsson, thanks for all your hard work on the manuscript – I learned so much in the process!

Maria Enberg and Edith Enberg of Enberg Literary Agency for your constant, unwavering optimism and support.

The staff at Bokförlaget Forum, who welcomed me so enthusiastically: Marie Björk, Sara Lindegren, Adam Dahlin, and others.

Maria Sundberg, who designed the new covers.

Ann-Catrin Sköld Pilback, my mentor and stickler for grammar, who believed in my books from the very start and toiled selflessly to make them better. And Magnus Pilback, for always spurring me on.

My test readers: Johan Zillén, Edith Enberg, Britta Larsson, Andrea Lindblom, Cecilia Lindblom, Jonas Ornstein, Helena Braggins, Jan Kammis, and Boel Persson.

Jenna Miscavige Hill, who helped me realize that the truth about children in cults was more terrible than I ever could have imagined.

Jonas Ornstein, who was there from the start and encouraged me to write and take risks.

Lars Elgeskog, meteorologist at SMHI, who taught me so much about storms and other exciting weather phenomena.

Ulla McLean at Skogome prison who gave me insights into the Swedish prison system.

Eva Sköld, who has always answered my questions about the legal system with great patience.

Lotta Olsson, for helping me understand how an outsider might view a cult, and for giving me tips that I use in my lectures.

Lawrence Wright, who made me realize it was my duty to write.

All my friends in the United States and Sweden who work on cult issues and help defectors.

Noomi Andemark, Erica Hindborg, Magnus Utvik, Håkan

Järvå, Helena Löfgren, Anna Emgård, Ron Miscavige, Becky Miscavige, Steve Hall, Leah Remini, Paul Haggis, Marc and Claire Headley, Marty Rathbun, Mike Rinder, Janis and Paul Grady, Amy Scoobe, and Mat Pesch, to name a few. Special thanks to Håkan for offering so many accurate diagnoses for my characters.

Geniveve Ruskus, for giving me greater insight into the world of lawyers, and for your friendship.

Anna Lindman. You are a rock. Thank you for making it so easy for me to speak out.

All the gifted journalists who helped spread my story: Anna Flemmert, Lotta Modin, Jonas Danielsson, Christopher Friman, Frida Funnemyr, Malou Sivers, Ebba von Sydow, Andreas Nordstedt, Annie Wernersson, Lars-Olof Strömberg, Linda Andersson, Patrik Ljungman, Margite Fransson, and Ola Hedin, among others.

My readers! Thank you for your intelligent questions and comments, and for cheering me on.

All the book bloggers who have posted about my books and kept the cult debate alive.

Maria Spångberg at Chapmansgymnasiet, Christopher Hall and Alice Leiding at Campeongymnasiet, Katarina Svensk at Tärna Folkhögskola, and all the students at these schools who helped spread the message in my books.

All the book clubs I've had the pleasure to meet and discuss my books with.

Ulrika Larsson and the staff at Akademibokhandeln in Halmstad, and all the staff at Halmstads Bokhandel. The passion!

Shadab Amoor, for all your book recommendations that have inspired my writing.

The marketing and sales staff at Bonniers Book Clubs, Adlibris, Bokus, and Storytel, for fantastic collaboration.

Jonas and the staff at Adviser Partner for your support that first tough year.

And finally, my former publisher Frida Rosesund. Because you believed in my books from the start and put so much work into them.